"Pratt's worldbu[...] [...]es up action and big [...] [...]his is definitely a series [...]"

Publishers Weekly (starred review)

"Fun, funny, pacy, thought-provoking and very clever space opera – a breath of fresh air."

Sean Williams, author of Twinmaker

"Through his wit, dialogue, and vast, diverse world, Tim Pratt has created a space opera for today – one filled with diverse characters and cultures that feel nuanced enough to be real – while still delivering the sense of wonder that made you love the genre in the first place."

Barnes & Noble Sci-Fi & Fantasy Blog

"Pratt gives all his characters and his galactic civilizations depth, his action sequences are page-turners, and the tone stays light-hearted (and sometimes even meta) despite the high stakes."

Book Riot

"*The Wrong Stars* is an amazingly good, extremely fun, very satisfying novel. *The Wrong Stars* is vital, visceral, energetic pulp. *The Wrong Stars* stands out, and right now, for me, stands alone."

Locus

"*The Wrong Stars* is purely, undeniably, excellent science fiction."

Book Wyrm

BY THE SAME AUTHOR

TIM PRATT

THE DREAMING STARS

Book Two of the Axiom series

**ANGRY
ROBOT**

ANGRY ROBOT
An imprint of Watkins Media Ltd
20 Fletcher Gate,
Nottingham,
NG1 2FZ
UK

angryrobotbooks.com
twitter.com/angryrobotbooks
Reach for the stars

An Angry Robot paperback original 2018

ISBN 978 0 85766 767 0
Ebook ISBN 978 0 85766 768 7

Printed in the United States of America

9 8 7 6 5 4 3 2 1

For Sarah

CHAPTER 1

Callie had been dead for three months, and she was sick of it.

She sat strapped into an ornate wooden chair decorated with carved comets and stars, glaring at a viewscreen, ostensibly browsing news feeds on the Tangle but mostly waiting for a message from an alien that might not even come today, or tomorrow, or next week. "Soon" was a word that contained a multitude of possibilities.

She shifted around, trying to get comfortable. Having chairs in microgravity was stupid, but what was the point in owning the throne of a pirate queen if you didn't sit in it sometimes? Besides, this kept her from pacing around the station, which was annoying everyone.

Her engineer Ashok floated into the control room and crowed, "It's Gravity Day! Soon you'll be able to stomp around and glare with your feet on the ground!"

"Unless you turn this ugly asteroid into a black hole by mistake."

"I only spawn singularities on purpose, cap." Ashok spun himself with puffs of compressed air from his fingertips and twirled in a mid-air cartwheel. "Gravity Day! You should make it a national holiday. You don't make nearly enough imperial decrees."

"To be an emperor, you have to rule multiple countries, Ashok. I'm in charge of exactly one asteroid in currently unincorporated space." She paused. "I do have two spaceships, though, so I could probably justify making you call me 'admiral'."

"O admiral, my admiral." He clucked his tongue, one of the few unaugmented organs in his head. "No, that doesn't work at all." He glanced at her screens. "No message from Lantern yet?" Their friend Lantern was a Liar, the race of pathologically untruthful aliens who'd opened the stars to humans... and kept dark secrets from them, including the existence of an ancient, now dormant race of near-godlike aliens known as the Axiom. Lantern had been raised in the cult of truth-tellers – Liars who didn't lie – but the cult itself secretly served the interests of the sleeping Axiom, hiding the existence of their ongoing, universe-altering projects from outsiders.

Callie's crew had stumbled upon an Axiom facility, and acquired forbidden Axiom technology, and as a result, the truth-tellers had tried to kill them. Fortunately, thanks to Lantern's infiltration and double-agency, the cult believed it had succeeded. Lantern had taken over the local cell of the truth-tellers in the Sol system, and as far as the elders knew, she was still loyal to them. She was checking their databases to make sure no record of their names, or the name of their ship, remained in the cult's systems. Callie didn't want to tangle with zealous assassins wielding unimaginable technology again. They'd only survived the first time by lucky accident. In the meantime, the crew was laying low.

"No word," Callie confirmed. "I appreciate her caution and thoroughness and all those other admirable qualities, but I'd really like to come back to life already."

"You talk like resurrection is inevitable, cap. If Lantern can't purge us from the cult's system without the big bad elders noticing, we might have to leave our old identities behind and start new lives in another system. That could be neat. I could be a chef named Reginald who specializes in algae-based dishes. You could be a saucy bartender who beats up drunks with a pool cue."

"I'm already that, except for the bartender part, and the saucy part, and they aren't always drunks."

"I was trying to hew closely to your essential nature. But cheer up. It's Gravity Day! I'm gonna flip the switch in–" He consulted some chronometer in his heads-up display "–forty-six minutes and eight seconds."

She glanced at the current local time on her viewscreen. "At 7:07? Why then? Does the gravity generator need to warm up or something?"

"No, but the gravitational constant is 6.674×10^{-11} m^3 kg^{-1} s^{-2}, so, you know."

Callie sighed. "So you want to start it sixty-seven minutes and four seconds after six. I'm not sure that even qualifies as a joke, Ashok. Not even by engineering joke standards."

"We've been stuck on a commandeered pirate base for three months pretending to be dead, cap. I've got to entertain myself somehow. I'm just glad Lantern got her hands – or pseudopods, or whatever – on this alien gravity-manipulation tech and was willing to share. Having a project has kept me from losing my mind."

Callie scowled. "You have so many lenses all over your face, I can't tell if you're giving me a pointed look or not. I haven't lost my mind." *Yet*. "I just want to get off this rock and do something useful with my time." She considered sending Lantern another message through the encrypted channels that the ship – now station – AI, Shall, had set up through the Tangle, but the alien would have gotten in touch if she knew anything for sure yet.

"How are things going with Elena?" Ashok asked.

Callie relaxed a little. "Good. She's the only thing that makes being here tolerable."

"Ouch," Ashok said cheerfully.

She ignored him. "This Sebastien thing is wearing on her, though." She glanced at one of the tattle-screens, and it showed a peaceful sine-wave of their prisoner-patient's sleeping brain. "She was hoping we'd see better results by now."

"I'm impressed every day you don't put him out an airlock."

She was always tempted. "Uzoma and Stephen are doing their best to fix his broken brain."

"Oh, I didn't think you'd put him out an airlock because he went psycho and tried to take over the universe and kill us all," Ashok said. "I know you wouldn't hold that against him. I meant because your girlfriend had a big crush on him and everything."

"I don't push my romantic rivals into space, Ashok. I just out-amazing them. Anyway, I think Elena's crush started to wane when Sebastien kidnapped her and tried to feed her to alien robot brain-spiders."

"I can see how that might have a chilling effect." He spun again, and waved. "I'm going to go tell everyone else that Gravity Day is upon us."

"You could just have Shall make a general announcement."

"Then I'd miss the opportunity to receive everyone's applause individually and in person." He paused. "I can't help but notice you didn't applaud. The thing you'd be applauding is my technological genius."

"I'll clap *after* you fail to turn us into a black hole, and when my feet are firmly on the ground."

"I love your optimism." He floated out of the control room and down one of the twisting corridors, cut long ago into the stony asteroid by miners and long since repurposed into living quarters by the pirates Callie had stolen the station from.

She sat and brooded for a moment longer, then got bored. Maybe she should take the *White Raven* out on a little run, not anywhere near inhabited space where they might be identified, just to make sure the ship was still in good working order. She wasn't built for this level of inaction. Even being on Meditreme Station between jobs for a couple of weeks at a time had made her antsy, and Meditreme Station had been the size of a city and home to fifty thousand souls, instead of the size of a city block and home to fewer than a dozen. At least Meditreme had bars, before it got blown up. She was rapidly working her way through the late pirate queen's stash of stolen liquors.

"Callie?" Shall spoke into the implant just behind her ear on their private channel. "I've got weird news and other weird news."

"Did we hear from Lantern?"

"I just received a voice message from her, yes, but it's not the all-clear you were hoping for. She has a line on some potential Axiom activity."

Callie grunted. If she couldn't come back from the dead, killing genocidal space monsters could be a nice compensation. "Let me hear it."

Lantern's voice, euphonious from her artificial

voicebox, spoke into Callie's ear: "I have been in touch with the elders of my sect, who report a troubling development in the Taliesen system. Our cell of truth-tellers there has gone silent, missing numerous scheduled check-ins, and the central authority has grown concerned. As you know, the elders value their secrecy, but they admit there is a major Axiom facility of some kind on the outskirts of that system, and that our cell has been monitoring it closely for millennia. I don't know for sure if they have gone silent because of Axiom activity… but it is certainly a possibility. I am investigating further, and will be in touch with any discoveries." She paused. "As concerns the other matter, I expect to have an answer soon – I have scrubbed details about your ship and crew from every database I can access, and only have a few last precautions to take and investigations to make before I know if you're safe or not. I hope to see all of you soon."

"Huh," Callie said. Taliesen had been a backwater for a long time, but now it was booming as a colony system – as of about a year ago, its innermost planet Owain had an Earthlike atmosphere, after almost a century of terraforming with Liar tech. Colonists were flocking to the planet now, hoping to grab their own little slice of paradise, and it had a certain wild frontier atmosphere. The settlers who'd moved in earlier, during the terraforming process, were a quirky lot, too. If the Axiom was waking up there, a lot of people could be in danger. "Michael's company was heavily invested in that system, right? Wasn't it his horrible uncle's pet project?"

"The company contributed heavily to the terraforming project in exchange for resource-exploitation rights in the future, yes," Shall said. "Uncle Reynauld runs the operation there, last I heard."

She sighed. "If I wasn't dead, I could investigate this from the human side – call up Michael and ask if he's heard about any unusual activity in the system."

Shall cleared his nonexistent throat. "Speaking of Michael, that's the other weird news I wanted to talk to you about. I've been monitoring the Tangle, flagging various keywords, and, ah, I found something you might be interested in."

"What's that?"

"Your funeral announcement."

"*What*?"

"Come in here with me and I'll explain," Shall said.

Callie started to protest, but it was just a reflexive reaction to anyone telling her what to do, so she refrained. She unclipped a slim silvery diadem from the arm of her absurd pirate queen throne and slipped it over her forehead. She ran her fingertip along the smooth metal, and it read her biometrics or some such crap, and her vision briefly went dark.

When sight returned, things weren't much lighter. She stood in a dark, empty warehouse lit by a single light high overhead. The temperature was cool, the air dry, and she couldn't smell anything except stone. She still marveled a bit at how *real* the world felt inside this Hypnos rig. She'd tried out an immersive system at a public arcade on Meditreme Station a decade earlier, a simulation of walking around some famous palace on Earth, and if you jerked your head around too fast, you could see the world filling itself in just a little bit too slowly, black polygons swarming away under a wave of color and texture and light. The smells of the flowers had been too strong and perfumey, the colors too vivid and oversaturated, the shadows too crisp, and there was a muffled quality to the sense of touch, like she was wearing double layers of latex all over her body, even when she'd tried to prick her finger on the thorn of a rosebush. The technology had progressed a lot since then. Ashok said the pirates must have attacked some plutocrat's pleasure craft and liberated this rig, because it was custom, and better than anything commercially available.

Callie thought the Hypnos as a whole was a frivolous waste of time, but access to a high-end virtual-reality system had probably kept her crew and the others under her care from getting asteroid fever from idleness during their months on this rock. Her pilot and navigator Drake and Janice in particular spent a lot of time in the Hypnos, immersing together and then blissfully ignoring each other.

Being in this simulation felt just like being in a real life... boring warehouse somewhere. The sensation of gravity was pleasant, though. She'd missed that in the past few months. Even during long hauls in space, she was mostly under thrust in a ship, the decks thrumming under her boots. She made a fist, wriggled her fingers, and rolled her head around on her neck. No twinges here, no muscle aches, no pain. That was nice. She looked down at herself and noted the utilitarian white jumpsuit with approval. "This is an improvement over the silk robe you had me wearing last time."

Shall emerged from the shadows. His current avatar resembled a spidery mining robot the size of a one-person escape pod, studded with glowing optics and covered in folded manipulator arms, and he danced toward her on spindly multi-jointed legs. It was a form Callie had a lot of fondness for: Shall had saved her life in that body once. "You love that robe," he said.

"Sure, but context matters, and talking about resource allocation isn't the right time for silk that stops at mid-thigh."

"You're welcome to create your own avatars for the Hypnos, or even select one of the pre-gens. Everyone else does."

"I don't need to be anything other than what I am." She looked around. "Why did you bring me in here?"

"It's nice, talking face-to-face."

"Virtual face to virtual faceplate, anyway."

Shall somehow managed to convey a shrug. "When you're an artificial intelligence and your body is an asteroid, it's nice to inhabit a form a little more approachable sometimes."

"I get that, but I meant, why are we in an empty warehouse? Last time we chatted in that weird tea house place. I liked that. The gunpowder tea was good. This is a dump."

"Ah, I see – it doesn't look empty to me, but I have a different set of filters running. This is a marketplace in the Tangle. It's where I come to order supplies, purchased through a complex series of anonymous shells and redirects and culminating in automated deliveries to nearby points in space for drone retrieval. Since we're supposed to be dead and everything."

"Huh." Callie walked over to a shelf and poked it. Felt like metal and plastic. "How's the marketplace work?"

"The interface should be pretty simple for you. Just name something you're interested in buying–"

"Potatoes," she said promptly.

The shelves around her instantly filled with hundreds of heaps of potatoes: mellow gold ones, waxy red ones, small ones the size and shape of thumbs, football-sized mutant baking potatoes. Another set of shelves included tureens of potato-leek and potato-broccoli soup, vast tubs of potato salad in the German, American, and Jovian styles, vats of mashed potatoes, and baskets of French fries. If she glanced at any particular item, a text display shimmered into existence noting specific details, including estimated delivery time, quantity available, and price.

"Why potatoes?" Shall asked.

"Shut up. I like potatoes."

"I remember." Shall gestured with an arm tipped with a diamond saw. "You keyword searched on 'potato,' which is why you got everything from latkes to compressed-air-powered potato guns." He gestured to more distant shelves in both directions. "Try 'raw potatoes' or a specific variety and you'll get more granular results."

She went to a vat of mashed potatoes, and a spoon helpfully appeared. Words appeared in a shimmering golden overlay: "Free sample!" She snorted, took up a scoop, and tasted. Creamy, garlicky, magnificent. "Would it really taste like this?" She dropped the spoon and it vanished.

"It would arrive in a sealed drum, dried and in need of reconstitution, and even then – no, probably not, but it would be recognizably the same species of food. It's easy to make everything taste delicious in the Hypnos. On habitats where there's nothing to eat but vitaminized slurry, the 'great restaurants of the galaxy' Hypnos package is popular. You can get the full experience of fine dining even if you're actually eating mush." He paused. "Human brains are stupid and easy to trick."

"You say the sweetest things," she said, then added, "I want a chair," and the throne from the control room popped into existence. She sat down and laced her hands over her stomach. "So what's this about my funeral?"

The surroundings blurred and became the galley on her ship, the *White Raven*, and instead of a mining robot, Shall appeared as a hooded figure in a black cloak. Callie was still in her throne, with a cup of coffee on the curved white table before her. Shall reached out with a gloved hand and slid a piece of paper across to her.

"Join us in celebrating the life of Kalea Machedo, this Saturday at 3 pm at the home of Michael Garcia-Hassan, thirty degrees on the westward curve of Ilus..." She looked up. "What in the shit is this shit?"

"Your ex-husband is having a memorial service for you this weekend," Shall said mildly. "Because you are dead, and he is the closest thing you have to a survivor, since your people on Earth are all gone."

She groaned. She'd considered sending Michael a note to tell him she hadn't perished when Meditreme Station exploded, but sending *any* proof of her survival, or the survival of the crew, was a bad idea.

Face-to-face communication – real, actual, non-virtual contact – was relatively safe. That's why spies preferred to meet that way, after all...

"What are you going to do?" Shall said.

"What makes you think I'm going to do anything?"

"You're Callie Machedo. You *always* do things. And I know you've been bored."

She grinned. "It's my funeral, Shall. It would be pretty rude of me to miss it, don't you think?"

CHAPTER 2

Elena Oh floated in the medical bay, one hand on the rail of her friend Sebastien's hospital bed. (Was he still her friend? True, he'd tried to take over the galaxy with a fleet of alien ships full of mind-control technology, and had almost hijacked her own brain with an implant, but he'd been under the influence of alien technology himself at the time. She was willing to forgive, if he could recover from brain-spider induced megalomania and psychopathy.)

Stephen, the executive officer of the *White Raven* and their resident doctor, floated in the corner, prodding a tablet with his fingertip and looking pessimistic, which was basically his default expression. Uzoma, the closest thing they had to an expert on the implants, was on the other side of Sebastien's bed, looking at him with no visible emotion, which Elena knew was no indication of their inner thoughts: Uzoma kept everything close.

Stephen and Uzoma had removed the alien implants from Sebastien's skull and brain, and the grafted skin around his temples and on the back of his head was pale and tender-looking. The rest of his flesh was unmarked, and less pale – his coloring was naturally Mediterranean, resistant even to the pallor of long cryo-sleep – and he was altogether lovely, like a statue of a young god in repose, dressed only in a pair of thin shorts.

Uzoma detached various bits of diagnostic equipment from his body, peeling off round metal sensors and unsnapping gleaming black bracelets, and unhooked the intravenous line that was keeping him fed and hydrated. They left the tube running sedatives into Sebastien's wrist in place, but otherwise, he was fully detached from the medical system.

"How is he?" Elena said.

Uzoma didn't have to consult any readouts. "His vital signs are good. His brain waves seem ordinary. But..."

But it's impossible to tell whether his mind is still full of writhing electric murder snakes, Elena thought.

"But his state of mind is still a mystery," Uzoma settled on saying.

They were going to try waking Sebastien up in a moment, and dread and hope warred within Elena. She still held out hope that the man she'd trained with, shared her dreams and hopes with, and undertaken an impossible mission to the stars with would return to her... but she knew he might never be the same. Or maybe he *was* the same, and she'd just never truly known him. The Axiom space station had tried to control Sebastien's mind and make him a slave, but it had failed, unable to cope with his unfamiliar human physiology: as a result, he'd retained his sense of self, but had lost all traces of empathy, and had embraced Axiom technology for his own galaxy-conquering ends. Maybe he'd always had the makings of a tyrant – certainly he thought he knew better than everyone else about almost everything, a confidence she'd once found attractive – and had just lacked a plausible path to conquest until he discovered the alien fleet.

But the alien implants *had* changed him. Whether they'd transformed Sebastien into a different person, or merely heightened his worst qualities and eliminated his good ones, was an open question. Stephen said the parts of Sebastien's brain that involved empathy and impulse control were those most badly damaged by the alien interventions. The pirate asteroid Glauketas, their home for the past few months, had an excellent medical facility, and Stephen and Uzoma had done what they could to repair the damage. The only way to tell if it had worked was to wake Sebastien up and see.

"Are you ready?" Uzoma quirked one eyebrow – a remarkable show of expression by their standards. Uzoma had been attacked by the Axiom mind-control devices too, but the implant hadn't taken as successfully as it did in Sebastien, and Uzoma's psychological recovery was complete. Uzoma still had visible lines from the skin grafts on their scalp, but those would be hidden completely once their fine fuzz of hair grew in a bit more. It was possible to come through an encounter with Axiom brain-spiders and emerge whole on the other side. It *was*.

Elena nodded, gazing down at Sebastien's face, so still and blank.

Uzoma swiped at the tablet in their hand. "He should wake up in a moment."

Sebastien's breathing sped up, his eyelids twitched, and then his dark eyes sprang open. His gaze rolled back and forth, passing across Elena without stopping, then returned to her. He inhaled sharply through his nose and sat up, so quickly that Elena pushed off the bed in surprise, the motion sending her spinning away in the null gravity.

Being startled backward probably saved her life.

Sebastien had spent a few months in a coma, but they'd kept his muscles pharmaceutically and electrically stimulated – therapies they all went through occasionally anyway, since weightless environments were terrible for maintaining muscle tone. He swiped at Elena with one long arm, but his fingers missed her as she floated backward. He snarled, teeth bared, and pivoted to lunge at Uzoma, on the other side of the bed, but the straps on his lower body, holding him down in the lack of gravity, prevented him from reaching them.

"Sebastien!" Elena shouted, steadying herself against a wall panel. "It's OK, you're not in danger!" She looked to Stephen. "Is this supposed to happen?"

"We expected some disorientation—" Stephen began, and then gasped.

Elena turned back to Sebastien. He'd wriggled out of his straps somehow, and as Elena watched, he braced his feet on the bed and launched himself at Uzoma, hands extended to grab their throat. Uzoma stabbed at the tablet with their finger, doubtless trying to dose him with sedatives, but Sebastien's violent escape had torn the needle out of his vein – the tube floated over the bed, drooling medication from its tip.

Uzoma raised their arms to fend him off, but Sebastien twisted in the air, graceful as an eel, and grabbed Uzoma around the waist instead, his momentum sending them both spinning against the wall. Uzoma battered at him, but Sebastien kept moving, coiling around Uzoma's body like a constricting serpent, climbing up their back and wrapping his arms and legs around them, pinning Uzoma's arms to their sides. Sebastien grinned at Elena from over Uzoma's shoulder, then lowered his head and bit into Uzoma's neck with the relish of someone tearing into the first ripe peach of summer.

Uzoma screamed as Sebastien jerked his head back, tearing out a hunk of meat and sending a spray of blood into the air, creating a constellation of crimson droplets that spun and floated in microgravity. Sebastien opened up his arms, planted his feet against Uzoma's back, and kicked hard. The force of the blow sent the glassy-eyed Uzoma flying forward and down, cracking their forehead hard against the rail of Sebastien's recently vacated bed. Uzoma bounced and then drifted, motionless, except for red streamers and bubbles spilling from their wounds.

The kick sent Sebastien up and backward, toward the place where the gentle curve of the wall met the ceiling. He twisted in the air, like he'd practiced zero-gravity combat a thousand times, and curled up his body, aiming his head downward and bracing his feet toward the ceiling.

"We need to sedate him!" Elena cried, and Stephen said, "Yes, I know." He was the XO in part because he was almost supernaturally calm in a crisis, famed throughout Trans-Neptunian space for his stoicism and implacability. He released his tablet, letting it float in the air beside him, and lifted the syringe of paralytic fluid he'd filled in case Sebastien became agitated or disoriented.

Sebastien didn't seem disoriented, or even particularly

agitated. He seemed to be enjoying himself, smiling down on them with bloody teeth. He pressed his feet against the ceiling and pushed off hard, aiming himself like a missile at Stephen. The doctor watched the approach for a moment, made some mental calculation, didn't like his chances, and tossed the syringe spinning toward Elena.

She snatched it out of the air and watched as Sebastien crashed into the XO, bulling him into the corner. Stephen was a big man, taller and heavier than his homicidal patient, and certainly stronger, but his height was no help in such a cramped environment, his weight was no help in a weightless one, and he didn't have the opportunity to use his strength. Sebastien slashed at the doctor's eyes with fingernails, and Stephen squeezed his eyes shut and flung his head back in an instinctive defensive motion. Sebastien took advantage of the moment to grab the handheld tablet Stephen had released out of the air, and swung it hard at Stephen's face. The metal, plastic, and smartglass smashed his nose in and cracked partly on impact, sending blood and gleaming shards in all directions.

Stephen howled. The force of the blow he'd struck sent Sebastien spinning, and he pulled in his limbs to conserve angular momentum, twirling fast – then lashed out with the tablet again when he came around, breaking the tablet in half against the doctor's face. Stephen slumped and floated, face obscured by a floating mist of blood.

Elena was not as cool in a crisis as Stephen, but she had a keen sense of responsibility, and this was her fault: she'd wanted to try this, she'd wanted to wake up Sebastien and get a sense of their progress despite

Stephen's concerns that their patient's brain was still too damaged. While Sebastien attacked Stephen, Elena pushed herself forward, syringe in her hand. She'd intended to glide silently through the air and stab him in the neck while his back was turned, but Sebastien's second blow spun him around to face her. His face was spotted with blood, and he smiled at her as she flew at him. There was no wall or furniture within reach to arrest her motion, and he spread his arms, as if to welcome her into an embrace.

She reached out with the syringe, but he batted her hand aside, sending the needle flying. The blow sent him spinning away from her, and she thought she might sail safely past him – until he grabbed her ponytail in passing and jerked her toward him. They slammed together, and he got his arms around her, spinning her body around until she faced him, then crushing her close to his chest. She wriggled, trying to escape, but his arms were bands of iron, his breath hot in her face. His mouth stank of blood and flesh.

Sebastien had kissed her, on the Axiom station, when the brain-spiders were still gleaming on his scalp, their legs punched through his skull, his eyes glowing red from the implants and nanomachines within. She'd taken advantage of his distraction, then – of his twisted affection – to punch him in the back of the head, but he'd learned his lesson, and she didn't have a fist free to repeat the effort.

Sebastien didn't try to kiss her now – just held her close. She looked into his eyes. "Sebastien. Calm down. You're safe. I know you're – confused. You were injured. But I'm here to help you–"

"Elena." His voice was low, a soft, insinuating whisper. "Missed you. Missed you. Missed you." He squeezed her harder, moved his face close, and took her lower lip in his sharp teeth.

"Failure!" she shouted as her flesh began to tear.

CHAPTER 3

Elena opened her eyes and removed the Hypnos diadem from her brow, setting it aside. She shuddered, wiping the back of her hand across her mouth – her lower lip didn't hurt, and she couldn't taste blood, but it seemed like she should.

Sebastien was still stretched out on the table in the medical bay, his own diadem resting on his sweaty brow. He had a faint smile on his face. That expression hadn't been there before. She shuddered. Was he floating above their bleeding bodies now? Gloating?

Uzoma walked over, removing their own diadem. "That could have gone better," they said. "I am surprised you did not stop the simulation as soon as he killed me."

Elena shook her head. "There was a possibility his violence was just a response to disorientation, mindless lashing out – Stephen said he might be confused and frightened. If that's all it was, we could have put restraints on him before waking him up for real. I wanted to give him a chance to calm down, to see if the real Sebastien emerged." She sighed. "But I guess he was calm all along."

Stephen, normally an unflappable figure of superhuman calm, floated in the farthest corner away from their patient, eyes narrowed. "I had my pain receptors turned off, and even so..." He shook his head. "I expected Sebastien to exhibit diminished function, because the implants we removed altered his brain in fundamental ways, but I wasn't anticipating quite that level of bloodlust."

"It's not his fault." Elena hated the wheedling, defensive note in her own voice. "The Axiom did this to him."

"On Earth in our time, dogs sometimes contracted rabies, and became aggressive and dangerous," Uzoma said. "It was not the fault of the animals that they became infected, but nonetheless, they had to be put down."

Elena stared at her. "Are you suggesting we kill Sebastien?"

Uzoma shook their head. "I am suggesting we continue searching for a cure for his rabies." They paused. "Space rabies."

The *White Raven*'s crew had a running inside joke about "space madness." "Did you just make a joke?" Elena said.

"I am very funny," Uzoma said.

"Right. Good. So. What's the next step, Stephen?" Elena said.

Stephen looked up from his tablet. His dark eyes were sad, but weren't they always? "The Axiom implants have been entirely removed, as far as we can tell, and there seem to be no lurking nanomachines – again, not as far as we can detect. We've done all we can with the resources we have here, I'm afraid."

"That's it, then? We just... give up?"

Stephen shook his head. "Not necessarily. I've been reading and researching, and there are experimental drug therapies that could repair the damaged portions of his brain. Combined with some other pharmaceuticals and some trans-cranial magnetic procedures, I suspect they could restore his higher functions, his ability to speak and reason – all the functions that were hijacked by the implants, and lost when we removed them. I don't know whether we can restore his empathy, or diminish the megalomania he exhibited on the Axiom station. There have been promising results on, ah, certain patient populations."

"What populations?"

Stephen sighed. "I believe back in your time they would have called them 'the criminally insane.' Incarcerated people with severe personality disorders and antisocial tendencies, with histories of violence."

Elena nodded. "That does sound like Sebastien."

Stephen said, "The studies are still ongoing, and it's difficult work to quantify because much of the research depends on the subjective self-reporting of people who lie and manipulate as easily as they breathe, but there's evidence of substantially increased empathy and decreased violence among the subjects. The therapies aren't commercially available, but... I know people. I'll need to visit the Jovian Imperative to acquire the necessary drugs and software. Fortunately, we can afford them."

They'd been broke for a while: the crew was afraid to access their personal accounts while the truth-tellers might still be monitoring the Tangle. None of them wanted to alert the members of a deadly alien conspiracy to the fact that they weren't as dead as everyone assumed. The time refugees from the *Anjou* didn't have any money either – they'd shipped out on a one-way journey to a prospective colony planet five hundred years ago, and hadn't left bank accounts behind accruing interest, more's the pity. For a while, the combined crews had subsisted on the supplies on Glauketas, which leaned heavily on a shipment of canned beets the villains had hijacked from some supply ship. Ashok's many borscht variations had lost their novelty quickly. The pirates had money, though, hidden in the darkest parts of the Tangle, and Shall had spent six weeks attempting to crack the password that would allow them to access the pirates' stash of cryptocurrency, without success. Then Callie found the password scribbled on a piece of metal with grease pencil, hidden behind a secret panel in the old pirate queen's bedroom, which Callie had taken as her own. Since then they'd had a decent bit of operating capital again, though it wasn't a vast fortune. Pirates, it seemed, were rather profligate with their funds. Callie didn't feel right spending blood money anyway, and said once they had a decent income again, they'd repay what they took from the pirate coffers and donate the lot to charity.

They'd have to find some kind of paying work soon, which meant they had to either take up the mantle of their old lives again (if Lantern declared it safe), or blow the rest of their money on false identities and relocate to a new system where murderous truth-tellers would be less likely to recognize them. They were all hoping for the former. People were attached to their identities, and

Callie was especially cranky at the prospect of having to rename her ship.

The door to the medical bay opened, and Ashok floated in, spinning around with his arms extended. "It's Gravity Day!" he crowed. Then he seemed to take note of the mood in the room, gazing down at Sebastien stretched on the table. "Ah. It's also 'wake up Sebastien in the simulation day,' isn't it. How did it go?"

"He murdered Stephen and Uzoma right away," Elena said. "Then he got his hands on me, and... well. We called the simulation off before he could kill me too."

Ashok kept gazing at the sleeping patient. "Huh. I mean, he couldn't do that, not really – Shall would have deployed drones to stop him when he got violent. At most he could have murdered maybe one of you."

"That's very reassuring," Stephen said. "We wanted to give Sebastien more options in the simulation than he'd get in reality, to see what he'd do if left totally unfettered."

"Maybe you could find him a good therapy module?" Ashok said. "Or put him in some kind of mental hospital sim?"

"His brain was altered by alien implants," Stephen said. "A psychiatric expert system wouldn't be much help at this point. Maybe someday. Right now, it would be like trying to put a fresh coat of paint on a house that's currently on fire. You have to put out the flames and then rebuild the walls first."

Ashok nodded, his cheerfulness undeterred. "Well, at least soon you'll get to be disappointed in *gravity*! We're going with maybe half a G to start, and if everyone clamors for more, we'll make it stronger. The artificial gravity system is adjustable to… honestly, a pretty terrifying degree. I could squish us all into mush." He waited for a moment, then sighed. "No applause? Really? OK. Gravity will hit in about fifteen minutes. Try not to be sleeping up near the ceiling when I turn it on. I'm going to go tell Robin and Ibn. Maybe *they'll* appreciate my genius, and also my wit." He spun out of the room.

Uzoma removed Sebastien's diadem. "There is nothing more you can do here," they said to Elena. "We will make sure he is comfortable."

Elena nodded. "Thanks, both of you, for trying. I know it isn't easy. I just… I'm not ready to give up on him yet. Not if there's a chance he can still be saved."

"We were on a ship together," Uzoma said. "I will continue my efforts for as long as it seems feasible, though now that I have assisted in removing the implants, I have no particular expertise to offer. I am good with machines. Bodies are so much… squishier."

"Fortunately, squishy things are firmly within my area of expertise," Stephen said. "I consider this a traumatic brain injury with personality-altering effects, and will treat it accordingly. I don't give up on patients if there's any hope left at all."

"Thank you. Both of you." Elena swam through the air, out of the clinic, trying not to cry. This was so hard. What if Sebastien couldn't be saved or changed? Even if they made him less psychotic, he might remain a homicidal megalomaniac who saw people as obstacles or pawns.

She wiped at her eyes, and tiny globules of tears were dashed into the air, floating away. She needed to feel better. And when she needed to feel better, she needed Callie.

• • •

The door to Callie's quarters opened, and Elena floated in. Callie was in the middle of stuffing clothes into a bag, but she left it hanging in the air when she saw Elena's beautiful, tear-stained face. "Oh, babe." Callie opened her arms, and Elena drifted into them, the momentum of their joining making the pair of them spin gently in the center of the room. "No good?" Callie murmured. She'd occasionally fantasized about taking Sebastien for a long ride in the *White Raven* and dropping him off someplace in deep space, but Elena still hoped he could be saved, in defiance of all evidence, so Callie supported her.

"It was bad. He woke up, but there was nothing human in him, as far as I could tell. I want to believe the old Sebastien is still in there somewhere, and Stephen says there's hope, but it's so hard to see him like that."

"I'm so sorry. Did he hurt you?" You couldn't feel more than mild pain, really just tactile feedback, in the Hypnos, at least not without special dangerous third-party mods, but terrifying things were still terrifying, and racing hearts and rushing hormones and clenched muscles could leave you shaky and wrung out even after the diadem came off.

"He would have, if we hadn't ended the simulation. He killed Stephen and Uzoma's avatars before he came after me. He was savage, but he was also *smart*."

Callie kissed the top of her head. Elena's hair smelled like the same shampoo they all used, but it somehow blended with her natural scent and became intoxicating. "What's the next step?" Callie wasn't sure if she was hoping for more options, or for Elena to declare Sebastien a lost cause. The latter would be sad… but freeing. They could stick Sebastien's comatose body on Lantern's

base and let her work on him for a while. At least
then Sebastien wouldn't be on her station, making her
girlfriend cry every day, dreaming psychopath dreams.

"Stephen says there are some promising experimental
therapies he can try, but he'll have to go to the Jovian
Imperative to get the necessary supplies."

Hope springs eternal, with feathers on, Callie
thought. "OK. I was thinking of organizing a field trip to
Ganymede anyway."

Elena didn't seem to hear that, lost in thoughts of her
own. "What if we can't save him, Callie? What if he's
just like this, forever? A monster?"

Callie thought of the exploded fragments of Meditreme
Station, her old home; of her friends who'd died there;
of her failed marriage to Michael. "Some things can't
be saved. It's sad, but there it is. You do your best, you
try hard, and when nothing else can be done, you do
your best to move on." Elena stiffened up in her arms,
and Callie stroked her hair and soothed: "Hey, I'm not
saying we're at that point yet. Even after Stephen and
Uzoma have done all they can, Lantern is researching
Axiom mind-control technology. There are references
to breaking Axiom conditioning among the rebellious
Liars, so there may be techniques we can adapt to work
on human physiology. We're a long way from the go/no-
go decision." *Unfortunately*. Callie had never known this
supposedly nice and thoughtful and kind and charming
version of Sebastien, only the megalomaniacal asshole
he'd been on the Axiom station, and she had her doubts
about the true nature of his allegedly good heart.

"I know you don't think much of him, and I don't
blame you." Elena pulled back and smiled up at Callie,

her expression open and warm, and Callie was warmed, too, by her proximity. "But it means the world to me that you're willing to help anyway."

"I just love you is all."

Elena wrinkled her forehead. "What's this about a field trip?"

Shall's voice, smooth and amused, broke in over the station's public address system. "Attention, denizens of Glauketas station. Gravity Day is upon us. Ashok reminds everyone to stow everything securely, though I pointed out that everything *is* stowed securely, because this is a weightless environment, and anything that's not secure tends to drift around, but at any rate – consider yourselves reminded. Please orient yourselves in relation to the agreed-upon definition of 'down' and prepare to feel the weight of the world again."

Callie and Elena drifted apart, but held hands. They were just a few centimeters above the consensus definition of the floor. "Bend your knees a little, darlin'," Callie said. "To take the impact better."

"If I had a nickel for every time I've heard that…"

Shall went on, "We're only going to half a G, but we're relying on barely understood alien technology, so be prepared in case–"

"*GRAVITY DAY!*" Ashok broke in. "Ten! Nine! Eight! Seven! Six! Five! Four! Drumrollllllllllll! Zero!"

Artificial gravity came on, but not from the expected direction. The new "down" wasn't below their feet, but behind their backs; the wall by Callie's hammock became the floor, and they fell a few meters, Elena shouting in alarm and Callie cursing.

They landed on a heap of blankets, but the impact was

still jarring enough to knock Callie's breath out. She sat up, groaning and gasping. "Are you OK?"

"Feel like I got kicked in the back," Elena said. "Oof."

The furniture they'd carefully bolted to the "floor" in preparation for this day listed and creaked and threatened to pull loose from their moorings, including a large dresser that was perfectly poised to fall from the opposite wall – now the ceiling – and squash them. One drawer, not fully closed, worked its way loose and flew across the room, and Callie had to roll over on top of Elena to avoid getting hit. Callie's underwear and socks spilled out of the drawer as it fell, and showered down around them.

"I do like seeing your clothes all over the floor," Elena said. "And I don't recall ever complaining about you being on top of me. But there are some drawbacks…"

Callie turned her head and shouted, "Ashok!"

"Oops," he said. "Sorry about that, everybody. Axiom tech is really weird in terms of spatial orientations. I think they operate in more dimensions than we do sometimes. Let me twist this value through a perpendicular… is everybody ready to go again?"

"No!" Callie shouted. "Not really!"

"Gravity Day!" Ashok crowed.

The room tilted. Ashok didn't turn off the artificial field, but just changed its orientation, and as a result, the room turned *around* them. It was like being inside a very roomy barrel, and rolling down a hill, or climbing into an old tumble-dryer. They clung to each other, Elena laughing uncontrollably, as they rolled up the wall in an avalanche of underwear, slid across what was supposed to be the ceiling, slid down the *other* wall (narrowly

missing the dresser, and it was a good thing the door
was shut or they'd have fallen into the corridor), and
finally thumped onto the originally intended floor. Callie
wondered if they'd just keep spinning, rolling around
the room, but the motion ceased.

Elena lifted her head and looked at Callie, a pair of
underwear stuck to her ponytail. "I don't know how that
was for you," she said. "But for me, the earth moved."

"I'd give myself a B-plus." Ashok spun around in a
swivel chair in the big central room the pirates had
used as a meeting hall. The space was vast and square,
topped by a "dome" – the concave ceiling was covered
in screens that looked like windows, simulating a view
of the stars around them at the moment, but capable of
displaying anything Callie wanted them to. The pirates
had stolen all sorts of odds and ends over the years,
including shipments bound for colony worlds, and had
storerooms full of things that were useless in a weightless
environment: sofas, footstools, tables, stand lamps,
desks, mattresses. Callie had furnished this room with
desks and a long conference table and chairs, suitable
for an all-hands meeting. "I know that thing where the
wall was the floor for a minute wasn't ideal, but I didn't
accidentally turn us inside out or spawn a singularity or
anything."

The whole crew of the *White Raven* was present, along
with the survivors from the *Anjou*. Drake and Janice
were there, in their egg-shaped mobility device, the
privacy screen drawn down and presenting a curved
mirrored surface; they weren't entirely comfortable
around the relative strangers from the *Anjou*. They'd

been in a terrible spaceship accident years before, their shattered and almost lifeless bodies plucked from the wreckage by a tribe of passing Liars who used advanced medical technology to put them back together again. Unfortunately, those particular Liars seemed unfamiliar with human biology, and had apparently thought Drake and Janice were a single organism; the pilot and navigator retained their individual minds and personalities, but shared a transformed body that now bore only a passing resemblance to the humans they'd once been. Stephen sat in an executive armchair, hands laced over his ample belly, eyes sleepy and bored. He'd been depressed lately – he was always doleful, but now he was dour – and Callie was worried about him.

"It is nice to have gravity, Ashok," Elena said from her chair beside Callie at the conference table. "And I wasn't *too* badly injured."

"It was like being inside a rock polisher," Ibn grumbled.

"I still don't understand it." Uzoma leaned over the table, fingers interlaced, scowling at Ashok. "How does the artificial gravity *work*? What happens if you stick your head outside the gravity field, but your body remains inside it? Why doesn't the *White Raven*, docked just outside, crash into the asteroid, since the asteroid has gravity fully half that of the Earth now?"

Ashok shrugged. "I'm not a theoretical physicist. I'm an engineer. I'm more about the hows than the whys, and since it works, I'm OK with not understanding *why* it works yet. Lantern and the rest of the Free don't understand it either." The Free was the name many Liars used for themselves, but almost never mentioned to outsiders. "They just know how to mess around with the variables – same as the bridges, and the short-range teleporting, and the wormhole generator on the *Raven*. The gravity field doesn't end abruptly, though, so don't worry about weird effects if you stick your nose outside. The artificial gravity kinda fades out in a gradient, so you'll feel yourself getting lighter as you get closer to the edges, and by the time you hit an airlock, you'll be weightless again. That same effect should keep ships and space trash from smashing into us. Glauketas has a gravitational field now, but only in a small, defined area. The gravity is pretty consistently half a G in all the living areas though. I can adjust that until we find a sweet spot."

Callie said, "You did good, Ashok. I wish you'd tested it a *little* more before activation, but I knew what I was getting into when I gave you permission to try this experiment. It'll be nice to do some weight training again."

"I'm looking forward to boiling pasta in an open pot," Stephen rumbled.

"Smelling coffee before I take a drink of it? Stirring it with a spoon?" Robin whistled. "That's civilization."

"Gravity sucks," Janice said. "We'll be going back to the *Raven* soon. Having weight again hurts."

"Are you having issues with pain?" Stephen flipped into ship's doctor mode instantly.

"Not really," Drake said. "No more than usual, considering the gravity. The gel padding inside the chair is still working well to support those things that need support. We've just had the pleasure of floating blissfully weightless for a while, and we got spoiled."

"Oh, yeah." Janice's voice was as dry as the surface

of Mercury. "That's us. A couple of conjoined hedonists, drowning in pleasure."

"Thanks for coming down," Callie said. "I'll cut you loose soon, and you might even get to do a little flying before long. I called this meeting not just so we could all applaud for Ashok–"

"Nobody actually applauded," he muttered.

"–but because we have some decisions to make."

"What decisions?" Uzoma said.

"Just little things," Callie said. "Like how you want to spend the rest of your lives. I'm going to Ganymede, to get some drugs for Sebastien and to chase down a lead on Axiom activity in another system... which means there's a chance for some of you to get off this ride."

CHAPTER 4

Elena invited Uzoma to her cabin after the meeting; she hardly ever used the room, since she slept with Callie most of the time, but it was good to have a place to keep her stuff, such as it was, and to immerse herself in educational simulations to catch up on the past few centuries.

The two of them sat side by side on the low bunk, the only furniture in the room. "I'm going to miss you," Elena said. "I'll miss Ibn and Robin, too, of course, but – well. All the work you and I have done on Sebastien together... it's made me feel really close to you."

Uzoma nodded. They were never a physically demonstrative person, but they reached out a hand and briefly patted Elena's own. "I did not decide to leave this fellowship lightly," Uzoma said. "What the Axiom implants did to my brain... it gives me some insights into their conceptual architecture. The way they see the world, and organize information. That understanding might be valuable to you." They paused. "I also hold a personal grudge against them, and celebrate your attempts to bring about their downfall. That said... I have done all I can for Sebastien. My knowledge of physics and mathematics and starship travel are of no particular value in this place and time – Shall exceeds all my capabilities in the theoretical areas, and I am hopelessly behind the times in terms of the practical ones. I do not enjoy being ignorant."

Elena nodded. Uzoma wasn't a warrior – they fought with their *brain*. "The crew has contacts that can help you catch up on education. Maybe get you into a college somewhere. Whatever you want."

"Yes. I have already discussed some options with Callie. She said, quote, 'I know people who donate so much money to the Jovian Imperative University system that there are buildings named after them on every campus,' end quote. We also discussed the possibility that I might rejoin the mission against the Axiom, once I feel I have more to contribute."

Elena relaxed at that. The idea of losing Uzoma again forever was heartbreaking, but if she thought of it as a brief separation instead, it was easier.

Uzoma went on. "I have talked with Lantern about the possibility of studying with her, too. The Axiom interest me. I think it would be fruitful to split my time between conventional education and delving into the databases of the truth-tellers." They narrowed their eyes, expression becoming fierce. "I cannot contribute enough to the fight with my current capabilities. I intend to change that."

Elena said, "That sounds wonderful. If you were into hugs, I would hug you right now."

"Consider me hugged in my metaphorical but not literal heart," Uzoma said.

• • •

Stephen stepped from the bright sunlight of the dusty street into the cool dimness of the restaurant. The walls were hung with tapestries in geometric designs, and the seating was mostly low tables with cushions scattered around them. That kind of layout was a recipe for back spasms in reality, but here in the Hypnos, nothing ever hurt too much. Stephen strolled around the empty tables, enjoying the scents in the air: hints of coriander and lamb, strong coffee, cinnamon. Much better than the way Glauketas smelled.

Ibn sat cross-legged on a cushion, a cup of tea on the dark wood table before him. Stephen eased himself down across from him. "I'll be sorry to see you go. I've enjoyed our talks."

Ibn opened one eye and regarded him gravely. "I will be glad to free myself from your endless blasphemies." Then he grinned. Ibn's smiles were rare and all the more lovely for that. "I will miss you, too, doctor. If I must be trapped, as Robin says, in a hollow rock full of farts, at least I had the pleasure of discussing philosophy during my confinement. I did have one query, though, before I go. Or perhaps two."

Stephen reached out for a cup, and it was there, full of spicy dark hot chocolate, because to hell with tea. "What's that?"

"Your religion believes that all thinking beings collectively make up the mind of God, correct?"

Stephen *hmmmed*. "My first teacher in the Church of the Ecstatic Divine, which is more a fellowship than a religion to my way of thinking, told me that all our minds were neurons in the mind of God. That we are all connected, in ways subtle and overt, and that we add up to something greater than ourselves, as proven by all the great works humans and Liars have created by working together. Some people used to believe our home world, Earth, was a single organism, and that all the living things on it were parts of that organism, just as our bodies are made up of thousands upon thousands of individual living cells, not to mention all those helpful microorganisms that dwell within us." Stephen took a sip. "Some of my people literally believe what you said – that, together, we are God, and that we cannot know the whole of God any more than a red blood cell in my body can comprehend the whole of me. But, sometimes, we can get a glimpse of the overarching grandeur, and be awed, and feel as if what we do matters – that our contributions are a small part of that whole. Some of us think of the whole 'neurons in the brain of God' idea more as a metaphor about how we're all part of this great ongoing experiment called 'living together in the universe.'"

"Which do you believe?" Ibn said.

Stephen considered. He liked to answer Ibn seriously and accurately, because Ibn always extended the same gravity to him. "It depends on how many drugs I've taken. Certainly when I take sacraments with my people, I feel the boundaries of my self disappear, and I connect to something greater than myself. As a materialist and a medical doctor I know those feelings are due to biological and chemical changes in my brain. That doesn't make them feel any less wonderful, though. In my lucid moments… I think that 'God' is best defined as a creative force that makes changes to the universe, directed toward the betterment of those beings capable

of imagining the future. Our sacraments – the drugs –
and the resulting feeling of connection to other people,
and to the divine, and frankly the occasional cuddle
pile, is just a pleasant way to remind myself of my place
within the context of a whole."

Ibn tapped his forefinger against his chin. "I think
I understand. My second question then: where do
the Axiom fit into your concept of God, if God is the
collective mind of all thinking beings?"

Stephen scowled. "They're a fucking brain tumor."

Ibn nodded. "And you are a doctor. You will do your
part to cut out that tumor."

"Yes. For as long as I have the strength. I'll probably
die in the process. I'm surprised we survived this long.
But it's meaningful work." That work was the only
thing Stephen had to live for, really, since his entire
congregation had died on Meditreme Station... and
frankly, the fight against the Axiom was a bit of an
abstract thing to live for. He wasn't sure how long he'd
hold out, with just that spiny, spiky task to fuel him.

"I am sorry I am leaving the fight behind," Ibn said.

Stephen waved his hand. "Don't be. There are different
ways to provide support. Having other people out there
who know about the Axiom is valuable. I was going to
ask if you'd be willing to safeguard the knowledge of
what we've learned so far. Fighting the Axiom in secret
makes sense, for now, but if something happens to my
crew, it's vital that others know the threat we face.
Callie has put some plans in place for that eventuality, of
course, but multiple backups are best."

"Of course. It is the least I can do." Ibn grimaced.
"Very nearly literally."

Stephen chuckled. "If I'd been frozen for half a millennium, and awakened on a nightmare alien space station, I wouldn't have conducted myself half so well as you. You've been through enough. You deserve such peace as you can find."

"This… Jovian Imperative? That's where I'm going? I don't understand the structure of the solar system now. In my day, it was just Earth, and a few scattered moon bases, all ruled by the One World Emergency Government."

"Earth is still ruled by the One World Government, which grew naturally out of the system you remember – they're just a bit less panicked these days."

"They don't have authority over Jupiter?"

"They wish. Earth and the Imperatives are allies, but not the friendliest ones. The OWG is far more closely aligned with an independent Luna, and Mars, which is also its own nation-state. Mercury is barely populated, but supplies power for much of the rest of the system. Those bodies make up the Inner Planets Governing Council, a coalition with a common currency and set of laws, but varied cultures. They're in charge of everything from the sun to the asteroid belt… except for Venus."

"Venus isn't inhabited?" Ibn said. "There was talk of building floating cities there someday, in my day."

"It's inhabited all right, but humans aren't welcome. Some of the first Liars that humans met, centuries ago, traded us some of their technology in exchange for permanent rights to live on Venus. They don't talk to us, and when we send probes, they never come back. We're not sure what they're up to there, if anything."

Ibn grunted. "That's not terrifying at all. What about

beyond the asteroid belt?"

"These days? The Jovian Imperative rules it all, despite a couple of the moons occasionally declaring independence or holding non-binding referendums to secede. Earth may be the seat of humanity, but Jupiter is arguably more important."

"Why? Jupiter can't be habitable. The storms, the radiation…"

"You'd be surprised where humans can live these days, with access to Liar technology, but yes, Jupiter itself doesn't have much of a population. They've got one advantage, though: the Imperative controls the wormhole bridge that allows access to the other colony systems in the galaxy, so they're an economic and cultural power on a par with the inner planets, despite having fewer natural resources. The Imperative is a classic port city, in some ways – closest to the bridge, taxing everything that passes through, with first pick of imports from all the other colony worlds. Though if anything ever happened to the bridges, the Imperative would find themselves starving before long."

"Is this Imperative a nice place to live?"

Stephen considered. "Depends on where you are. The storm cities floating in the upper atmosphere of Jupiter itself are remarkable, but they're the playthings of the impossibly rich – palaces with views of the titanic forces whirling underneath. Ganymede, Callisto, and Europa are all well built up and heavily populated, with their own individual cultures. Io is settled mostly by immigrants from Mars, and they're one of the moons constantly trying to declare independence, so as a result, the rest of the Imperative makes life hard for them – I wouldn't recommend settling there. Beyond that, there are smaller outposts on other moons, and space stations that are city-sized themselves. Ilus, on Ganymede, where we're going, is reckoned to be one of the great cities of the system, possibly of all the colony systems, host to a thriving series of domes and underground caverns. You could do worse as a place to begin, and from there, you can go back to Earth, or to any colony world."

"Are you from Ganymede?"

Stephen shook his head. "I was not born in the Imperative, and it's not the home I chose. I was born and educated on Earth, and spent most of my adult life in territory held by the Trans-Neptunian Authority. The TNA used to be the biggest player from the orbit of Neptune out into the Kuiper Belt. It was a corporation that acted like a government, and made lots of money mining the countless icy planetesimals on the edges of the system. There was a definite frontier aspect to the TNA – it was the place you came when all else failed, a place of high risks and high rewards. With the TNA gone, the seat of the corporation destroyed by the truth-tellers, everything is still in flux, but the Jovian Imperative has never lacked territorial ambition, and the word on the Tangle is they're trying to gain all the mining rights the TNA had, and may build a successor to Meditreme Station. There's just too much money to be made on the outskirts, too many trillions of tons of valuable minerals, not to mention water ice, to be mined. There's a power vacuum, and someone will fill it, whether the Imperative or someone else. It won't be the place it was, though. The home of my heart is gone."

"I am so sorry for your loss," Ibn said.

"Thank you. Losing my congregation… that was hard. I'm hoping to attend services on Ilus, and I'm sure that will give me some comfort, but it won't be the same. Would you like to join me?"

"I appreciate the offer, but the sacraments you take are haram – intoxicants, forbidden by my faith." He smiled. "I'd invite you to my services, which Shall assures me are still held, but I fear you would find it dull."

"As long as it gives you comfort and offers you meaning, my friend," Stephen said. "That's all any of us can hope for, and more than many of us get."

CHAPTER 5

The *Golden Spider* wasn't always called the *Golden Spider*.
According to the records on the pirate base, they'd
named it the *Inevitability of Death*. Callie supposed that
name was intended to frighten potential enemies, but
given the poor condition of the vessel, it sounded more
like a promise about the ship's own imminent demise.
The ship was a freighter, originally, with some guns stuck
on it here and there as aftermarket additions, but it was
much patched and battered. Ashok, with the help of
Shall's repair drones, had done their best to undo the
decay caused by years of slovenly maintenance and "good
enough" repairs on the part of the pirate mechanics. The
ship was, at least, reliably spaceworthy now, though she
wouldn't want to take it out into deep space or enter it
in the Araboth Regatta. It was good enough for a trip to
Ganymede, though.

The *Golden Spider*'s interior was mostly bare metal,
scuffed plastic cladding, and shiny new metallic caulk.
Nearly every curve and corner sported the bulging,
fungal-looking brown growths of spray-and-set
insulation Ashok had used to seal a million rattling,

whistling holes throughout the interior. Ideally, every compartment of a spacecraft could be made airtight, so a single hull breach wouldn't kill everyone, but the pirates, unsurprisingly, had believed in living dangerously – or lazily, which amounted to the same thing.

Callie sat in the cockpit, keeping her eyes on the screens because the navigational system had a tendency to glitch, as they cruised toward Ganymede. Drake and Janice had opted to stay home, floating in the *White Raven* and enjoying themselves in the Hypnos, and Callie hadn't objected. She was adequate behind the controls, though she lacked the intuition, elegance, and quick thinking under pressure that made Drake such a fantastic pilot when the going got heavy or violent. She wouldn't have minded some heaviness or violence. They were going as fast as the ship's abused Tanzer drive could take them, and the trip wasn't a long one by system standards, but the tedium still chafed.

Especially since there was an alternative. They had a wormhole bridge generator on the *White Raven*, allowing instantaneous travel to any point in the galaxy – they could have jaunted from Glauketas to Ganymede in under a minute. Their bridge generator was the only such drive in all of human space, a bit of salvaged Axiom technology that could revolutionize life for everyone if it could be reproduced... except that, soon after revolutionizing life, it would *end* life, because the Axiom security systems would notice a bunch of new sapient creatures popping up all over the galaxy from tiny wormholes, and wake from their slumber long enough to kill everyone. The use of such engines was forbidden even among those Liars who were still secretly loyal to their ancient masters and had access to Axiom technology, because with such an engine, they could go anywhere. People with that kind of mobility might disturb the slumbering Axiom, or disturb the millennia-long projects with which the old aliens hoped to reshape, or transcend, or outlive the universe.

Callie had a magic door she couldn't walk through: it was too dangerous to use the bridge generator to go someplace as thickly inhabited as the Jovian Imperative. Someone would see them appear out of nowhere, and want to know how they'd done it. So they had to go the slow route.

"Approaching Imperative space," Shall murmured. Or, rather, a budded-off, limited copy of Shall's artificial consciousness murmured. The *Golden Spider*'s computers weren't sophisticated enough to house a full copy of his mind, but it was still useful to have even a reduced version of him on board, monitoring communication channels and making sure the ship stayed cobbled together properly. Even if he wasn't as good a conversationalist as usual.

"Good." Callie double-checked the fake transponder. The pirates had a handy little gadget that could spoof various ports of origin and ship names, so they could glide into civilized parts of the solar system without being immediately fired upon, much like ancient maritime pirates had falsely flown the flags of other nations to take their victims unawares. As far as any Jovian Imperative authorities scanning them were concerned, the *Golden Spider* (née the *Inevitability of Death*) was a small freight-hauler called the *Bloedworst*, registered to a chemical processing corporation on Titan.

"That's Saturn!" Elena said over her headset, and Callie smiled at her enthusiasm.

"What, you've never seen Saturn before?"

"We kept well away from gravity wells when we set out in the *Anjou*," she said. "Oh, wow. Look at the rings."

Callie turned on her viewscreen and tried to see the familiar scene with fresh eyes: the pale yellow gas giant, tinged with orange, surrounded by those admittedly majestic glittering rings. From here, the whole was stately and beautiful, though up close the rings were whirling rivers of ice, a torrential spin of matter ranging in size from dust particles to space glaciers bigger than her ship. There were mining vessels in there too, whipping alongside the larger chunks, harvesting ice. The dark shapes of mining platforms drifted in the gas giant's atmosphere, like leaves floating on a pond, sucking up raw material to feed the fusion reactors that drove the system's Tanzer drives, and provided for most of the other energy needs in the Imperative. Several of Saturn's moons were visible against the backdrop of the planet too. There were certainly enough of them, more than sixty, and Callie couldn't remember all their names; some were too small to be useful, and even some of the larger ones were still wholly undeveloped. Saturn and its satellites marked the outer edge of absolute Jovian Imperative control, though the Jovians had extended tendrils out to Uranus and, lately, even into the orbit of Neptune and beyond.

"There's Titan! Do people live there?"

"It's one of the more populous moons, yeah. Titan has a nice thick atmosphere, so it's not too cold by local standards, which makes settlement easier. There are lots of domed bubble cities on the surface."

"Why not stop there instead of going all the way to Ganymede?" Elena said.

Callie hadn't told Elena about her plans to attend her own funeral yet – it was an awkward subject, since it involved her ex – but fortunately there was a different, and equally true, answer. "Titan isn't the nicest place in the solar system. The wormhole bridge in this system is tethered to Jupiter, so Jupiter is the center of everything out here. Culture, technology, high society, low society, arts, entertainment, commerce. Saturn is rich in resources, but the Jovian Imperative uses Saturn and its moons as an industrial base. Think chemical plants, processing centers, mining towns, as compared to restaurants, night clubs, museums." She paused. "Also, there's liquid methane on the surface of Titan. Lots of it. No matter how good the air filtration systems are, well... If Robin thought Glauketas smelled like farts, she would not enjoy visiting Goya."

"Goya?"

"The capital of Titan. Sometimes affectionately called the 'rose on the shitheap,' but one rose doesn't make much difference in a setting like that."

"Ah. So Saturn is sort of like New Jersey to Jupiter's New York."

Callie frowned. She'd heard of New York – it was a common setting in historical fiction, like Rome and Constantinople and Paris – but... "What's New Jersey?"

"New Jersey! Just across the river from New York, but a million kilometers away culturally? Butt of endless jokes? Their state bird is an inferiority complex?"

"Huh," Callie said. "Before my time. It's probably part

of the Eastern Inundated Area now. They do scuba tours to look at the submerged ruins."

"Ugh. The future is the worst. Nobody gets my jokes."

"Truly you bring us the wisdom of the ancients."

"Ancients, huh? I am young and vigorous. You're the one who tapped out last night."

Stephen cleared his throat. "This is not a private channel, Elena."

There was a long pause as Callie suppressed laughter.

"Crap. Sorry about that," Elena said. "I'm still getting the hang of the comms."

"It's fine," Robin chimed in. "Go ahead and remind me of my horrible loneliness. I haven't had sex in five hundred years is all, but who's counting?"

"I'm sure you'll make new friends on Ilus," Callie said. "We've got a long stretch ahead of us before we get to Ganymede, so keep yourselves occupied as best you can. We can do family dinner tonight if people want."

"I miss the Hypnos," Robin said. "The crappy little immersive media goggles here just don't compare. Totally convincing virtual reality is the only non-terrible thing about the future. Uh, present company excepted."

"You haven't seen our time at its best," Stephen rumbled. "Being abducted by sadistic alien space monsters and pretending to be dead for months inside an asteroid are actually fairly unusual pursuits."

"As long as there are bars. There was nothing to drink on Glauketas but crates of triple sec and crème de menthe! You can't even mix those without getting a whole orange-juice-and-toothpaste combo."

"It's probably hard to stock a bar adequately when you depend on robbing passing supply ships," Elena said.

"Still, you'd think they would have had more rum on board. If only for the sake of tradition."

Callie tuned them out, glancing over the course Shall had calculated to Ganymede. The *Golden Spider* was following it well enough so far, despite its tendency to gradually list starboard. Now that they were sailing past Saturn and its satellites, there wasn't much of interest until they reached Jupiter. After the destruction of Meditreme, the rescue on the Axiom station, and helping Lantern stage a coup and take over the local cell of truth-tellers, Callie had been ready for some down time... but she'd overdosed on idleness. It felt good to be doing something again. At least this voyage was a voyage *toward* something.

Callie spun around in her chair and stood up, enjoying the thrum of the engines through the decking under her feet. Thrust gravity was her favorite, better than the spin gravity you got on big space stations, better than being down a gravity well, and better even than the eerie artificial gravity they had now on Glaukctas. Thrust gravity meant you were going somewhere. She should hit the gym, get some exercise...

"Callie," Elena murmured in her ear. "I figured out the private channel."

"Well done."

"Would you like to explore some *other* private channels?"

Callie grinned. "I was just about to go work out."

"Yes?" Elena said. "I don't see any conflict there."

"See you in our quarters, then." She switched to another comms channel. "Shall, take the helm?"

"I *already* took the helm," he said. "I never relinquished

the helm in the first place. This is a spaceship, not a sailboat. Squishy organic brains can't be trusted in such circumstances."

"Squishy organic bodies have more fun, though."

"Pfft," Shall said. "Have fun crudely manipulating your nervous system and brain chemistry through tactile physical inputs. If you're lucky you might vaguely approximate the kind of transcendent pleasure I can experience at will just by altering my own sensorium."

"Oh, Shall. There's nothing wrong with masturbation, but I've always had more fun collaborating."

"You have no idea what goes on in the machine-intelligence-only parts of the Tangle, do you?"

She made a face. "Nor do I wish to. If the crew wants anything, tell them it can wait, unless it can't wait, and then... you deal with it."

Callie dropped down the ladder and turned toward the corridor that led to her quarters – then drew her sidearm and crouched, staring hard at an empty bit of passageway. Because, just for a moment, it hadn't *looked* empty: she'd seen something, a shimmer, like heat haze rising off a badly insulated engine. "Shall, is my infiltration suit still in storage?"

"Checking... yes, the transponder places it in the locker in your quarters. Why?"

She had a special suit with active camouflage, that allowed her to blend in with her surroundings – it was almost as good as magical invisibility, except for a slight shimmer when she moved fast. "I thought I saw something in the corridor here."

"Crap. Truth-teller assassins?"

"Ugh. If you want to go all worst-case scenario about

it." The Liars who secretly served the Axiom had all kinds of exotic technology, including short-range teleporters that could let them board her ship, and they might have stealth tech to rival her own. "Could someone have teleported on board?"

"The *Golden Spider* isn't equipped to scan for those signatures – it's not like they're a common threat. Ashok had to build the sensors we have on the *White Raven* and Glauketas."

"What *can* you scan for?"

"I'm not getting any life signs, heat signatures, unexplained motion, inexplicable sounds... of course, a stealth suit could mask a lot of that, but they're not common. Yours is a one-of-a-kind experimental model. How sure are you that you saw something?"

"Maybe sixty percent." She thought about how many repairs Ashok had done on the ship, and how poorly parts of it were still insulated – she might have *actually* seen a heat shimmer. "Maybe less."

"You do have squishy human eyes, Callie, and you've been staring at screens for a while, and also you've been pretty bored. Maybe the shimmer was just a visual artifact?"

"You're saying I have space madness?"

"I'm saying you might have space madness, yes."

"It's possible," she said. "Keep a close eye on things, though, would you? Ratchet up the security protocols another notch."

"My vigilance is eternal."

Callie tried to put it out of her mind, but she watched the air closely and kept her hand on her weapon until she reached her quarters, and got properly distracted.

• • •

Afterward, Elena and Callie lay curled together in the captain's bunk – the nicest bed in the nicest cabin on the *Golden Spider*, which was rather worse than the worst berth on the *White Raven* – just pleasantly afterglowing.

"So," Elena said. "Why are we really going to Ganymede?" She pushed herself up on her elbow and looked down at Callie, half-smiling. "I did a little research. You're right that Titan is a craphole, but Callisto is closer than Ganymede at the moment, and by all accounts it's bigger and better."

Callie sniffed. "Callisto is too fancy. It's a step below the floating cities, but it's still crammed full of rich people, and the people who make a living sucking up to rich people. Ganymede isn't a shithole like Io, but it's not totally gentrified, either. There are still artists there, people doing interesting music, young professionals just starting out. It feels alive. Callisto is great if you're rich, but if you're not, you're just standing around looking at the exteriors of places you'll never see the interiors of, and getting glared at by clerks who can smell the lack of money on you. It's like walking around in a museum, or visiting that elderly relative who covers the furniture in plastic and only has hard candies to eat. Ganymede is more vibrant."

"So that's the only reason you picked Ganymede? Your reliable reverse snobbery?"

"Ha." Callie sighed. "OK, it's kind of awkward, and I've been waiting for the right moment to bring it up, but... I used to live on Ganymede." She cleared her throat. "It's where I got married."

"Ah. So the ex is still there?"

"The ex is still there. The ex's family has extensive

business operations in Taliesen, which means I can ask them if they've seen any weird activity that might connect to the disappearance of the truth-teller cell there. Also… the ex thinks I'm dead, and he's holding a memorial service for me."

Elena smacked her on the chest and said, "Oh, *shit*!"

Callie glared. "Ow. You don't have to hit me."

Elena smacked her again. "You're going to your own funeral?"

"It's more like a celebration of my life," she grumbled. "Though I don't have a lot of friends left on Ganymede. Michael kept most of them in the divorce. He was always more fond of other people than I was. Which… was kind of the problem."

Elena wrinkled her forehead in that adorable way she had. "How so?"

"Michael was so fond of other people that he had sex with many of them behind my back."

Elena winced. "I guess social mores haven't changed that much in the past five hundred years. Cheating is still cheating."

"We got married, which is pretty old-fashioned anyway. Michael works in the financial arm of his family's corporation, and that family is old Jovian money, so it's a conservative crowd. He actually had a travel pass, is the thing – I told him he was allowed to have casual sex, if he took proper precautions, while I was out in the big empty working for long stretches. He promised to be monogamous when I was home, though, to focus on me when he had me… and he broke that promise. Repeatedly. The sex didn't bother me much. But the betrayal of trust? That's different. Without trust, what have you got?"

Elena murmured sympathetically.

"Of course, when I got suspicious, instead of confronting Michael about it, I snooped on his personal devices and read all his correspondence. At one point I threw a tablet in the general direction of his head, though I gave him plenty of time to duck. It's not like I covered myself in glory, either, is what I'm saying. Self-righteousness is a wonderful drug, but the come-down is brutal."

Elena whistled. "Was the divorce nasty?"

"Not when we finally got around to it. He was very mea culpa about everything when I caught him, and begged for counseling. I tried, for over a year. Eventually I told him that since counseling couldn't turn back time and take his dick out of all those other people, I didn't see the point in going forward with it. We separated for a while – I moved out of the house in Ilus and made my home base on Meditreme Station instead – but officially we were still married, and I even did holidays with his horrible family for a while longer, to keep up appearances, and leave the door open to reconciliation. When we decided there was no going back, and agreed to formally dissolve our relationship a couple of years ago, he was open to my offer for how to separate our finances. I took a little money and the *White Raven*, and he kept the house and most of our savings. The alternative was to sell them both and split the money, and he loves the house like I love my ship, so." She sighed. "Though it wasn't easy, having an artificial intelligence based on Michael's mind and personality as my ship's computer."

"He Who Shall Not Be Named," Elena said. Shall was an AI based on a template of Michael's mind, and seeded with his memories. Using human minds as conceptual frameworks was the only way to create artificial intelligences that took any interest in humankind at all; pure machine AIs just withdrew from all human contact and lived their own inscrutable lives of the mind… or else tried to murder everyone.

"The very same." Callie rolled over and looked at Elena's face. She could read every emotion there, and she saw a lot of sympathy and not much pity, so that was good. "The original idea was that having my ship's AI based on Michael's personality would help our marriage. Hearing his voice, talking to someone so much like him, would allow me to feel connected to Michael when I was elsewhere in the galaxy, so I wouldn't miss him as much. But it turned out to be more like talking to Michael's twin brother, the one who *doesn't* have a wandering dick. Maybe I should have put an AI based on me in the house, to keep him company on my voyages. Robo-Callie could have gotten in some nice nasty remarks when he brought lovers over, at least."

Elena chuckled. "And now he's having a memorial for you. Wow. And you're crashing it. I don't know if I'd have the courage to do that."

"Is it courage? It feels like guilt. I hate that he thinks I'm dead. We haven't spoken in over a year anyway, but that was my choice, not his. He still cares about me, and I want him to know I'm alive, even if it's still better for the rest of the world to think I'm dead."

"What are you going to say to him?"

"I'm not sure. I try to run through the scenario, you know, imagine how it might go, but my thoughts just skitter away from the subject. Thinking about Michael…

it pisses me off, is the thing. He's sad, but I'm *mad*. That's why I was so shitty to Shall for so long – because hearing his voice, his idioms, the jokes he makes, even the compliments he pays me, it all reminded me of Michael. But Shall saved my life on the Axiom station, so I decided to get over myself. It's not Shall's fault that his mental model has poor impulse control. Just because Michael betrayed me doesn't mean Shall ever will."

Elena nodded. "I'm glad you and Shall made up. He's great. Is he really a lot like Michael?"

Callie *hmmmed*. "They've diverged a lot, of course, over the years. Shall is a machine intelligence, but he's still a person, and he grows and changes based on his experiences, which have been very different from Michael's. Chasing down space pirates is a lot different than adjusting spreadsheets and massaging databases. But even so, they're a lot alike. Shall is what Michael might be if he'd spent the past several years in space with me, and didn't have the physical apparatus necessary for cheating." She frowned. "The funny thing is… Never mind."

"No, what?" Elena nudged her in the shoulder. "I knew you had an emotional landscape, but the terrain was largely mysterious. I'm enjoying this rare glimpse behind the curtain."

"More like into the abyss. When we were in counseling, Michael said he felt like I was cheating on him, emotionally – with Shall. I don't think that's fair, but I'll admit, the situation was… confusing at the time. The two of them were so similar, in voice, and in mannerism, and I spent a lot of time on the ship talking to Shall, often while in my bunk, in the dark, so it was almost pillow talk. When I'd come home, I'd mention some story, but Michael wouldn't know what I was talking about, because I'd only told Shall, not him, and I'd forgotten. Or I'd make some inside joke, or refer to some previous conversation, and when Michael looked at me blankly, I'd remember I'd actually had that exchange with Shall, not him. Michael tried to laugh about it at first. He'd joke about how Shall was my 'other husband,' or say I'd replaced him with a newer model, someone faster and smarter and always available – shit like that. It took me longer than it should have to realize they weren't really jokes. In one counseling session, Michael said that's why he cheated – he wanted to feel close to someone again, because he'd lost my heart to his digital doppelganger." She paused. "At which point I said, 'OK, but did you need to feel close to, like, *seven different someones*?'"

"Oh, good," Elena said. "For a minute there you almost had me feeling sorry for Michael." Then, perkily: "So, do I get to meet him?"

CHAPTER 6

Callie switched her viewscreen mode so she could get a real-time look at the vast curve of Jupiter, filling the lower two-thirds of the screen. They were almost at the end of their trip, and she was glad, because the voyage had been gnawing at her nerves. She'd seen two more shimmers, once in the gym and once in the shower, but the former could have been sweat in her eyes, and the latter an artifact of swirling steam. She'd spent a long night stalking through every corridor of the ship in her *own* infiltration suit, with Shall scanning each millimeter with the best sensors he could muster, telling the others it was just an exercise to keep her skills sharp, without finding any sign of intrusion. She'd sent a discreet message to Lantern, who said there was no indication that any truth-teller assassins knew about them or were pursuing them. She hadn't wanted to cause panic by telling the crew there might be an intruder, and Shall had very delicately suggested she was just antsy and bored and jumping at shadows. She wasn't at all sure he was wrong. If there was a secret killer on board, it was taking its time with the killing, and if it was a spy, it wasn't seeing anything too interesting.

Elena strolled in, bouncing on the balls of her feet. "We land today!" She dropped into the co-pilot's chair.

"That we do."

"Look at Jupiter!" Elena spun around in her chair, taking in all the viewscreens. "It's gorgeous!"

Callie couldn't disagree. In terms of visual grandeur, nothing beat the king of the planets: the swirling patterns of a thousand storms interacting, the endless churning of unimaginable titanic forces, great clouds of ammonia and ice forming cyclones and hurricanes and sine waves of colliding atmospheric fronts. The view was even better from the floating storm cities, but those bubbles were playgrounds for the ultra-rich, because building a structure that could float in an atmosphere of hydrogen and helium required access to ruinously expensive Liar-made smart matter. Callie had only visited a storm city once, while doing bodyguard work for a visiting Lunar dignitary, and even her jaded soul had been awed by looking down through a transparent floor into a storm bigger than the planet Earth.

They were going someplace more modest now. Not the craphole of Io, at least, and not the claustrophobic underwater cities of Europa, but the gleaming overlapping domes of Ilus. Her old home, once upon a time, when she'd made a living running freight and passengers through the bridge to other colony systems and back instead of scrounging scrap and chasing bad guys out in Trans-Neptunian Space... and well before she was in the freelance being-dead-and-saving-the-universe business. Old memories were swirling inside her like a Jovian storm.

"It'll be good to stand on dirt again," Elena said. "The closest I've come to being on solid land since I shipped out for my goldilocks mission is Glauketas. Otherwise it's been all ships and stations. Ganymede is practically planet-sized!"

"Nearly half the size of Earth," Callie said. "Not very massive, though, so don't expect much, gravity-wise. It's like a tenth of a G down there."

"Point-one-four-six," Shall corrected.

"Are you excited to go home?"

"The *White Raven* is my home these days, but if you have to go down a gravity well, Ganymede's not so bad."

"Not so bad! That's high praise from you, Captain Callie. Tell me something you *liked* about it. Be excited with me."

"The views are good," Callie conceded. "Ganymede is tidally locked, so the same side always faces Jupiter – that's the fashionable side, where Ilus is. The planetward surface is covered in dome cities. They're pretty, if you like that sort of thing."

"Ganymede has its own magnetic field, too," Shall said. "So it has beautiful aurorae at the poles. Much redder than the aurora borealis on Earth, for, well... physics reasons."

Callie didn't wince. She'd taken a trip to the pole with her ex-husband, early in their marriage, to stay at a luxury hotel with a spectacular view of the aurorae. Shall had memories of that experience too, of course, but here she was, thinking about Michael. Her typical approach to dealing with complex emotions was to seal them up behind a wall in her mind and never think of them again, and now the halls of her mind were full of escaped memories, rampaging up and down. His face, under the reddish lights of the Ganymede aurora... his face, covered in tears in the soft light of their therapist's office... his face, stony and still while he watched her pack her things to move out forever...

She shook herself back into the present. Shall was telling Elena various Ganymede facts. "Galileo called Ganymede, and the other three moons of Jupiter he discovered, the 'Medician Stars,' in honor of his patrons, the Medici family."

"Suck-up," Callie said.

"The name didn't stick, obviously. The Galilean Moons got their current names from another astronomer, Simon Marius, who discovered them independently, around the same time Galileo did. Io, Europa, Ganymede, Callisto – all named for the Roman god Jupiter's lovers, a convention that continued for the other moons. It's a good thing Jupiter was so promiscuous, because there are a lot of moons."

Elena nodded. "In the twenty-first century, when they sent a probe to explore Jupiter's moons, they named it Juno – Jupiter's wife, coming to check up on his lovers."

"Ha," Callie said. "Cute." It was sort of cute. Mostly it reminded her of Michael's myriad infidelities. That association, at least, helped soothe her complex mixed feelings about seeing Michael again, tilting them away from heartbreak, and regret, and the smoldering remnants of love, and more firmly toward anger and self-righteousness. She was much more comfortable with the latter feelings.

"Marius didn't name the moons so elegantly at first," Shall said. "First he just numbered them, and then tried to name them after his own patron, the Duke of Brandenburg, but no one else liked the idea."

"Good. That family got all those Bach concertos anyway," Elena said. "No need to be greedy."

"Marius's third idea was to name the four moons after other planets in the solar systems, since the moons orbited Jupiter as those planets orbited the sun."

Elena wrinkled her nose. "What, he wanted to name them Mercury, Venus, like that?"

"Not quite. He proposed calling them the Venus of Jupiter, the Mercury of Jupiter, the Saturn of Jupiter – like that. Do you know what he called Ganymede?"

"What?"

"The Jupiter of Jupiter."

Elena burst out laughing. "The Jupiter of Jupiter! It's elegant in its simplicity. I can't imagine why that didn't catch on."

"It's a mystery. Then Marius hit upon the idea of extending the mythological naming structure for the planets to the moons, and here we are."

"If I'd discovered a bunch of brand new moons, I wouldn't have named them after some patron, or any imaginary old gods, either," Callie said. "I'd have named them after *myself*."

"The... Callielean moons?" Elena said. "I don't know. Doesn't have much of a ring to it."

"Kiss my ass," Callie said. "Then kiss the *ass* of my ass."

The *Bloedworst* AKA the *Golden Spider* AKA the *Inevitability of Death* didn't have a nice observation deck like the *White Raven* did, so Elena, Ibn, Robin, and Uzoma all crammed into the cockpit with Callie. She had the viewscreens on the walls set to simulate a window view of the satellite below them.

Much of the surface of the Jupiter of Jupiter was smooth gray ice, mottled with darker areas that were predominantly rock; they looked almost like continents adrift in a sea of ice, which wasn't all that far from the truth. Callie hit the zoom function and the view of the moon jumped closer to them, its pocked and striated surface filling the screen. She magnified again, and then again. "There. That's Ilus, the best city on the best moon of the second-best planet in the system."

"It looks like... did you ever blow bubbles, as a child?" Robin said. "Sometimes you'd blow a lot of bubbles all at once, and they'd get caught on the ground or a leaf or whatever, and the bubbles would stick to each other, and you'd have these overlapping hemispheres..."

Callie nodded. "That's pretty much the aesthetic down there, yeah." Ilus had an immense central dome, covering a huge green park and most of the grand public buildings, but that dome sprouted a cluster of three dozen more domes of varying sizes from all sides, and some of *those* domes had their own smaller domes lampreyed on as well. Most of the bubbles were transparent, revealing gleaming towers or factories or forests, but some domes were pale pink or green, and some were opaqued into blackness.

"It's like a single dome covered in parasitic growths," Elena said. "Or, no... like a Portuguese man-o-war. A colony organism, made up of multiple independent creatures, conglomerated together."

Callie shuddered. She'd visited relatives in the Algarve

back on Earth as a child, and one of their favorite reclaimed beaches been closed one summer due to an infestation of those stinging, tentacled terrors of the sea. The invading men-o-war had transformed a beautiful, familiar place into a dangerous and threatening one. She looked at the city below. Maybe the Portuguese man-o-war wasn't such a bad metaphor for Ilus, after all. After what happened with Michael down there, she'd avoided returning to Ganymede, and indeed the whole Jovian Imperative, as much as she could, because everything she'd once found beautiful and comforting had turned poisonous instead.

"Ilus is less toxic," she said at last. "For the most part, anyway. Stay out of the blacked-out domes if you're concerned about your safety. They're mostly unregulated decriminalized areas, and you agree to a waiver as soon as you enter that acknowledges you're no longer under the protection of local authorities: enter at your own risk. It's where you go for strange drugs, stranger sex, unsanctioned medical procedures, and things like that."

"I thought you said Ilus was a nice city?" Ibn said.

"Eh," Callie said. "It's a good city. The dangerous parts are clearly marked and set aside for people who want to explore them, and the rest of the city is pretty safe. It's your own fault if you stray from the path. Callisto doesn't have any black dome districts at all – the super-rich have their own personal drug dealers – and it's a lot less vibrant and more boring because of that. Io is nothing *but* bad neighborhoods. I like a place that has some life and options but where you won't get mugged every time you take a walk. Ilus is best for our purposes." Stephen wouldn't have been able to acquire his sacraments on Callisto, for one thing. The bespoke psychotropics favored by the Church of the Ecstatic Divine were generally frowned upon by the conservative oligarchs who ruled the Imperative, as was the church itself – the CoED wasn't illegal, but they operated mostly in the shadows.

"Callie," Shall said. "I have an incoming splintercast from – well, another me, from Glauketas."

CHAPTER 7

"Talking to yourself again?" Callie said. "I always heard that was a sign of a weak mind."

"On the contrary, it's a privilege enjoyed by those of us with better mental architecture than you squishy types possess," Shall said.

"What's a splintercast?" Robin asked.

"Encrypted communication," Callie said. "Military – or pirate – grade. It embeds a concealed signal in other comms traffic, like a splinter under the skin. You need a corresponding cryptographic key to extract the message – to pull out the splinter."

"Are the decryption codes called tweezers?" Elena couldn't help herself.

"Ugh. No. Please don't make that joke in front of Ashok, or he'll start calling them that and never stop. Is this a message for my eyes only, Shall, or can we share it with the rest of the class?" Unless the signal was marked private, Shall would have already digested the contents.

"It's for all of us in general, and I think it will make you happy."

"Good news? That's unusual. Put it up on the screen, then."

Ashok's face appeared onscreen, too close to the camera, and thus even more distorted than usual. He pulled back far enough to wave jauntily. "O captain my admiral! And anybody else still on board the *Inevitability of Boredom*. We have a visitor." He stepped away, revealing his machine shop, and a squidlike Liar clambered up onto the worktable and undulated two of her seven pseudopods in greeting.

"It's Lantern!" Ashok said from offscreen.

"I think they know that," Lantern said, in the warm and familiar tones of her artificial voicebox. Elena was pleased to see Lantern's face. Not that she had a face; she had seven eyes, arrayed around the domelike central bulge of her body, and "front" and "back" were all the same to her. Her pseudopods pulsed briefly with undulating lines of dark purple and pale blue, which meant affectionate greetings, if Elena was reading the body language correctly. Liars communicated among themselves primarily non-verbally, with pheromones and chromatic shifts and movements, and even when talking to humans, those other channels kept working. Elena was doing her best to learn the language, a gesture that Lantern seemed to appreciate.

Lantern said, "Callie, Elena, Stephen, and any other humans I do not know as well but nevertheless possess generally positive feelings toward – greetings. I have glad news. I have thoroughly studied the data banks on my station, and examined all the outgoing and incoming communications from the past several months, and made discreet inquiries where necessary… and I have determined that your identities are safe."

Callie leaned back in her chair, and Elena was pleased to see her visibly relax. Then she frowned. "I wish this was a real-time transmission. I know Lantern's sect does a lot of in-person communication, to keep things compartmentalized and undetectable. What if she missed some hand-off of information, or–"

"I'm certain of my findings," Lantern went on. "It has taken me months to be comfortable announcing this conclusion, because the price of error is death. You must understand, my sect does not like to admit any difficulties to the central authority. No one wants a visit from our leaders, because their evaluations have a tendency to become purges. As a result, our reports... minimize problems. The elder of my cell only told our leaders that humans had discovered a piece of Axiom technology – they did not even say it was a wormhole generator – and that steps were being taken to recover and destroy the artifact and silence the humans. After you helped me take over the local cell of my sect, I personally sent a report confirming that the technology had been destroyed, and the humans eliminated. Your names, and the name of your ship, were never transmitted beyond the bounds of the cell, and those who *did* know your names here perished when we staged our takeover. None of the other truth-tellers know you are alive." She paused. "I'm sorry you were not here to receive the news in person, but I hope to see you again soon."

Ashok stuck his face between Lantern and the camera, grinning. "We're alive again! It's *Resurrection Day*!"

The screen blanked.

Callie swiveled around in her chair and grinned at the

others. "I am no longer one of the undead." She exhaled heavily. "That is a nice feeling."

"It makes crashing your own funeral a little easier," Shall said. "You won't have to be as subtle."

"Subtle? I was looking forward to seeing Callie dress up like a ghost," Elena said.

"I was leaning more toward putting on my infiltration suit and sneaking into my ex-husband's office and ambushing him after the memorial was over, but I can do a more direct approach now." She paused. "If anyone asks, though, this ship is still the *Bloedworst* out of Europa. I'm allowed to be alive, but I probably shouldn't be on a stolen pirate ship with a false transponder." She shooed them. "Ibn, Robin, Uzoma, go strap in – we're landing soon."

After they were gone, Elena took the co-pilot's chair without asking and allowed it to enfold her. "What are you planning to do, now that it's the first day of the rest of your old life?"

"Get a job," Callie said. "While Lantern is investigating possible galaxy-saving missions for us, we still have bills to pay. At least now we can access our own accounts, and buy stuff openly from public marketplaces instead of the dark parts of the Tangle – the mark-ups for privacy are brutal – but we still need to get income flowing."

"Also, you like working," Elena said.

"Also that."

"What kind of work will you look for?"

She shrugged. "Transporting things, or people, or chasing things, or people, or making sure things, or people, don't get blown up while someone else transports them or chases them. That's basically my whole skillset."

"I wouldn't say that."

Callie chuckled. "My whole skillset in terms of moneymaking skills, then."

"I don't know about *that*, either," Elena said.

"Ha. Nothing against people who do that kind of work – it's as good a way to earn a living as any, and better than many I could name – but I enjoy it more when the motivation is purely intrinsic. I've never been to bed with someone I didn't have romantic feelings for."

"Really? No drunken tumbles just because you like the look of someone in a bar? Your will is like unto adamant."

Callie shrugged. "It's not that. It's not even a philosophical stance. I've just... I can admire how someone looks, sure, but I don't want to sleep with them. If I start liking someone in a certain way, though, lust follows."

"That's really sweet." Elena gazed at the viewscreen. "In the interests of disclosure, I'll admit I did a fair bit of sleeping around for sport when I was younger, and it was more enjoyable than not. What you and I have is different, though, and I like it, too. Better, even. And not just because we get to practice and refine our techniques."

"We haven't talked about... us... too much," Callie said. "Our configuration, or whatever. It hasn't really been an issue, since you didn't seem interested in anyone else on the station, except maybe Sebastien–"

Elena shook her head. "That ship has sailed. And crashed into a star."

Callie snorted. "I can't say I'm sorry to hear it. But if you ever want to, you know... discuss things, or whatever... we can do that. I don't really know what, this, dating, relationships, whatever, was like in the time you came from, and this is important to me. I don't want to mess this up because we didn't talk about things, or because we made bad assumptions."

Elena reached out and put a hand on her arm. Callie was so absolutely confident in other areas, it was kind of sweet to see her trying to navigate matters of the heart. "I like being with you, Callie. I'm in love with you. I'm not interested in being with anyone else right now. If that changes, I'll talk to you about it. And if you start *liking* someone else, in that way that turns to lust, you'll tell me, too. OK?"

"Absolutely."

Elena nodded. After the way Callie's marriage had ended, dishonesty in *that* arena wasn't something she was too worried about. "Good. I think that's all I need for now. Labels don't matter to me all that much. How about you?"

"Me neither." Callie paused. "But they can be useful. Like... how should I introduce you to Michael? What should I say we *are* to each other?"

"I can't wait to see how you handle that situation." Elena grinned, and before Callie could do more than wrinkle her forehead and open her mouth to reply, Ilus ground control was giving them instructions about their landing site.

Shall broke into Callie's private comms after she strapped in for the landing. "There was an additional voice message from Lantern, for your ears only."

"Let's hear it."

Lantern said, "Callie, I wasn't sure if you'd want me to share this in front of the whole crew, or if you'd like to consider your options before telling them. The leaders of my sect are very concerned about the situation in the Taliesen system. They want to send a representative to the base there to investigate in person, and to check on the Axiom facility, and I believe I can secure that mission for myself without raising suspicions. I am a new elder, after all, and they will believe I am trying to prove myself and my value by volunteering. Let me know if you discover anything in your researches on Ganymede… and if you'd care to join me on the voyage. I'd be very happy to have you, but I know you may want time to adjust to getting your lives back. If this were a certainty, I would ask for your help more ardently, but the lack of communication may have nothing to do with the Axiom at all – it could just be an accident or a technological failure."

"Well?" Shall broke in when the transmission was over. "What did she say?"

"I'll tell you later," Callie said. "She might have some unpaid interstellar work for us to do."

"Saving the galaxy isn't very lucrative, is it?"

"No, but at least it makes people try to kill us."

Callie, Stephen, Elena, Ibn, Robin, and Uzoma disembarked at the docking station, one of a network of small domes a bullet-tram ride away from the city proper. They had a brief wait on the platform before piling into an otherwise empty tram car, a gently lit lozenge that zipped along, humming through a subterranean tube.

"Here we go." Robin clung to a pole, eyes bright

through the screen of her hanging hair. "Off to the next thing." She bounced on the balls of her feet, and given the low gravity on Ganymede, it was a lot of bounce.

Ibn nodded. "I am attempting to consider it an adventure." He paused. "Unfortunately, I dislike adventures."

Uzoma nodded. "Agreed. I have had enough adventure. I look forward to the controlled conditions of a physics lab."

Elena sighed. "I'm going to miss you all so much."

"We'll miss you too, but the pirate's life isn't for us," Robin said. "Ibn and I were talking – the destination of our goldilocks ship, all those centuries ago? There's actually a colony there now. The wormhole gate for that system is located about a month's journey from the planets, so it's not the most popular colony, and they're actively looking for more immigrants. It's called the Kur system now, and there are two habitable planets, Ki and Nammu. Ki is the colony candidate we were aiming for. We might have actually made a start there, if we'd arrived like we were supposed to, and other people hadn't beat us to it."

"You want to go there?" Elena asked.

Ibn nodded. "We're interested to see how it all turned out… and to see what we can do to help."

"We've set you up with personal accounts, with a share of the take from Glauketas," Callie said. "You aren't set for life or anything, but it should be sufficient to pay your passage and get you established."

"Thank you," Ibn said. "Stephen put us in touch with members of his blasphemous hedonistic sect in Ilus, and they've offered to help us sort out the logistics of travel. We're going to meet them shortly."

"We're very helpful blasphemers," Stephen said.

Uzoma nodded. "They have offered to help me find housing. I will pursue independent study in the Tangle while I apply to the university here. Shall tells me the Ganymede branch has the best physics and computer science departments in the Imperative University system."

Callie nodded. "I've got some strings I can pull there, and I'm going to pull the shit out of them for you."

The tram slowed and stopped, and the doors slid open. This station was right in the middle of the main public market beneath the central dome, and the tram filled with scents of roasting meat and wafting spices. The sound of buskers on ur-pipes played above the low background thunder of hundreds of people going about their lives.

Callie led them into a white-and-black tiled plaza dotted with trees in planters, and smiled as the refugees from the past craned their heads back and marveled at the dome, tinted a pale blue to suggest an open Earthly sky. Immense pieces of kinetic sculpture – new since Callie's last visit; the public art was a rotating collection – filled the space overhead with shimmering shapes of silver and gold and brass and copper. They resembled impressionistic versions of fish and rabbits and birds and serpents, all slowly twirling and rotating on invisible filaments.

This was where their paths diverged. Callie said her farewells to Ibn and Robin and Uzoma, then stepped aside to let Elena have her more emotional goodbyes, with lots of hugging and promises to be in touch frequently. Even Uzoma opened their arms to Elena, who said "Really?

It's okay? I know you prefer your hugs metaphorical."

Uzoma nodded gravely. "I would like a literal one, just this once." Callie was glad Elena and Uzoma had grown so much closer during their attempts to cure Sebastien.

Stephen and Ibn conferred for a long moment, then embraced. Callie was glad they'd become friends too. Space was big and lonely, and Stephen had been in a bad way emotionally after losing his congregation when Meditreme Station was destroyed. He was still clearly hurting, but his relationship with Ibn had helped.

Robin and Ibn gave their last waves, and Uzoma a businesslike nod. The three of them set off, with Shall doubtless murmuring in their earpieces to make sure they didn't get lost on their way to meet their contacts from the church.

Elena leaned up against Callie, wiping tears away from her cheeks. "It's funny. I always thought of them more like co-workers than friends, you know? We trained together, and we were psychologically compatible, but we were there for the mission, not for each other. And now... there go three of my oldest friends."

"Three of the oldest possible friends in the whole galaxy," Callie said. "There are only about a hundred known time refugees, and you're among the oldest, from the first wave of goldilocks ships and the earliest cryo-sleep systems."

"Lucky for me you like older women," Elena said.

"You had this whole sleeping beauty thing going. How could I resist?"

Stephen cleared his throat. "Not to interrupt your flirting, but shouldn't we go to your funeral?"

"It would be gauche to show up late," Callie said.

"Should I... I don't know... call Michael and tell him I'm alive? Since we're allowed to be alive again, and I can make a call without worrying that truth-tellers will blow up Ganymede if they overhear?"

"Mmm," Stephen said. "You could. That would be nice of you. On the other hand, didn't he surprise you rather rudely once?"

Callie nodded. "There's that."

"What happened?" Elena said.

"Oh, I found out Michael was cheating on me in the traditional way: I came home early to surprise him, and found him in bed with someone else instead."

"Ugh," Elena said. "Popping up out of your coffin and yelling 'boo' seems like reasonable retribution for that."

"Are you going to run your errands now, Stephen?" Callie said.

"And miss seeing your glorious resurrection? Absolutely not. My errands can wait."

"Resurrection Day," Callie muttered.

They took an auto-cab two domes over to the residential district where Michael lived, and it dropped them off out front. Elena whistled, gazing around appreciatively. Callie tried to see it through her eyes: the dome above in swirling orange and yellow sunset colors, the house a deliberately retro design of metal curves and glass panels. Callie thought the structure looked like the skull of a giant Art Deco robot monster, but in a good way. The house was on its own large plot, with steps leading up from the street, and the neighboring houses were hidden behind artful combinations of fencing, ornamental hedges, and other landscaping details to make the place seem even more private. Life-extension technology being what it was, Michael was still a relatively junior member of his family's corporation, and the house was more "comfortable executive" than "rapacious oligarch." Michael got a lot of bonuses working in the financial services division, though, so the interior was always cutting-edge. Callie came home from more than one trip to find the inside utterly transformed, except for their bedroom, which he never changed without consulting her. Though that probably wasn't the case any more.

The windows were partially tinted, but Callie could see figures moving around inside, holding glasses and chatting. The grieving masses. "Enter, three wraiths," Callie said, and pulled her hood up over her head.

CHAPTER 8

Callie was afraid the house would greet her by name, spoiling the effect of her entrance, but apparently Michael had changed the settings in the expert system. No one took much notice of her, or the similarly hooded Stephen, and she spotted a few other people in matching garb – stupid cloaks were apparently in fashion again, and they looked close enough to the norm that no one looked twice.

Michael had changed the layout, replacing all the furniture and artwork from the day she'd moved out. Had he changed it just because the whim struck him, or because looking at the furnishings reminded him too much of her, and caused him pain? Why did she wonder about that? Ugh. Feelings were horrible things.

Callie moved quietly among the crowd, not catching anyone's eye, but looking around for familiar faces. Most of the people she recognized were Michael's relatives and friends, which made sense. She'd never made a lot of close connections on Ilus, and those she did have were more itinerant, like her, venturing out and treating Ganymede as a home base. She'd always had more in

common with people who plied the spaceways and
traversed the bridges than with those content to stay in a
gravity well, even one as mild as Ganymede's.

The overall mood was somber enough, but there
wasn't much in the way of open sobbing or rending of
garments, which peeved her, but only mildly. They all
thought she'd been dead for months, after all, killed
when Meditreme Station exploded. The memorial
had only taken this long because Michael had held
out hope she'd turn up miraculously alive, probably.
The windows and wall screens were cycling through
photos and short video clips of her, taken from happier
times: their wedding in the floating gardens, Michael
in beautiful formal robes, Callie in a bespoke suit made
by his family tailors, both with starlight charms in their
hair. Their honeymoon in the polar resorts of the Silla
system, hurling snowballs at each other on the slopes.
Callie laughing at a dinner party. Callie smashing a bottle
of real Earth champagne against the nose of the *White
Raven* on its naming day. Michael and Callie on their first
anniversary, and then a run of photos showing every
anniversary after, in a succession of fine restaurants, on
up to the eighth; that was as far as they got, at least in
terms of celebrating. Their final wedding anniversary
before the divorce had passed unremarked by either of
them, though not unnoticed – at least by Callie.

The photos were hardly her life story, of course. There
were no pictures from any of her many trips through the
bridges (she'd been to every system at least once, except,
of course, the Vanir system); no videos of her piloting
the *Raven* in pursuit of assorted fugitives; no photos
of her clowning around with Ashok after a successful

salvage; no footage of her playing Go with Stephen, or climbing around on the hull with Shall's repair drones, or getting drunk with her late friend Hermione at the Spinward Lounge or some other bar on Meditreme. It was a celebration of her life, yes, but only the parts of her life that had intersected with Michael's.

But even that much sent a poisonous wave of nostalgia through her. Callie's eyes stung, and she gritted her teeth. Elena put a hand on her arm, and Callie looked down at her, trying to smile. "I'm OK," she murmured, and returned to scanning the room. Where was Michael, anyway? What kind of host didn't come to greet–

Ah, there he was, with his mother and father and a representative sample of aunts and uncles, all seated in a cluster around the freestanding fireplace in the center of the living room. Callie started toward him, then hesitated when Michael patted his mother's hand and stood up. He looked tired, and regret stabbed at Callie for not letting him know she was alive as soon as she could have. Just because he'd been a trifling asshole didn't mean she had to be petty as well, but it was too late now.

Michael glanced around, then stepped up onto the stone hearth, which suited him like a pedestal for the statue of a philosopher king. Why did he still have to look so good? He'd grown more attractive to her when she fell in love with him, so why hadn't he become ugly in her eyes when he broke her heart? He wore an immaculate dark suit woven with glittering threads, his dark hair was swept back (with a little picturesque gray at the temples), and his eyes were bright and blue. The bags under those eyes were darker than she'd ever seen before, even during the divorce. He cleared his throat, and the house's expert system cut off the background music. The room rustled as everyone turned to face him.

"Thank you all for coming," Michael said. "We've gathered here today to celebrate the life of Kalea Maria Machedo – Callie, to her friends. All of you knew her, and many of you loved her. She was courageous, brilliant, ambitious, stubborn, difficult, but always completely her own person. For a decade I was lucky enough to call her the love of my life, and even when we separated, my admiration for her never faded. Most of us have lost people out there, in the cold and the dark. The galaxy is a dangerous place, out beyond the safety of our domes, and I often wished she would stay here, with me, where it was safe. But staying locked away under glass was never Callie's way. She lived for the opportunity to stand beneath new skies, in the light of new stars. Those stars all shine a little dimmer, for me, in her absence."

Pretty good speech, Callie thought.

Michael looked around. "Would anyone like to say a few words?"

Callie had always possessed a good sense of the dramatic. She threw back her hood and stepped on top of a low coffee table made of pale green stone. "I guess I should probably say something."

There was a beat as everyone turned and looked at her, and then Michael's Aunt Simone fainted, or pretended to, and there was a lot of gasping and shouting and milling around. Michael just stared at her, mouth agape – at a loss for words, for once.

Callie cleared her throat. "Hi, everyone. Reports of my demise were greatly... you know how the saying goes." No one laughed. Fair enough. "I'm so sorry you all thought the worst. I wasn't on Meditreme Station when it exploded. I was on my ship, out in the depths, chasing bad guys, and didn't even know about the disaster until it was old news." That wasn't even remotely true, but it was the most plausible story she'd been able to come up with on the ride over. "I only recently returned, and found out about this memorial service, and… here I am." She stopped talking. Everyone seemed to expect more. She scratched her chin. "Feel free to keep saying nice things about me, though? Michael throws a good party, and now you can dance and laugh without feeling like insensitive jerks."

Michael started toward her. The crowd parted. She stepped down off the table before he reached her, because she didn't want to be looking down at him when they reunited. She was already a little taller than he was. They stood, looking at one another, and she wondered if he was going to yell at her, or hug her, or both. Instead he said, "It's so nice of you to come. You could have RSVP'd, though."

"It was kind of a last minute thing." She gestured. "I brought a couple of people – you remember Stephen?"

Her XO was standing by the buffet with Elena, sucking a shrimp off a toothpick. He swallowed. "Hello, Michael. Always a pleasure."

"Stephen. Welcome." Michael inclined his head.

"And that's Elena, my, ah…"

Elena beamed. "Yes? Your what?"

"My, ah… the person I'm with."

"Elegant," Elena said. "Succinct. Hello, Michael. You have a lovely home, and I'm sorry about all this. Maybe we should have called ahead, but you have to admit, Callie does have a flair for the dramatic."

He nodded gravely. "I have often observed that quality in her. It's very nice to meet you, Elena." He turned away and raised his voice. "Everyone! This is no longer a memorial, but since we're here, please enjoy yourselves. I'm just going to have a… private word with my… with Callie. We'll return soon."

"We're having a private word?" Callie half-whispered.

"I think that would be preferable to a *public* word, given the circumstances, don't you?"

"It's your house, so we can do it your way."

They threaded their way through the crowd, with people Callie barely remembered murmuring their congratulations at her ongoing survival, and proceeded down a hallway she remembered well, though the walls were a different color. She was afraid they were going to their old master bedroom, which would have stirred up all sorts of memories (some good ones, sure, but mostly overshadowed by the one where she found him in bed with a financial analyst named Gerald). Fortunately, they went into Michael's study instead. That had always been his private domain, but given the circumstances, Callie was willing to cede him the home field advantage.

His study was a high-ceilinged, airy space lit with full-spectrum light globes, decorated with shelves and tables of faux blond wood. The room was dominated by an exquisitely ergonomic desk that appeared made of silver latticework, and on either side of the desk stood self-configuring chairs that paid attention to how you shifted around in them and algorithmically altered themselves to fit your body perfectly. Callie sat down on the visitor side, and her chair wriggled around her subtly, lending her support where she needed it – physically, at least. Michael took a seat on the other side of the desk. Callie felt like she was at a job interview, and dealt with her nervousness by affecting nonchalance and taking in the décor.

In contrast to the rest of the house, the study hadn't changed much, though there was the odd bit of new art on the wall, mostly Jovian spacescapes executed with more enthusiasm than skill. Callie figured Michael was probably fucking the artist – his taste was too good for any other explanation – but decided not to speculate on that aloud.

Michael stared at her, his face perfectly blank. She stared back until she got bored, then gestured vaguely behind her. "The house looks nice. I like the new dining room table. Is it real wood?"

"Yes, please, let's discuss my decorating. I can think of no more pressing matter."

Callie sighed. "All right. I'm here. Get it out of your system."

He took a deep breath. "First, of course, I am so happy that you're alive. Relief, and even joy, are my foremost emotions."

"I can tell, from the relieved and joyful look on your face."

He didn't even crack a smile. "My neutral expression is the result of joy and relief conflicting with a certain amount of horror and outrage, because I thought you were dead, and you didn't tell me otherwise. I realize we're divorced, and that you don't owe me anything, but–"

"No, you're right."

He blinked. "I think that's the… third time you've ever said that to me?"

"Is it?" She considered. "There was the thing with the lobster, but what… Oh, right, the karaoke bar in the Irani system. Add this to those cherished moments. Yes. I should have let you know I was still alive. I'm sorry."

"Were you really so far out in the depths that you didn't know about Meditreme Station until, what, today?"

Callie couldn't tell him the truth, but it was hard to keep lies straight, so she decided to split the difference. "No. That was just the simplest way to explain things to a crowd. I was pretty far out for a while, it's true, but then I was dealing with a lot of chaos, and after that… I was investigating."

"Investigating? Ah. You mean, trying to find out who destroyed Meditreme Station? It wasn't an accident, like the official reports say?"

"It wasn't an accident. It was a deliberate attack." True, but there was no need to tell him it had been an attack aimed at her, and her ship, and the alien tech they had on board.

"Pirates?" he said. "Was it Glauketas? I heard that theory, but it didn't make sense to me. Why would the pirates want to destroy the station, when they preyed on traffic to it?"

Huh. Well, why not? "The TNA was getting tired of the pirates. They'd been nibbling at the edges of our trade routes for a while, and we'd tolerated that, but they got bolder, and started seriously impacting operations – kidnapping and killing people instead of just looting, taking down bigger vessels, hitting us more often. Warwick, the security chief on Meditreme, commissioned me to destroy the pirate base, and loaded up the *Raven* with cutting-edge armaments to make it easier. It was all-out war between us."

Michael winced. His work never involved anything more violent than fighting over who would pay the check at a business lunch. "So the pirates decided Meditreme Station was an existential threat and destroyed it. How horrible. And... you couldn't reveal that you'd survived, because then the pirates would know you were hunting them?"

"Something like that," Callie said.

"I assume you finished your mission?"

"The pirate fleet has been eliminated. My crew, and some survivors of a wreck we found, took up residence in the old pirate base." She shrugged. "It's safe to reveal that we're alive now, so here I am. I'm really sorry you were worried. I didn't expect you to hold a memorial for me."

"At least now you can be the guest of honor." He looked down. "I'm very sorry for everything you lost. I know Meditreme was your home, after this wasn't any more."

"I've got some practice at losing things," Callie said. "But thanks."

"I'm glad Stephen and the others, at least, are all right. I know how much your crew means to you."

"They're my family," she said simply.

"And... Elena?"

"What about her?"

He raised one eyebrow, something she'd always found

painfully endearing, and it made her heart ache a little now too.

"She's... I don't know what we are, really. Besides in love, which you and I both know is necessary but not sufficient. We're figuring it out together. I think you'd like her. She gets along really well with Shall."

"Shall?"

"Michael Mark II. The Michael Bot. Robo-Michael. Especially after the divorce, it got awkward, calling him by your name, so we started calling him Shall."

"An understandable innovation," he said. "Do give my digital doppelganger my best."

"Will do." She swiveled back and forth in her chair. "So. Um. How are things with you?"

"Since I'm no longer in mourning, I'd say they're looking up."

"How's the family business?"

He chuckled. "Since when are you interested in that?"

She lied breezily. "Oh, I just noticed your horrible uncle Reynauld wasn't here. Is he busy with Taliesen now that the terraforming project is done? Or is it just that he never liked me?"

"Why not both?" Michael said. He leaned back in his chair. "Since you mention it, yes, Taliesen is keeping Uncle Reynauld very busy, though not for good reasons."

Callie tried not to look too interested, or too worried. Surely if the redoubtable utopian artsy-fartsy scrappy pioneers in the Taliesen system had been attacked by a race of heretofore unknown advanced genocidal aliens, Michael would have led with that information. "What's going on?"

"Various disasters. A team of surveyors went

missing, and the people who went looking for them also went missing. Reynauld sent a crew of our special auditors to find out what was going on... and they never returned, either."

"Huh." The special auditors were very good, within their limitations. "Pirates?"

"It's hard to believe so. The company has mining rights in the asteroid field out there, but the project is in the early stages. They've only just begun setting up crew quarters and equipment, so there's not much for pirates to prey on, unless they specialize in stealing extruded plastic and plasma drills."

"A rival company, maybe?" Callie said. "Or wildcat miners taking out your people, maybe even stealing the equipment to help their own operations?" Or the Axiom.

"It's possible," Michael said.

"So send a hundred mercenaries to kick their asses," she said.

Michael sighed. "Would that it were so easy. Reynauld took a lot of risks investing so heavily in that system, and though the investment looks poised to pay off, his position is delicate. He's kept the problem quiet so far, and only confided in me about it, but if word gets out that they've lost that many personnel, including a team of auditors? It would make his position more precarious. He could even lose his place on the board."

"Couldn't happen to a nicer guy," Callie said. "So you need someone capable and discreet to investigate, huh?"

Michael chuckled. "You just came back from the dead, and now you're angling for a job?"

"There are precious few money-making opportunities in the grave. It's better for my mind and mood if I have a job, and neither one of us wants Ashok to be bored and unemployed."

"True enough." He swiveled back and forth in his chair, thoughtful. "Reynauld did reach out to me about hiring a freelance team to investigate the disappearances discreetly. It's so hard to know who you can trust – any company that contracts regularly with Imperative corporations is going to have spies and moles reporting to rival corporations, after all, and Uncle Reynauld has no shortage of enemies."

"I've always said the Jovian Imperative is a sack full of snakes."

"I thought you said it was a bucket full of scorpions?"

"The bucket is *inside* the sack. Keep up."

He smiled, which was as good as a laugh from most people. "You know, that's not a bad idea, Callie. You're discreet, at least professionally. You won't go tattling to the board, whatever you find out. And I do trust you."

"Glad to hear it. I'm the one in this room who's never betrayed a trust, after all."

He winced. "A fair hit, and a palpable one. Let me continue making amends by helping fund your resurrection. Uncle Reynauld has a certain amount of discretion in his budget, so it should be worth your while."

Callie smiled. She'd planned to ask Michael for favors, which galled her, but now they were just negotiating a benefits package, and she was very comfortable with that. "Maybe you could help me out with another thing, too."

"I live to serve."

"My crew is pretty well-settled on Glauketas now. As

much as I enjoy the outlaw life, I'd rather not have my new home get eminent-domained by the Imperative, or blown up by a passing gunship because it's still flagged as an illegal haven of slime and villainy in some security contractor's database."

"Yes, I can see how you might crave a little security."

"You set up that holding company for me when we bought the *White Raven*, right? I'd like you to get Glauketas added to the Machedo Corporation's asset sheet."

"You're taking squatter's rights a bit far, aren't you? Or did you happen to have the pirate queen sign over the deed?"

Callie snorted. "Please. Like the pirates bothered with a paper trail. Nobody owns the asteroid, officially. I had Shall dig into the records. Glauketas used to belong to a minor mining concern incorporated under the auspices of the Trans-Neptunian Authority, but the company dissolved without reassigning the rights, and since the company *and* the polity that held its paperwork have both ceased to exist, the asteroid has no legal owner, and since it's already been modified for human habitation, it's not just an asteroid, it's a derelict station – so I claim it by law of salvage."

"Hmm. Salvage laws in the Imperative aren't quite as liberal as they were in the Trans-Neptunian Authority–" She glared, and Michael held up his hands. "Yes, all right. I'll take care of it. The company lawyers can register it as one of your assets. Since Glauketas is beyond the Imperative's borders, it's not subject to most of our laws, though. Your legal status will just keep other Imperative concerns, or the government, from making claims on the asteroid. Don't expect any help from our emergency services or security forces."

"I'm all the cops I need, thanks. I have one other request."

"You're the one who asked *me* for a job, you know," he said.

"Please. I'm the answer to your horrible uncle's prayers. I've got a time refugee I rescued, Uzoma, staying with some friends of Stephen's now. They were a brilliant physicist and mathematician and starship engineer – five hundred years ago. They've got the brains and dedication and drive to excel, but they're way behind on the literature. They were still using astrolabes and sextants or whatever back in their day, probably. Uzoma wants to go back to school. I owe them – I'd probably be dead without them. I want to help."

"Uzoma wants to attend JIU Ganymede, I suppose? It's got the best physics and engineering school in the Imperative."

"That's the one."

Michael nodded. "I can call the dean. She's an old friend, and we bought her a new administration building last year. I don't suppose this time refugee left behind a bank account that's been gathering compound interest for five centuries?"

"Nope."

"All right. We'll handle tuition, too. How does the Kalea Machedo Scholarship for Displaced Persons sound?"

Callie winced. "Make it the Meditreme Station Memorial Scholarship, how about that?"

Michael nodded. "Consider it done."

"I have to run the job by the crew, but I'm sure they'll be on board." Especially since it was just an excuse to pursue their real mission of fighting the Axiom.

"Who could say no to you?" Michael said. "Should we go take part in the celebration of your life? Since you're alive to celebrate it, and all?"

"I suppose slipping away without a word would be ungracious." They rose, and started toward the door.

"I really am… joyful," Michael said. "I know it's too late for us, and I accept that, but I'm glad it's not too late for you to… to live. To have a good life."

She groaned. "This estrangement would all be a lot easier on me if you were a complete piece of shit instead of just a partial one, Michael."

"I'll try to live down to your expectations more in the future," he said.

CHAPTER 9

Elena went out to the garden, marveling at the sight of flowers growing out of the *ground*, something she hadn't seen in months of conscious time and centuries of real-time. Sure, the dirt was probably imported at great expense, the flowers were doubtless genetically engineered, and the sunshine was artificial full-spectrum light – but it *felt* like being outside, even if the low gravity prevented it from feeling like Earth. She sat on an ornamental bench and looked at the great silver blossoms bobbing on long stems, and listened to the slow burble of a nearby fountain. She started thinking about life in low gravity, and how animals would adapt to these conditions – did they have squirrels? butterflies? – so she was surprised when someone sat down on the bench beside her. Michael.

Elena looked at him sidelong, and supposed she could see what Callie had liked about him, at least superficially: he was handsome, and smiled like he knew interesting secrets, and had a casual ease and confidence that could be appealing. "So," he said. "You and Callie."

He sounded *exactly* like Shall, and Shall was probably

Elena's best friend in the galaxy apart from Callie, so it felt natural to talk to him casually. Too natural. Probably she'd better be careful. "Me and Callie," she agreed.

"How did you two meet?"

"She found me in a glass coffin and brought me back to life."

Michael chuckled. "Very fairy-tale. But really."

"Really. I'm from the twenty-second century. I was in cryo-sleep, on a wrecked ship, and Callie and her crew rescued me. We went through some... rough experiences... and got pretty close, pretty quickly. We've been working on getting closer."

Michael crossed his legs. "That's remarkable. It's like something from a story. A woman from the distant past falls in love with a hard-bitten space captain."

"I don't bite her *that* hard," Elena said.

Michael burst out with a brief but genuine-seeming laugh. "That's very good. You have to be quick to keep up with Callie."

"You two were together for a long time, weren't you?"

"Ten years from first date to finalizing the divorce, more or less. Eight of them were even good."

"Any tips for me? I really care about Callie, and I don't want to mess this up."

"My first piece of advice, obviously, is don't have sex with several other people behind her back. That is an approach that historically has bad outcomes."

"That's a really useful note, Michael."

"I am a fount of wisdom." He looked domeward, thinking. "I can only say... Callie doesn't trust easily. She never did, and what I did... made things worse. If she trusts you, cherish that. She'll do anything for you, as long as she knows the two of you are in this together. But if you betray her, lie to her, mislead her... she'll never forgive you."

"No pressure there."

"It's not quite as bad as I make it sound. You can make mistakes. Just talk to her. Admit your errors. Include her in your process. Don't make her feel like a fool." He shifted on the bench, glancing at her and then looking away, focusing on the flowers instead. "Callie is an ideal captain because she's always prepared for catastrophe – when something goes wrong, she doesn't waste time thinking about how unfair it is, or how unlikely, or what could have been done to prevent it. She just figures out how best to address the problem. She's practical, and pragmatic... but she's also a romantic. She wouldn't admit it, but she loves plying the spaceways, visiting new places, seeing new vistas, having extraordinary experiences. She gets bored easily."

"So the advice is, don't be boring?"

"I might phrase it more like, 'Don't worry about surprising her.' Don't be afraid to try new things or suggest new adventures. I realized too late that she was never going to settle down on Ilus – this world is just too small for her. *I* was too small for her, and I knew it. I hated that, but it's true. Have you joined her crew?"

"Not in any kind of official capacity, but I'm tagging along, and helping where I can."

He nodded. "I think that's the only way we could have worked. If I'd been out there, with her, growing and changing by her side, who knows? So I stayed here, thinking I could be her home – the person and place she returned to. Instead, we grew apart, until the distance between us could be measured in light years. If you're with her, out there, you have a better chance at keeping her than I ever did. Does that help?"

Elena smiled. "I was asking more like, what kind of flowers does she like, and does she like poetry, and is it really important to her if people make a big deal about her birthday, but sure, this other stuff is good too."

"She likes alcohol more than flowers, she's not much for poetry, and she doesn't care about birthdays, but she likes anniversaries."

"Oh, no," Callie said, and Elena turned to see her strolling into the garden with that light-footed low-gravity bounce in every step. "My ex and my current, talking about me. This isn't at all literally exactly like a nightmare I've had." She bumped Elena with her hip, and Elena obligingly scooted into Michael to make room for Callie to sit.

"Michael was just telling me about all the times you did super embarrassing things," Elena said. "I couldn't believe the one about the low-gravity swimming pool and the tequila shots."

"A classic," Michael murmured.

"I must have blacked that one out," Callie said. "You threw a good party, Michael. I'm sorry I spoiled it by not being dead."

"Your survival doesn't really fit the theme, but I'll let it pass."

"Do you mind if I talk to Elena for a bit? If you're done conspiring against me."

"We would only conspire in your favor, Callie." Michael rose, and gave Elena a small bow. "It was lovely to chat with you."

"Likewise."

He went back inside to the party, and Callie visibly relaxed once he was gone.

"He seems nice," Elena said.

"He's a good eighty-five, maybe even ninety percent nice. It's that last few points that get him in trouble. He offered to help us out with Glauketas, though, getting us some legal status, and he's going to set up Uzoma with a scholarship."

"That's good! Was this all out of the kindness of his heart?"

"Out of the depths of his guilt, really, but there is some pro quo to go with his quid. He wants to hire the *White Raven* for a job."

"Oh? What kind?"

She leaned closer to Elena. "You know the disappearances in the Taliesen system that Lantern mentioned? It's not just the truth-tellers who vanished. Some employees from Michael's company went missing, and the people the company sent to look for them never reported back, either. It might be accident, or sabotage, or pirates, but… put together with what Lantern said, it may be Axiom."

Elena shivered. "So we might be getting paid to fight the Axiom? That's a bonus, at least. Usually we do it pro bono."

"Your ability to find the bright side is one of my favorite things about you. I think you'll like Owain."

"What's that?"

"The terraformed planet in the Taliesen system."

Elena grabbed her arm. "We get to visit another planet? An actual planet with an actual atmosphere where actual humans live?"

"Yes? Yes."

Elena bounced, rather dramatically due to the low gravity. She drifted back down to her seat, grinning. "Callie! I am from the past. We had Earth, and a space station or two, and a really sad little base on the moon. We did not go to other planets, except for a couple of trips to Mars, which is like walking to the corner store in astronomical terms. I was one of the first people who even got *sent* to another planet outside our system, and you know how that turned out. This here, Ganymede, is the only natural celestial body I have ever set foot on, besides the Earth. This is amazing."

"We may be eaten by space monsters."

"Yes, but before that happens, I will get to stand on *another planet*." Elena snuggled in closer. "We should have sex here on Ganymede. And then we should have sex on Owain. We should collect various celestial bodies. I like collecting things."

Callie seemed a bit stunned, but not in a bad way. "I... yes. I approve of this plan."

Elena kissed her. She didn't think keeping things exciting was going to be a problem, at least not for a good long while.

Stephen went to a black dome district to shop for Sebastien's medication (and, doubtless, some sacraments for himself), while Callie and Elena strolled around the market district, browsed in shops, and basically soaked up the pleasure of being among other people after long months of isolation. They passed by a commercial Hypnos parlor, and the holographic avatar of the expert system hailed them from the doorway. "Come experience a reality realer than real life!" it promised. "Sail the storms of Jupiter in our newest exobody sim! Ski the slopes of Sedna and compete in our Ice Olympiad multiplayer competition! Stalk the mean streets of the lost city of New York in the latest installment of the award-winning Midnight Noir series!"

Elena peered in at the gleaming pods arrayed inside, tubes snaking out of them and up to the ceiling. "These people live on Ganymede. They can look up through the domes and see Jupiter looming in the sky above them. But they still want to play in imaginary worlds?"

"If you grew up in the Imperative, Jupiter isn't that exciting – it's just the big swirly thing in the sky. Wherever you are is normal, and people like to get away from the familiar. Me, if I get tired of where I am, I get on a ship and actually go someplace else, but not everyone is built that way." She paused. "Poor bastards."

Elena chuckled as they walked on. "I shouldn't judge. I spent some time in the Hypnos on Glauketas, though mostly in educational immersives meant for children, soaking up a few centuries of history. I was never big on games, though back in my day, you couldn't actually mistake them for reality – even the best virtual reality couldn't pass for real life."

"I thought in your day people kicked cans and rolled wooden hoops down the street with a stick and whittled for fun?"

Elena nodded solemnly. "Sometimes, on special occasions, we had bear baiting."

When Stephen got in touch to tell them he'd finished shopping and was on his way back, they returned to the *White Raven*. Stephen arrived a bit later and found them in the galley. He took off a backpack, presumably full of drugs, and frowned at them. "I met up with some members of my church, to make sure Ibn and Robin and Uzoma were being taken care of – they're fine. But we started talking about other things, and I mentioned the Taliesen system, and there's troubling news from the congregation on Owain."

"Were some of the lost surveyors members of the church?"

Stephen nodded. "Yes, a few – and the church sent their own mission to search for the missing congregants, without success. In fact, the searchers never came back, either."

Callie frowned. "When was this?"

"The news is fresh through the bridge from the Taliesen system. They went missing no more than a week ago, apparently."

"Huh. This is sounding less and less like a series of bad accidents, and more and more like coordinated enemy action."

Stephen nodded. "There's something else, maybe unrelated, but… Last year, a member of the church went on a month-long solo trip in a small ship, traveling in the void, taking various sacraments and plunging deep into his inner self."

"In my day, people just did peyote in the desert for a few days," Elena said.

"Outer space is the greatest desert of all," Stephen said. "He had a vision, on the far outskirts of the system, where there's an extensive asteroid belt, apparently. He said he saw an asteroid, quote, 'turning to dust and nothingness, devoured by the dark.' He found this vision profoundly disturbing, and the ship's life-support systems detected his distress, sedated him, and returned him home early."

"Bad trip," Callie said. "In a couple of senses."

"Oh, yes. Those sacraments can cause hallucinations, of course, and it could have simply been a case of shifting shadows, but when the congregants went missing... they disappeared near the same place where he had his vision. When he heard about the missing people, he said, 'What if the darkness devoured them, too?'" Stephen shuddered.

"Don't worry," Callie said. "If there's darkness out there, we'll bring the light."

The voyage back to Glauketas was quieter, and somehow melancholy, with so many fewer people on the ship. At least Callie didn't see any more shimmers. Maybe it had just been stress-related anxiety. When they were within real-time communication distance, Callie opened a voice channel. "Ashok! How's my asteroid?"

"Still drifting in the endless dark, cap. You almost home?"

"I am. Why?"

"Lantern's back. Let me put her on."

Lantern spoke into Callie's ear. "Callie, the elders have agreed to send me to Taliesen to investigate the disappearance of our sect there. Ashok tells me humans have been disappearing too? That's troubling. It's hard to believe the situations are coincidental."

"You're not wrong," Callie said.

"Are you leaving to investigate soon?"

"Sooner than soon. We're basically just coming back to get the *White Raven* and pick up the rest of my crew. Are you calling me to bum a ride?"

"I thought you might like the opportunity to beg abjectly for my expert assistance on your mission," Lantern said.

"This is my groveling voice," Callie said.

CHAPTER 10

The *White Raven* floated just beyond the orbit of Jupiter's moons, waiting in a line of ships to pass through the bridge to the Taliesen system. They had a specific time for departure, a "bridge window," but there were always small delays that sometimes added up to big ones. Unfortunately, if you showed up late, the Jovian Imperative's Bridge Authority would auction off your spot to last-minute travelers on standby, so you had to join the queue on time, even if you ended up motionless for a long delay.

Elena and Lantern, the two people (at least, the two conscious people) on the ship with no specific responsibilities, were in the observation deck, looking out the high, curved windows at the other ships. There were bulky gas transport freighters that were little more than clusters of tanks with engines on one end and cockpits on the other; large passenger vessels that looked like apartment buildings uprooted from Earth and set adrift in space; and smaller ships that moved like minnows among whales, some sleek and gleaming and pointlessly aerodynamic, others ramshackle and patched with sealant and panels that didn't match the rest of the hull in color. There were even a couple of starfish-shaped Liar vessels. Ship upon ship full of emigrants, merchants, politicians, dreamers, fugitives, scientists, and more, all waiting to pass through the bridge to one of the twenty-seven other systems accessible through it.

"There's the bridgehead." Lantern gestured with a pseudopod. An array of cylindrical buoys hung in empty space, thirty-six of them all glowing red, arranged in a circle easily a couple of kilometers apart. "The gate itself is invisible when it's inactive – the buoys are there to mark the position of the bridgehead. You don't want your ship parked in the middle of that space when the bridge opens."

Elena nodded. She'd seen what happened to a ship when a wormhole opened up in the middle of it. The ships didn't fare well.

As they watched, the buoys flashed from red to yellow, and then to green, and the space the buoys surrounded darkened as the stars that had been visible through the "circle" a moment before suddenly vanished from sight. The darkness within appeared to thicken, tendrils of inky blackness reaching out, and the small ship at the front of the queue was surrounded by the darkness, then snatched into the bridge. The darkness rippled for a moment, then dissolved, and the stars were visible again. The buoys flashed back to red.

Elena shook her head, awed. "It's so much bigger than the bridges the *White Raven* makes."

Lantern rippled a pseudopod in a way that Elena knew conveyed assent and affirmation. "Your bridge generator is portable, and meant to transport a single vessel. These fixed bridges are different – each one is linked to a celestial body, and follows that body in its orbit, maintaining a constant relative position. These bridges were used to send entire Axiom armadas to systems at once, in order to subjugate, overwhelm, and exterminate – or to transport equipment for larger projects. The bridgeheads were left in place as threats and promises, before the Axiom empire crumbled. Now they are ruins. Useful ruins, though."

"Why is there a bridge near Jupiter anyway? The Axiom never came to this system, did they? They don't even know humans exist as a species, or they'd turn over in their sleep long enough to exterminate us."

Lantern crossed two pseudopods: the equivalent of a shrug. "The records are incomplete, but there are rumours of a pre-human race of ocean-dwelling sapient creatures on Earth that the Axiom may have abducted en masse, or killed by raising the temperature of the ocean enough to disrupt their reproductive cycle, or sterilized by chemical means. There are regions of deep space that are more thoroughly explored than Earth's oceans are, so there may be all sorts of secrets hidden in the depths. Or maybe there was some other reason the Axiom wanted to visit this place, millions of years ago. Many of the records are garbled, or lost."

"The Liars – sorry, the Free – only shared the location of twenty-nine bridges with humans, but there are more, right?"

Lantern fluttered partial agreement. "There are hundreds. We only told humans about ones that were deemed to open a safe distance from any Axiom projects. It's better if the humans never suspect there are more gates. We feared that humans would experiment with different radio frequencies and forms of radiation and manage to open bridges to new locations, but fortunately the combinations are so complex and specific that the odds of a human stumbling on one that works by accident is small. The various port authorities in the colony systems discourage such experimentation anyway."

They swayed as the *White Raven* put on some thrust, moving closer to the bridge. A couple of other ships heading to the Taliesen system moved up with them. They were second in line – almost there. The *White Raven*'s crew was on official business, so they couldn't just use their own bridge generator to travel, without leading to a *lot* of questions about how they'd traversed light years of distance so quickly without leaving a trace. Literally all extra-system travel from the Sol system went through the Jupiter gate: that was what made the Jovian Imperative so powerful. They took a toll from every ship that passed through, ostensibly to pay for security and traffic control and so on, but really just because they could. Elena supposed that was the way of the world, even when "the world" comprised nearly thirty systems scattered randomly across the galaxy.

The buoys flashed, turning from red to yellow to green as the Bridge Authority bombarded the bridgehead with the specific forms of radiation that caused it to open a path to another system. The ship ahead of them, an immense passenger vessel, slowly moved into the inky tendrils of the gate and vanished. The buoys turned red again.

The *Raven* and its cohort moved closer. "Here we go," Elena murmured, then waited the long moments for the lights to change and the empty space to thicken. The tendrils of the gate reached out, surrounding them, like the grasping tentacles of some undersea abomination.

The journey was surprisingly unexciting. Everything went black, and though there was a sensation of movement, it wasn't particularly dramatic. "That's it?" Elena said, and after twenty-one seconds, they emerged into a new star field, close by a large asteroid with a domed facility clinging to its side like a tumor: the Taliesen system's Bridge Authority. The system's star, which seemed to Elena a paler orb than the one back home, was bright enough that the observation deck's windows darkened several shades to compensate. A dot was just visible in the distance: Owain, presumably.

"That's it," Lantern said.

"Weird," Elena said. "When we go through our bridge, there's a tunnel, and there are lights – it's clearly a created passageway, something built on purpose, not just a boring trip through the dark. Though now that I think about it, going through a tunnel where the lights have all burned out, or been switched off, is kind of creepy." She pressed up close against the windows, looking at the distant speck she took to be Owain. Another planet, inhabited by humans, so far across the galaxy from her homeworld that it would have taken a goldilocks ship ten thousand years to reach it. These people had achieved the dream of her bygone age: they were out there, making lives among the stars. Tears started to well up in her eyes.

Callie's voice boomed over the PA. "We're here. We'll go to Owain to check in with the company liaison, and then we'll go investigate the disturbance." She paused. "Or lack of a disturbance. The anomaly. Whatever."

"I can't believe she doesn't sound more wonderstruck," Elena muttered, looking out the viewport. "We just traveled through a wormhole to another inhabited solar system. This is objectively amazing."

"Those native to this time view traversing bridges as akin to commuting on those… trains you had in your century. The ones underground," Lantern said.

"Subways," Elena said.

"Yes. Remember, the bridges were in use longer than any of the crew has been alive. Familiarity can make anything routine." She paused. "I do not mind routine. I suspect we'll have plenty of opportunities to be surprised in the future."

"This part at least gets to involve wonder, and not terror," Elena said. "I'm going to enjoy that while it lasts."

The trip to Owain was going to take a while, even with the Tanzer drive on full thrust, because the planet was at almost the farthest point in its yearly orbit from the bridgehead. No one knew why the gate was tethered to an asteroid of no particular distinction, but then, no one knew *how* it was tethered, either; the builders of the wormhole bridges had done things their own way for their own reasons with their own methods. Fortunately, the asteroid was never all that far away from the planet – they didn't have to travel for a month like Ibn and Robin would to reach their colony world – but it was going to take a few days. At least they could afford to use fuel profligately now, since they were on the Almajara Corporation's payroll.

Callie hit the gym with more regularity than usual

on the trip, working the resistance bands hard, because it had been a while since she'd been down a real gravity well, and Owain was a hair over a full G. Even Stephen joined in for occasional workouts, though he grumbled that he had adaptive medications that could give temporary boosts to muscle performance, and the side effects weren't *that* harmful when used sparingly. Ashok was content with his mechanical augmentations – he could bound around in multiple Gs with aplomb – and Lantern found it all baffling, since her particular offshoot of Liar physiology got by just fine with nothing but isometric exercises.

Elena loved working out, though, taking obvious joy in movement and the endorphin rush of a hard workout. For Callie, exercise was more like checking the air filters or keeping the reaction wheels lubricated: dull, but necessary in order to maintain functionality. Watching Elena sweat in her workout gear did improve the whole gym experience, though. One morning when they were alone, working out on machines across from one another, Elena broke the companionable silence. "I hope it's OK if I'm objectifying you a little right now."

Callie chuckled from within her tangle of straps. "And here I was under the impression you loved me solely for my mind."

"Your mind is good. The housing for your mind is also a factor." Elena puffed a sweat-sticky strand of hair off her forehead. "How long will we be on the planet, before we have to zoom off into the dark?"

"A day or two, probably. Almajara Corp will put us up."

"Almajara." Callie thought the word sounded pretty

in Elena's mouth. There was probably no such thing as a "twenty-second-century accent," but Elena had it anyway: her vowels were softer and more rounded than Callie was used to. "Is that Spanish?"

"Spanish, sure, but it's also Arabic, or close enough. Two words that happen to sound sort of the same – false cognates. In Arabic the word means 'galaxy.' In Spanish it means, like, a cultivated field? Or, more specifically, a field that's been freshly fertilized – I used to tell Michael he worked for the Spreading Bullshit Through the Galaxy Corporation." Elena laughed, and Callie grinned. "Michael's great-great-whatever grandfather was from the Barcelona flotilla, and his great-great-great grandmother was from a vertical city in the Emirates, and when the couple founded the company together they wanted to choose a name that would reflect their two cultures. There's a whole speech the personnel resources directors give new hires, about how the company is devoted to growth across the galaxy. Basically, it's a bilingual pun."

"Ha. Personnel resources, huh? In my day that was called human resources, but I guess when you might hire the occasional Liar, the whole 'human' thing could come across as insensitive. This living-in-the-future situation still takes some getting used to."

Callie strained against the bands, bringing her wrists and elbows together slowly. "You'll figure it out. As well as anyone does, anyway. One nice thing about living in a galaxy where you can jump from one solar system to another in twenty-one seconds is that most people have a high tolerance for strangeness. A million subcultures have bloomed, and if you do something really strange by local standards, people will just shrug and figure that kind of thing is normal in your system. Don't break any laws and you'll be fine."

"What kind of subcultures does Owain have?"

Callie grunted through another rep, then let the straps drop. "Owain has a reputation as a haven for philosophical types and artists. The very first charter colonists, who spearheaded the terraforming effort, came from a now-defunct religion that preached the importance of abstinence and... who remembers? The holiness of cruciferous vegetables or something. The abstinence is what did them in – conversion rates weren't high enough to keep them going when they weren't raising their own children in the faith, such as it was. When the sect dissolved, their claims were sold off for cheap, because living on a half-terraformed world isn't exactly easy. Various other utopians and artist collectives snatched them up – people with more vision than money, you know? Now that the planet is actually habitable, it's attracting more mainstream sorts of colonists, but it's still got, I don't know..."

"A bohemian flavor?"

"If you say so. I don't know who the bohemians were or what they were like. But it's a place for experiments, and big ideas, and beauty for its own sake. The place should be interesting, at least compared to the conservatism of the Jovian Imperative." She paused. "Do you want to stay on the planet, while the crew and I go do our investigatory thing?"

Elena scowled at Callie from her own tangle of straps. "Absolutely not. Maybe when I thought it was just a corporate job, but after what Lantern said about losing contact with their sect out here – what if the Axiom is involved?"

"Maybe it's a coincidence. Whoever took out the surveyors, whether they're pirates or freelancers or fixers from a rival corporation, could have stumbled on the truth-tellers and killed them too."

Elena shook her head. "Come on. The entire pirate fleet from Glauketas attacked a truth-teller space station and couldn't take it down. They got massacred, because they were up against Axiom tech. No wildcat miners are going to fare any better."

Callie nodded. She'd come to the same conclusion. "You're right. I just hate seeing you in danger."

Elena growled at that. "I hate seeing you in danger too, but I'd rather be by your side than sitting down some gravity well, waiting for word. People have disappeared out there. There's *devouring darkness*. If you're going to disappear, I want to disappear with you. Besides, you don't object to Drake or Janice or Ashok or Lantern or Stephen going along with you into whatever terrifying hall of endless rending awaits us out there."

Callie sighed. "Yes, but they knew what they were signing up for, more or less, when they joined the crew. And they're trained for this kind of work, at least to the extent that anyone can be. You didn't choose this life, though. You were supposed to be starting human colonies on faraway worlds, ensuring the survival of the species, not hunting down villains in the deep black."

"I am ensuring the survival of the species. Just with more punching and less lab work. I've had some on-the-job training too, as you know. You don't think I have anything to offer? I'm a good medic – I don't have

Stephen's surgical expertise, I know, but I took two years of medical training, and I was going to be the closest thing to a doctor on our colony world. I'm an asset."

Callie held up her hands. "You don't have to convince me. I've seen you in action. You're absolutely useful! All I'm saying is – you don't work for me, unlike the rest of the crew. You're a volunteer, and that gives you the option to sit this one out. If you want to take part, though... I'm going to cut you in. Put you on the payroll. You can have a ten percent stake in the Machedo Corporation, same as the rest of the crew. I get more, but all the ship's repairs and upkeep come out of my end."

Elena stared at her. "I was prepared to be super mad at you for thinking I was incapable, or for trying to protect me when I don't need protecting, and then you go and say just exactly the right thing. Really? You want me on your crew? This isn't just because you love me and everything?"

"I never invited Michael to join my crew, and I was married to him. Yes, I want you. You are an asset, and you deserve recompense."

"Then I accept. Do I get a title? Can I be a boatswain? I bet I could swain a boat."

"You can be the ship's scientist, how about that? We could use one, with all the weird shit we're discovering lately, and, as Ashok always reminds me, he's an engineer, not a scientist. Since I know you like keeping busy, you can also be assistant medical officer, and help out Stephen as needed."

Elena beamed. "I like it. Does this mean I have to take orders from you?"

"Only when you're on duty, and only in ship-related matters. I will try not to abuse my authority otherwise."

"Do I get to boss anybody else around?"

"You do not. You listen to me, and then you listen to Stephen, and otherwise, you listen to yourself."

"Hmm. Does this mean we can't play 'rear admiral and insubordinate captain' any more? I guess it could be weird since I'm in your actual chain of command."

"Maybe it would just add verisimilitude. This isn't anybody's navy, though. We're a private vessel with civilian positions, not military ranks. I thought you liked playing pirate and plucky captive better anyway?"

Elena gave her a sloppy salute. "As long as there's a strong narrative, I'm pretty flexible."

"I have noticed that about you," Callie said.

CHAPTER 11

"All set?" Ashok said.

Elena nodded. "Thanks for doing this."

Ashok shrugged. "We've got some downtime before we hit the planet, and I find the process interesting. Are you sure you're ready, though?"

"I am. Why do you ask?"

"Because your heartbeat is very thumpy and your pupils are doing some stuff pupils do when the people those pupils are attached to get nervous, and also you're sweaty," Ashok said. "Simulated sweaty, but your avatar is mimicking real physiological responses right now, so."

She sighed. "Of course I'm nervous, but that doesn't mean I'm not ready. Stephen said I shouldn't get my hopes up, that the drug therapies are still in progress, but we may be too busy to run these tests once we reach the planet, and I'd like to see if there's any improvement. I can't help but be worried and hopeful all at once."

"Gotcha." Ashok looked around. "Being in this homebrew Glauketas simulator is weird. Usually when I plug into Hypnos I'm in a giant mech suit punching planet-eating space leviathans."

"Just be yourself," Elena said.

"Every minute of every day," Ashok said cheerfully. "OK, I'm waking Sebastien up." Ashok drew his fingertip across the surface of a handheld terminal, easing back on the levels of sedation that kept Sebastien in his induced coma. A moment later his eyes fluttered, and Sebastien turned his head toward Elena. She braced herself for an attack. Instead, a lazy smile bloomed on his face. "Elena?"

Her heart eased in her chest, like a fist unclenching. "I'm here, Sebastien."

"I… Are we there? Did we arrive, at the colony world?"

Elena glanced at Ashok. He shrugged. "Stephen said there might be some memory loss. His brain's been through a lot."

Sebastien started to sit up, then groaned, touching his temple. "Was I injured? What happened?"

"We were awakened from cryo-sleep early, Sebastien." Elena took his hand. "Do you remember? We encountered an alien space station? It seized our ship, pulled us on board?"

He frowned. "I remember waking up, maybe? Arguing with Robin and Hans and Ibn, seeing something on the viewscreen. Something big, all strange angles…"

"That's right. The station captured us, and started to cut open the *Anjou*. There were machines, security devices, and the crew was scattered for a while."

He grimaced. "I don't remember that at all. My last clear memories are from launch day, Hans shouting 'Nighty night!' and Ibn muttering something about, 'In this sleep, what dreams may come.' Then I got into the cryo-sleep pod, and I might have dreamed? Or were those flashes of the station, the... metal spiders? Those can't be real."

"They were real. They were alien."

He shook his head. "Aliens. There are aliens? Are they... friendly?"

Elena almost smiled. "I wouldn't say friendly. But the aliens weren't at home – the station was abandoned. The automated systems were still active, though. The station thought our ship was broken and in need of repair. The ship thought *we* were broken and in need of repair. You..." She tried to think of how to explain it. For accuracy she should say something like:

You were attacked by a robot spider that stuck electrodes and injected nanotechnology into your gray matter and tried to transform you into a compliant slave, but because the technology was made to mind-control a *different* species of aliens that we call Liars, it didn't work properly on your human physiology, and instead of making you into a servant, the implants made you into a psychopath, and then you decided to hijack the station's offensive capabilities to build and launch a fleet of automated warships that would enable you to take over the galaxy, oh and also you kidnapped me because despite having your brain scrambled you decided you were in *love* with me, and you might have succeeded in your mad plan of conquest if I hadn't taken advantage of your attempt to kiss you by punching you in the head while wearing basically a set of electrified brass knuckles –

"You got a head injury," Ashok said.

Elena nodded. "Yes, that's exactly right."

Sebastien's gaze slowly tracked over to Ashok, and his eyes widened. "You... You must have been hurt terribly. Was it the aliens?"

Ashok shook his armored head, then thumped some of the metal on his skull with the manipulator cluster at the end of his prosthetic arm. "Oh, you mean the metal plates and the augmented limbs and all that? Nah. These upgrades were collected painstakingly and with great care over time, and only a few of them were due to grievous catastrophic injury. Most of them I just have because they're more useful than whatever I was born with. I'm Ashok, by the way – part of the crew that rescued you guys off that alien space station. While you were snoozing in cryo-sleep for all those centuries, humanity was keeping busy. We've upgraded and expanded and spread through thirty colony systems in the galaxy. The future is a wonderful place. You're gonna love it." He grinned.

"But our mission," Sebastien murmured. "Everything we trained for..." Elena squeezed his hand. She sympathized. It was a lot to take in. Their mission had been launched as a desperate bid for survival by a species on the brink of extinction, and then he'd slept through the human galactic renaissance. "It's good humanity didn't go extinct, at least," he said. "However they may have... changed."

"Ashok is not entirely typical," Elena said.

"I'm an early adopter," Ashok said. "Majorly into radical self-improvement. Most people are too timid to really seize all the technological advances the modern world has to offer."

"Not everyone sticks a computer directly into their

face, he means," Elena said.

"Modern world," Sebastien said. "How long were we frozen?"

"About five hundred years," Elena said. "Welcome to the twenty-seventh century."

Sebastien sat up, more successfully this time, the straps around his legs holding him to the table so he wouldn't float away. "Where are we now? Is this a ship?"

"An asteroid," Ashok said. Of course, in reality they were on the *White Raven* in an entirely different star system, but they hadn't seen any reason to change the simulated setting from the last time they tried to wake Sebastien up. "Big one, a real lumpy space potato. Started out as a mining operation, and then they smoothed the tunnels down and cleaned it up and turned it into a habitat. It's called Glauketas."

Sebastien looked at Elena. "Does everyone live on asteroids? Are we the only ones here?"

"People live all sorts of places. Right now the only people here are you, me, , and the crew of the ship that saved us – Ashok, Callie, Stephen–"

"What about *our* crew?"

"Ibn, Uzoma, and Robin are all right. I'm afraid Hans didn't make it off the alien station. It... was a very dangerous place."

Sebastien winced. "Hans. I can't believe it. I always thought he was too mean to die. So, we're on an asteroid, but – where? Gliese 3293 C?"

Their original destination – and the colony world where Robin and Ibn were going right at that moment, amusingly enough. All that was too much to get into now, though. Time enough for full disclosures later, if

Sebastien proved cured. "No. Glauketas is in Earth's solar system, way out near the orbit of Neptune."

"How did we get... no, never mind. I won't ask you to catch me up on several centuries of old news. I *will* ask if I can have some water, though?"

Ashok said, "Sure thing."

"Are you my attending physician, Ashok?"

"Nah, I mostly fix the broken machines, not people. Stephen Baros is the station's doctor, but I've been helping him out."

Ashok didn't mention that Stephen had declined to take part in this test, after being murdered in the last one. Ashok passed Sebastien a bulb of water, who sucked it down greedily, then plucked at the straps holding him down. "Can I walk? Well, not walk, but, ah... float around?" He waved his arms vaguely. They'd opted not to have gravity turned on in this simulated Glauketas, because it would lead to questions about the nature of reality that wouldn't be diagnostically useful.

"You can try." Elena and Ashok loosened the straps around Sebastien's legs, and he turned gently on the bed, stretching out his limbs, pointing his toes. He was entirely unselfconscious about wearing only a small pair of undershorts, a quality Elena remembered from training with him for their voyage – he would always wander out of the shower smiling and completely oblivious to the fact that no one else strolled around naked, until Hans barked at him to cover up, this wasn't a damned naturist colony. Sebastien had murmured something about cultural differences and mostly remembered to wear a robe after that, though it wasn't always fastened very tightly. Elena tried not to let her eyes linger on the planes of his body. The emotional parts of her infatuation with him had been completely burned out by his homicidal behavior on the Axiom station, but apparently her lust remained. Oh well. Callie probably wouldn't fault her for looking, though she might question her taste.

"Give me the grand tour?" Sebastien said, and took her hand.

"As soon as you put some clothes on," she said, taking her hand back.

They floated through the corridors of Glauketas station, perfectly replicated in the simulation. (Elena actually found herself homesick for the place. The *White Raven* was rather cramped by comparison, if nicer overall.) The passages were old mining tunnels, reinforced with metal in some places, still exposed bare rock in others, and tall and wide enough to accommodate elephant-sized mining drones. The pirates who'd lived here had carved, cut, and blasted living quarters, storage areas, recreation, and other facilities as needed. The new inhabitants were still inventorying the mishmash of equipment left behind by first miners and later pirates. Elena pointed out some of the highlights as he walked: the gym, with its low-gravity resistance equipment; the cargo bays, full of as-yet-unsorted pillage the pirates had acquired; the machine shop, which Ashok had made his own, with every wall covered in magnetic clamps and cargo netting to keep his tools in place; the room full of strap-covered chairs and Hypnos diadems (which she vaguely described as "entertainment centers"), and the galley. She started daydreaming about which room he could stay in when they got home, if he was really better now, as he seemed.

She drifted into that gleaming stainless-steel-and-tile space and did a little spin, gesturing all around. "The galley – which I say should be called a kitchen, because this isn't a ship, but tell that to a bunch of people who spend all their time on space boats – is amazingly well kitted out. It's mostly food warmers and microwaves, like you'd expect, but there are weird pressure cookers and things too, and apparently a good chef can reproduce just about any dish you could get someplace that has gravity and open flames. You're a pretty good cook, right? I remember you talking about it during training."

"I dabble," he said, in the way that means, *My skills are exceptional, but I am modest, and also sexy.*

"The coffee is good, too. The pirates hit some kind of gourmet food shipment and got heaps of beans."

"Oh, coffee. I didn't even dare to dream." Elena took the hint and filled a couple of bulbs from the dispenser, flicking one to spin toward him. He deftly caught the bulb, gave it a suck, and widened his eyes. "This... is the best coffee I've ever had. And I'm not just saying that because I haven't had any at all in five hundred years."

Elena sipped hers and nodded. It tasted of chocolate and cherries. "It really is." Simulated food was *always* the best.

"This really used to be a pirate base?"

She nodded. "We repurposed it." They'd actually won it by right of conquest, but that was a long story.

"Huh. Actual space pirates."

"Oh yes. We're in a sort of lawless region here, beyond the jurisdictional reach of the Jovian Imperative – that's the major polity in the area – but close enough to zip out and hit the shipping lanes."

He shook his head. "Pirates. I bet they left a lot of weapons lying around, huh?"

Was his tone nonchalant, or just *faux*-nonchalant? "What, like cutlasses and cannons? Grapeshot?"

"Or the higher-tech equivalent, I guess."

She sipped her coffee before answering. Sebastien had a curious mind, that was all. "Sure. They left a few things behind, and there's an armory, but the weapons weren't well maintained, and most of it's junk. The pirates had their best weapons on their ships, and Callie destroyed those."

"Ah, the famous captain. Is she ferocious?" He mimed clawing and growling, like a tiger. Or a housecat. Elena wanted to kick him in the shin, but that would send them both spinning away in the null gravity.

She settled for a shrug. "I guess she can be, if you're on the wrong side of her. She's the reason I'm alive, and you're alive, and Ibn and Uzoma and Robin too. We'd all be dead if she hadn't rescued us."

"Shame she couldn't save Hans. But nobody's perfect." He sipped meditatively. "I suppose I'm in this Callie's debt, then. I should thank her. Where is she – and everyone else, for that matter?"

"They went on a supply run. There's no one on the base but me and Ashok right now."

"Really? That seems like a lot of people to go fetch groceries."

Elena snorted. "We've been cooped up here for months, and going off-station is a treat people line up for, even if it's just to run errands."

His eyes widened in alarm, or a good facsimile. "Are we stranded here, then? What if we suffer some disastrous failure of infrastructure? I can't imagine pirates are scrupulous about doing safety checks. Are there escape pods or anything?"

This is a natural and reasonable thing to worry about, she told herself. "Oh, no. We've got two ships. They took the *Golden Spider*. We still have the *White Raven* in case of emergency."

"Mmm." Sebastien spun the empty bulb in the air before him, and watched it twirl. "Where are the bathrooms? I gather I've been peeing into a tube for some months, and I look forward to reasserting my agency in eliminative matters."

"I'll show you." They floated out into the corridor. "There's a whole locker room, basically. Showers, toilets, even a sauna." She led him through a hatch and pointed. "Stalls over there. The toilets are basically the same as the zero-gravity ones we trained on. I'd sort of hoped five centuries of technology would make them more elegant, but nope."

"Straps and vacuums? Charming."

"That's the word for it. There are lockers over there, and towels in this dispenser here. The showers are nice." She pointed to a row of gleaming silver cylinders standing upright on the other side of the room. "You get in, slide the door shut, and water and optional soap sprays at you from various adjustable directions, then the water gets slurped out by fans at the top and bottom, and there's forced-air drying. It's really quite refreshing. You should try one."

Sebastien looked over the showers. "Hmm. They look big enough for two."

Elena's face warmed up, and she shrugged. If he could fake nonchalant, so could she. "They're nice. The pirates weren't very good housekeepers, but they stole quality fixtures."

"If you'll excuse me?" He drifted off to one of the toilet stalls and swung the door shut behind him.

Elena floated over to look at the showers. Big enough for two... maybe she'd mention that to Callie.

Ashok murmured in her earpiece: "How goes the tour?"

"Fine so far."

"No warning signs?"

"No red flags yet." She thought about his questions regarding weapons and escape pods. Curiosity, or *pointed* curiosity? "Maybe a couple of pink ones. Things are going a lot better than they did last time, though."

"There's not blood everywhere, it's true." Ashok signed off.

Sebastien emerged from the stall, shaking his head ruefully. "That process will never feel natural. It would be nice to live somewhere with gravity again." He floated to the towel dispenser and pulled out a strip of cloth, then drifted toward her. He cocked his head. "I haven't had a shower in five hundred years. I think I'd like one. Care to join me?" He began to slide down the zipper of his jumpsuit.

She put her hand on his chest – just below the unzipped portion – and lightly pushed him away, sending him drifting backward. "Sebastien, I..." She swallowed. "I'm flattered. But I'm with Callie now."

He regarded her for a moment, his expression blank and unreadable, and then smiled widely. "But that's wonderful! To find love, across the centuries! How marvelous. *Is* it love?"

Elena nodded. "As far as I can tell. You're not upset?"

"Upset? No, no – she's the daring space captain who saved your life. It's only natural for you to show your appreciation. Rank has its privileges and all that."

She frowned, but before she could formulate a response, he went on.

"I'm disappointed, of course – I always thought, once we reached our destination and set about the great work, that you and I might... explore our relationship further. But hopes are not the same as expectations, and neither of those is the same as a requirement. I *would* still like a shower, though, even a lonesome one. Show me how it works?"

Elena decided to let his shitty comment roll off unremarked-upon. He'd been through a lot, after all. "Of course." She slid open the nearest cylinder. "There's a button there–"

Sebastien shoved her into the shower, and she yelped as she crashed against the interior wall. She spun herself around in the small space, but he was already sliding the doors closed. She hit the release button, and the doors tried to slide open, but something had them jammed – he'd tied the towel around the door handles, trapping her. He looked at her through the crack in the door. His expression was utterly blank.

"What are you doing?" she said.

"Pursuing my destiny, Elena."

She darted forward, slipping her hand through the crack to try to jab him in the eyes, but he pulled back and vanished from her sight.

Elena sighed. "Ashok?"

"Yes."

"Sebastien just locked me in a shower pod."

"I see."

"Where's he going?"

"He's coming toward the medical bay. I could tase him or something but I guess we're supposed to see how this plays out?"

"That's the idea."

"Standing by, then."

Elena listened to the low hiss of the open channel for a long moment, tense, waiting for sounds of violence.

Finally Ashok said, "He didn't come in. He switched on the infirmary's quarantine mode and sealed me inside. We knew those Axiom implants gave him great computer skills, and I guess his brain remembers them. I've still got him on the monitors, though. Now he's systematically checking all the parts of the station you *didn't* show him on the tour."

"He's looking for the armory," Elena said.

"I assume. Oops, there we go, he found the guns. Huh. So... do we call this a failure? I can punch us out."

"Give it a moment? Obviously it's not a success, but... let's see what he does. Maybe we've made some progress. For a while there, he really seemed like his old self. He hasn't murdered anyone yet. Being less homicidal, that's a big step, right?"

"I feel like you're setting a pretty low bar there, Elena, but sure, let's see where he goes from here." Pause. "He's at a terminal, consulting the station map. Now he's pulling up the technical schematics for Glauketas, but I can't tell what he's looking for." Pause. "Now he's heading for the airlock, where the *White Raven* is docked. You think he's going to take off? We could yell at him over the public address system if you want."

"I don't know what we'd say." Elena rested her forehead against the smooth, cool wall of the shower pod.

"He's boarded the *White Raven*." Pause. "He's powering up the engines."

"Well. At least he went non-lethal this time," Elena said. "He just locked us up. Maybe his conscience is starting to grow back–"

"He's firing on the station now." A distant thud made the room vibrate. "He... yep, he's definitely targeting our life support systems. I guess that's what he was looking at the schematics for."

"All right, fine," Elena sighed. "It's a failure."

She sat up in the medical bay, where Ashok was unplugging himself from his own Hypnos rig. Sebastien slept on, diadem still sparkling on his brow.

"Sorry that didn't go better," Ashok said.

Elena nodded. "Me too, but... even so, there was progress. It's not like last time, when he just murdered everyone. This time he was calm, conversational, even seemed like his old self until the end." As she spoke, Elena realized that wasn't as reassuring as it had seemed initially.

Ashok shrugged. "OK, sure, but this time he was manipulative and made plans to escape before killing us. He went from homicidal maniac to cold-blooded premeditated murderer. In some ways, a total beast is easier to deal with than a mission-driven psychopath."

"I know." Elena looked at Sebastien. "Still, getting his higher functions back is a start. He's not his old self yet, I know, but it seems like elements of his old self remain.

If the drug therapies keep doing their work, maybe his empathy will come back."

"That would be nice," Ashok said. "He seems like he'd have a lot to offer if we could tone down the killing-spree stuff." He handed Elena a bulb of coffee, and she sipped the lukewarm contents. Not nearly as delicious as the coffee in the Hypnos, of course. That was the joy of virtual reality, at least when using the absurdly high-quality gear they had here: everything was its best self.

Except Sebastien.

CHAPTER 12

The *White Raven* was built for space, and it was going to stay in space, under the care of Drake and Janice and Shall. The rest of the crew took the canoe – their transport-and-landing vessel, usually tucked snugly into the *Raven*'s cargo hold – down to the planet's surface, a bumpy ride through atmospheric turbulence. Lantern was especially miserable, since the canoe had been made with human passengers in mind, and they'd had to improvise a webbing of straps to keep her in place. Once they got about ten thousand meters above the surface, Callie switched them over to auto-landing mode, letting the ground control tower at the spaceport outside the planet's main settlement, Rheged, guide them in. They landed with barely a bump, but the unaccustomed gravity dragged them all into slumps.

Their doors were sealed while the port's sniffer-sensors made sure there weren't any nasty radioactive substances or pathogens on board. Then the airlocks unlocked, and Callie opened both the inner and outer doors to the world beyond.

Owain smelled like–

"It smells like Halloween!" Elena said.

Ashok took a deep breath through what he had instead of a nose. "Oxygen, water, assorted aldehydes, alkyl benzenes, some oxygenated monoaromatics, and various polycyclic aromatic hydrocarbons."

"Burning leaves," Stephen said. "Or wood smoke."

"Burning," Lantern said. "Is there danger?" Lantern hadn't spent much time on any planet, and in ships and on space stations, the smell of smoke was almost never a good thing.

"I don't think so." Callie stepped out of the canoe, blinking in the sunlight. There was a certain brightness and harshness to the light that she associated with deserts on Earth, which was just due to the fact that Owain's star didn't shine at precisely the same wavelength as Earth's, though the relative distance between the bodies was roughly equivalent. The air here was crisp, but not cold, and that tinge of smoke in the air really did remind her of her childhood autumns spent camping on Earth.

They were in a landing zone, surrounded by a dozen ships parked in their own little marked-off areas. There were stands of leafy green trees off in the distance, and buildings of a curiously jumbled-looking design nearby. The sky was remarkably Earthlike, blue and scattered with low clouds, but that made sense, upon reflection – the terraforming engines the Liar and human engineers built had attempted to recreate as Earthlike an atmosphere as possible.

Callie waved to a ground control officer, dressed in a jumpsuit decorated with a constellation of sparkling tiny lights in various colors. Good for visibility for night landings, probably, but also clearly just the local – what had Elena called it? – bohemian style. "What's on fire?" she said.

"Hmm?" The officer cocked their head, then grinned, showing off a mouthful of teeth somehow carved into tiny skulls. "Oh, that's the wood-fired pizza ovens. It's the lunch rush." They pointed to a cluster of buildings across the landing zones, beyond the parked ships. "That's the Welcome Center. Over there we've got food, drinks, rooms for rent, entertainment for weary travelers, all that sort of thing."

"Food isn't a terrible idea," Callie said. "What do I do for ground transportation?"

"Just hit up the local channel on the Tangle, should give you all the options in the world. The port has an expert system to help you winnow down the choices and find the right option for your budget and business needs, blah blah blah. Welcome to Rheged!" They waved and bustled on about their business.

Callie turned and looked over her crew. Stephen prodded gingerly at the smooth, hard surface of the landing zone with the toe of his boot, his customary slouch even more slumped than usual. Ashok was peering at the Welcome Center through his external optics, probably reading a menu from five hundred meters away. Lantern delicately ambled around the nearest ship, a low-slung rich person's toy – just about every Liar Callie had ever met had a deep and abiding interest in machines, and Lantern was no different.

Elena was… well, she was gamboling. Bouncing on her toes, doing little pirouettes, stretching out her arms and spinning. Callie half-expected cartwheels. The gravity was heavy, but Callie felt good, too. You had to take care of yourself in space, and she'd kept up on her supplements and electro-stimulants, and they'd all taken small doses of Stephen's personal blend of muscle enhancers before departure. She wasn't up for running a marathon, but she could probably manage a sprint if she had to.

Elena bounced over to her. "Callie! I am on another *planet*. I am an interplanetary explorer! I've been on moons before, sure, but, pfft, *moons* – this is another planet! Humans live here, did you know?"

"It is, and they do, and I did. In that restaurant over there they probably have food made with things that grew in the dirt in the open air. And maybe made of some things that ate those things, if you're feeling carnivorous. The prospect of fresh food from planetary soil sounds exciting to me, and I'm not even an unfrozen prehistoric caveperson biologist."

"Do you think they have cheese made from actual milk and not nutritional yeast?"

"I live in hope. Why don't you amble over that way while I make arrangements to meet our contact at Almajara Corp?"

Elena bounced over and gave her a kiss. "Do you know what you are, Kalea Machedo?"

"What?"

"You are the heart of my heart." Elena zipped away and herded the others together and toward the restaurant with the force of sheer enthusiasm.

Callie opened her comms. The *White Raven* was in orbit, close enough for real-time communication, so she reached out to Shall. "We didn't crash." That was her traditional way of saying "We arrived safely," a message she'd once upon a time sent without fail to Michael, now deployed only on occasion with his estranged digital twin. "We're going to get something to eat at the spaceport."

"You humans and your need to consume organic material in order to replenish energy," Shall said. "It's like you've never heard of nuclear fusion."

"Could you reach out to our point person at Almajara and let them know we're here and ready to start solving all their problems for money? Maybe set up a meeting?"

"I live to serve."

Huh. Michael had said the same thing to her when she asked him for a favor on Ganymede. The similarities between the two of them were more glaring now that she'd had an ex-husband refresher. "Do you? I hadn't noticed that." Callie checked in briefly with Drake and Janice – "We're fine," Drake said; "We know how to make a ship fall continuously in a circle around a planet without crashing, thanks," Janice said – and then strolled along after her crew, enjoying the feel of her muscles moving against the gravity.

Her crew made an odd-looking group, viewed from a little distance: the alien, the cyborg, the woman out of time, and the doleful mountain of a man. Callie felt a sudden rush of love for them – for her whole crew. They'd gone through unimaginable things together. Attacked by hostile cultists, lost on a deadly space station, witnessing the deaths of fifty thousand of their friends and neighbors on Meditreme Station, months hiding out and pretending to be dead – and they were still together, still willing to fight for each other, still walking together companionably toward a meal. These were her people, along with Drake and Janice and Shall, and these moments, when they were all as safe and happy as their individual capabilities allowed them to be, were precious, and to be savored. They were what she fought for.

She ran a little to catch up.

As they drew closer to the Welcome Center, Elena vocally marveled at the architecture, and even in the depths of his grumpy heart, Stephen had to admit it was all rather cute. "Is that building shaped like a giant mushroom?" Elena said. "And that tower at the end... is that a carrot? Look, it even has a big green sprout on top! That one looks like a rocket, but the old-timey kind–"

"So, like, the kind they had in your day?" Ashok's tone was all innocence. Was he capable of such dry teasing? Stephen wondered. No. He was probably being sincere... but if he was developing a new degree of conversational nuance, that was a development that bore watching with suspicion.

Elena was apparently unoffended. "Even earlier than that, if you can imagine it – it's like the way people in the past imagined rockets of the future would be. Look at those round portholes, and those fins at the bottom! Why are all the buildings shaped like *things*? That one over there looks like a giant snail with a rainbow shell."

"Artists," Stephen shook his head as he tromped along, feeling every kilogram of his body's weight for the first time in ages. "Owain is lousy with them. They get in everywhere."

"Give materials science its due," Ashok said. "Most of the buildings here are made of ultragel."

"An innovation of the Free." Lantern spoke from an artificial voicebox, of course, but still managed to sound smug.

"Hey, now, ultragel is a true collaboration," Ashok said. "Look at that building over there! It looks like someone threw a bunch of sticks in the air and then froze them in the act of falling." The tower at the far end of the plaza was an organic and chaotic assemblage of eight or nine rough cylinders of assorted lengths, all painted and sculpted to resemble twigs half-stripped of their bark, subtly joined at peculiar angles. It reminded Stephen, unpleasantly, of the internal-structure-of-an-anthill organic shape of the Axiom space station where they'd rescued Elena's crew. "That would be a pain to build with concrete or steel or wood, if you actually wanted people to be able to live and work and walk around inside. But ultragel makes it easy."

"I wonder if it is a reference to xylomancy." Lantern rose up on her walking pseudopods, as if to get a better vantage on the structure. "An ancient form of human divination. Practitioners would throw sticks onto the ground and discern portents from their arrangement."

"Like using yarrow stalks to interpret the *I Ching*?" Ashok said.

"No, they didn't throw the stalks for that, they just sorted them," Elena said. "It was coins they threw. This stick-tossing business must be some kind of European thing."

"I wonder what it portends?" Lantern still gazed at the building.

"A lecture on the origins of ultragel, if we're unlucky," Stephen muttered.

Ashok grinned. "Did they have aerogel in your time, Elena?"

"Sure we did, though we used it for insulation mostly. We had some on our ship. Light and strong, but not strong enough to make buildings out of, and it had some unhealthy qualities – the particles were a skin irritant, and bad for the lungs."

Ashok nodded. "Some human engineers got together with some Liars and said, 'How do we make something like aerogel, but stronger and cheaper?' They worked together and made ultragel. It's incredibly light, and strong, and before it sets you can sculpt it into almost any shape. The mineral compounds you need to concoct ultragel occur naturally in quantity on this planet, and the organic compounds are freely available too, since the planet was terraformed. They build a lot of things out of ultragel here."

"So what's the drawback?" Elena said. "Why isn't everything everywhere made out of ultragel?"

Callie had caught up to them. She snorted. "Because if I had a big truck, I could crash into any of these buildings and knock them right over. Using ultragel is like making a house out of pumice or balsa wood. I mean, they won't break, and they'll take your weight, but ten people with crowbars could lever one out of the ground and load it onto a flatbed and drive it away. Ultragel can't stand up to any kind of attack, either. On Earth they're mostly used as government-provided housing. Ubihuts, we call them." She frowned. "I'm not sure why."

"Comes from 'universal basic income,'" Stephen said. "Ubihuts, ubimeals, ubicars, all that."

"Oh, right." Callie glanced at Elena. "On Earth,

everybody gets a place to live and a stipend sufficient to buy the basics, but if you want a house that isn't made of air and dust or whatever, you have to make up the difference yourself with some kind of outside work."

"We used to dream of instituting those kinds of reforms in my day," Elena said. "And you couldn't even remember what they were called!"

"Welcome to our glorious post-scarcity future," Ashok said.

Callie snorted. "We still have plenty of scarcity. We just moved it around. One breakdown in a supply chain, and people start starving. Though the infrastructure situation is more stable down in gravity wells, I'll grant you. It helps when you can scoop up water off the ground and pluck food off a branch."

"I'd love to live in a house shaped like a nautilus shell or a jellyfish," Elena said. "I don't care if it can't stand up to a siege engine. I doubt any of the dorms I lived in would have stood up to a trebuchet either."

Stephen chuckled. He liked Elena. He had reservations about making her his assistant in medical matters, as Callie had rather blithely proposed, but as a person, he got along with Elena better than almost anyone on the ship. "If the reanimated armies of the Ottoman empire do attack your ultragel house with cannons and it collapses on you, you stand a better chance of surviving than you would if you were in a house made of stone. I was at a scene once, in my first responder days, where a sinkhole opened and collapsed half an ultragel house, and the resident dug himself out of the rubble before we even got started on rescue efforts. We treated him for a scratch on one cheek and sent him on his way."

"Let's hope the pizza isn't made of ultragel." Callie led the way into a building shaped like a green mushroom with red spots on its cap. The underside of the cap even had individually sculpted white gills. Stephen half-expected it to dump a load of artistic spores on them.

The pizzeria was bustling, a big open space full of long wooden tables with bench seats (most low for humans, a few higher ones for Liars) with employees of the spaceport and visitors mingling together, elbow to elbow. The lights inside were all mushroom-shaped, too, some of them exotically so, and Stephen was amused to see death caps and destroying angels hanging among the various edible varieties. He hoped that didn't portend poisonous menu options. He doubted the colonists had imported deadly mushrooms to their terraformed world.

A few mechanics rose from a table, and Callie swooped in to claim it. Elena nuzzled up beside her, and the others arrayed themselves as best they could. There were actual menus, printed on paper. Stephen tried to remember the last time he'd seen that. There were, predictably, several mushroom-themed specials, but there were lots of other choices too, and after some friendly wrangling and declarations that certain toppings were absolutely essential or irredeemably disgusting, they settled on an order. (Lantern just wanted a bowl of raw garlic cloves in oil, which was on the menu, and apparently a popular choice among her people.) The server was a cheerful woman with long dark braids woven with sparkling lights, wearing a silver diadem on her forehead, and she took their order without writing anything down.

"What was that on her forehead?" Stephen said. "It looked like a Hypnos headset, almost."

"Basically," Ashok said. "Augmented reality gear. I've got something similar built into my optics, but mine's better than that commercial stuff, of course. It probably just gives her a heads-up display, tags objects in the real world with metadata, things like that. She can look at us and see what we ordered hovering over our heads in glowing green letters or whatever. Though she could also be watching armies of meter-high orcs and centaurs have a bloody battle using the tables as terrain, or there could be a projection that erases the walls and makes it look like we're in the middle of a tropical rainforest – who knows."

"Nothing's real any more," Stephen grumbled.

"This from the man who does massive doses of psychedelic drugs on a monthly basis?" Callie said.

"My sacraments connect me to a greater reality," he said. "Though now that you mention it, some of the congregants have talked about using augmented reality to enhance the experience – projecting animated mandalas in the air, or exploring tranquil underwater scenes, to ease the comedown."

Stephen could tell Elena was about to ask him something – he had some hopes that she might join his church, or at least give it a try – but then Callie got a faraway look and said, "Acknowledged." She focused on the crew again. "Turns out our contact at Almajara was at the spaceport on business this morning anyway, so she's walking over." Callie looked around the restaurant, then raised a hand in greeting. "There she is."

Stephen turned on his bench, and entirely failed at trying not to stare. The woman approaching them was perhaps in the first years of middle age, her skin a deep and lustrous brown, her hair a dark cloud, her face lovely, though troubled. She was short and wide-hipped and walked with confidence and purpose, and she made a simple gray jumpsuit look like the robes of an empress. She stopped at the table, took them in, and then nodded once, briskly, as if deciding they would have to do. "You must be the crew of the *White Raven*. I'm Q Fortier. You can call me Q."

I'll call you anything you want, Stephen thought.

CHAPTER 13

Callie pointed Q to a short bench at the head of the table, next to her. "Have a seat." Once the woman was settled, Callie made introductions, then said, "You can give us the rundown while we eat." The server had just reappeared, carrying trays that smelled divine.

"*Cheeeeeeese*." Elena made grabby hands toward the platters.

"You're welcome to share," Stephen said to Q. "We have plenty." He'd edged a little closer to her on the bench, though Ashok and Lantern were between him and Q. Callie hadn't seen that look on Stephen's face before, but she recognized it anyway. She considered whether him making eyes at their corporate liaison would be a complication, and decided it probably wouldn't. Stephen was so professional he made Callie look like a frivolous dilettante, and even if he developed a crush, she doubted he'd let it affect his duties.

"Thanks, but I already ate." Q leaned forward, elbows on the table, lacing her fingers together. "On behalf of the Almajara Corporation, I welcome you to Owain. We're stretched a little thin here, so a team of experienced surveyors like yourselves will be a big help." She spoke a little louder than necessary, and Callie resisted the urge to roll her eyes. She was doing the deniability thing, of course. "The specifics of your assignment have been sent to your ship's system. I'm here to show the corporation's full support and to offer any—"

"Ashok, cone of silence," Callie interrupted.

Ashok paused in the act of shoving a whole slice of goat's cheese and pesto pizza into his face in order to fiddle with a panel on his prosthetic arm. There was a brief buzzing sound, and then he gave a thumbs-up and went back to chewing.

"We're in a sonic exclusion field," Callie said. "Anyone more than a few centimeters from the back of our heads will hear us talking about, whatever, the weather, local architecture, small talk stuff. Ashok's anti-surveillance suite samples our voices and then has an expert system remix them into something halfway between inane banter and word salad. There are also countermeasures in place to prevent surveillance. You can speak freely without being overheard, at least until the server comes back to refill the water glasses."

Q nodded, smiling. "Thank the Green Lady. The situation here is *fucked*."

"Give us some background," Callie said. "We know people disappeared from the outskirts of the system, but that's about it."

Q nodded. "OK. The short version is, we've lost multiple survey ships, and a team of corporate auditors. They all just vanished. No beacons, no last messages, nothing."

"You'd better go ahead with the long version too," Callie said.

Q took a deep breath. "Right. Owain is a wonderful planet, but its accessible mineral deposits are limited. There is, however, a vast asteroid field on the outer edge of the system. The scientists think there used to be a planet there, but it was blown up, maybe by whoever built the bridgehead however many thousands of years ago." She shivered. "Ancient aliens who blow up planets. I'm glad *they* don't live in the neighborhood any more."

We hope, Callie thought.

"Anyway, it's rich pickings out there in terms of mining, and the corporation donated generously to the terraforming of Owain in exchange for the right to exploit the asteroids. The people in charge here, the weird conglomeration of artists' organizations and utopian communities who have the charter for this system, wouldn't allow any mineral exploitation at all until the terraforming was finished, though."

"Ha. They may be artists and optimists, but they aren't fools," Callie said. "Corps aren't famous for fulfilling their obligations after they get what they want, and they have whole armies of lawyers and expert systems devoted to wriggling out of the spirit of contracts. Definitely smart to extract full value from the corporation before letting them extract any from you."

"Exactly."

Callie quirked an eyebrow. "'Exactly?' Usually employees of the corp would say something like, 'We would never renege on a contract, and we always act in good faith and in the best interests of the shareholders,' or some similar bullshit."

Q shrugged. "Cone of silence, right? You said I can't be recorded, and I doubt you'll report me to personnel resources for acts unbecoming a corporate drone anyway. I only started working for Almajara a year ago, when they began hiring people to prepare for harvesting the asteroids. I guess I'm not all the way indoctrinated yet. I've been on Owain for years, helping with the terraforming efforts – I'm a resource management person, really. I do supply and logistics work, and you're all resources, which is why I'm managing you."

"When did your other resources start to go missing?" Callie said.

"About six weeks ago. We had survey teams out, marking the most valuable targets among the asteroids, and they were sending back reports, until… they weren't. All the teams in one segment of the asteroid belt went dark. Other surveyors in adjacent segments went to look for them, to see if there'd been an accident. We didn't hear from them, either. The people Almajara sent to look for the missing surveyors all stopped communicating too. We sent a couple of locals, more familiar with the system, to check on things, and they didn't come back. The locals won't even go in that direction any more. Almajara finally sent a crew of specialized auditors, who went from the bridgehead straight out to check the last known locations of our survey teams. They were never heard from again. You know what our corporate auditors are like, don't you, Captain Machedo? When an outpost or a development goes dark, it could be anything – pirates, catastrophic infrastructure failure that could make the company liable for damages, rival corporations, sabotage from disgruntled employees, militant separatists who think you've encroached on their turf… Our auditors are prepared to deal with *any* of those things. But whatever they found was too much for them." She hung her head. "Something out there is killing my people."

You hope, Callie thought. Killing, at least, meant an end to suffering. If the Axiom was involved, there were worse fates than death. "We'll figure out what's going on."

"I'm sure that's what the auditors thought too."

"Corporate auditors are made for breaking strikes, hitting back at corporate rivals, hunting down money launderers, and frightening employees into submission. Eighty percent of them came up through the security services. They're good at breaking stuff and containing a perimeter, and that's about it. Those are useful skills, don't get me wrong, but my crew can do those things too, and more besides."

"Almajara auditors are famed for their investigative techniques, I thought," Q said. "Or is that just public relations talking?"

Callie shook her head. "No, it's justified, just... limited. The other twenty percent came up through accounting or data mining. They're great at hunting down hidden records and following twisty financials and ferreting out spies – I'll admit there's nobody better – but this doesn't seem like a money laundering thing, or industrial espionage. We're qualified to approach things with a wider perspective."

"Single-purpose tools are inefficient," Ashok said. "We're a multi-tool."

"I hope you're the right tool for the job," Q said.

"You have a personal connection to this, don't you?" Stephen said.

Q grimaced. "Is it that obvious?"

Stephen shook his head. "Probably not, but I'm CoED."

"Coed?" Elena wrinkled her forehead. "Where I'm from, that meant men and women going to the same college, and it was considered a pretty outdated and binary term even then."

"He means the Church of the Ecstatic Divine," Q said.

"Ohhhhh," Elena said.

Q cocked her head at Stephen, seeming to really look at him for the first time, and Callie noticed him straightening up under the attention. "But how did you know... oh, that's right. I said 'thank the Green Lady,' didn't I? So you know my affiliation. What's yours?"

"Most of my congregation were machine elf. I've always been open to various guides, but I've personally had the best experiences with fractaline entities."

Elena leaned over to Callie. "What are they talking about?"

Callie shrugged. "Religion. Drugs. Religion drugs."

Q smiled at them. "Members of our church take sacraments that connect us to one another, and to the wider universe. The Church of the Ecstatic Divine is a syncretic religion, incorporating ecstatic and hallucinatory traditions from assorted cultures. We differ from those traditions mainly by attempting to more rigorously control the dosages and compositions of our sacraments."

"Instead of eating funny mushrooms they found in a pile of cow shit or taking a pill they got from someone at a club, they have custom-made psychedelic drugs tuned for different intensities and effects," Callie said.

"Close enough," Q said. "My congregation, probably because we were engaged in terraforming efforts to create a paradise on Owain, gravitates toward nature-based experiences. We seek a sense of oneness with the living world and all that world's organisms. Sometimes, during our ecstasies, we encounter a figure we call the Green Lady, who guides us. Other affiliations focus on other entities – like the machine elves."

"They're remarkable," Stephen said. "I watched the elves build a solar system once, moving with lightning speed, creating something from nothing. It was inspiring. Then there are fractalines – figures of pure abstraction, with shapes that shift and twist and offer insights along the way."

"I had a friend in college who did salvia and DMT and stuff," Elena said. "She talked about those kind of things."

Q made a face. "Salvia? They still do that? Where are you from? I thought that sort of thing went out with bloodletting and trepanning and electroshock therapy."

"Oh, I'm like five hundred years old," Elena said. "I spent a lot of that time sleeping though, so I look pretty good for my age."

Q looked at her uncertainly. "Really?"

"She's a time refugee, yeah," Callie said. "Anyway, not to interrupt all this fascinating talk about your various hallucinations–"

"Those entities are messengers from the greater mind of God," Stephen countered.

Q nodded. "Or possibly just manifestations of our own subconscious minds, helping us work through personal and philosophical issues. The guides are helpful, anyway, whether they have objective reality or not. Some people see their own personal guides – bees, frogs, talking fountains, ocean waves – and others never see the same thing twice, but many people see the same entities over and over again, which suggests either that they possess some external reality, or that we share an underlying pool of archetypes."

"Or they're just primed to see the Green Lady because they heard all their co-religionists talking about her, or read accounts about her on the druggier parts of the Tangle," Callie said.

"Or that," Q agreed cheerfully. "The church is a practical religion. Our practice makes us feel better, and makes us better people, so I don't care too much about why or how it works." Her face fell. "But, yes, that is why I take these disappearances personally. We had congregants on some of the survey teams. The leader of my branch here and some of my friends went out looking for them when they vanished, and they were lost too."

"I'm so sorry," Stephen said. "I... My congregation was on Meditreme Station, so I know what it's like, to lose people."

Q leaned back. "Oh, Stephen. I'm so sorry. I didn't realize there were any survivors from Meditreme at all."

"We happened to be off the station at the time," he said.

"Have you found anyone else to practice with?"

He shook his head. "I've done some solo sacraments, of course, but without the group element, well. What's the point of connection with no one to connect with? I've missed at least two Festivals. It's been hard."

She stood up, walked around the table, and stood by him. "May I hug you?"

"Churchgoers." Callie shook her head.

"Please." Stephen rose, and the two of them embraced for a long moment.

Q drew back, but kept her hand on his shoulder. "Come to our meeting hall tonight, all right? I know the Green Lady isn't your preference–"

"No, I begin to see the appeal, now that I'm on a planet, where things are growing," he said. "I'd be very pleased to join you."

Ashok, in an incredibly rare moment of social awareness, left his spot on the bench and sat on the other side of the table, allowing Q to sit beside Stephen. She looked over at Callie. "I'm here as an agent of Almajara, but I'd also like you to look for any signs of my fellow congregants. They may merely be lost. I hope so."

"We'll find out what's happening," Callie said. "We'll bring back any survivors too." Wishful thinking, but also the truth: in the unlikely event anyone was still alive out there, she'd bring them safely home.

"I'll have space for a few passengers on my ship, too," Q said.

Callie closed her eyes, counted silently to five, and then said, "Do you mean to suggest you're going with us?" She didn't bother to hide her disapproval of that idea.

Her disapproval didn't appear to bother Q a bit. "I am. Almajara wants a representative and observer, but I don't want to interfere with your operations, so I'll follow in my own ship."

"And hang back a bit, so if we get eaten by the devouring darkness, you can turn around and burn for home and send a splintercast back to Uncle Reynauld telling him what happened to us, right?"

"Something like that," Q said. "Did you say Uncle Reynauld? Reynauld Garcia-Hassan is your *uncle*?"

"Only by marriage. Not even by that, any more. But old habits die hard."

"I had no idea you had such close connections to the family." Q was clearly regretting her not-entirely-loyal-to-the-company talk from earlier.

"Don't worry about it. I met Reynauld at my wedding and at a funeral or two, but since he wasn't interested in sleeping with me, he didn't pay me much attention. We don't sit down for friendly chats about the relative loyalty of his down-the-line employees."

Q breathed out. "That's comforting. I've only ever seen him projected on a viewscreen, four meters high, complaining about production targets and our anticipated failure to meet them."

Callie chuckled. "He's a lot shorter in person. All right. I understand your position. You can follow along, but stay a ways back. We've got some experimental stealth technology on our ship, and we're going to try to creep in where others rushed." Callie was privately annoyed. She'd planned to use their bridge generator to jump to the far side of the asteroid belt and approach the region of the disappearances from an entirely unprecedented angle, but now they'd have to settle for stealth and a roundabout approach, maybe dipping way below the plane of the ecliptic and then rising up toward the danger zone. At least Q didn't want to ride on the *White Raven*: the crew could still discuss the possibility of an Axiom threat openly on the way. "I'm giving the crew tonight to get some rest and relaxation, and we'll set off in the morning refreshed. Shall – that's our ship's AI – will be in your comms tomorrow with an hour's warning, so nobody overindulge tonight." She looked at Stephen and Q sternly.

"You know our sacraments don't give us hangovers," Stephen said.

"Yeah, but staying up all night bonding over imaginary green machine fractals might tire you out, and I need you at peak. If we find any survivors out there, they may need medical attention."

Stephen sniffed. "I have never yet failed to discharge my duties, captain."

"Fair enough, XO. I'm glad you're going to get some of your old-time religion, anyway. I know you missed it."

"I like it when you call him XO," Elena said. "It sounds like what you'd sign at the end of a love letter – like hugs and kisses." She made smoochie noises.

"People from the past are so strange," Callie said.

"You should try hanging out with people from the future sometime. They don't even laugh at super funny jokes reliably."

CHAPTER 14

The crew was given quarters in Almajara Corp housing, but the company had contracted out the building to the same whimsical crew who'd designed the restaurant at the spaceport, and as a result, Elena and Callie slept inside what looked like a huge hollow tree, albeit with better amenities. The windows were knotholes, and you could take a spiral staircase up the center of the trunk and go through a hatch to a rooftop patio among the "branches," which had real living vines twining all over them.

There were two bedrooms in the vast trunk, a master and a junior, and they shared the big one: the bed was immense, with a headboard and footboard in the same branches-and-vines motif. The bed itself stood on a slightly raised platform, like it was on stage. Callie bounced on the edge of the bed, finding the mattress pleasingly firm. "Are you sure you don't want to take a walk around Rheged, see the sights?" Callie said. "I know being on a planet is new and exciting for you—"

"You know what else is new and exciting for me? Sex on another planet. I wasn't kidding about collecting all the celestial bodies." Elena pounced.

• • •

After they showered – the showerhead was shaped like a tulip blossom, which was way over the "this is twee" line for Callie's taste, prompting complaints that Elena stifled with a kiss – they got dressed and set out, taking a small electric cart along a winding landscaped path to see the sights, such as they were. Despite being the capital, Rheged wasn't a huge settlement, and only merited being called a city because it was adjacent to the planet's main spaceport. Most of the experimental communities and artist colonies had their own properties where they did things their own way, scattered elsewhere on this edge of the continent, most within a day's drive of the capital.

The people who lived in Rheged were either employees of Almajara or support staff for the spaceport, dealing with incoming and outgoing passengers and freight (Owain was already sending tons of food through their bridge to other colonies and stations from the auto-farms to the south, and they hardly imported anything except art supplies and finished goods). The city center was full of more ultragel buildings, many whimsical and representational, clearly the work of a crew that enjoyed making buildings shaped like boots and boats and goats and so on, but there were other more avant-garde and abstract designs, too – structures that incorporated curves and spirals and unexpected angles. Many of those were ugly, and some were sublime. The latter ones made Elena think of Stephen's machine elves and fractalines. He'd hinted once or twice that Elena might find his church's sacraments helpful: she was a woman from another time, coping with the trauma of her arrival in a universe stranger and more hostile than she could have imagined, and that sense of connection and belonging might ease her path. Maybe. She had never dabbled overmuch in mind-expanding or enhancing drugs, and not even Stephen could claim that CoED's sacraments were, strictly speaking, medicine, though he did stress their therapeutic value. In truth, Elena felt she was coping pretty well with her displacement. She'd always had a "change what you can, accept what you can't" mentality, and she found what solace she needed beyond that with Callie.

She looked at her partner, driving the cart with her usual fixed attention, and smiled. Callie didn't believe in accepting what she couldn't change. She'd just change the circumstances until she *could* change whatever needed changing. Elena worried sometimes that she might be getting dependent, but she didn't worry about co-dependence: as far as she could tell, Callie didn't need anything or anyone, and was with Elena solely because she chose to be. That could be a little scary, admittedly – what if Callie got bored and wanted to move on? They were together on a great endeavor, protecting the universe from the Axiom, but that mission didn't require romance. If Elena lost Callie's heart, how adrift would she be in this strange universe, without a guide? She wasn't with Callie just because Callie offered security and a sense of stability in an uncertain world, but that was certainly a nice side effect. Elena's talk with Michael had made her feel better, at least. She had no intention of betraying Callie, and it sounded like Callie was the loyal sort, when it came to love – maybe even loyal to a fault. Elena would try to be worthy of that.

They found a café (bulbous, with an open inner

courtyard, like a torus) with live music – traditional instruments with a local twist, apparently – that wasn't too cacophonous. They settled down in a shaded corner of the courtyard to sip some very creditable coffee and tea. "This is a London Fog." Elena closed her eyes and inhaled the steam from the cup. "That means they had to grow tea leaves and something akin to bergamot oranges to make the Earl Grey, raise bees for honey, and keep cows for the cream. The way they've recreated so much of Earth here... it's incredible. Almost as incredible as them still knowing what London is. Unless they don't even associate the name with the city any more."

"London is still a place. It was raised from the sea floor and refurbished, hundreds of years ago, and now it's one of the rotating capitals of the One World Government. It's not especially foggy nowadays as far as I know. It probably looks a lot different from the city you knew, though they kept the historic structures intact where they could." Callie offered one of her rare, sweet smiles: what Elena thought of as her secret smiles. "You're a genuine time traveler, you know that?"

"Ha. Only like everyone else: moving forward at the rate of one second per second. Time travelers in the stories can go back and forth. They can return home with knowledge of the future or the secrets of the past, and actually make a difference. Me, I just took a long nap."

"Still. The way you look at the world, it helps me. I try to imagine I'm you, sometimes, and attempt to see everything with fresh eyes. It's good for me. You're good for me."

"Be careful, captain. You'll use up your allotment of romance for the year."

"It's OK, I'm done. I'm glad your tea is good. The coffee is merely adequate, and it'll be a decade before there's any Owain whiskey worth drinking. You can't rush the aging process."

"A decade doesn't sound like very long to me at all." Elena sipped, then grinned. "So. Stephen and Q. What do you think?"

"Ha. You saw that too. He's smitten, and I've never seen him smitten before."

"I didn't even know he was interested in that kind of thing. I thought he was maybe aromantic, like Uzoma."

"He used to be married to a woman. It ended badly – I think she died."

"You think? I thought Stephen was one of your closest friends."

Callie nodded. "One reason we're so close is because we don't pry too much into one another's pasts. The kind of people who end up – ended up – working out in Trans-Neptunian space are usually trying to get away from something. That's definitely the case for Stephen. He wanted to go someplace that wouldn't intersect at all with his old life. When I met him, he was performing gray-market body modifications – he did some work on Ashok. He used the money from that to help fund a free clinic for the families of Kuiper Belt miners – he kept on donating a chunk of his pay to the clinic even after I hired him as XO and ship's doctor." A look of fleeting sadness crossed Callie's face, and Elena realized the clinic, like the rest of Meditreme Station, must be just so much irradiated dust now.

"You moved to Meditreme full-time after your divorce, right? Were you trying to get away from your old life too?"

"I don't think too deeply about my own psychology, if I can help it, but probably. I was doing lots of work out there on the fringes anyway, even when my marriage was going well. I wasn't running away from anything then – I just wanted to explore. To see everything. To see something new more days than not." She smiled. "Drake and Janice wanted to live someplace where no one would care what they looked like, or ask what happened to them, as long as they could do the job. They found that."

"What about Ashok? He doesn't seem like the dark-past type."

"Ha. Ashok wanted to live someplace with very few regulations about self-improvement. He wanted to be able to buy black-market prototypes and stick them on his body without anyone arresting him for using unlicensed tech, or trying to treat him for mental illness. If we ever master mind-uploading in a way that doesn't make the subjects go insane from not having a physical body any more, he'll be the first to load himself into a robot."

"Various outcasts by choice and circumstance, and me, the amazing unfrozen woman. It's quite a crew."

"The best I could ask for."

"Except for Sebastien, I guess."

"He's not crew. He's cargo."

Elena chuckled. "For now. Stephen says we should give the new drugs some more time. He is so good at his job. I hope Q is smitten back. Stephen has lost so much. He could use some comfort. She did jump right into hugging him, at the restaurant."

"Sure, but they're churchy. She might just think of him as a wounded bird that fell out of the nest, or an amputated finger that needs to be reattached to a hand."

"I suppose," Elena said. "I might have the soul of a matchmaker. I'd hate for Stephen to feel like a fifth wheel."

"What... are the other four wheels supposed to be?"

"You and me are a couple, of course. And, you know. Ashok and Lantern."

Callie stared at her. "What do you mean, Ashok and Lantern?"

"Haven't you seen how they are together? I can't claim to read Liar body language perfectly, but come on. They're at least best friends. I don't know if there's anything more between them, but then, I don't know if humans and Liars ever, you know... get involved. Do they?"

Elena knew there were things Callie didn't much like to think about, and judging by the look on her face, cross-species romance was one of them. "I mean... yes, you hear about it. Liars and humans, sort of, bonding. Saying they're in love. It's tricky, probably, with the way Liars lie about everything. How you have a relationship with no basis of trust is beyond me. At least Lantern is from the cult of truth-tellers. That would make it easier. We barely even understand how Liars relate to one another. Some Liars pair bond, some form group relationships, some are purely solo – I don't even know if they think about romance the way some humans do. Asking them doesn't help – one of them will tell you all Liars are beings of pure logic, and another will say they're the greatest creators of love poetry in the universe and our feeble human minds simply can't apprehend their genius."

"Sure, but there are some things that can be viewed objectively – what about Liars and sex? I ask, of course, as a xenobiologist." Elena actually knew about all there was to know regarding the practicalities of Liar sexuality already, having done research on the Tangle to satisfy her scientific curiosity during their months on Glauketas, but sometimes it was amusing to make Callie wince.

Callie winced. "That's not something I've looked into. I know Liars don't have reproduction and pleasure intermingled the way humans do – they reproduce in a bunch of different ways, and some of them only require getting friendly with an incubator – but they do have bodies and nerve endings so who knows. I don't browse the parts of the Tangle that would educate me about their sexual habits. As for Liars who are involved with humans, I can't even imagine. I'm sure there's someone who's tried everything, and if it's between consenting sapient creatures with a basis for common communication, it's none of my business."

Elena chuckled. "There were xenophiles in my time, fantasizing about sex with aliens. The world is wide."

"Too wide, sometimes. Forgive me if I don't want to speculate on the logistics. Ugh. Now I'm speculating on the logistics. Ashok has so many options for *attachments*."

"I hope he and Lantern are happy, if I'm right. They sure seem to enjoy one another's company." Elena looked around at the laughing couples and groups, at the musicians sawing and blowing away at their instruments, and suddenly felt a cold spot open in the midst of her warmth. She leaned back in her seat. "It feels strange, Callie. Enjoying myself, joking, being with you… all while knowing there are people out there who need rescuing."

Callie hunched her shoulders and looked down into her coffee cup. "There are no survivors."

"That's what you thought about my crew, when you went to rescue them – you didn't think there was any hope at all. You admitted that afterward."

Callie nodded. "That's true. But rescuing them was one of very few exceptions in a lifetime made up mostly of rules. Your crew was only lost for a couple of days. It's been well over a week here, and that's just the auditors. The others have been missing for over a month. I am not hopeful we'll find any survivors, but we might find some answers, and keep more people from being killed. We'll do a better job if we set out tomorrow well rested and with a sense of calm and clarity. Rushing ahead only risks getting us killed too."

"I know. You're right. I just have a soft spot when it comes to thinking of people lost in space."

"It's an easy place to get lost in. There's lots of it."

"Space is big," Elena said.

Callie gave another secret smile. "How about that. You do listen to me." She sipped, and then put on a changing-the-subject face. "I hope Stephen isn't hitting the sacraments too hard. *Inner* space is big too, and I don't want him to get lost in there."

Stephen was lost in a world of green. He spun, bodiless and slow, traveling through unimaginable verdancy: there were leaves and vines all around him, yes, but also green waterfalls, green soil, green air. A presence – unseen but feminine, motherly but stern – beckoned him onward, onward, onward...

And down. A tunnel of blackness opened beneath him, and then engulfed him, and he plummeted. The tunnel walls began to glow, showing bands of light at regular intervals, flashing past: much like the tunnel they traversed in the *White Raven* when they used their personal bridge generator, so different from the unlit passageways people traveled through with the big fixed bridges. These lights, though, were green, not white, and soon the smooth stone of the tunnel was encroached upon by lichen, mold, vines, and creepers. The tunnel was no longer the sterile ancient conduit created by the Axiom, holes punched in the fabric of space, but instead a living place, a natural cavern in the ground, full of life. Was there a lesson there? Something about life conquering the Axiom's drive toward subjugation and death?

He reached the bottom of the tunnel and floated, shimmering leaves on all sides. His breath, in his body, somewhere far away, made the leaves rustle in time. He sensed the presence again, the Green Lady, looming over him, but he felt suddenly unwelcome, that this was not his place, that he didn't belong here, that he was an outsider, an invader, a despoiler–

Stephen opened his eyes, gasping. He shivered, though the dim, cushion-filled room was warm. The dose Q had given him was fast-acting and also cleared the system quickly, and the green tinge at the edges of his vision receded rapidly. Q was right there, holding him close, her arms around him, helping to ground him in his body as he gulped for air. "I… There was a bridge of fog, and then a forest, and then a jungle, and then there was a *tunnel*, and, and caverns, and I was out of place, I knew it…"

"Oh, no," Q said. "I'm sorry. I was hoping you'd find her in a more welcoming aspect. That's how she manifests most frequently, these days, as a nurturing figure. But early on, lots of us had the experience you did – she made us feel like we were weeds in her garden."

He nodded. "Yes. Exactly." He twitched, the Green Lady's disapproval in him like a fever, and she held him closer. That helped.

Q said, "Some people think it's just a bad molecule in the compound. That the feeling of transgression is due to a tension between the physical and the mental, a border that hasn't been properly erased, a connection to the body that's too strong and insistent, so we feel unwelcome in the inner space. Others think…" She trailed off.

"What?"

Q sighed. "Some of those who believe our visions are messages from something outside ourselves, from entities with independent existence, think the Green Lady is telling us we shouldn't be here on Owain. That we shouldn't have terraformed this place. There was life here, you know, when the Liars first brought us here – very simple life, the local equivalent of slime mold, but still. That's why the planet was such a good candidate for terraforming – it was already capable of sustaining life, though not Earth life. By terraforming we destroyed the conditions that allowed those simple lifeforms to thrive, and they're all gone now, except for a few samples.

In addition to killing that simple life, though, we also destroyed what that life might have *become*. What might that slime have evolved into, given time, and an undisturbed environment? Would it have developed into multicellular life? Sentient life? Sapient life? A few members of the church left the terraforming project because they thought the Green Lady was enraged at us for destroying the opportunity for new forms of life to grow here. I've actually got a sort of hybrid art project and science project devoted to that idea."

"Oh?"

She nodded. "I had some environmental science friends build a dome on my property, enclosing a full acre, and pulled some strings with biologists to fill it with samples from the pre-terraforming days. The interior of the dome mimics the conditions on the planet from before we arrived as perfectly as possible, matching the original character of the geographical location – it's swamp, basically – and I'm just letting it grow wild. It's a miniature ecosystem, as balanced as we can make it. I'm good with systems management, and confident I can sustain it for a long time. It's small, of course, and it's not like I expect a civilization to rise up inside, and it's all a cheat because there are no outside forces acting on it, but… it's something. A memorial to the world that might have been, at least. That was the accommodation *I* made with the Green Lady."

"That's a beautiful idea," Stephen said. "I'd like to see it sometime."

"I'd really like to show you," she said. "That's not the only theory about why the Green Lady is displeased, though. Some people think there used to be advanced life on this planet, thousands or millions of years ago, and that the Lady is angry on *their* behalf – that we're dancing on the graves of a dead civilization, tearing down even their ruins."

Knowing what he did about how the Axiom – and the truth-tellers, acting as stewards of genocide in the absence of their masters – treated intelligent life, that idea didn't strike Stephen as impossible. "Is there any evidence of past life on Owain?"

"Not really. We've unearthed a few bits of metal that probably didn't occur naturally, but Owain is the closest planet to a bridge, and the Liars used the bridges long before humanity did. They probably left some junk behind."

Or else there was some other civilization here, long ago, and the Axiom destroyed it, and their works vanished under the growth of millennia.

"She usually only rebuffs you once," Q was saying. "The second time you seek her, she is almost always more welcoming, and it gets better from there."

"I'd… rather not risk it just now."

Q smiled. "Maybe you'd like to take something else, then? I could call in a few other congregants, and we could share a sacrament of comfort together? Something entactogenic, maybe some of the oxytocin-derivatives…"

"I'd like that," Stephen said. "I'm not sure I'm up for meeting another batch of people, though – I'm feeling a bit vulnerable after that experience. Maybe just… me and you? Something more personal?" Outsiders often assumed membership in the Church of the Ecstatic Divine was an excuse to have orgies, and yes, there were naked cuddle piles from time to time, but sexual (as opposed to sensual) activity was minimal, and almost nonexistent. For one thing, having sex with someone when your perception was altered such that their flesh appeared to be rippling like the surface of the ocean was distracting, but more importantly, you didn't need to have sex with someone when you were on drugs that made you feel connected to them on a level that transcended the physical, and when the stroke of a fingertip on your skin was more pleasurable and sustained than orgasm. When the doses and conditions of the sacraments were right, the barriers that divided one person from another seemed to vanish, until you couldn't tell where you ended and your fellow worshippers began. He missed that feeling so much.

Q looked at him for a long moment. "Huh," she said. "That's interesting. Do you feel a desire to connect with me, in particular? Or just to form a close one-on-one connection with someone, and I happen to be convenient? Both are fine. I'm just curious."

Stephen knew he was known among his crew for being quiet, doleful, self-contained. But here, in the safety of the church, he could open himself in ways that felt safe nowhere else. He *could*, but it wasn't easy, and his voice croaked a bit when he said, "You. In particular."

"Huh," she said again. Then she smiled, and that smile looked so much better on her face than pity and sympathy had. "Let's give it a try."

CHAPTER 15

Callie sat in the cockpit with Drake and Janice, watching their progress through the dark. The nose of the *White Raven* was a segmented dome of smartglass panes hardened for space travel, and the glass was currently toggled to transparent. There wasn't a lot to see out there, though: just blackness and distant stars. They'd been traveling for a while, and had left the bridgehead and its asteroid base far behind. They hadn't encountered any signs of life, but so far they hadn't encountered anything that *took* life, either. There was plenty of darkness, but it wasn't devouring anything.

"Are the long-range sensors picking up anything, Janice?"

"Space rocks in space," she said.

"Helpful as always." Ashok had once made reference to a "falling star" and Janice had launched into a lecture on proper terminology, with an extra dose of condescension, because she was feeling bored and obstreperous, probably: "Falling stars are called meteors, Ashok. They aren't stars. They're the flash of space rocks burning up in the atmosphere. Not to be confused with

173

meteorites, which are space rocks that make it to the ground partly intact."

Ashok hadn't been offended. "So what are asteroids?"

"Space rocks in space." Janice didn't bother calling him an idiot. When Janice talked to you, you could usually take that part as given.

Callie's terminal was set to combat readiness, a screen full of glowing options to deal out devastation, and nothing to use it against. "Are any of the space rocks secretly space monsters? We're getting close to the zone of death. Or disappearance. No reason to be overly pessimistic."

"I'll tell you if there's anything noteworthy, captain," Janice said. "If I notice a giant alien interstellar meat separator covered in spikes, you'll be the first to know."

Callie sighed. "If there's nothing but rocks, at least light them up so I can see what we're dealing with."

The screen lit up suddenly with hundreds of green specks, as if the asteroids were mossy rocks. Some of the specks were large, and some were small, but they were all getting bigger with every second of forward thrust. The ship was approaching the asteroid belt from beneath the plane of the ecliptic, but from Callie's perspective, it looked like they were falling toward a shattered land. "That's a lot of space rocks in space."

"It's like a wall around the system," Drake said. "This makes the asteroid belt back home look like more of a cummerbund. Admittedly, a wall you can fly over or under isn't much of a wall, but still."

"Look at all that fancy metal just whizzing around in space, unattended," Callie said. "Even after the cost of extracting it all, Almajara will clear billions of lix on this deal. Wow. I hope the Owainians – Owainites? denizens of Owain – negotiated for a big percentage for themselves."

"Mining rights aren't much good if there's something eating all the miners," Janice said. "Maybe these asteroids are secretly baby Axiom eggs and we've stumbled into their well-protected nursery, with ship-killing robot nannies."

"I'll file that under 'plausible hypotheses.'" Callie toggled the comms and connected to the machine shop. "Ashok, is Lantern with you?"

"Of course. Why break up a duo of such distinction?"

"Did the Axiom blow up a planet in this system, Lantern?"

Lantern's voice was tentative. "I can't be sure, Callie. The surviving records from the time of the empire are fragmented, so our accounting of Axiom exterminations is partial at best. The fact that there is a wormhole bridge here suggests the Axiom had an interest in the system, and their interest was often inimical to local life. It's entirely possible the asteroid belt is the remnants of a planet they destroyed for their own reasons."

"Like because there was some annoying race of sapient creatures they needed to eliminate," Callie said.

"It's certainly possible," Lantern said. "But it's difficult to understand the motives of the Axiom. Perhaps they destroyed a planet simply to test the efficacy of a new weapon, or it might have been a casualty of one of their factional skirmishes. There is an Axiom station a few days beyond the asteroid belt, near the truth-teller base – perhaps the planet's orbit brought it too close to their project, and they wanted to clear space? There's no way to know."

"If the Axiom *did* destroy a planet, is there a chance they left the weapons that did it lying around?"

"Ah," Lantern said. "I see. You think the surveyors might have run afoul of such a weapon, still operational after all these millennia, like unlucky people stepping on a land mine from a long ago war. The Axiom did build things to last, but I don't know… using a planet-destroying gun to destroy ships seems like overkill, even by Axiom standards. It seems like a weapon capable of destroying a planet would produce some sign we could perceive, in terms of radiation if not in the visible spectrum."

"I'm not picking up any unusual radiation, captain," Janice said. "I've just got… huh. That's weird."

"What?"

"There's something warm up there, among the asteroids," Janice said. "I'm picking up some bright heat signatures." Heat regulation was always an issue in space. The vacuum was a perfect insulator, and there was no easy way to dump waste heat, so hot things tended to stay that way for a long time unless you took steps to cool them down. There were whole branches of engineering devoted to solving the problem, and various human and Liar-made technologies designed to keep parts of your ship from melting, and hiding your heat signature from detection when you wanted to be sneaky.

"Is it a ship?" Callie leaned forward, as if she could see anything through the windows besides green rocks.

"Our sensors aren't showing me anything ship-shaped. When I account for the asteroids, I'm not seeing any other masses out there at all. It's like there's heat, but no surface radiating that heat." The screens changed, the green vanishing, and in its place, a fuzzy blob of reddish dots appeared, dense among the asteroids, larger than the largest space rock.

"What is that?" Callie said

"It appears to be a cloud of hot gas," Janice said.

"Like... a cloud of hot gas left over from a ship being blown up?"

"Eh, if the ship was vaporized, maybe, because that's what we're dealing with – vapor. This isn't debris. It's just... hot dust."

"Let's send out a probe and get a sample. Shall, want to go for a walk?"

The ship's computer spoke. "Have you ever worn boots that are two sizes too small? That's how it feels when you put me inside a probe."

"I'll take that as an 'aye, aye, sir.' Besides, you can just run the probe by remote control, you don't need to bud off a copy of your consciousness. Prep for launch." She switched to shipwide communication. "We've got something worth looking at here, folks. I'm going to call Q and give her a heads-up. Nobody talk about ancient alien super-monsters over the open channel, OK?"

Everyone affirmed their infallible discretion, and she contacted Q's little ship, the *Peregrina*, hanging a few kilometers back. Q's face appeared in one of the dome's panels as the window transformed into a viewscreen. "We're picking up some unusual heat signatures," Callie said. "We're going to cut thrust, and send a probe to take a closer look."

"Understood. I'll stop my engines so I don't overtake you. Are there, ah... any signs of life?"

"No." That was probably too brusque. Q was a

corporate drone, but she wasn't all *that* drone-like, and Stephen liked her, so Callie softened her tone. "We're just beginning our investigations, though."

Q nodded. "I'm a realist, Captain Machedo. Just a hopeful one."

"That's a good combination, if you can manage it," Callie said. "Ashok, Shall, are we ready?"

"Shall is all linked up to the probe," Ashok said. "And it's loaded in the launch port. Just say when."

"Shall is your ship's expert system?" Q asked.

"I'm an AI, actually," Shall said.

Q blinked on the screen. "That's... wow. Those are expensive."

"Shall was an anniversary gift from my ex-husband," Callie said.

"A gift?" Shall said. "I feel so objectified."

"Wait. You have an AI based on a template of Reynauld Garcia-Hassan's nephew?" Q said.

"Grand-nephew, but yes," Shall said. "I was created nearly a decade ago. My template and I don't have all that much in common any more. For one thing, Callie's still on speaking terms with me."

"Let's have less speaking and more probing." Callie winced. "Please, no probing jokes."

"Launching," Ashok said. A few moments later, a pumpkin-sized orb bristling with sensor studs and nodules appeared on the viewscreens, hurtling toward the glowing red cloud. Janice lit up the probe in blue so they could visually track its progress.

"Whee, I'm flying," Shall deadpanned. "I see cold space and cold rocks in space and... lots of little hot things. Very little, and very hot. They are specks, they are motes, they are dust. I think there's some mineral content in there... They could be fragments of a ship, I suppose, but I hate to think of the force necessary to pulverize them so thoroughly. Let me get closer and I'll grab a sample and see what the precise chemical composition of this dust is."

The probe had small thrusters, and they fired, adjusting the orb's course more to Shall's liking. Callie watched as the probe slowly approached the cloud, a shimmering fuzz of red against an infinity of black.

The orb cut its thrusters, and Callie zoomed in the view until the screens were filled with a blue ball against a field of red. "All right," Shall said. "Let's eat some dust and... huh. That's not good."

Callie leaned forward. "Shall? What is it?"

"They're... corrosive. The particles are breaking down the probe. I don't understand it. They're not acidic. I... Callie, the cloud, it's *moving*. It's swarming me, it's breaking me down, it's..."

The blue orb was suddenly surrounded by the red, and within seconds, the blue had vanished entirely.

"Communication with the probe lost," Shall said. "That was unpleasant."

"What the hell is that crap?" Callie said.

Shall sounded remarkably calm. "It's a nanomachine swarm, Callie. They're hot because they're tiny matter-conversion engines. The dust disassembled our probe and turned it into... more dust. That swarm is eating the asteroids, and maybe anything else it encounters, rearranging matter at the molecular level – maybe the atomic level – to enlarge itself."

"That's unreal." Callie stared at the jittering motes

on the screen. Humans and Liars both made use of nanotech, especially in medical technology, but they'd never managed to realize the science-fictional dream of utility fog, molecular machines that could alter matter at the atomic level to create anything you needed. Callie hadn't thought scientists ever would create such technology – as far as she could tell it was just the old dream of alchemy updated, the idea of turning lead into gold and mortality into eternal life. A place for people to put their dreams and try to allay their fears. Of course, no one had ever created the nightmare corollary to utility fog, either: gray goo, out-of-control nanomachines that transformed everything in their path into more of themselves.

The Axiom could create machines like that, though. They'd been able to alter the fundamental laws of physics, at least in localized areas, generating artificial gravity and controlling inertia. They'd injected nanites into Sebastien's brain and cut away his empathy and sense of proportion, among other things, with wicked precision. What was the creation of a little gray goo to beings like that?

"This is it," Callie said. "That swarm is what killed the ships and the surveyor teams." All those people, miners and auditors and the members of Q's church, they'd all been broken down and turned into... more of the swarm. Members of the Church of the Ecstatic Divine like to talk about dissolving their consciousnesses into a single universal mind, but Callie didn't think this was the sort of thing they'd imagined.

"We have to warn Owain!" Q said.

Callie silently cursed. She'd forgotten Q was on the

channel. At least no one had actually mentioned the Axiom. But if this swarm was part of some Axiom project, and humans came out and investigated, that could awaken the aliens (or their security systems, more likely) and make things even worse. The Axiom had probably already destroyed one planet out here. If they didn't proceed carefully, Taliesen system might end up with a second asteroid belt – this one a lot closer to their sun.

"The swarm should be a lot bigger, though, if it's been out here eating asteroids for, what, at least six weeks?" Shall said. "Before the probe was destroyed, I detected a sort of... wisp of heat, leading out of the system. I thought it was just the outer edges of the cloud, but... Oh no. Captain, the swarm is moving. It's approaching us. I think it *noticed* us."

Callie's blood thudded in her ears. She considered opening up a wormhole with their personal bridge generator so they could escape, and swearing Q to secrecy later, but it was too dangerous. The opening of the bridge wasn't instantaneous, and the bridgehead didn't close immediately after they entered it, either – what if some of the swarm reached them, and came through the bridge to Owain? Even a handful of this dust could destroy the whole planet, given time. The bridge generator had originally possessed an emergency system that opened up a wormhole automatically when the ship was in danger to allow its escape, but they'd deactivated that system after it sent them light years away, into orbit around a ruined Axiom planet: the escape had almost been more dangerous than what they were escaping from. Callie was glad they'd turned that feature off. Spreading this poison dust to some random point in the galaxy would be disastrous. They'd have to escape by conventional means. "Fire EMP torpedoes. Q, get out of here, head back to Owain as fast as you can. Drake, follow her. Let's outrun that swarm."

Three electromagnetic pulse torpedoes burst from the *Raven* and arrowed toward the swarm. The torpedoes were low-velocity, because they were designed to disable the electrical systems on enemy ships, not tear holes in their hulls. There were failsafes that prevented the torpedoes from going off while the *White Raven* was within their field of effect, so they wouldn't cripple themselves, but she set the pulse to trigger as soon as the torpedoes reached a safe range.

The swarm got to the torpedoes before that happened, though, and they were devoured before Callie's eyes. Janice groaned, and Shall softly said, "Shit." Callie didn't even know if an EMP would work against such nanomachines, but she'd hoped the pulse might at least thin out the cloud. No such luck.

The *White Raven* was a fast freighter, made for high-end courier jobs, and improved beyond its impressive base specs to function as a skip-tracer, security escort, and pirate-killer. Drake got the ship turned around quickly, the reaction wheels whirling mightily... but it just wasn't fast enough. Shall said out loud what Callie had already silently determined from the data streaming on her terminal: "The swarm is going to overtake us, Callie!"

They were going to die. Callie knew it with a cold and chilling certainty. You couldn't fight nanomachines.

You couldn't shoot them – there was nothing to shoot, and any projectiles you fired would just become more of the swarm. A nuke might destroy the cloud, or part of it, but at this range, the *Raven* would destroy itself in the process – and Q's ship, too. There was still hope for her. Maybe the swarm would take long enough eating the *White Raven* for Q to get away. That was the best-case scenario at this point: that their death would aid someone else's survival.

They were falling into the heart of a volcano. They were being lowered into a pool of acid. They were a feast for the devouring darkness.

Elena, Callie thought, with an infinity of sorrow. Knowing Elena would die was worse than dying herself. Was there time to reach Elena? To end, at least, in her arms? No. Not even close.

How would it feel, to be disintegrated by a swarm of tiny machines? Maybe it wouldn't hurt. The swarm would eat the hull first, after all, and let the vacuum come rushing in. The contents of the ship, crew included, would spill into space. They'd die quickly, exposed to the vacuum, but the swarm would eat their bodies in time. There'd be nothing left of them.

"Contact," Shall said. "I... They're all over us. There's nothing I can do."

"Fuck," Drake said.

"Finally," Janice said.

The viewscreens went red, covered by the cloud of motes. The dots weren't really red, Callie knew – they were invisible, microscopic flecks of rapacious almost-nothing – but it was better, somehow, to see the thing that was about to kill them.

"It's been an honor to serve with you all," Callie said. And then, for maybe only the tenth or twelfth time in her life, she said, "I'm sorry."

CHAPTER 16

Callie almost kept talking, because what else should a captain do in the last moments but try to give some comfort to her crew? At the very least she should profess her love to Elena. Elena would probably appreciate that... for the couple of minutes she had left to appreciate anything.

Except there were no alarms going off. If a swarm of nanomachines was eating her ship, chewing up the hull, there should have been alarms going off – all manner of beeps and wails and klaxons. The shimmering red still covered the viewscreens, but they were still *viewscreens*, and not gaping holes full of murder-dust. "Shall? Why are we not dead?"

"I have no idea, captain. The swarm approached us, the cloud enveloped us, and now... the cloud is streaming away."

"Does it only eat... uninhabited things?" Elena said over the comms.

"If it's that picky, then it couldn't have killed the surveyors and the auditors," Callie said. "It seems like a hell of a coincidence for there to be *two* deadly mysterious things happening out here in the asteroid belt."

The red motes receded from the viewscreens, leaving darkness behind. "The swarm is coming toward your ship now, Q," Shall said.

"Oh, good." Q's voice was understandably tense. "Should I jump up and down and wave my arms and shout 'occupied' so the swarm knows there's a person in here?"

"The swarm shouldn't know anything," Shall said. "Unless it's made for more than just self-replication. A percentage of the motes could be sensors, I suppose. That makes sense, in terms of choosing targets better... maybe the swarm can only manipulate matter on the molecular level, and not the atomic – then its requirements for new material would be more specific. Maybe the swarm ate *some* people because it needed to collect organic molecules that weren't present in the asteroids? But, no, carbonaceous asteroids are the most common ones out here, and humans are mostly carbon. There's plenty of calcium and oxygen out here, too. Maybe they needed nitrogen for something, but that makes up such a small part of human bodies... The swarm is about to contact your ship, Q."

Suddenly alarms *did* scream – but across the comms, from the *Peregrina*. "Uh, Captain Machedo?" Q said. "I turned my ship around, trying to rush back to Owain like you said, and now my sensors show microscopic hull breaches where the swarm is making contact, at the back of the ship – sorry, uh, aft? The holes are self-sealing, but... no, there go the seals."

"Get into your environment suit now!" Callie said. "Get off that ship! Shall, launch the canoe and go get her *now*." There was a distant *thunk* as the canoe dropped from the *White Raven's* belly, with Shall's favorite many-armed mining-drone body clinging to the top, as usual.

Q stared at the screen, wide-eyed, her face bathed in pulsing red lights from the ship's emergency system. "I... My suit is in the next compartment, in a locker next to the airlock. I can't get there now. The cockpit is sealed. There's... That part of the ship is exposed to vacuum."

"Her ship is about a quarter gone already," Janice said. "The cloud is getting bigger, too." The viewscreens shifted to a different set of the *Raven's* external cameras, allowing Callie to see Q's ship. The swarm wasn't lit up in red in this view, and so the *Peregrina* seemed to be simply melting away, like cotton candy dipped into a stream.

Q closed her eyes and murmured to herself. Callie couldn't make her prayers out, apart from a mention of the Green Lady. Q opened her eyes, and locked her gaze with Callie's. "I wanted to die on Owain," Q said. "I wanted to be buried on a planet I helped bring to life."

Stephen's voice cut into the channel, eerily calm. "Shall, how long before the canoe reaches her?"

"Barely more than a minute, XO, if the swarm doesn't try to eat me first, but I don't see–"

Stephen ignored him. His voice was as solid as a mountain. "Q, we're going to shoot out the window of your cockpit. You'll need to lie down on the floor so we don't hit you by accident. When the window breaks, you'll be sucked into the vacuum. Don't be afraid. Shall will grab you and put you into the canoe before any harm comes to you."

Q shook her head. "That's... No, that's insane, I'll die–"

"No you won't." Calm, calm. That's why Callie had made him XO, and why he was a good surgeon: chaos and crisis made Stephen more steady, not less. "You can survive up to two minutes in space, Q. We're going to give you a countdown, and when we hit zero, you're going to *exhale*, hard – expel every bit of breath from your lungs. Do you understand?"

Q stared at Callie, who did her best to put on an encouraging face. Q's eyes glistened. "I don't know if I can–"

"Do you trust me, Q?" Stephen said. "After last night, do you?"

She wiped her cheeks, then nodded. "I do."

"Get me a firing solution, Shall," Callie said. "An expanding ballistic round that will knock out her cockpit window and *not hit her*."

"Lie down now," Stephen said gently.

Q nodded and dropped below the view of her camera. The canoe appeared on the viewscreen, approaching the front of Q's ship, which was now easily half gone. The swarm hadn't noticed the canoe – yet.

"Counting down from five," Shall said. "Five. Four. Three. Two. One. Zero."

"Exhale!" Stephen shouted.

The round struck Q's ship at an oblique angle, blowing a door-sized hole in the nanoglass, without leaving an exit wound – the remnants of the round were embedded in the ship's ceiling. That kind of round was made specially for knocking holes in ships without going through-and-through: it was designed to disable pirate vessels without totally destroying them.

Fragments of Q's cockpit spewed out into space,

chunks of metal and plastic and her terminal – and one
human figure came tumbling out along with the rest.
Shall's many-armed probe launched from the canoe and
had her within seconds, grabbing her and darting back
to the canoe's airlock, depositing her swiftly inside. The
little ship was on its way back to the *Raven* before the
airlock was even closed after her, Shall's drone body
squatting on top of the opening like a guard dog. "She's
secure."

"I'll meet you in the cargo bay," Stephen said. "Elena,
come down? I'll need your help."

Callie watched as Q's ship gradually vanished, like a
sandcastle eaten away by the incoming tide. Why had
the swarm killed the *Peregrina* and not the *White Raven*?
It didn't make any sense.

Then, suddenly, it did.

"You can survive for two minutes exposed to space,
huh?" Callie said. Their ship had withdrawn some
distance from the asteroid belt, and the swarm hadn't
followed them, appearing content to return to snacking
on the asteroid belt after it finished eating the *Peregrina*.

Q was unconscious, strapped down in a hospital bed,
next to Sebastien. She looked and sounded bad – her
skin was puffy and badly sunburned, and her breathing
was raspy – but she was alive.

Stephen sighed. "Honestly? More like ninety seconds.
To survive without permanent damage. In theory. That's
if you don't have any air in your lungs to expand when
you hit the vacuum – if you don't exhale first, your
outcomes are far worse, because your lungs burst, which
is not conducive to continuing life." He reached out as if

to touch Q, but then stopped, his fingertips just short of her swollen skin. "She exhaled, fortunately. But hypoxia causes loss of consciousness in ten to fifteen seconds. Your skin begins to swell within fifteen seconds, as the water in your tissues expands. She had on a tight-fitting jumpsuit, which helped mitigate that at least. There's a bit of frostbite around her nose and mouth, where the moisture boiled off and then sublimated, and we're close enough to the star even way out here that solar radiation gave her a mild sunburn. But it could have been so much worse, Callie. If she'd been out there much longer her blood would have boiled." Stephen closed his eyes, and his lips moved soundlessly for a moment, in some prayer of his own. Then he looked at Callie, and she was shocked to see tears glistening at the corners of his eyes. "I don't want to lose anyone else. My entire congregation on Meditreme Station wasn't enough?"

"Do you need to take Q back to Owain?" Callie said. "We could open up a wormhole, and send you two back through in the canoe. When you get to the ground, just tell them her ship had a catastrophic failure on the journey and you brought her back for care."

Stephen considered, then shook his head. "It's tempting, but it isn't medically necessary. Shall reached her fast. Once her swelling goes down, she'll be basically recovered. Sore, and tender, but entirely functional. Also... I think Q would be furious if she woke up back home. We talked a lot, that night on Owain, and we've kept talking on private channels during the journey out here. We got very close, very quickly, which is an advantage of my church, when you take the right sacraments. There's nothing more important to Q than figuring out what happened to her congregants, and making sure it doesn't happen to anyone else. She's in the business of making things *work*, and this whole problem, these disappearances, it's a terrible failure point in the system. She can't abide that." His eyes narrowed. "And, personally speaking, I'd like to destroy whatever sent that swarm here. Do you think it's the Axiom?"

"I am entirely one hundred percent certain it's the Axiom," Callie said. "At least, I'm sure the swarm is Axiom technology, originally. As for what unleashed it... that I don't know. It could be humans or Liars, playing with Axiom technology they found. Or even setting it loose by accident. I can imagine someone stumbling on an Axiom facility, opening the wrong door, and finding themselves disassembled by the swarm before they realize what's happening." She looked at Q's swollen face. "But... I don't think it was an accident. There's intentionality here. The swarm isn't just mindlessly devouring. It has mission parameters and rules of engagement. I think the swarm is part of one of those millennia-long Axiom projects Lantern told us about. I don't know what the sleeping uglies are working toward, or why they need a matter-conversion cloud to do it, but whatever their plan, it's probably not good for any other living things in the system. Speaking of things that aren't good for living things..." She nodded toward Sebastien. "How's our other patient?"

Stephen swiveled toward the other bed, frowning. "My tests are promising. The regenerative drugs have done remarkable work, even over the past few days – as of this morning, his brain scans are now identical to those of a healthy person who's never had a brain-spider clinging to their skull. Whether that's improved his personality, I couldn't say, but he's not brain-damaged any more. Any time Elena wants to do another simulation with Sebastien, she's welcome. It's *possible* he won't try to murder her this time."

Callie *hmm*ed. "Maybe I'll run his next simulation."

"Really? I thought the theory was that interacting with Elena would be more effective, because they were friends – she'll be better able to reach him, and provoke an empathetic response in his abused brain."

"That's the theory, but look at the practice, and the evidence from the simulation she ran with Ashok. Sebastien thinks he can trick Elena – and he might be right. He can deceive her a lot more easily than he could me, anyway. I'm not waking him up and letting him walk around on my ship in the real world unless I'm sure he's not going to murder everyone – and even when I *am* sure, I'm going to have Shall follow him around with one of the little snatch-and-grab drones we brought from Glauketas." The pirates had a cache of small bots loaded with non-lethal suppression measures, from tranquilizers to nets to stun-guns, designed to neutralize targets selected for kidnap and ransom. "Maybe it's time to test Sebastien against the *worst* case scenario: me."

"You're the captain," Stephen said. "You might want to mention your plan to Elena first."

"We'll talk about Sebastien later, assuming we live that long. We have more pressing concerns, like figuring out where this swarm came from, and how to turn it off. I need to go see Lantern, and figure out our next move."

"Oh? You haven't already figured it out?"

Callie smiled. Her XO knew her well. "Of course I have, but it's always gratifying to have someone knowledgeable tell me I'm right."

Callie floated into Ashok's machine shop – and then fell onto the floor, thudding down hard. "Ow." She scowled, getting up and rubbing her knee as Ashok rose from behind a work table.

"Crap, cap! Sorry, I've got a gravity generator going in here. Drake and Janice like it floaty, so I didn't do the whole ship, but it's just easier to work in here when down is down."

"Ow," Callie said again. Then: "Maybe we should set this up for my quarters, too, and the infirmary. Can you put it on a switch, like the lights, so people can turn the gravity on and off as needed?"

"I can cobble something together, sure."

Callie nodded. "It's not a priority, obviously, but when you have time. Where's the squidlet?"

"Is that a term of endearment?" Lantern clambered up onto the same tabletop Ashok was standing behind. What had they been doing back there, on the floor? *Just engineering*, Callie thought firmly. Curse Elena for putting thoughts... of cross-cultural communication... into her head.

"It's a term of endearment when I say it, anyway. Is the term offensive to Liars? I didn't mean it that way."

"You call my entire species *Liars*," Lantern said. "The Free are used to humans insulting us."

"In our defense, ninety-nine percent of you lie almost all the time about almost everything, including what you *want* us to call you."

"That is true," Lantern said. "Anyway, you should hear some of the things we call you."

"I'm sure I've heard worse." Callie dropped onto a stool. She could get used to this gravity-on-demand thing. "So. This swarm of nanomachines. They were made by the Axiom. Do you know how I know?"

"Yes," Lantern said.

"Wait," Ashok said. "I don't know how you know. I don't even know *what* you know. Why don't I know?"

"Nobody knows everything," Callie said. "Not even you. The reason our ship is still intact and Q's ship is swarm food is because we have one of *those*, and Q didn't." Callie nodded toward the greasy black cube on a nearby table, hooked up to cables that snaked into the depths of the ship's propulsion and navigation systems. Their greatest treasure, their most dangerous weapon, the reason Meditreme Station had been destroyed and the reason they'd been able to rescue Elena's crew from the Axiom space station: their personal bridge generator.

"Yes," Lantern said. "Many Axiom systems are designed to protect, or at least not harm, other Axiom property. There must be sensors in the swarm. They scanned us, detected the bridge generator, determined we were Axiom servants – because at the height of their empire of extermination, no one *but* Axiom or their servants could possibly possess such technology – and spared us accordingly. Q's ship was... less fortunate. But I am confused about something else."

"What's that?"

"My working theory was that whatever killed the surveyors also killed the local cell of truth-tellers," Lantern said. "But their station has Axiom technology on board, too, so the swarm should have left them alone. Maybe the cell has gone dark for some other reason, though as you say, it's unlikely there are *two* mysterious deadly situations happening simultaneously."

"Huh," Callie said. "Is the truth-teller station nearby?"

"In astronomical terms, yes, but it would take days to reach it by conventional propulsion – we like to stay well away from the local population."

Callie nodded. Lantern's cell back home was hidden deep in the Oort cloud. "We'll check up on the station as soon as we can, and you can see how your fellow genocidal zealot lapdogs are doing."

"Only the elders of my sect are knowingly loyal to the Axiom, Callie," Lantern said firmly. "The junior members, like I once was, truly believe we're *protecting* the people of the galaxy from the Axiom – not protecting Axiom projects from interruption."

Callie nodded. "I know, I know. It was a bad joke. We won't go in with weapons hot or anything... and I hope the innocent junior truth-tellers turn out to be OK. Maybe the station is just suffering communication problems. For now, though... tracking down the source of that swarm is the most important thing. It's going to keep eating ships, and Almajara is going to keep *sending* ships to look for its missing property, and eventually the Corp will send a force too big for the swarm to eat all at once, and some will make it back alive, and then word will get out. I'm not just worried about the Axiom in that situation. Uncle Reynauld would *love* to get his hands on gray-goo-level nanotech. He is not a responsible individual. He has a strip mine for a soul. If he managed to isolate some particles, study them, and program them to his own ends? Ugh. That would be the worst."

Lantern said, "Dealing with the Axiom requires discretion and delicacy – if they feel threatened, if their security systems even feel threatened, they could destroy Owain. Does your ex-great-uncle-in-law possess those qualities?"

"Reynauld is about as discreet as a spaceport crash and as delicate as a sledgehammer."

Shall cleared his non-existent throat over the room's speakers. "I wouldn't worry too much about Uncle Rey. We have a more pressing issue. I've done some calculations, and it won't be long before the swarm finishes chewing through that segment of the asteroid belt and moves on to eat Owain."

CHAPTER 17

There was a moment of shocked silence, which Callie broke, rather inelegantly, by saying, "Wait. What?"

"Based on my limited observation of the swarm's activity, I've made some extrapolations," Shall said. "The swarm was devouring its way through the asteroid belt, but along a fairly narrow path. The swarm doesn't seem to be following the ring around, which would keep it occupied for a long time. Instead, it's chewing its way straight through. I think it's just devouring the asteroid belt along the way to its actual target: Owain itself."

"How the hell does a swarm of dust-sized machines even know there's a planet in the system?" Callie said. "I thought the swarm was purely reactive, just eating anything in its path?"

"In its *path*," Lantern said. "That suggests it has a path. The Axiom have a bridgehead here. They had charts of the system. Even their automated systems are smart enough to examine the available data and direct the swarm accordingly. Owain is the greatest conglomeration of matter in the system, and is the obvious target.

Converting an entire planetary mass would be faster and more efficient than picking at asteroids here and there. A planet's worth of mass spread across thousands of kilometers of space in a huge orbital ring is harder to convert than a planet's worth of mass neatly compacted into an oblate spheroid. The swarm is just consuming and converting anything it encounters on the way to Owain, because that is convenient."

Callie did not like this theory. She'd been feeling pretty smart and pleased with herself for figuring out why the swarm had spared them, and now she felt two steps behind again. "Are we sure the swarm has a plan? Maybe it's just some ancient machinery that got turned on accidentally, and it's just drifting around eating what it finds. Hell, it could have been chewing on the asteroid belt for decades, and it's just that nobody noticed until surveyors stumbled on it and went missing. Right?"

"Ah, no," Shall said. "Not right. Wrong. Because of exponential growth."

"Yes," Lantern said.

"That's true," Ashok agreed.

Callie scowled. "Use your words, people."

"The swarm should be larger than it is," Shall said. "*Much* larger. If it's been operating in the asteroid belt for a minimum of six weeks, it's converted countless metric tons of matter into copies of itself already. The cloud should get bigger with every asteroid it eats, and once it's bigger, it can eat even more asteroids even more quickly, and so on, exponentially, until it goes from consuming a few asteroids an hour to a few asteroids per minute to a few per second – and so on. The classic exponential growth curve for self-replicating machines was laid out by the ancient philosopher Eric Drexler, who posited a single such machine, making copies of itself, with every subsequent copy making copies of *themselves*. Say it takes a thousand seconds to make one copy – in the first thousand seconds, one copy is created. In the next thousand seconds, each of the two replicators makes another copy of itself. In the next interval, those four replicators build four more, and then those eight build eight more. Within a day, there are tens of billions of replicators, and despite their microscopic size, they weigh more than a ton. Before two days pass, the replicators have more mass than the planet Earth. A few hours after that, they have more mass than all the bodies in the solar system combined – including the sun. The growth rate curves *that fast*."

Callie thought about that. "Damn," she said at last.

"The swarm seems to replicate rather faster than one copy per every thousand seconds," Lantern said.

Ashok nodded. "This entire system should have been converted by now – instead, the swarm has been slowly munching its way through the asteroid belt for weeks, at least."

Callie considered. "Right before we thought we were going to die, Shall, you said the swarm, what, has a tail?"

"Yes," Shall said. "I detected a steady stream of hot particles, moving away from the system, toward the outer darkness."

"So most of the matter the swarm is converting is being sent *back* someplace," Callie said. "That's why it hasn't gone all exponential on us. Why? Where's that matter going? What's it being used for?"

"I shudder even to speculate," Lantern said.

"Huh," Callie said. "Sounds like there's a trail, though. And we can follow a trail, right back to its source." She smiled. "This is just like your thing about the ants, Lantern."

"Ants?" She sounded baffled.

"Right after we met, when you were first telling us about the Axiom, and trying to convince us to leave them alone, you said humans were like ants. If we see a single ant walk across a picnic table, we ignore it. If we see a couple of ants, and they're heading for our food, we brush them away. But when it's ten, twenty, a hundred ants, or a thousand, swarming all over our food, crawling into the house, getting into our clothes – then we get pissed off, and follow the trail of ants back to their nest, and burn them out. You were afraid that if humans kept messing with Axiom facilities, we'd become that swarm of ants, and the Axiom would wake from their slumber and destroy us."

"Ah, yes, I remember," she said. "I still think it is an apt metaphor."

"Me too. The swarm went from nibbling on rocks to nibbling on ships to nibbling on people, and we've noticed, and we're pissed off, and we're going to follow the trail back to *their* nest... and burn it out. Shall, coordinate with Drake and Janice, and let's start following that trail, at a respectful distance. I don't want to test our immunity to the swarm too vigorously."

"Aye, captain," Shall said.

Callie turned and strode out of the machine shop, thinking, "This time, we're the exterminators, and the Axiom is the ants." She stumbled when she hit the null-gravity in the corridor, momentum carrying her until she banged up against the far wall. "Ow," she said. Way to spoil a good exit line.

Elena waited in Callie's quarters, sitting in a chair (thanks to thrust gravity) as they powered along, following the tendril of heat swarming above them. The door opened and Callie stepped in, smiling, and then stopped smiling when she saw Elena's face. "What's wrong?"

"I asked Stephen how Sebastien was doing, and he said good, and I said I was ready to do another simulation, and he said *you* want to do it."

Callie raised up her hands. "I was going to talk to you about that. Like, right now. As in, I came in here to talk to you about it."

"So talk."

Callie explained – in rather more diplomatic terms than Stephen had – that it might be time to test Sebastien a bit more stringently, against a less sympathetic audience. Elena didn't think that, after being attacked in one simulation and locked in a shower in another, that she was all *that* sympathetic any more, but she conceded that Callie was even less so. She also recognized that Callie was trying to protect her from another round of pain and heartbreak. "What if I said no?" Elena said finally.

"I'd respect your decision and try not to worry about you too much," Callie said.

Elena sighed. "I know you would. I know you're right – or at least, not entirely wrong. Even after everything, I still have a soft spot for Sebastien. But *you* have a hard spot for him."

Callie scrunched up her face and stuck out her tongue.

"That sounds kind of dirty."

Elena shook her head. "No jokes. You hate Sebastien, don't you?"

Callie seemed to consider the question seriously. "Hate? It's not that strong. I don't have a reason to feel good about him, though, Elena. I hope you're right, and there's a good person in there, and that we can bring him out again. I hope your friend can be recovered. It's not hate. It's… caution. I approach the situation with a certain amount of skepticism. Which could be a good thing, if we want to make sure he's really himself again."

Even if she met with Sebastien and he seemed fine, Elena had to admit, she would wonder if he was just playing her again. She made her decision. "Just give him a fair chance, all right? Expect the worst, be prepared for that, I know you always are – but leave yourself open to the possibility of the best."

Callie bowed her head, then looked up. "All right. I will. I just… don't want you to get hurt. Hope is great, until it becomes…"

"Delusion?" Elena said.

"Dangerously unrealistic, let's say." She softened. "Do you want to sit in and watch? You could plug into the simulation without an avatar, just an invisible observer hovering on the ceiling, looking down on us, yelling in my ear if I do a bad job."

Elena considered, then shook her head. "No. I trust you. It's important that I trust you. I'd like your opinion. About whether it's worthwhile to keep working with Sebastien, or if it's a waste of time. Whether Sebastien should just be locked up in a cell on Glauketas, or plugged into the Hypnos for the rest of his days. I still don't think he deserves punishment for the things he did, but he might require... containment. I know that."

"I'll observe with an open mind and tell you what I think," Callie said.

"When are you going to do it?"

She shrugged. "The trail extends into space for quite a distance, as far as our sensors can tell, and we don't want to jump ahead via wormhole bridge, since we don't know what's waiting for us at the other end, so. No time like the present, right?"

Elena rose from the chair and gave Callie a kiss. "Thank you. I know having Sebastien on the ship feels a lot like having a ticking bomb on board to you."

"We'll disarm him," Callie said. "Don't you worry." She stood up, then frowned and lifted her arm, gesturing to the corner. "Did you see, it was like a shimmer..."

"What?" Elena looked, and didn't see anything but an empty corner.

Callie shook her head. "Nothing. My eyes are tired. Just a touch of space madness."

"Happens to the best of us," Elena said.

Elena helped fit the Hypnos diadem onto Sebastien, then came over to adjust Callie's, looking into her eyes for a long moment, fingers lingering at Callie's temples. "Good luck in there," she said.

When in doubt, fall back on bravado. "Luck is for amateurs." Callie gave Elena a wink, then closed her eyes.

The darkness receded, and she was... in the infirmary still, but this time sitting on a bench next to Sebastien's bed. The simulation was excellent: it even smelled of the sick bay's aggressively filtered air. Sebastien opened his eyes, blinked in a fluttering flurry, then looked at her. "I... know you. Don't I?"

"You tried to kill me once."

He sat up, looking around. "No, that doesn't sound right. I... locked you up? I was afraid you were going to interfere with something important."

"That 'something important' was a plot to transform the entire human race into your obedient slaves using mind-control implants. Which I class as murder, so, I stand by my statement."

"I think... were you with Elena? Did you... oh, God." He put his face in his hands. "I tried to change her." He looked up, then touched his skull all over, tenderly, as if expecting to find implants there. "The way... I was changed. But I'm all right now? You helped me? Like you helped her?"

"Cut the shit, Sebastien," Callie said. "You remember what happened just fine, don't you?"

His face lost its twist of worry and went briefly blank. Then he sighed. "Yes, all right. I was just trying to make a good first impression."

"You blew your chance at that on the Axiom space station," Callie said.

He turned toward her, leaning slightly forward, a bit of intimacy-building body language – or manipulation. "I remember you, Captain Machedo. I remember what I did. I don't remember why it seemed like a good *idea*, because now it strikes me as absolutely insane... but I did it. I don't dispute that. I remember waking up a couple of other times, too, though they seem more dreamlike, somehow. They weren't dreams, were they?"

"No." She crossed her arms, closing out his attempt to connect with her, whether it was unconscious or not. "They were simulations – what you'd call virtual reality, though a lot more advanced than the stuff they had in your day."

He frowned. "Why wake me up in a computer program?"

She snorted. "We weren't sure if our attempts to get the brain-spiders out of your head worked or not, and I wasn't about to wake up a genocidal lunatic on my ship, so we did it in a safe space. A good thing, too, since you attacked people and tried to blow up my house."

"Ah." He waved his hand in front of his face. "Is this real?"

"Wouldn't you like to know?"

"I think, based on what I know of you... no. This isn't real. You aren't actually here."

"Oh, we're really right next to each other. I'm in a hospital bed next to you. But yes, this is a simulation, so strangling me here, like you did to Elena the first time you woke up, won't accomplish much. Won't even hurt me, because pain responses are dialed way down for me. Not so much for you, though, so watch yourself. You can feel pain, and I'm good at inflicting it."

He swung his legs over the edge of the bed. "Threat duly noted. I feel... different, though, captain. Before, it was like I was looking at the world through a pane of thick, dirty glass. Everything was dim and muffled. Like instead of inhabiting my own body, I was in a sort of... control room, inside my own skull, looking out, manipulating my body like it was a robot under my remote control. You *all* seemed like robots, everyone – and moreover, you were malfunctioning, or programmed in ways that conflicted with my own goals."

Callie didn't let herself shudder. She wasn't going to show Sebastien anything that could even remotely be construed as weakness. "What goals were those?"

"I think… freedom? Yes. Freedom."

"Last time we woke you up in a simulation, you stole my ship and blew up my station. For freedom?"

He sighed. "Freedom for me, anyway. Maybe… less so freedom for everyone else. I don't feel that way now, though, captain. I don't have that sense of… estrangement from myself, and from others, any more. I am so ashamed of the things I did, even though it doesn't really feel like it was *me* that did them."

Callie considered his look of anguish. "How do I know you aren't lying?"

Now he just looked tired. "You can't detect lies with your fancy future technology?"

"Not with perfect reliability, though believe me, your brain is being scanned very thoroughly, and we'll get some indications about your general truthfulness from that."

"Something changed, though. I feel it. You, or the doctors, must have done something to me, to clear away that fog, to let me out of the cage inside myself. Am I wrong?"

Callie shook her head. "No. Parts of your brain were damaged by the Axiom intrusion. Our ship's doctor, Stephen – you killed him once in a simulation too, remember? – gave you some very expensive experimental drugs that regrew some of your brain tissue. You've regenerated the bits that got chewed up by nanobots. Some of your mirror neurons, he said, and parts of your prefrontal cortex, and the temporo-parietal junction, and your… something… supramarginal gyrus. Brain bits associated with empathy and impulse control, apparently. The Axiom didn't think you needed those. We disagree. Stephen said the treatment might make you less megalomaniacal."

He looked sheepish. "Well. Probably. But I was always a *little* megalomaniacal."

She actually laughed. "I bet you were. How about the homicidal part?"

"I was never particularly homicidal. I don't feel at all like murdering anyone right now."

"I won't take your word for it."

He slumped. "Elena must despise me."

"She's the reason you're still in therapy. She hasn't given up on you. But I wouldn't expect her to make out with you."

"Ah, no, of course. Maybe I can be her friend again, though. I… Do you know, I forgot what guilt *felt* like? It feels terrible. I want to crawl into a hole and pull the hole over me."

"That was my suggestion for how to deal with you, though it was going to be more like me *throwing* you in a hole than letting you crawl into one."

"Point taken. You don't like me. I don't blame you. Where do we go from here?"

"I'll unplug myself, and talk to the doctor about what your brain scan says. If it looks good, we'll wake you up in the real world… and you'll be closely monitored. Like, a small machine the size of a hummingbird, with the mind of a hyperintelligent AI inside it, will fly around with you at all times, keeping you under surveillance."

"Ah. There was a writer, before my time, named Iain M Banks, who wrote about something similar – criminals on an alien world were assigned robot minders to keep them in line. They were called slap-drones, I think."

"Ha. You *wish* you'd only get a slap from these machines. They're more like a stab-drone."

"I always used to say, science fiction helps us imagine the future, which helps us create it," he said. "And here we are."

"Huh. You're less humorless than you were with large parts of your brain burned out. I'll take that as a good sign." She stood up. "Oh, hey: Elena and I are together now. Like, together-together. The only reason I didn't let you die on the Axiom space station along with your fleet of mind-control ships was because she cares about you, and I care about what she cares about." Callie stepped toward him, crowding into his personal space, and spoke low and quiet. "But it also means I protect her. Obviously if all this 'I feel so bad' crap is a ruse, I'll shove you out an airlock. But even if you are a person again instead of a monster, watch yourself. If you hurt her, if you so much as *disappoint* her, you'll contend with me. Do you understand?"

He didn't shrink away, but held her gaze, and nodded. "I do."

"Yeah. So you say. We'll see." She snapped her fingers, and left the simulation.

CHAPTER 18

"How did it go?" Elena tried not to sound too eager, but she was bubbling over with hope. It would be so nice if Sebastien was *OK* – or at least OK enough that she could stop worrying about him all the time, and free up her mind to worry about *other* things.

Callie sat up. "He said all the right things. I don't know how reading body language works when the bodies aren't even actually real, but that all looked right, too, unless he's very good at faking, which I think takes more social awareness than he's shown in his last couple of iterations. How's the brain scan, Stephen? Is he a lying murderer who murders people and lies about it?"

He grunted, consulting his terminal. "You know my reservations about using brain scans to try to detect lies – it's so inaccurate it's barely better than chance – but I didn't see any strong indications that he was making things up in there. Otherwise, and without going into technical details you neither have the training to comprehend nor particularly care about... everything looks good. His past scans showed almost no activity in the parts of the brain that involve empathy, or guilt, which wasn't a surprise, because they were badly damaged by the Axiom machines. This time, he's lighting up in ways that indicate real emotional engagement. The responses are a bit muted, perhaps, but his pathways are still forming, and I don't know what his original baseline capacity for love, kindness, and understanding was anyway."

"Sebastien was… always more interested in systems than people, I think," Elena said. "He could get interested in individual *persons*, sometimes – he was interested in me, that way – but he was a big-picture sort of thinker, let's say."

"We might not get a big weepy breakdown and show of penitence, is what you're saying," Callie said. "My question is: can he be trusted not to kill everyone?"

"I refuse to promise that," Stephen said. "About anyone, really. But based on these scans, if Sebastien kills us all, he might at least feel bad about it afterward."

"He could be useful to us," Callie mused. She glanced over at Q, probably to make sure she was still deeply asleep, but lowered her voice anyway. "He can understand Axiom language at least as well as Lantern, and has a better sense of their – what did Uzoma call it? Conceptual architecture? – than anyone else on the ship. If we're headed to an Axiom facility, that insight could be helpful. But I don't want him thinking, 'Ooh, a nanobot swarm, I can use that to conquer the galaxy.'"

"At some point, we have to decide to trust him, or not," Elena said.

"There's an ancient Earth proverb," Callie said. "'Trust, but verify.' Shall, spin up one of those snatch-and-grab drones for me? Actually, make it two. Nothing wrong with a little redundancy. Test them really thoroughly, and then send them to the infirmary."

"Will do," Shall said.

"You're going to wake him up?" Elena couldn't tell if she was happy or scared or an amalgam of both.

"We're going to give him a probationary period, under close supervision. When the drones arrive... yeah, bring him out of the coma, Stephen. Keep an eye on him, Elena. You knew him before. You're the one who'll be best able to tell if he's back to whatever his version of normal is. I'll alert the rest of the crew." Callie gave Elena's arm a squeeze and left the room.

"How do you feel about this, Stephen?" Elena asked.

"Your friend attempted to murder me in a simulation. I am conflicted. But we are all parts of the mind of God, and so forth, so I'll try to give him a fair chance, and trust in Shall to stop him from doing anything too dangerous. At the moment, I'm a lot more concerned with Q."

Elena turned her attention to the woman in the other hospital bed. "She looks a lot better – the swelling has gone down."

"I expected her to be awake by now, though," Stephen said. "I don't see anything too serious on the scans, and people recover at different rates, but I'll feel a lot better when I can hear her voice."

"Is there anything I can do to help with her care? I am supposed to be junior medical assistant in training."

Stephen turned slightly away from her. "Yes. Have you been doing the reading?"

"As much as I can. I was always a good student."

"I don't doubt it."

Elena could even read Liar body language pretty well at this point; reading human body language was far easier.

"You don't want me as an assistant, do you?"

Stephen winced and rubbed his jaw. "Ah. It's not that, exactly, though I've never worked particularly well with others – it's part of why I became a ship's doctor and a generalist instead of continuing to work in hospitals as a surgeon. I like you, Elena – a lot, actually, and I don't warm to people easily – and you are obviously very intelligent and dedicated. It's just, when Callie came to me and asked if I could teach you, she talked about your years of studying field and emergency trauma medicine…"

He trailed off, but Elena understood where he was going. "Right. Callie basically said, 'She learned how to chop off legs in the American Civil War, so she'll be a great surgeon,' huh? 'She was at the top of her Miasma Theory of Illness class!'"

"Mmm."

Elena thought for a moment, then nodded. "Worse than that, huh? My knowledge is basically medieval from your position, isn't it? So it's more like, 'This plague doctor from the Middle Ages with the giant beaked mask and the censer full of burning incense is going to be your new bacteriologist.'"

"A somewhat closer analogy," Stephen admitted. "In your time, they still treated cancer by irradiating and poisoning the patients, and hoping the cancer would succumb before the patient did. They almost seemed to treat cancer like it was *one thing* instead of scores of related maladies with some similar properties. Doctors in your day barely had access to basic genetic scanning, and targeted therapies were almost nonexistent. They'd send new mothers home with codeine even though some people process the drug into morphine more quickly than others, and the children would die from drug overdoses after nursing! They treated emotional disturbances by sticking icepicks into their patient's brains, they electrocuted people in the hopes of curing so-called sexual deviance, and they *punched holes* in people's skulls to drain out fluid because they didn't have any better options!"

"A few of those things were actually before my time," Elena said. "But from your vantage point, I can see how they all look contemporaneous. OK. Here's the thing: what I learned, basically, was how to do emergency resuscitation, how to stop bleeding, how to clear airways, how to set broken bones, how to remove bullets, and how to stich wounds. That stuff probably hasn't changed too much, right?"

"The principles are likely similar," Stephen said grudgingly. "Though I'm sure our techniques are greatly refined."

She smiled at him. "Excellent. So refine me. I don't have that many bad habits to unlearn. Teach me what you can, and send me into the Tangle to study everything else, and I will make you proud. I promise. I want to contribute. I want to lighten your load."

"Hmm," Stephen said. "My loads are rather heavy. I wouldn't mind having someone who could insert catheters and run tests… All right. I'll put together a list of immersive classes for you to take in the Tangle, and begin giving you some practical instruction as well."

The door opened, and two blurs flew in: the hummingbird-sized drones that would act as Sebastien's minders.

"Starting with how to wake someone from an induced coma," Stephen said.

• • •

"I'm sorry about… everything," Sebastien said.

Elena walked down the corridor beside him, the two drones softly buzzing along, one in front of him, one behind. The bots were nearly, but not completely, silent. "I believe you," she said.

"Part of me wants to protest, to say it wasn't me who did those things, that I wasn't myself, and that's true, but… I remember doing it. I feel responsible. I feel guilty."

"Sometimes guilt is our mind's way of telling us not to do something. Listen to that part."

He stopped walking. "Elena. You haven't looked me in the eyes since I woke up."

Not so long ago, his eyes had been glowing, lit from within by the strange workings of the Axiom machinery in his brain. "That's probably true." She tried to keep her voice bright, but it was mostly brittle.

"Are you afraid of me?"

"A little bit. You shoved me in a shower and tried to explode me last time we talked."

"I hate that." His voice was low but somehow ferocious. "You shouldn't have to be afraid of me. I'm going to fix this, Elena. I'm going to prove myself. Win back your trust."

"Just… refrain from trying to murder anyone to conquer the galaxy for a few months… or years… and I'm sure everyone will relax around you. Me included."

Sebastien laughed, but it was a sad and rough sound. "I was sick before, and now I'm well. You'll see that. Everyone will. I promise."

"You've made some other promises. Maybe… less with the promises, and more with the follow-through, OK?"

"Right. Good advice. You always gave such good advice.

I just haven't been good about taking it."

Elena didn't know what to believe. In the last simulation, when Sebastien had professed remorse and said he'd changed, she'd wanted to believe him – and look how that had turned out. He was behaving himself better now, but he was also being followed by ping-pong-ball sized robots capable of stunning him into paralysis if he stepped out of line. It was going to take time for her to relax around him. It might take longer than she had to live.

"What happened to the rest of our crew?" he asked. That was a good sign, she thought – showing interest in people outside himself. Right? Unless he was faking. Or trying to get a headcount of the ship's personnel, so he could do a threat assessment, and figure out how many people he had to neutralize. Ugh. All this second-guessing was exhausting.

She filled him in on Ibn and Robin and Uzoma's plans as they walked to the galley. Callie wanted to have family dinner, since they might be going into the teeth of death and all that soon, and she'd reluctantly agreed that Sebastien should be there as well – let the crew get a look at him, and maybe start to get used to him. Everyone would be there, except Stephen, who was staying with Q until she woke.

They went into the galley, and everyone else was already in place. Callie sat at the head of the table, Ashok beside her, Lantern beside him, an empty seat for Stephen beside her. Drake and Janice were in their chair at the end, their privacy screen down, because Sebastien was a stranger, and they didn't like being exposed in front of strangers, even in the best of circumstances. Elena sat down across from Ashok, and gestured for Sebastien to join her.

Everyone stared at him. He smiled, with all his old charm. "Hello, everyone. Thank you for having me."

"You hungry?" Ashok said.

"I haven't eaten solid food in... I'm not sure how long. At least months. But Doctor Baros says I'm cleared to try."

Ashok nodded and rose, pulling two trays from a heating pod and popping off the lids. An enticing garlicky aroma wafted throughout the galley. "You've got a treat tonight." Ashok put the trays down in front of Sebastien and Elena, along with utensils; no knives, Elena noticed, but it wasn't like they were eating steaks. "We re-upped our supplies on Ganymede, and then picked up some actual grown-in-the-dirt vegetables on Owain, so I made my famous garlic tofu stir fry. Lantern is mostly just eating the garlic."

"The garlic is pretty good," Lantern said. "Could be more garlicky."

"Garlic and broccoli, on an enclosed spaceship," Callie said. "This is truly a dish preferred by someone with an artificial nose they can modify so it doesn't detect stinky things."

"It's not my fault you haven't chosen to modify your factory equipment, cap," Ashok said.

"The Machedo nose is a family heirloom," she said.

Elena closed her eyes and inhaled. "Oh, Ashok, this is wonderful."

Sebastien took a bite, swallowed, and smiled. "This is wonderful. Truly. I can't imagine a better first meal."

"Don't encourage him," Callie said. "You know there's too much garlic. Ashok is whatever the opposite of a supertaster is. He spices everything into oblivion."

"Guilty as charged, cap," Ashok said. "And utterly without remorse. I'll get an augmented tongue one of these days, don't worry. I can configure it to match your boring taste buds and cook accordingly."

"Finally, a useful upgrade." Callie gestured around with her fork. "Sebastien, you met Ashok, and I know you remember me. Our navigator and pilot, Janice and Drake, are in the chair over there. This is Lantern – remember her?"

"Ah, yes, from the servitor–" He turned the word into a cough. "The, ah, what is it? The Liars?"

"That's what humans call us," Lantern said. "We call ourselves the Free. The Axiom called us servitors. Or vermin. You called me vermin, I'm told, when you were on the Axiom station." She fluttered her pseudopods in a gesture Elena hadn't seen her make before, but she thought it meant disgust, or disdain. "You used to be human. Then you were at least partly Axiom. What are you now?"

"Forgive me, Lantern. I was not myself back then. As for now, I am all too human, and thus prone to terrible social errors. I apologize." He lowered his fork and looked at each of them in turn, even gazing for a moment at Drake and Janice's mirrored visor. "I apologize to all of you. I was sick, but I still did terrible things, and I know it will take a long time to earn your forgiveness. I intend to do my best, though."

"You might get your chance," Callie said. "Can you still understand Axiom writing?"

"I think so," Sebastien said. "There is… a lot of information in my brain, and that's part of it. I seem to know a lot more than I used to about very strange information retrieval systems – computers, but not like any computers from my time – than I should, too."

"The Axiom liked to make their mind-controlled flunkies useful, so they put some helpful things in your head. We're on our way toward something – we don't know what – but we think the Axiom built it. We'd like to figure out why they built it, and how to turn it off, or destroy it."

"I will render any assistance I can, of course. It's the least I can do."

"Good. You owe me a lot of back rent and medical expenses, so consider yourself on call." Callie turned back to her meal, and Elena exhaled in relief. That could have gone a lot worse. Callie seemed willing to give Sebastien a chance, and the others would follow her lead.

"Do you always do the cooking, Ashok?" Sebastien asked.

"Nah, we take turns, me and Callie and Stephen. Drake and Janice have weird stomachs, so they prepare their own meals, and one time Elena burned some oatmeal so she's strictly relegated to sous chef duty these days, and Lantern doesn't really do human cooking."

"Insufficient garlic," Lantern said.

Ashok nodded. "Callie always makes spaghetti. Every third night, spaghetti. She grew up eating Hawaiian and Portuguese food and I assume some really interesting fusion cuisine and still – just pasta. Let me tell you, you haven't lived until you've tried to eat spaghetti in microgravity." He considered. "Stephen makes lots of different things, at least. They're all pretty good, actually. Not as good as mine, because he's not a famous gourmet, but, you know, comfort food stuff. I guess he's gone to a lot of church potlucks."

Sebastien cleared his throat. "You know, I was considered a good cook back on Earth. I'd be happy to pitch in and join the rotation. Or even just take over the job of ship's cook entirely, and free the rest of you up for more important things."

No one answered. Callie stared at him, as if aghast at his presumptuousness, and the others just looked down at their trays.

"Er... not that cooking isn't important, too... obviously, food is important, I didn't mean to offend anyone." Sebastien looked around, clearly baffled. "It's just, I'd like to contribute to the... life of the... ship." Elena put a hand on his arm, but he kept talking. "What is it? I don't understand. What's wrong?"

Ashok paused from scooping broccoli into his mouth to say, "We're not going to let you cook for us, because you might poison everybody. The drones would *probably* stop you, because our ship's AI is running them and he's good at paying attention, but if you were quick, you could slip something into the food. It's the same reason we wouldn't let you run the ship's defenses or life support or the water filtration system." Ashok shrugged. "You were all kinds of murdery for a while there, is the thing."

Sebastien set his fork down carefully, with a small *tink*. "Ah. Yes. Of course. I'm sorry. I didn't think."

They finished eating in silence, and then Sebastien pushed back and rose. "Thank you for the meal. Elena showed me my room – I think I'd like to go and get some rest."

"I'll walk with you." Elena started to rise, but Sebastien shook his head.

"No, that's all right, stay with your friends. I'll be all right. I have my... minders." He gestured at the buzzing drones, and they preceded and followed him out the door.

Elena sighed. "Ashok. Did you have to be so direct?"

Ashok cocked his head. "What? Sorry?"

"She wishes you'd used some tact," Callie said. "Remember tact? That thing you don't have any of?"

"Oh. Right. It's not like I said he was a hundred percent definitely going to murder everyone. Just that we're legitimately afraid he might try." He cocked his head, thinking. "Oh. That's one of those very-small-distinction things, huh?"

"Pretty small," Callie said. "Basically nano. Are you all right, Elena?"

She nodded. "I am. Just... a little tense. It's hard not to be hyper-vigilant around him, after everything. I thought I'd feel better when he was awake, but I'm a lot more anxious now that he's walking around. But... he seems better, honestly. Even just now, him being hurt and going off to sulk – that's not something galaxy-subjugating conqueror Sebastien would have done."

"It was more of a human reaction than an Axiomatic one," Lantern agreed.

"As if humans are so great," Callie said.

"Better than the Axiom," Drake's voice said from their chair.

"That's not a high bar to clear," Callie said.

CHAPTER 19

"Stephen?" Q's voice was harsh and cracked, but Stephen had been waiting to hear it for so long, he was off his stool and by her side in an instant.

"Q? You're all right. Or you will be. You're recovering."

She groaned. "What happened?"

"Your ship was destroyed," Stephen said. "We rescued you, but you got a little banged up in the process." Her swelling was almost entirely gone, thanks to the combination of her body's self-regulation abilities and his anti-inflammatories, and her sunburn was healing. He'd treated the frostbite, too, and kept her hydrated intravenously. She didn't look good, but she looked so much better it might as well have been perfection.

"I feel like I've been beaten very thoroughly with hammers," she said.

"That doesn't surprise me. I've never experienced explosive decompression personally, but it seems to fit."

She groaned. "Oh, Lady, that's right. You shot my ship!"

"Only the cockpit window. The rest, we fed to a swarm of self-replicating machines."

"Of course. Can't have them going hungry. Can I sit up?"

"I hope so. Let's see."

He helped her swing her legs around and straighten her upper body, which she managed with much wincing and gritting of teeth and zero complaints. When she said she wanted to stand, he helped with that too. She groaned, and after swaying on her feet for a moment, sat down on a chair fixed to the floor. He tried to avoid fussing over her, but it was hard. They'd done very intense sacraments together, gazed deep into one another's essences, poured out truths and secrets and fears and hopes and dreams, felt themselves merge and separate and merge again – and they'd strengthened that relationship during the long journey from Owain to the asteroid belt, murmuring on a private channel through the long days and uneventful nights, opening up about their regrets from the past and their hopes for the future.

The only thing Stephen hadn't shared with her was the truth about the Axiom, and it had taken an effort of will to hold that back. He still felt intermingled with her. Her pain ached as much as if it were his own.

He hadn't loved anyone since the moment his wife died on an operating table while he watched through a window as the second-best surgeon in the city botched the procedure he would have performed flawlessly, if he'd been allowed to operate on his own wife. He'd fled that life, repudiated his faith in those systems, and gone to a place where those kind of rules and regulations didn't apply. He looked back as seldom as possible.

Now, after meeting Q, he was looking, for the first time in a long time, toward the future with something other than resignation or dread.

"Are we going back to Owain?" she said. "We have to warn them about those *things*."

Stephen hesitated. He'd talked this over with Callie, and she'd ultimately said, "Tell her as much as you feel like she needs to know." He should probably keep the details to a minimum, but it would be hard, given the strength of the connection between them. "We're not going to Owain. We're tracking the source of the swarm. Callie wants to find out where it originated, so we can try to deactivate the machines."

"We have to warn them," Q said again. "We have to tell them not to send anyone else out there! What that swarm did to my ship, what it must have done to the *other* ships, the people inside them…" She hugged herself.

He put a tentative hand on her shoulder, and she leaned into his touch. "We can send word. I doubt anyone is going to visit that part of the asteroid belt – certainly no one from Almajara will, not until we report back, or fail to report back in the allotted time. Everyone on Owain has heard about the disappearances, and I'm sure they're being cautious. But, yes, to be safe, we can send a message. We just have to figure out what to tell them."

Q's forehead bunched up in confusion. "We tell them there's a cloud of mysterious self-replicating machines feeding on the asteroid belt and destroying any ships they come in contact with!" She frowned. "Except for this ship. Wait. *Why* didn't they destroy this ship?"

"Ah. We have a theory, but I'll have to give you a bit of background in order for it to make sense."

"Well?" she said.

"We think the swarm is alien in origin."

"I should think so," Q said. "The only humans in this system are on Owain. We have the records of passages through the bridge, going back for over two centuries, and all the people who passed through are accounted for – nobody set up a secret tech lab in the asteroid belt. It must be some previously unknown group of Liars. You're going to find them and, what, ask them to stop?"

Stephen shook his head. "If it were Liars, this would be easier, because Liars will listen to reason, and there are plenty of uninhabited systems we could encourage them to experiment on instead. We think it's... other aliens."

Q thought for a moment and then said, "Could I have some water?"

Stephen brought her a bulb, and she sucked on it pensively, deep in thought. She got a worry line between her eyes when she did that, and he wanted nothing more than to smooth it away with kisses and reassure her that things would be all right... though the truth was hardly all that reassuring. Finally she said, "Are you speculating about the existence of alien life, other than the Liars, in this system? Or do you *know* about the existence of such aliens?"

The moment of truth. Stephen decided Q needed to know a lot of things. "The latter. We've encountered these other aliens – or, more accurately, their artifacts – before. We're pretty sure the swarm is one of their projects."

Q ran a hand through her hair and gave a scattered, manic-sounding laugh. "I'm going to need some details here, Stephen."

He nodded. "Last year, we discovered a wrecked goldilocks ship, light years away from where it should have been. We found a strange device hooked into its propulsion and navigation system, and only one crew member still in cryo-sleep, beside a bunch of empty pods…" He told her the whole story, of finding Elena and rescuing her crew, and discovering the terrible threat of the Axiom, and the devastation and upheaval that had followed afterward.

When he was done, he needed some water himself. Q sat with the story for a long time. Then she said, "So, OK, but you didn't answer me: *why* didn't the swarm eat your ship then?"

"Ah, yes. The original question. We have the bridge generator on board still. Lantern says the swarm can detect Axiom technology, and leaves it alone. The swarm sees us as allies, essentially, or, at least, not a potential source of fuel."

Q leaned back in the chair. "That's an incredible story. How could an ancient alien race, with a dead empire that spanned the galaxy, stay hidden?"

"To quote one of Callie's favorite sayings – space is big. It's easy to lose things out in the black. That said, I'm sure some humans *have* stumbled on evidence of the Axiom, the same way we did. We're just the only ones who've survived. The truth-tellers have bases in every system, keeping an eye on things, preserving the secret of the Axiom, and they're armed with technology beyond anything humans have. They're ruthless. When they realized we had a bridge generator, and could go places humans aren't supposed to go, they blew up Meditreme Station in an attempt to contain the problem. The truth-tellers are the ones who introduced humans to the bridges, because it was better for them to guide us toward relatively safe systems than to let us explore on our own. They convinced everyone the big bridges can only access twenty-nine different systems, when, in reality, there are probably hundreds of accessible destinations – the others are just too close to Axiom projects. The truth-tellers have shepherded us and kept us hemmed in. The only reason they haven't exterminated humankind is because there are too many of us, and there are still goldilocks ships sailing to their destinations. We're too hard to get rid of. The only reason we aren't at war with the truth-tellers is because they opted for a strategy of containment instead of murder."

"*Safe* systems? If Taliesen is safe, why are there nanobots heading toward my home?"

"The Axiom facility is a long way outside the system, floating in empty space, according to Lantern," Stephen said. "It's watched over by a cell of truth-tellers. Space being big, it probably never would have been discovered by humans… but something changed. The truth-tellers went silent, and the swarm began eating ships."

"Lantern. A *Liar*." She almost spat the word. "She was part of this conspiracy? Why did she decide to betray her people?"

Stephen shook his head. "It's not like that. Only a few of the truth-tellers know their true purpose. Lantern believed her elders when they said they were trying to protect the galaxy from the Axiom. When she realized her elders were loyal to the Axiom, and protecting them, Lantern joined our cause. Most of the Liars know their people were once servants of a vast, oppressive alien hegemony, though the details were largely erased. They're all trying to forget. The Liars make up new stories about their origins, their existence, their purpose in the universe, trying to construct new stories for themselves. They've lost their real history – it was *stolen* from them when the Axiom erased every record, even every memory, of their home world after destroying it, to punish the Liars for their attempted rebellion. The Liars are creating new histories for themselves as they go along. They're attempting to create a reality they can bear to inhabit. That's why they lie, Lantern says. Because the truth is too hard for most of them to bear."

"If all this is true…" She sighed. "Of course it's true. You asked if I trusted you, before you blew a hole in my cockpit and sucked me out into space and saved my life, and I said yes, because I do. If I trusted you with my life, I trust you to tell me the truth about this. So… if we send a warning back to Owain, they might investigate, and stumble onto the Axiom without knowing what they're getting into. If we go public about the Axiom, the truth-tellers might try to murder everyone – and you say they have weapons that can actually do it."

"They've erased planets in the past," Stephen said. "Even if we fought them and won, the casualties would be incomprehensible. It wouldn't help, anyway. If word got out about the Axiom, people would *go looking*. Humans being what they are. Personal wormhole generators? Mind-control technology? Those are just a couple of things we know for sure the Axiom have. Humans would lust for such power. They'd go pillaging the tombs of the Axiom like the grave-robbers of old, looking for treasure... except these ancients aren't really dead. They're just sleeping. Their pyramids really *are* cursed. Our strategy, insofar as we have one, is to creep up on the Axiom facilities one by one, learn about them, and quietly disable them or disrupt their plans, without alerting the aliens themselves to our presence. Lantern has infiltrated the cult of truth-tellers, and though their organization is highly compartmentalized, she hopes to assemble a comprehensive list of known Axiom facilities, and we'll pick them off strategically. The Axiom are dangerous... but they don't know humans exist, and they still slumber. We think we have a chance to kill them in their sleep."

"But if you die?" Q said. "Not just you, but the whole crew? If some alien security system wakes up and smears you to goo? If the next swarm of nanobots you encounter *doesn't* have a lucky flaw in its friend-or-foe detection system?"

"We *do* have a failsafe in place – if we go missing for too long, crucial information will be transmitted to some people in the church, and to Callie's ex-husband, and a few others we can trust. Knowledge of the threat won't die if we do."

She nodded. "Good. Well. Now that I know this, what, am I sworn to secrecy? If I talk, I die?"

That hurt. "I'm not threatening you. I hope we can make you understand the importance of secrecy. We're not the ones you need to worry about if you start talking about the Axiom publicly. The truth-teller cell in this system went quiet, possibly fallen victim to the same swarm that ate the surveyors, but their central authority will be sending a new branch of the cult here soon. If you so much as say the word 'Axiom' over an open channel, they'll investigate you, and if they deem you a threat, they'll kill you. They'll kill everyone you might have talked to. They'll kill Owain itself, if they think it's necessary, and as an organization, the truth-tellers err on the side of overkill."

Q slumped. "That's a lot of weight to carry." She reached out and took his hand. "And you've been carrying it yourself, all this time, without a congregation? I'm so sorry, Stephen."

He stared at her. "You're wonderful. I tell you these worldview-destroying secrets... and you're concerned about my wellbeing."

She laughed. "I don't know how wonderful I am. Maybe I just can't face the bigger implications. But as for caring about you... we're connected now."

"The power of drugs," he said lightly.

"That helped, but I've shared that sacrament with others, without feeling this level of attachment. The shapes of our souls aren't identical, but they're complementary. I want to fix broken systems and make them work. You fix broken bodies and make *them* work. We're both pulling in the same direction. I like the idea of us pulling together."

Stephen kept the elation off his face. "I like that, too."

"So. We're following a breadcrumb trail to the witch's house?"

"Essentially."

"How long until we–"

Callie's voice cut in over the PA. "Turn on your screens, everyone, and take a look at this."

Stephen obeyed, putting the external camera view up

on the largest screen in the infirmary. Q leaned forward
to look, and winced in pain from her injuries. Stephen
winced in sympathy.

Callie said, "The image is a little grainy, because
we're zooming in from a long way off and doing some
enhancement, but… that's where the swarm is going."

"Is that what the other Axiom space station looked
like?" Q said. "It's incredible."

"No," Stephen said. "The station we found was like
a jumble of branching corridors, cylinders crossing at
odd angles, more like a tangle of tree roots or a nest of
snakes than anything humans would make. Immense
and organic and strange. This… this is *beautiful*."

The structure on the screens – machine? space station?
– looked like an immense silver-white gyroscope, with
half a dozen unconnected rings all spinning lazily in
different directions around a spherical floating hub that
looked like an oversized ball bearing. The outermost ring
of the structure was still being constructed, and it grew
visibly larger as they watched, the ends emerging from a
fuzzy blur of matter in motion.

"How big is that thing?" Stephen asked.

"Big," Callie said. "We're still pretty far away. The
central sphere is almost the size of Earth's moon, and
every successive ring is larger than the last. It's still
growing, as you can see. That's what the swarm is doing.
It's converting matter in the asteroid belt, bringing it
back here, and rebuilding that matter into… more of
that structure. I have no idea why. Theories?"

"It could be a habitat," Ashok said. "Though the way it's
spinning in all those different directions is weird. They don't
need spin gravity anyway. They have artificial gravity."

"Artificial *gravity*?" Q blurted.

"Ah. Did I not mention that?" Stephen said.

There was silence on the comms for a moment, then Callie said, "So. Q. You're awake. And Stephen filled you in."

"He did, captain."

Another moment of silence. "All right, then. It is what it is. I hope he told you the importance of maintaining operational security here."

"He did, captain," she said again.

"Let me tell you again anyway. Loose lips explosively decompress ships. If you go around telling people what you know, that endangers me, it endangers my crew, and it endangers Lantern. Believe me, Doctor Fortier, you don't want to put my people in danger, because then you'll be in even worse danger – from me."

"I understand, captain. Don't worry. Stephen made the stakes clear to me. I want to protect Owain. We're on the same side." She paused. "And it's just Mx Fortier, if you want to be formal. No doctor."

"Really? I just assumed. I'm used to being the only human on this boat who doesn't have an advanced degree in something. All right. Ashok thinks it's a habitat, and it's certainly big enough to house a sizable population, but it's not like the Axiom are big into having babies these days, so what do they need more room for? Why are they building additions?"

"The structure could be some sort of machine," Lantern said. "I have heard rumors about some of the mega-scale Axiom projects, operations with matter and energy requirements that would require pillaging entire systems over the course of hundreds of millennia."

"What would a machine that takes a million years to build even *do*?" Callie said.

"Provide the ultimate answer to life, the universe, and everything?" Elena said.

"What do you mean?" Callie said.

"Never mind," Elena said. "Literary reference. Nobody reads the classics any more, I guess."

"It could be a machine meant to punch a hole into a neighboring universe," Lantern said. "Supposedly there was an Axiom faction that wanted to do that, as a way to escape their inevitable extinction due to heat death here. I'd heard that project was shut down by a rival faction of the Axiom, because attacking the structure of reality that way would threaten both universes, and almost certainly cause a chain reaction that would destroy this one. But there are just scattered references to the conflict in the records I've been able to access."

"Oh good," Callie muttered. "Like worrying about the fate of *one* universe wasn't enough for me? So, it could be a habitat, or it could be a trans-dimensional drilling machine. Other ideas?"

"Maybe it's just an art project," Q said. "The Axiom had the power of gods, it sounds like. Maybe they just wanted to create something beautiful. It could be a kinetic sculpture, or some kind of monument."

"That is… unlikely, Mx Fortier," Lantern said. "We have a few examples of surviving Axiomatic art, in my sect's museum of subjugation. They mostly depict the enemies of the artists in the midst of unimaginable torments."

"Ah," Q said. "Carry on."

Callie said, "How about you, Sebastien? You had

Axiom tech deep in your head for a while. Does this spark any associations?"

"I have no idea what it is, captain," Sebastien said. "But it scares me."

"Who's Sebastien?" Q whispered.

"Long story," Stephen whispered back. "Tell you later." He briefly muted his mic. "Just… don't go anywhere alone with him."

Q gave him a look that was more quizzical than alarmed.

"It's real interesting to try to figure out what that thing is," Janice said. "I'm real interested. You're all really interesting, with all your really interesting theories. But I know a way to remove all doubt. Let's fire every weapon we have at that pretty spinny thing, and blow it up, and then we'll know for sure what we're looking at: an expanding ring of irradiated debris."

"Janice always cuts right to the heart of things," Drake said. "That's why I love having her as a roommate."

Callie said, "Total annihilation is tempting, but I want to know what I'm annihilating. We're going to have to get closer, and figure out what we're dealing with. My hope is, the swarm will keep thinking we're authorized personnel. We need a better scan of that central sphere – maybe it's a control center, or a barracks, or a cockpit, or something. Maybe there's an on-off switch in there for the swarm. I want to shut the whole project down."

"Exploding it would be a good start," Janice said.

"I'm not sure blowing it up will be enough to stop the swarm, and if it *is* some kind of reality-cutting drill, exploding it could cause more damage than we intend. What if the swarm just starts rebuilding what we blew up? What if an attack doesn't deactivate the swarm, but does disrupt the swarm's protocols, so instead of doing a building project, it just grows exponentially and eats Owain and then everything else in the galaxy?"

"Ugh, fine, those would be bad outcomes," Janice said. "I still think total destruction is a good fallback plan."

"It's my usual one," Callie said.

"Hey, Janice," Ashok said. "Are there some other masses, between us and the system?"

Dark shapes on the screen lit up green. "They're asteroids," she said. "Pretty big ones – all roughly twice the size of the *White Raven*. Huh. All nearly exactly the same size and shape, actually, within a couple percentage points of variance. That's odd."

"It's probably not an ornamental rock garden," Q said.

"There are a dozen of the asteroids arrayed around the station, if it is a station." More green dots lit up on the screen, forming a spherical array of points with the silvery gyroscope in the center.

"Why hasn't the swarm converted *those* into more of itself?" Ashok said. "They're perfectly good multi-ton asteroids, sitting right here. We thought the swarm was chewing up the asteroid belt in passing, because it was valuable material conveniently in its path, but these space rocks are even more convenient."

"I… don't think those are asteroids," Shall said. "I'm probing them with our sensors, and they're nowhere near as dense as they should be. They're not hollow, in the sense of being entirely empty inside, but there are large voids within them."

"Are they mines, or something?" Callie said. "Full of tunnels?"

"That makes sense, but there's no sign of any openings on their surfaces, though," Shall said. "No doors, no hatches – it's all rock and metal."

The camera zoomed out and refocused on the nearest asteroid, a looming potato-shaped lump in their viewscreens. They all watched as it grew incrementally larger.

"It just looks like a *rock*," Callie said. "Are we scared of rocks now?"

Then the asteroid on the viewscreen cracked open like an egg broken neatly in two.

CHAPTER 20

"What the hell is this now?" Callie zoomed the camera in closer, on the dark shape revealed when the asteroid broke open. "Give me some data, Shall!"

"It's some kind of machine, hidden inside the asteroid. I'm getting energy signatures. Whatever it is, it's waking up."

"Like a nut in a shell," Callie said. "Or one of those toy eggs with a surprise inside. Janice, are our countermeasures operational?"

"Of course," she said. "Stealth deflection mode is engaged, and all the active systems are primed and ready." The *White Raven* was equipped with a special mode that made it appear to be kilometers away from its actual position, capable of fooling even advanced sensor systems, and thanks to a series of projectors all over the hull, the trick even worked against direct visual observers. Of course, their displacement system had been acquired from Liars, and was quite possibly based on Axiom technology, so Callie couldn't be certain it would work against... whatever this was.

The broken halves of the asteroid tumbled away in

opposite directions, and the thing inside... unfolded itself. Janice adjusted the contrast and false color in the viewscreen image so they could get a better look, and what they saw was not reassuring.

The machine inside the asteroid was shaped like a teardrop, and it unfurled a score of spindly, many-angled manipulator arms, some of them tipped with hooks, others with barbs, others with spikes. The manipulator arms wriggled, and the machine spun slowly around. Spikes and pointed fins popped up along its (for want of a better word) back, and the new eruptions began to glow a deep and worrisome shade of red. Slits of yellow light opened along the machine's sides, each slit a downward curve, like frowns full of fire.

"It looks like a radioactive mutant black widow spider with too many legs," Ashok said.

"Oh no. Oh no, oh no." Lantern's voice was low. "I've seen a machine like this before, in the museum of subjugation. Half of one, anyway, ruined in some battle, the wreckage embedded in a transparent cube of unbreakable smart matter and put on display – but the machine was *still operational*, still glowing from within, still trying to escape. There is no right term for it in your language. It's a sort of guard. But also, a deterrent? Its very presence is meant to frighten away any who might stray too close. You might call it... a terror drone. Does that sound right?"

"Unfortunately," Callie said. "If we kill it, does it call for reinforcements?"

"I would imagine," Lantern says. "Also... I do not wish to cause offense... you cannot kill it. The capabilities of your ship are very impressive by human standards, but the *White Raven* is a toy by the standards of the Axiom."

"I'm aware of my limitations," Callie said. "Even if I don't like to acknowledge them. The drone isn't doing anything yet. Maybe it just wants to say hello, or escort us to the station, if it's a station – maybe it thinks we're on the same team, like the swarm did."

"Terror drones are much smarter than the swarm, I suspect," Lantern said. "The Axiom fought amongst themselves, all the time. Teaching the swarm to avoid all Axiom vessels is good sense – you wouldn't want to accidentally destroy the ship of an ally, or escalate a conflict with a rival faction by accident. The swarm has to be more conservative, because it goes so far afield. The terror drones can be more discerning, and if a ship they don't recognize attempts to breach their perimeter–"

Lantern abruptly cut off as the terror drone moved toward them – or, rather, toward the place where they *appeared* to be – with incredible speed, its manipulator arms blurring into invisibility, its spiderlike ugliness looming in size and filling half the viewscreen. A white-bright burst of light flared off on their port side – dead centered on the illusory version of the ship, Callie was sure. The *White Raven* rocked, just from the backwash of whatever attack the drone had made, and Callie's body bounced hard against the straps holding her into her seat. Janice and Drake's chair stayed upright thanks to its fancy gyroscopic balancing system, but alarms blipped plaintively throughout the cockpit.

The false ship didn't take any damage at all, of course, and the terror drone stopped abruptly – more abruptly than normal physics could account for. Some kind of inertial dampening technology? The terror drone extended a set of six manipulator arms, and began to slowly weave them around in a complicated pattern. "What is it doing, casting a spell?" Callie said. "Making a cat's cradle with no string?"

"I don't know, but it's building up a *lot* of energy," Shall said. "I think it's going to unleash something bigger than… whatever it unleashed before."

"Shit. We need to rethink our approach. Let's pull–"

Everything exploded into whiteness, and then into black.

Elena woke up in the sick bay, weightless, head pounding, her body held down by straps. She blinked around in the dim red emergency lighting. "What happened?"

Sebastien appeared above her, floating. No thrust gravity here, or artificial gravity, either. "You're OK. Oh, thank God, I was so worried."

She groaned. "Where's Stephen?" If anyone should be looming over her in the infirmary, it was him, and not Sebastien.

"He's still unconscious. Everyone is. I was in bed, so when everything went spinning, I was more padded than everyone else, I assume. I think I blacked out for a bit, even so. I don't know what hit us, but it hit us hard."

Something was different about him. His head was shaved, so it wasn't like he could have changed his hair – wait. "Where are your drones?"

He shook his head. "They went dark and floated away. The ship's AI – Shall? – doesn't respond at all. I think he's offline. I dragged you in here, and Callie, and Lantern. Stephen was already here. Ashok was too heavy to move – there's a lot of metal in him. I couldn't figure out how to open Drake and Janice's chair. I hope they're all right."

Someone groaned, and Elena recognized the voice: Callie. She struggled with the straps, freed herself (with Sebastien's help), and pulled herself through the dimness to the next bed. "Wha' hit us?" Callie said. "Elena?"

"The terror drone did... something," Elena said. "Knocked us all out, and disabled the ship somehow. We're drifting, I guess? I don't know why the drone didn't just tear us apart once we were disabled."

Callie fumbled with the straps, and Elena helped her. "How is everyone?"

"Unconscious, mostly."

"You brought me in here?" Callie pressed a hand to her forehead. Elena had almost never seen her look so vulnerable.

"No. Sebastien did. He helped us. All of us."

Callie turned her head. Sebastien gave her a funny little bow. "Like I said. I want to help."

"Even without your tiny flying babysitters." Callie looked at Sebastien for a thoughtful moment. "OK. Elena, you're our only conscious medic, so see how everyone is doing. I'm going to see if I can get Shall and the rest of the ship back online." She pushed herself awkwardly across the room, floated through the open door, and on down a corridor.

Elena checked on Sebastien and Q, who both seemed unharmed – no new bumps, blood, or bruises, anyway, though Q wouldn't feel good when she woke up, still being tender from her earlier snuggle with death. Elena opened one of the supply cabinets and found capsules of ammonia inhalants, for rousing people from faints or snapping them back to wakefulness after injuries that left them dazed. In gravity, you could often wake someone up by putting them on their back and elevating their legs to increase their venous return and pump oxygenated blood to the brain, but that wasn't very effective in a weightless environment. She broke one open under Stephen's nose. He jolted awake at the first inhalation and batted Elena's hand away.

"Oof. We're alive? We're alive. All right. To work." He held out his hands for the vial of salts and went to Q. "Elena, go check on Ashok and Drake and Janice. I'll try to figure out how to wake up Lantern."

"I think I can help with that." Elena had studied Liar physiology a bit, and though it was hard to know anything for sure given the species' penchant for self-experimentation and modification, there was usually a nerve cluster at the base of the two major pseudopods, and if she gave that spot a hard poke with two stiffened fingers...

Lantern flailed and spun, shoving herself away from Elena and floating halfway to the ceiling. "Ah! What!"

"Sorry, sorry, you were unconscious!" Elena said.

Lantern oriented herself in the air and fluttered distress. "Oh, no, the drone, the terror drone, they were made for stopping escapes, for quelling riots, for crowd control, for disabling... Ashok!" She twirled and shoved and went hurtling down the corridor.

"I think Lantern can be counted on to check on Ashok." Stephen looked up from helping Q and made a shooing motion. "Drake and Janice might need you. Go!"

Elena went, and Sebastien trailed after.

• • •

"Come on, come on," Callie muttered. She was in the depths of the ship, below the engine room, in the usually-sealed cylindrical space where Shall's brain lived. The banks of processors around her should have been warm and humming and glowing with soft white light, but they were cold and quiet and dark. There was a backup of him on Glauketas, and an instance of his consciousness running on Lantern's base too, helping to rear the Liar children they'd rescued, so Shall wasn't *dead* – he'd just lose his memories of this trip, and everything that had happened since they left their home asteroid. But if she couldn't wake up this version of him, they might not survive to fill him in on everything he'd lost. Repairs that would take hours with Shall's drones scuttling around on the hull and deep in the guts of the ship would take days or weeks if Ashok, Lantern, and Callie had to do it all by hand, and she did not relish the idea of being wherever they were, disabled and helpless, for that long.

After she finished checking all the physical connections, she pressed down hard on a bright-red stud in the center of one wall and held it, counting slowly to thirty under her breath, then released it.

Nothing happened. "Come on," she said. "Resurrection Day, goddamn it."

Another five seconds went by, and then a light flickered, and then another, and then a whole array of lights, all around the cylinder, and she heard the ship wake up too, with a deep and reassuring *thrum* – the first thing Shall did when he came back online was set things right again. He was the best ship a captain could hope for.

"Callie," Shall said. "I was dead for a little while there. I hate being dead."

"I know the feeling. You're OK?"

"Self-diagnostics check out. Something knocked everything offline. Some kind of electromagnetic pulse attack, I assume?"

"No, I... The blast didn't just knock the ship offline – it knocked our *brains* offline. All of us passed out for a while. I don't even know if everyone is all right."

"Checking life signs... they're OK. Everyone's awake accept Drake and Janice. Let me restart their chair, so it can administer medication, maybe stimulants if the expert system thinks it's warranted... There it goes. Oh, dear. Janice is swearing a lot. Not an EMP, then. Some kind of Axiom weapon, that disrupts electrical systems *and* biological ones. That's not terrifying at all."

"Where are we?" Callie said.

"Drifting, a few dozen kilometers away from the Axiom station. The blast the terror drone hit us with must have had some concussive element as well as a disabling one – or else it followed up the disruptor with a more conventional blast."

Callie nodded. "That makes sense: disable any security systems, then *kablammo*."

"The attack caught us glancingly, because the drone was aiming at the spot where it *thought* we were. We only got hit with a fraction of the weapon's full intensity. That was enough to send us spinning, though. When we went dark, our displacement projectors stopped working, and the illusion vanished – maybe the terror drone thinks we're dead. At any rate, it must not have noticed the real version of us twirling through the dark, or else it's satisfied we're no longer a threat, because I don't see it on my scans. Its asteroid is there, though... and it's whole again. Looks like an innocent stone potato. I can't even detect the seams, and I know where they are. That's bizarre. But the spider has crawled back inside its egg." He paused. "I don't think the direct approach is going to work for us here, Callie."

"But that's my favorite kind of approach," Callie said. "Running straight ahead, with a dagger in my teeth."

"Alas. Life is little more than a pageant of disappointments."

"I think that line was in our wedding vows."

"The good news is, we aren't dead." Callie looked over the assembled crew in the galley, their de facto meeting room since forever and always. It was strange to see Q there, but she seemed a decent enough sort – she hadn't freaked out or made impossible demands when she found out about the Axiom. It was even stranger to see Sebastien there, but at least his drones were buzzing around his head again – that made her feel better. He hadn't objected to the reinstatement of his minders, or even sulked about it, which was either reassuring or worrying, depending on how you looked at it. "The bad news is, the swarm isn't dead, either. Or the terror drones. Or the really big, terrifyingly big, giant-sized big Axiom facility. Walking up to the front door didn't work, and there's no back door. So. Suggestions?"

"Evacuate Owain, seal off the bridge to this system, and leave forever?" Q said. "I don't want to do that – I worked hard to make that planet what it is – but if the alternative is horrible death or being turned into raw material to build a giant robotic alien eggbeater, a retreat is worth considering."

"We'll call that Plan C," Callie said. "It would be tricky to implement without letting everyone know about the Axiom. Even if we could convince the artists and utopians to leave a planet they have finally terraformed to their liking – ha, that would be easy, I bet – the Corp isn't going to want to walk away from an investment of this size."

"You have connections at Almajara, though," Q said. "Maybe you could come up with a story that would convince them?"

She snorted. "Yeah, no. Uncle Reynauld isn't going to take the advice of his grand-nephew's ex-wife, or even his grand-nephew. He's got that thing where he thinks he always knows best, even when he doesn't know shit. Still, it might come down to saving as many people as we *can*. Let's try to come up with a Plan B first, though."

"The truth-tellers," Lantern said. "Their station is only a few days' journey from here – beyond the Axiom facility, and so not really in the path of the swarm. I thought the cell must have been destroyed, but perhaps they've gone silent for some other reason? They may have answers. My sect has been watching this Axiom facility, and secretly protecting it, for thousands of years. I'm sure there's data there."

"I prefer blowing up enemies to paying them friendly visits, but I appreciate the necessity of doing the latter before I can do the former," Callie said. "Does anyone else have a better candidate for Plan B?"

No one did. "Are you going to use your, ah… personal bridge generator for this trip?" Q said.

"Stephen told you about that, huh?" Callie shook her head. "Despite my natural inclination to move fast, we should take a minute. We still have to run a lot of diagnostics to make sure the ship is in good working order, and frankly, after that encounter... we could all use a little down time before we have to risk someone *else* shooting at us." She turned to Lantern. "Go talk to Janice about the coordinates, and she can chart us a course that takes us the long way around the Axiom base. The rest of you, get some rest, center yourselves, take painkillers if you got banged up, whatever. We'll reconvene when we have something to reconvene about." She felt pretty banged up herself, and went to take her own advice.

When Elena came in, Callie was in bed, staring at the ceiling. "Want some company?"

"Only if it's your company." Callie scooted over, and Elena folded in next to her.

After a long quiet moment, Elena said, "I'm glad we're alive. I would have missed you, in the endless abyss of nothingness that lies beyond life."

"Likewise." Callie wrapped her arms around her. "We had what, in technical terms, is called a failure today. But my ship still works, and nobody died, so I'm declaring it a draw."

"How about Sebastien, though?" Elena said. "That's a win. He was the first one to wake up. No drones watching him. Total freedom. And what did he do? He helped."

"Mmm," Callie said.

"What, mmm?"

"Nothing mmm. Just mmm." Callie shifted around, drawing Elena closer, nuzzling into her hair. "I am acknowledging that I heard and processed the words you spoke."

"Hold on, I need to adjust my mental state," Elena said. "Let me look at the world through your eyes for a second. I just need to be sixty percent more suspicious, twenty percent more cynical–"

"Forty."

"Forty percent more cynical... Ah. So maybe Sebastien *didn't* prove himself today. Maybe he took an opportunity to trick us into trusting him. Am I on the right track?"

"No comment."

Elena took her own turn staring at the ceiling as she worked it out. "The ship only had emergency power anyway. No engines, no weapons, and no wormhole generator. Sebastien had his freedom, but he couldn't *go* anywhere. There was no incentive for him to throw our bodies out an airlock, at least not right at that moment, because he needed us to fix the ship. So instead, he played helpful junior crewman and did good deeds, so we'd start to trust him and let our guard down, all the better for him to murder us *later*."

"That interpretation fits the available evidence just as well as your theory, you must admit."

"Such a dark worldview for one so young," Elena said.

"Yours is bright enough for both of us."

CHAPTER 21

"We should be close enough to communicate with the truth-teller base now." Lantern was in the cockpit, perched in one of the chairs behind Callie. "Assuming it wasn't devoured by the swarm. Janice, can you broadcast a message from me? I need to establish my credentials before we can talk directly."

"Queue it up and I'll send it."

Lantern's pseudopods tapped at the terminal attached to the chair for a moment. "Transmit that message, on the frequency I noted."

"Whatever you say."

"What did you tell them?" Callie asked.

"It's just… what would you call it, a code word? A secret handshake? Something to let them know I am of the truth-tellers. They will ask me why I'm on a human ship, and I'll…"

"Tell a lie?" Callie said. "I hope you're going to tell a lie."

"Yes. I must. I hate to knowingly tell a falsehood, it goes against all my training, but as the elders deceived me, so I must deceive them. It's true that I was sent by the central authority to determine why they lost contact. I will tell them that, and that I acquired a human ship so I could travel to Taliesen without attracting attention, as the Free are a minority there. I will be indignant, and demand answers on behalf of the central authority. As the head of our cell in the Jovian system, I have high-level authorizations, so they might even answer me, if there's anyone alive to do the answering."

"The *Jovian* system?" Callie said. "Why isn't it called the Earth system? When the Liars found us, humans only lived on Earth and the moon and a few space stations."

"Jupiter is where the bridge is," Lantern said. "From the point of view of secret servants to the Axiom, that's the important part. I'm sorry. I didn't devise the nomenclature."

"Jovian system," Callie muttered. "If they heard *that* in the Imperative, they'd be even more smug and insufferable."

"We got a reply," Janice said. "Audio only." She played a few seconds of whistling and screeching.

"That's… extremely odd," Lantern said.

"What?" Callie said.

"You must understand, sound is only one of the ways my people communicate among ourselves – movements of our limbs and alterations in color and even pheromone discharges are crucial for adding nuance and detail. Hearing just the audio is the human equivalent to a sentence spoken in monotone, with no adjectives or other modifiers. But the closest translation is probably something like… 'Praise the masters, and welcome.'"

"Do they mean that like, 'Thank God, you've come to rescue us,' or is 'praise the masters' a religious greeting like 'peace be unto you,' or what?" Callie said.

Lantern fluttered her pseudopods in dismay. "'Praise the masters' *is* a ritual greeting, but only among the elders of the truth-tellers, the ones who know our sect's real purpose. But Callie... no elder would send that greeting over an open channel. Or *any* channel. It's something that's only said face-to-face, and there's a thrill of secret danger even then, because if anyone overheard it, there would be questions. I'm very confused. I'll request permission to dock and board the base."

Another message sent, another wait, and then another audio response that Lantern translated in bewilderment. "It says we should enter the... I don't know if there's a word in your language for this. The term refers to a part of sleep, just before you begin to dream? 'Enter the place before the dream begins.' That phrase, 'the place before the dream begins' is sometimes meant literally, to describe the time right after you've fallen asleep, but it's also an idiom among my people, referring to the... time of mental and practical preparation that comes just before you commence a great work of some kind. The moments before you begin the work of making something imagined or talked about into reality. But without some visual cues, I have no idea if the transmission means it literally or metaphorically – and no idea what it would mean in either case."

"I heard 'welcome' and 'enter' so that's good enough for me," Callie said. "Let's get ready. Are we taking weapons? We could fire up Shall's military combat drone."

"That might make the wrong impression," Lantern said. "I come cloaked in the raiment of our sect's authority, and a show of overt force would be unnecessary… unless things have gone badly wrong here. I should go alone – or, at least, apparently alone."

"Got it. I'll come along in stealth. Death from the shadows."

"Perhaps just inconvenience from the shadows, at first?" Lantern said. "There may be junior members of the cell on board who are blameless."

Callie scowled. "Even your junior members are happy enough to kill any innocent person who stumbles across Axiom technology."

"Because they think it is necessary to protect all life, Callie." Lantern was patient but implacable. "The sincere truth-tellers see Axiom technology as an infection, and if that infection is allowed to spread, it could kill every thinking creature in the galaxy. They take whatever steps they believe necessary to contain that infection, and regret when innocents are harmed."

"I'm sure their regret is a great comfort to the dead thousands on Meditreme Station. But all right. I'll stick to non-lethal solutions, unless there's no other choice. How long until we reach the base?"

"We'll be in visual range by the time you get dressed," Janice said.

"That is so not your color," Elena said, as Callie dressed in the ruinously expensive prototype environment suit she'd acquired from a canceled Trans-Neptunian Authority research project.

Callie looked down at the eye-wateringly bright electric blue of the suit. "What do you mean? I'm a winter, right?"

"Just because your heart is cold doesn't make you a winter. You'd look good in, oh, burnt orange."

"I'd look like a human-pumpkin hybrid, you monster."

"My delicious pumpkin monster." Elena squeezed her hand through Callie's glove. "Be careful over there, and stay in touch."

"The point is for me to be stealthy, so I doubt I'll be doing a lot of talking, but I'll be all right. The truth-tellers won't be on the lookout for an invisible human."

Elena kissed Callie before she put on her helmet, "in case you die over there."

"Thanks for that." The suit fit Callie well – it was custom made to fit her measurements as of a couple of years ago, and remained close enough – but it was still a full-body environment suit, a little bulky and clunky by definition, so she wouldn't be doing yoga poses or cartwheels. She switched on the active camouflage, and the blue shimmered as the micro-projectors all over the suit and helmet came online to mimic her background. "Can you see me?" Callie said.

"A little, but only because I know to look for the shimmer, like you taught me."

Callie thought of the possibly hallucinatory shimmers she'd glimpsed on the *Golden Spider* and the *White Raven* in recent weeks, but pushed the idea out of her mind. She had to focus on the mission now. "Liar eyesight isn't as acute as human, unless they make an effort to upgrade, but they're better at sensing vibrations." She turned on the sound-dampeners, and stomped her boots and clapped her gloved hands together a foot from Elena's face. She didn't respond. Callie had never been clear on how the sound thing worked – something about creating sound waves that countered the ones she created, so the net result was no waves at all? During testing she'd been more interested in sneaking up on people and kicking them in the back of the knees than listening to the technical explanations.

She switched the dampeners and camouflage off, shimmering back into view. "Seems operational. Let's go steal some secrets. And maybe the front door code into the Axiom facility, if we're lucky."

The Liar space station was shaped like a starfish, a common shape for their structures. This one had seven arms radiating from a central hub, and cylindrical rings intersecting the arms to take advantage of spin gravity... not that it was spinning right now, which was odd.

"That's not the only strange thing," Lantern said. "There are no ships here." She gestured to the viewscreen, and Janice zoomed in on a few domed bulges on the central hub. "Just those short-range single-seat pods, the kind we use for escape, and for boarding enemy vessels. Where are the ships?"

"Let's find out," Callie said.

They went down to the belly of the ship and boarded the canoe, Lantern taking the controls while Callie activated her camouflage. The canoe dropped from the *White Raven* and made the short trip to the Liar station, docking easily at the end of one of the starfish arms. "Let's see if they open the door," Lantern said.

They waited, and waited, and Callie was about to call for Shall to come over in his hull repair drone to cut a hole in the airlock, when the hatch finally irised open with a hiss. Lantern scuttled through, Callie following close behind, invisible – or as close as technology could make her.

The inner airlock door opened when Lantern pressed a button, and they stepped onto the station, thumping to the floor when they hit the artificial gravity.

Lantern thumped, anyway; Callie didn't make a sound, thanks to her suit. "That's strange," Lantern murmured into her comms. "We almost never turn on the artificial gravity on truth-teller stations. Even having it installed is controversial within the sect – you know we limit our use of Axiom technology, lest humans stumble upon it. Artificial gravity is supposed to be for emergencies only, to facilitate repairs if the station is damaged, or to disable intruders by flattening them against the floor with heavier gravity. Maybe the station was harmed? It's not spinning, but I don't see any signs of damage."

Callie silently agreed. She'd been on a truth-teller station before, but only one that had been battered by a pirate attack. This station was pristine: all the lights glowed softly, the shining floors gleamed, and the walls and low ceilings were carved with repeating figures of Liars in various poses – probably conveying all kinds of information via body language that was opaque to Callie.

"Hello?" Lantern called through her artificial voicebox. Liars often preferred to communicate in human languages even amongst themselves, especially when they were in space or communicating at a distance, since it was easier to convey nuance without body language or pheromones in those tongues. There was no reply, and no one came to meet them.

They went down the long corridor of the starfish arm until they reached another door, and then onward to

the center of the base. There was a ring hallway that
ran around the perimeter of the hub, with doors set at
regular intervals, some of them open, and they looked
inside: sleeping quarters, an armory, what looked like
a media room, a few work spaces with terminals and
screens designed for Liar anatomy. There were no
cultists in sight, though, and the whole station had an
abandoned, almost haunted-house feel. One of the
doors was larger and more ornate than the rest, with
an arched door of some shimmering, iridescent metal.
"The elder's quarters," Lantern said, probably for Callie's
benefit, though she could have guessed.

Lantern pressed a button next to the door, and a
moment later, it slid open.

The interior was similar to the inner sanctum Callie
had seen on the station in the (feh) Jovian system:
palatial and ornate. The floor was made of that same
iridescent material, the ceiling was vaulted, and pillars
carved with figures of Liars stood at irregular intervals,
each column glowing with an inner light to illuminate
the room. A large bowl-shaped water tank stood in the
center of the space, and a huge Liar, easily three times
as big as Lantern, splashed over to the side and hauled
himself partway out of the tank, gazing at them over the
rim. The last elder Callie had met had worn ceremonial
garb and assorted jewelry and marks of office, but this
one was naked, pseudopods dangling lazily in the water.
He had well over a dozen eyes, scattered seemingly
at random all over the central dome, and they all had
different colored irises, blue and gold and green and red.

"Elder Trogidae," Lantern said. "Praise to the masters.
I am Elder Lantern."

"Praise." The voice boomed from the walls, and the ceiling – the elder's artificial voicebox must be hooked into the station's public address system. "Welcome, Elder Lantern. Sent by the central authority to check up on me, I assume? It was bound to happen." He paused, spun one hundred-eighty degrees in the pool, and now looked at Lantern with a single yellow eye, as big as a saucer. "Aren't you a bit young to be an elder?"

"I am, though not the youngest recorded. I had what you might term a battlefield promotion. Most of my cell was killed in the course of recovering a bridge generator discovered by a group of humans. The elders died around the same time, in a pirate attack – given the diminished staff on the station, they were unable to repel the invaders without taking substantial losses. Elder Mizori had been grooming me for a leadership position, and inducted me into the mysteries in her final moments."

"Gave you the codes to her computer system, you mean, so you could educate yourself."

"As you say, elder. The central authority ratified me soon after, at any rate."

"I've heard of you. You watch over the Jovian system, don't you? Birthplace of the human infestation. Is it a difficult post?"

"I find it amenable."

"I heard about all that… business, with the bridge generator. I found it very surprising. There are no works by the great masters within light years of that system, and yet, humans appeared there with a sacred artifact. The humans are a pestilence, aren't they? Always going where they shouldn't. It's a shame it was deemed impractical to exterminate them."

Callie gritted her teeth.

"As you say, elder," Lantern said again. She was usually polite. "I offered to check on your cell, since you missed multiple scheduled check-ins?"

"You wriggled your pseudopod as if that were a question, child. But I heard no query."

"Elder, not child," Lantern said sharply, and Callie was impressed. Lantern was normally as mild as milk.

"Of course. My apologies. You deserve the title in recognition of rank... if not age or experience. Was there a question?"

"It was clearly implied, I thought, elder, but I will make it explicit: why did you stop reporting to the central authority?"

"There was nothing to report. There will be nothing to report, rather, and as I always found the process of compiling those coded messages tedious, I stopped sending them a bit earlier than dictated by necessity."

"Yet you communicated with me."

"You came all this way. If I'd ignored you, you would have cut your way onto my home. This seemed simpler."

"You spoke to me without our sect's... customary discretion, though."

"Secrecy only matters when there is a future to keep those secrets in."

Lantern waved her pseudopods in frustration. "You seem to enjoy being mysterious."

"This surprises you? Did you think I joined a secret cult within *another* secret cult because I'm such a great believer in transparency and forthrightness?"

"I require direct answers. Our superiors demand them. Where is the rest of your cell? What *happened* here?"

Elder Trogidae gave another lazy, contented spin in the pool of liquid. "Ah, the others. I was the only initiate of the inner mysteries here, did you know that? Until recently this was an uneventful post, and hardly needed much in the way of oversight. True, there is a great work of the masters nearby – have you seen it? It's beautiful – but there were only a handful of humans in the vicinity, close to the nearest star, working tirelessly to transform the planet into a more comfortable habitation. They were focused entirely inward, rather than outward, and never ventured farther than the asteroid belt around their system – they seldom went as far as that. Alas, it's become so much more crowded now that they finished their terraforming. So many more humans to worry about."

"You could have sent for more assistance," Lantern said.

"No, no. I liked the devotees I had. They knew just how I liked my meals, exactly what temperature to make the water in my meditation tank, the tone and timbre of the ritual chants that least displeased my highly developed aesthetic sense, the proper way to massage my limbs. They were good children. That's why I sent them to such a glorious reward."

"What reward?"

"They fuel the dream."

CHAPTER 22

The elder clambered out of the tank, slopping water everywhere, and languidly dragged himself toward an alcove on the far wall. Callie moved a few steps to the left so she could keep an eye on him, just in case he went for a weapon. He didn't: he stood in an alcove, forced air blowing across his body to dry him, and then pulled on a sort of robe made of silky black fabric before scuttling back out, moving closer to Lantern.

"Whose dream?" Lantern said.

"*The* Dream," Trogidae said. Callie caught the proper-name emphasis this time. "The Dream is the great work of the masters here. The secret only I know. That vast station of the masters, floating between here and the system the humans have occupied? It is the engine of the Dream. Of all the long, slow projects of the masters, the Dream is the most noble, and the most glorious. The slumbering masters there are creating the future, Elder Lantern."

Callie scowled and clenched her fists. The kind of future the Axiom wanted to create wasn't a future anyone else would want to live in – or be *allowed* to live in.

Trogidae continued to rhapsodize. "How can you create the future if you can't imagine it?" Hadn't Sebastien said something similar to her, when she was in the Hypnos with him? "The Dream is a place for the great masters to test their various schemes and stratagems – a virtual world where they can control every variable. Everything within the Dream is theirs to control, and in that place, they perform great experiments, and plan for the future. The world within the Dream seems absolutely real to them, and this faction of the masters has lived there for tens of thousands of years, refining and perfecting their visions."

The Dream sounds like the Hypnos, Callie thought. *A fancy alien version of the same virtual reality humans use for schooling and gaming and porn.*

"I imagine that the masters might someday be able to overwrite this reality with the reality of the Dream." A happy-sounding sigh rustled from the speakers in the ceiling and walls. "Wouldn't that be glorious? For the visions of the masters to become real in the physical world?"

"Praise the masters," Lantern said in a perfunctory way. "What are they… dreaming about?"

"Things more amazing than the pitiful, limited mind of a servant like myself could possibly imagine, I'm sure."

"But if it's a virtual world, then what is the swarm doing? Why is it devouring all the matter in the system?"

"The swarm? Ah. You refer to the gatherers. They are servants of the masters, too – they reach out from within the Dream to touch this world directly. I only wish I had their clarity of mission."

"Yes, fine, the gatherers, but *why* are they gathering?"

"Even infinite dreamworlds can become cramped, elder," Trogidae said. "We have seen this happen before, though not for many centuries – the gatherers go out, and bring back matter, and convert that matter into dreaming crystals."

"You mean... computronium? Programmable matter? Those huge rings, they're... just vast computers, running the masters' virtual reality program?"

"The way you explain it lacks poetry, Elder Lantern. You have been living too close to humans for too long."

"So when the Dream reaches its computational limit and needs more processing power, they send out the gatherers to pillage local systems for material," Lantern said.

"So it has been, and so it will always be – until the masters waken from their slumber and bring their Dream to life. This new expansion is the largest yet – each is larger than the last, by orders of magnitude, as their needs seem to grow exponentially. To complete the latest ring of dreaming crystals, the gatherers will need to consume the planet the humans spent so much time changing, along with a fair portion of the asteroid belt, at a minimum."

"Oh, no," Lantern said. Callie, standing invisibly nearby, clenched her teeth and both fists. "When you said you sent the rest of your cell to fuel the dream – you sent them into the *swarm*?"

"I sent them to be gathered, Elder Lantern, so their feeble bodies might serve to glorify our masters. It is a great honor. The very particles of their bodies were transformed into dreaming crystals: they will hold the visions of the masters in their own cells."

"Did they go… willingly?"

"I told you," Trogidae snapped. "They weren't initiates into the inner mysteries. They believed their only purpose was to keep the Axiom from being disturbed – to protect the *humans* from the masters, instead of the reverse. When the Dream began to expand again, the gatherers moved in the direction of the planet the humans occupied. I had long predicted such a possibility – they'd already gathered most of the available mass in the vicinity, after all. The junior members of the cell wanted to send a delegation to the Dream engine! They wanted to try to switch off the gatherers, before they reached the humans. To *save* them, and prevent the discovery of the engine. The children knew I'd studied the engine for years, and believed I had knowledge that would allow them to approach safely, without triggering the engine's defenses."

"Do you?"

"Of course I do. But I didn't give it to them. I told them to transmit a certain sequence of digits on a certain frequency, and they would be protected, but I just gave them random data. I sent them all, every child from my cell – I told them it was *too important*, too vital a mission, to leave anyone behind – and of course, they never returned. They were transformed. They were blessed."

"You've lost your senses," Lantern said. "The whole purpose of our sect is to keep the Axiom a secret – to keep anyone from disturbing their work! What do you think will happen when an entire human colony planet is devoured?"

"I think the other humans will be *afraid*." Trogidae moved closer quickly, looming over Lantern, an act of physical intimidation that made Callie want to plant a boot in the elder's side. "When the Taliesen system goes silent, and humans eventually come to see what happened to them, and the planet is simply *gone*, vanished without a trace? This will become a haunted system. A cautionary tale. An object lesson, teaching those vermin: do not explore. Do not push into the dark, or you will die. You will die and vanish utterly. You say I've lost my senses!" The elder lashed out with a pseudopod and struck Lantern, sending her tumbling. Callie raised her arm to fire a tranquilizer dart, at the very least, at the elder, but then Lantern struggled upright, and Callie held off.

"I am *brilliant*!" Trogidae bellowed. "The humans will huddle in their other systems, terrified, wondering if the fate that befell Taliesen might befall *them*. This will become a forbidden system, the bridgehead sealed off, just like Vanir – which I hope has also become deadly thanks to the glorious work of the masters. It is a shame we lost contact with the cell there so long ago – it would be nice to have confirmation. At any rate, I am not violating the purpose of our sect – I am epitomizing that purpose. By allowing Owain to be devoured, I am protecting the Dream definitively. I'll make sure no human ever dares venture here again."

You don't know much about humans, Callie thought.

"You fail to understand humans," Lantern said. "Your assumptions are wrong. I have observed them, closely, for all my years, in the system where they are most numerous. Humans, on the whole, do not run from danger. They do not hide from mysteries. Oh, there are individual exceptions, but as a rule, cautionary tales mean nothing to them. If Owain disappears, they will want to know why, and they will come, and they will investigate, and they will find the Dream. They might even destroy it."

"Nonsense. They are nothing. Cowards, unfit to serve the masters. They gave up on Vanir, didn't they?"

"Only because every ship they sent failed to come back, and they eventually decided there must have been some terrible malfunction with the bridgehead there, but they sent *scores* of expeditionary missions first. The missions they send here *will* return, though, with news of a mystery, and they will investigate that mystery. Cowards? Centuries ago the humans sent hundreds of primitive ships, barely crewed, out into the dark, in the faint hope that they might find planets where their kind could survive, and keep their species alive when their home world seemed in danger of dying. Does that sound like *cowardice* to you?"

Trogidae fluttered his pseudopods. "You are a child, *elder*. Do not presume to tell me my business. Protecting the work of the masters is my vocation and my religion. You've spent too much time with humans – you have become like them. You *admire* the vermin."

"I'll need the codes," Lantern said. "The ones that allow safe approach to the engine of the Dream."

"Why do you imagine you need such a thing?"

"I'll stop the swarm. I'll switch it off."

"Ha. Fool. Do you imagine there is a switch to throw, a button to push, a lever to yank down? The great masters slumber in this physical realm. Do you imagine they rouse themselves to send out the gatherers? How absurd. The controls are located *inside the Dream*."

Oh, shit, Callie thought.

Lantern was unperturbed. "Then we'll just have to destroy the machine itself."

"Ha! Codes or not, the swarm won't ignore you if you try to damage the Dream, and whatever pitiful damage you do, they will repair, using your ship and your body as raw material."

"Then I'll... I'll warn the colonists."

"Mention the existence of the great masters to the humans and our superiors will punish you so thoroughly you'll feel like an exhibit in the museum of subjugation."

Lantern rose up on her walking tentacles, dignified. "I won't tell them anything about the Axiom. I can say that some Liar experiment in programmable matter got out of control, and that they're in danger, and need to evacuate. I'll help them escape—"

"Oh, no, elder infant. It's too late for that. I have monitoring stations out in the asteroids and throughout the system, disguised as small asteroids, the size of pebbles – small enough that the gatherers hardly bother with them. I've been watching their progress. The gatherers aren't intelligent, but their programming is complex. Several ships came from the direction of Owain, after all. The gatherers became... curious about that – or perhaps they fear interruption. For whatever reason, they've sent a delegation ahead to the planet. A small cloud of gatherers, moving slowly, conserving energy, but by the time you make it back and organize an evacuation, it will be too late. The swarm doesn't even have to reach the planet to make your plan fail – it just has to reach the bridgehead, and devour the base that allows the gate to be opened from this side. That will happen before you even reach the asteroid belt from here."

Callie silently swore. She'd thought they had more time to deal with this – Shall's calculations said the swarm would be slowly chewing its way through asteroids for weeks or even months, leaving ample time to organize an evacuation if their attempt to stop the Axiom project failed. She hadn't planned on the swarm *adapting*. Now the humans were the ants again, annoying the swarm with their frequent incursions, and the swarm was following them back to *their* nest.

Trogidae sidled closer to Lantern. "You should join me, Elder Lantern. You can do something that's actually meaningful with your life. Take one of the escape pods, and give yourself to the swarm. Become part of the mind of the masters."

"Join you?" Lantern fluttered her pseudopods derisively. "Is that your plan? To give yourself to the Dream? The gatherers have been active for weeks, and you sent your people to die some time ago – what are you waiting for?"

"I… Nothing. I'm not waiting. I'm *preparing*. I want to ready myself, spiritually, to enter the Dream in my… purest state…"

"Sacrificing for the masters is easier when it's someone *else* you're sacrificing, isn't it, elder?" Lantern said. "You sit here, and feast, and float, and meditate, and revel in your own cleverness, but when it comes down to it, you're afraid to give yourself to the swarm, because you know it will hurt to die. You know even if you become part of the Axiom's Dream, it will be the end of *your* dreams, and your pleasures. You want to stay forever in this – the moment before the dream begins."

Trogidae rose up. Callie had never been in a room with a Liar this size. They were usually the size of toddlers – this one was more like the size of a tiger. "You were not invited here. The courtesies I have extended to you, as a fellow elder, begin to seem ridiculous. Soon enough, I will dissolve into the Dream. I won't allow you to meddle, and I grow tired of your voice. If you refuse to join the Dream willingly, I will shove you into a pod and launch you there myself."

Callie fired several darts into Trogidae's body just as he reached out to grab Lantern with several thick tentacles. The elder listed, stumbled, and then fell to the floor in a tangle of limbs and robes. His many eyes slitted, blinked, and then closed.

"I hope that was OK." Callie turned off her active camouflage, shimmering into bright blue visibility. "I felt like we'd moved past the 'useful information' portion and into the 'deranged ranting' part of the program."

"Your timing was excellent," Lantern said. "I can use the elder's biometrics to unlock the computer systems and find the access codes he mentioned, and any other information about this engine of the Dream."

"What do we do with the elder once you're done using his tentacle-print to open the files?"

"We'll do what he wanted. Put him in a pod and launch him toward the Axiom station, so he can become part of the Dream." Lantern picked up a portable terminal from the room's workstation and carried it over to the elder's body.

Callie blinked. "Whoa. You were pretty opposed to me executing Elder Mizori last year."

"I have the authority, as the leader of a cell sent

on a fact-finding mission by my superiors, to pass this judgment."

"OK, but it's not like you actually believe your superiors deserve that authority."

Lantern pointed to the elder with a trembling limb. "This... This monster sent an entire cell of junior initiates to their deaths, knowingly, without remorse, without cause, because it suited his vanity! His hunger for reflected glory!" Lantern let out a keening sound – not from the artificial voicebox, but from her own mouth – and Callie hunched her shoulders, because it was a sound of such pure anguish and sadness.

Lantern's own cell was populated by young Liars rescued from the incubators of an Axiom facility, and she took shepherding the younger generation as a sacred trust. No wonder the loss of those young truth-tellers hit her so hard.

The keening cut off abruptly. "I am happy to do it if you do not wish to take part. I can find a power loader to help me move his body–"

"No, Lantern." Callie spoke softly. "I've got this. You focus on finding the information we need."

Lantern pressed the elder's pseudopod to the terminal, then said, "Just a moment, let me change the authorization to my physiology instead... there. We don't need... that... any more." Lantern gestured at the unconscious Liar, then bustled off to begin her work.

Callie picked up the elder. It was like lifting an octopus-shaped sack of gelatin, but she was strong, and she lugged the elder out into the hub, and toward the pod bay. Some weightlessness right now would come in handy. The pods were round fishbowls in a hangar near the top of the hub, each one in its own cylindrical tube with its own airlock. She got the outer and inner doors open, then shoved Trogidae into one of the pods, not bothering to secure him in the seat before she sealed him in. His ungainly tangle of pseudopods made him look sad and shapeless and harmless, which just proved you couldn't tell much by looks. She called Lantern on their comms. "He's in a pod."

"I'll take care of the rest," Lantern said.

Callie left the hangar, and she was halfway down the hallway when she felt the vibrations and heard the *thump* of the pod being fired, launching the murderous elder into the devouring darkness of the Dream.

CHAPTER 23

Elena and the others on board the *White Raven* had listened in on the events on the Liar station, through Callie's comms. When Lantern clambered out of the canoe, Elena was there to greet her. "Are you all right?" Elena said.

Lantern fluttered her pseudopods in a gesture of uncertainty. "I did what was necessary, with leaden limbs. Or, you would say, a heavy heart? To take a life is no small thing, though Trogidae treated it like one. I should... go review the data I found on the station, with Ashok, and Shall – and Sebastien. Would you send him?"

"Oh. Of course. I think he'd be happy to help."

"His happiness is of little importance to me, as long as he can render assistance. He is the closest thing we have on this ship to the mind of the Axiom."

Elena didn't like the sound of that, though she knew it was fair enough, in its way. "I'll let him know."

Lantern bustled away, and Callie hauled herself out of the canoe next. Elena said, "How are *you*?"

"Pessimistic." Callie began to strip off her bright blue suit. Elena was glad – that color made her think of poison dart frogs. "Lantern says we can probably get past the terror drones, and make it to the station's central hub, but what do we do once we're in there?"

"Are there Axiom inside? Like, physically? Or are they just… uploaded digital minds?"

"They have real bodies, apparently. Lantern said they could change their physical forms to a remarkable degree, but they do still *have* physical forms – having strong bodies that can crush and devour their enemies is important to them, and anyway, the best housing for their terrifyingly complex minds is a biological one. The Axiom are sleeping, or at least reclining, in life-support pods in there, plugged into the Dream, just like those hardcore Hypnos addicts who put themselves on IV drips and get auto-nurse beds to turn them over so they won't get bedsores while they do marathon sessions. Except in this case, the Axiom have been in the Dream for thousands upon thousands of years. Apparently they solved the whole 'physical immortality' problem a long time ago, which is why they're concerned about surviving heat death."

"So… what's the plan? We go in there and tear open their pods and stab them all in the neck, if they have necks?"

Callie smiled, but it was a weak effort. "I'm game to try, but I don't imagine the codes we found to get us past the terror drones will protect us if we start actively smashing stuff up. There's no telling what kind of defenses those slumber-pods have – the records Lantern was able to access are pretty short on details. It's not like we've got schematics of the place or anything." Callie sat down on a crate in the cargo bay, radiating exhaustion and worry.

"The swarm doesn't just build more computing power. It also does repairs. According to the records on the base, the swarm is always hovering around the engine, touching things up, doing maintenance, maintaining the life-support pods inside. If we break something, the swarm will just fix it. We need to turn the swarm *off* to save Owain, and the controls to do that are only accessible inside the Dream of the Axiom."

"Ugh," Elena said. "What are you going to do?"

"I did what captains do best: I delegated. I called Shall and Ashok and told them to work with Lantern and figure out a solution." She shrugged. "I've got a couple of really smart engineers and a big fancy AI at my disposal. Just because I can't find a solution doesn't mean there isn't one."

"There's no solution," Ashok said at family dinner.

"That's not what I wanted to hear," Callie said.

"We can probably destroy the station," Ashok said. "The *White Raven* is pretty solid when it comes to firepower. That would kill all the Axiom lurking on board, and them being dead is a good outcome. But... we don't know if killing them would save Owain. No reason to think it would, really, knowing how the Axiom like to leave their automated systems running even in their absence. The swarm is programmed to go out, to gather, to come back, and build. Even if we destroy the station, the swarm is out there, heading to Owain, and it might just keep eating stuff, and rebuild the station, whether the Axiom inside are dead or not."

"Is there any way we can fight the swarm itself?" Callie said.

"If we can get our hands on a terror drone, without disabling it too badly in the process, Lantern and I can try to use its disabling weapon – it knocked out the ship's systems, and our brains, so it might work on the swarm, too. If we can render the swarm inert for even a little while, we can try to destroy it. Even dust will burn. Of course, if the disabling blast doesn't work on them, they might see us as hostile, and come eat us."

"Even if it does work, how would we know we got the whole swarm?" Callie said. "If even one speck survives, a single replicator, it can regrow the whole swarm in, what, hours?"

"Yes," Ashok said. "That's why I said there's no solution. It's awfully hard to know if you've burned every single speck of dust in the system."

"I have an idea," Sebastien said.

Callie looked toward him, and the drones buzzing around his head. They made her think of those ancient cartoons, where, when someone got knocked hard on the head, little birds would appear and fly and chirp around them. Sebastien had been knocked on the head, all right – inside and out – but she was desperate. "What's your plan?"

"There's an on-off switch for the swarm inside the Axiom's Dream," he said. "So let's go into the Dream and turn it off."

"Elegant in its simplicity," Stephen mumbled.

"How do you propose we do *that*?" Callie said.

Sebastien shrugged. "I can't speak to the technical requirements, but you've all used the Hypnos. How is the Dream any different, at least conceptually? Find a way to plug yourselves into the Dream, go find the controls for the swarm, and turn them off. With the swarm disabled, we can destroy the station without fear of it being rebuilt."

"That's a... huh." Ashok scratched his chin. "I mean, it's not a good idea. But it's an idea. Obviously we know almost nothing about Axiom physiology or how their brains work. You're not going to be able to climb into an Axiom pod and plug into the Dream the way they do. Best case, you'd melt your brain. But... it's not like we lack experience combining Axiom technology with human and Liar machinery. Lantern and I have done a bunch of that, with the bridge generators, the artificial gravity, the short-range teleporter, all kinds of things, and we've worked out a lot of the basic principles." He leaned forward, warming to the idea. "If we could find a way to patch our own Hypnos rig into the Axiom system, we could theoretically use our hardware to project ourselves into their sensorium. I have no idea what an alien VR landscape would be like, what sensory data they take in, but Lantern says the Axiom had all the same senses we have – they just had *more*. A human mind might not be able to process all the information coming at it in the Dream, but I bet we could set up filters to strain out extraneous information so you could at least function. It would be the equivalent of going into a cheap Hypnos arcade, with low-resolution rigs and lag and everything."

"Do you think that's possible?" Callie asked Lantern.

The Liar waved her pseudopods in assent. "I do. Axiom technology is highly adaptable. They didn't use just one sort of body – they had many forms, and altered their physiology often, to adapt to different circumstances. Any virtual reality equipment they built would require multiple forms of input to accommodate those variations. Patching in hardware developed for use on humans... I won't say it's a trivial problem, but it's possible, especially given our experience hooking the bridge generator into the *White Raven*'s systems."

"The difference is, if you burn out a Tanzer drive, you can take it out and get a new one," Elena said. "If you burn out someone's *brain*, they're dead."

"I was thinking the same thing," Sebastien beamed at her like she was a student who'd made a good point, which annoyed the shit out of Callie. She was never going to like that guy. "I would be happy to help you there. My... unique mental architecture... might make me better suited to navigate their virtual world. At the very least, I stand the best chance of understanding how to operate the controls for the swarm – I grew quite adept at operating Axiom systems during my time on their station."

"He is right," Lantern said. "His grasp of their engineering principles far exceeds even my own."

"No way am I letting you loose in the Dream," Callie said.

Sebastien nodded. "I know. You won't even let me prepare your food – you certainly won't let me near the controls for a swarm of galaxy-devouring nanobots. I accept that. Isn't it possible for two people to enter the Hypnos together, though, inhabiting a single avatar?"

"Sure," Ashok said. "There are some cooperative games like that – one person controls the avatar, and the other sort of whispers in their ear. Or two people take the form of a ship, say, and one of them pilots it and the other handles the guns, but they're essentially working together."

"That's my proposal," Sebastien said. "We enter the Dream. Callie gets to control our avatar. She decides what we do, where we go, and when we leave the Dream. I'll be a passenger, offering advice and suggestions."

"How can I trust that advice?"

Sebastien sighed. "Because if I gave you bad advice, the worst possible advice, murderous destructive device, you could leave the Dream and *kill me*. I'm cured, but even if I weren't – even if the worst version of me you can imagine is the one sitting before you – does that version strike you as suicidal?"

"No," Callie admitted. "Self-preservation seemed pretty high up on your hierarchy of needs."

"Precisely. I don't want to be devoured by the swarm, captain. I want to get out of here, and live a life, and achieve things. Whether I'm 'good' or 'evil' doesn't even matter – in either case, it's in my best interest to help you, and I think I can be trusted to act in that interest."

Callie swiveled in her chair. "What do you think, Elena?"

She shrugged. "At some point, you have to trust."

"I knew you'd say that."

Callie hated this whole plan, but it was the only Plan B they'd come up with. She didn't even like going into the Hypnos, because it seemed like such a self-indulgent waste of time, and now she had to go into an *alien* virtual reality? What would it even be like in there? Could the Axiom smell geometry? Taste magnetism? Was she going to have seizures when she looked at their mood lighting?

Lantern assured her that her mind would process the
sensorium on whatever level it safely could – that
human brains were *excellent* at extracting useful things
from torrents of data and ignoring everything else, and
that the Hypnos headsets had safeguards in place, too.
Even if she didn't perceive things exactly as the Axiom
in the Dream did, she should at least be able to navigate
the place.

The thought of going with Sebastien in her head,
whispering in her mind's ear... Ugh. The idea made her
feel like she was coated with a thin layer of slime, but
on the *inside*.

Still. Needs must. It would be good to get something
useful out of Sebastien's messed-up brain.

The gyroscopic shape of the Dream engine loomed
up in the viewscreens. Was the partial outer ring half
as big again already? What new imaginary continents
or planets or galaxies were the Axiom creating in there,
that they needed so much processing power?

"Send the code," she said.

"Sending," Janice said.

The records in the Liar base had included a frequency
and a number string that would apparently make the
terror drones stand down. There was no answering code
– no acknowledgment at all – and they weren't sure
whether to expect one. They sent the canoe ahead first,
uncrewed except for Shall's repair drone squatting on top.
The asteroids failed to crack open and disgorge glowing
death spiders from outer space. That was a good sign.

They called the canoe back, and this time Ashok,
Lantern, Stephen, and Callie boarded it – with Shall's
vastly larger and more useful military drone on top. That

body had been scavenged from the depths of the pirate base in a broken and ruined state, and subsequently repaired and augmented. There wasn't a better war machine in this system... except for the terror drones, and whatever else might be lurking in the hub of the Dream. They had a few Hypnos headsets, a toolbox the size of a steamer trunk, and Ashok had cables and connectors of various sorts looped around himself, along with a portable fabricator strapped on like a backpack, in case he had to custom-make hardware to fit the Axiom connections.

They said their farewells, and launched. The canoe moved slowly, and all of them hunched their shoulders and tensed up as they passed the nearest terror drone asteroid – because what if it only attacked vessels with killable human flesh on board? But their alarm code worked, and the space rock in space didn't disgorge its dark heart.

Callie piloted the canoe toward the central sphere, choosing a moment when the slowly turning rings opened a nice wide gap. Getting clipped by a few thousand tons of dreaming crystals moving at unspeakable velocities wouldn't do the canoe any good, and it would be a stupid way to die, when they'd survived so much.

From a distance, the moon-sized sphere at the center had looked like a solid ball of silver, but up close it was filigreed all over with lines in sinuous patterns, some faintly glowing, some dark.

"Here goes." Lantern transmitted another code taken from the elder's files – one rather cryptically titled "Request an Audience." What if the station refused their request? What if an Axiom woke up and opened the door, pissed off at the interruption? Callie sort of wanted to see one in the flesh – to *kill* one in the flesh, even – but another part of her hoped that she never would.

The sphere rippled, and an opening just big enough to accommodate the canoe appeared before them – not like a door opening, but like a whirlpool forming in a puddle of quicksilver. There was no landing assistance, no tractor beams, no runway lights, so Callie guided the canoe in by hand, exterior lights shining into the sphere's black interior.

Here we go, she thought. *Into the moment before the dream.*

CHAPTER 24

The hangar bay inside – if that's what it was, and not a ballroom or an unoccupied torture chamber – was vast and empty, and the canoe settled down on the floor gently. There was gravity inside, though considerably less than a full G, Callie judged. The door behind them rippled and closed, and lights came on – but not from lamps or bulbs or banks of LEDs. Callie peered out the viewscreen. "The light is coming from clouds. Glowing bright white. Like swarms of high-wattage fireflies."

"Utility fog," Ashok said. "Am jealous."

Callie had the canoe's sensors sample the air, and it wasn't remotely breathable by humans... except, a few seconds later, it was – in fact, it was identical to the atmosphere inside the canoe, down to the last part per million. "How did they alter the composition of the air so quickly?" she demanded.

"More swarms," Lantern said. "Flying around, eating molecules of one gas and pooping out molecules of a different one. How... hospitable."

"I'm going to keep my suit on anyway, in case they decide to change the air back to toxic soup." She tried hailing the *White Raven*, without success. "Just like the last time we visited the Axiom – I can't get an outside line."

"Hmm," Ashok said. "Clearly the interior of this sphere can communicate just fine with things outside – the processor rings and the main body of the swarm are controlled from in here. Maybe if we figured out *that* frequency we could communicate..."

"Maybe, but we anticipated being cut off," Callie said. "Remedying that would be nice, but it's way down on the priority list."

"I know. I can't help *thinking*, cap. My brain just does it, is all, whether I want it to or not."

"No use sitting in here. Let's do what we came for." Callie ordered a last check of gear and suits, then opened the airlock. They stepped out into the hangar – and the illuminated swarms flew down to eye level and lined up at precise intervals, creating a curving path into the darkness. "Is it worse to follow the path, or stray from it?" Callie said.

"We requested an audience," Lantern said. "Let's see where they take us."

Shall clumped up behind them, his tank-sized drone body bristling with weaponry and manipulators and sensors. He had a local version of his consciousness loaded, since they'd anticipated losing connection with the ship, which meant he was stupider than usual, but still so much smarter than most humans that no one would be able to tell the difference. "There are many rooms and corridors all around us," he said. "Some of them are changing, and reconfiguring, as the matter rearranges itself."

"The *walls* are made of the swarm?" Callie said.

"Some of them appear to be."

"So we could just, what, get sealed into a room and left to starve forever?"

"I doubt they'd leave us to starve," Lantern said. "If they decided not to let us leave, the swarm would just convert us into more of itself."

"Shall we go?" Sebastien sounded entirely too eager, which made Callie sure he was planning something. She couldn't even tell if she was being fair or unfair any more... but he still had his drones, buzzing along and keeping an eye on him, remotely controlled by the splinter of Shall inside the war-drone. His intentions didn't matter, as long as he was being closely watched.

They followed the glowing swarms into the darkness. After they passed a cloud, it would go dark, and then another would light up farther ahead, and so it went for dozens of iterations, until they reached a wall – which conveniently melted open to reveal a door big enough for them to pass through, war-drone and all. Clearly the swarm was unconcerned about their firepower. Why not? The swarm was the ultimate apex predator. It could eat anything, and nothing could eat it.

The corridor they entered gently wavered through slow s-curves. The walls and ceiling were gently curved, and all the same color as the great rings, silvery white. Were they walking on computronium? Probably. Why waste valuable space on inert matter when you could use those corridors to help run your galactic genocide simulator, or whatever the Axiom was doing in the Dream.

Lantern had explained that the Axiom had factions,

with different goals and methods, sometimes mutually exclusive ones, but it was still bizarre for Callie, seeing how different this place was from the twisty anthill tunnel aesthetic of the last such station they'd explored. The Dream engine was actually pretty, in a simple, clean, elegant way, while the other facility had seemed designed to disorient and distress. That had been a factory station made to create two things, though: ships, and obedient Liar slaves. The goals of this place were very different, and that might account for the differences.

Or maybe she should stop trying to understand the mindset of sadistic alien demigods entirely.

They emerged from the corridor into a room shaped like a cylinder stood on end. There was no discernible ceiling, just overhead space that extended up farther than Callie could see. It was like being at the bottom of a well. The floor here was different, made of lightly pitted stone or metal, and even in the dimness, she could tell the walls weren't smooth. Were they surrounded by tiers, or galleries, or shelves, stretching up and up? There were no more glowing swarms showing them the way.

"We're in the center of the sphere now," Shall said. "The matter here is cold, dead, and more stable – I think this is the core of the station."

"The Axiom wouldn't want to sleep in a place composed of programmable matter," Sebastien said. "They'd want something more stable – something that would last for millennia, even in the case of disabling radiation or system failures. The heart of the heart of the station is stone."

"How do you know?" Callie said.

Sebastien shrugged, the motion barely visible in his

environment suit. "It's how I would do it." He pointed behind them, toward the door they'd passed through. "Look, the swarm isn't even coming in here – the glowing clouds stopped at the entrance. There's probably a safeguard, to keep them from coming in here, where they might disassemble vital things – like the bodies of the sleeping Axiom. They are an immensely paranoid people." He paused. "I know. I was for a while there, too."

Callie grunted and walked forward. In the very center of the hub, there was a strange object – roughly the size and shape of a bathtub, but made of some stiff brown material, leathery and fibrous – it looked almost like a split seed-pod. There were greasy-looking black cables inside, with sharp silver spines protruding from the ends. Those reminded her of the claws of the brain-spiders that had changed Sebastien, digging into his brain and stimulating certain areas while destroying others, and injecting nanites to do the fine work.

"This setup is meant for my people." Lantern approached the pod tentatively, prodding at it with a pseudopod. "I've seen these sort of connections before – they're meant for deep immersive learning, mainly. They hook into our nervous system."

"This is where you go for an audience," Callie said. "Huh. You plug in here, and what? You appear in the Dream, and some Axiom asks what you want and why you're bothering them?"

"Probably not an actual Axiom. An automated system, maybe. The Axiom only bothered to interact with their servants directly for purposes of punishment... or entertainment."

Callie considered. "Still, I'd rather not show up in a place where visitors are expected, if there's another way. Shall, shine a light around, would you?"

The war-drone was equipped with spotlights capable of everything from gentle illumination to searing brightness, and he extended an array of arms to light the way. Callie walked alongside him, guiding him toward a side wall.

Her impression of the space was correct. The perimeter wall was made of oversized shelves, each level about four meters high, rising up, and up, and up... Every shelf held a dozen or so pods, generously spaced apart, like the one in the center of the room... except three times as big. The Axiom were not small creatures. Callie tried to count the shelves and gave up after ten – Shall's lights didn't reach the ceiling, and the shelves disappeared in the gloom. "There could be, what, hundreds of Axiom here?"

"Most of the pods are open and empty, though," Lantern said. "I think this place was built with more capacity than they needed."

Shall deployed a hover-drone from his back, and it did a quick circuit, rising up the cylindrical space and scanning the shelves, one by one. The drone buzzed back down, and Shall said, "There are hundreds and hundreds of pods, but only forty-seven are occupied, as far as I can tell – at least, that many are closed, and giving off heat signatures."

"It's so demoralizing when you invite people to a party and they don't show up," Callie said.

"The Axiom were in disarray by the end of their active period," Lantern said. "They made war among themselves. It's possible that a score of ships were meant to converge here, and only one or two made it, with the rest lost in skirmishes with other factions."

Forty or fifty Axiom. She could exterminate that many of them, personally. What percentage of their total numbers was that? A surprisingly large one, if Lantern's estimates were correct. "How are they protected? There's no swarm in here, and the pods seem totally undefended."

"They aren't," Sebastien said.

"Agreed," Lantern said. "There are certainly defenses we can't see. Even allies didn't trust one another. Treachery was their religion."

Callie peered into the nearest open, unattended pod, on the ground-level shelf. "Then for now, we'll settle for using one of these, assuming they're plugged into the Dream? Presumably they were fully set up with the expectation of having inhabitants."

"There's one way to find out," Ashok said cheerfully. He leaned over a pod and pulled out a cable, taking a look at the end. "Oh, yeah, I've got this. Lantern, this, uh, well, *spike* is meant for the visual center, right? That's what this little squiggle at the base means?"

The Liar clambered up onto the pod and took a look. "Yes, and this one is auditory, and this one – that's for the electromagnetic sense, so we can do without that…"

"Or we could cross-patch it with one of the other cables, so Callie could, I don't know, smell oranges in the presence of a magnetic field, or whatever."

"Synesthesia might be distracting, though," Lantern said.

Callie left them to their work (and easy camaraderie), and stood beside Shall. Her footsteps echoed hugely in the cavernous space. "This place is like a tomb full of things that don't know they're supposed to be dead." She put a hand on the side of Shall's body. "Watch over them."

"Them, and you," Shall said.

"What about me?" Sebastien strolled over to join them, pretending to ignore Callie's glare.

"Oh, definitely," Shall said. "I'll cherish and protect you, like you're my own sweet baby child."

"I want you to scan these pods, occupied and otherwise, and figure out what kind of defenses they have," Callie said. "Passive scans only, though, to start. We don't want one of the sleeping monsters to wake up and take an interest in current events. I'm worried enough about entering the Dream through an unused pod. What if all the Axiom get a message flashing 'Welcome new user' or something when we go in, and decide to throw me a welcoming party?"

"I wouldn't worry about that," Sebastien said. "You don't understand the Axiom. They aren't social creatures, in the way humans are. Their interests in others are limited to domination. They might ally with one another, but only to further their own agendas, and even then, it's only a matter of time before they betray one another. Even their factions were cobbled together out of convenience and necessity. No one is going to greet a newcomer, though they might note your arrival – and they'll certainly take an interest in you if you get in their way, or if they think you can help them further their goal."

Callie shook her head. "How did creatures who can't cooperate for more than five minutes without trying to murder each other create an empire that spans a galaxy?"

"They're smarter than we are," Sebastien shrugged. "*So* much smarter. The Axiom are better than us, in almost every way – except for that inability to cooperate."

"And the sadism. And the lack of empathy. And the slave-holding."

"Yes, of course, that goes without saying."

"It would make me feel better if you said it anyway."

Sebastien ghosted her a smile. "Your preference is noted. The Axiom were ultimately smart enough to realize their limitations, too, and so the factions were born, working toward their various long-term goals, cooperating to achieve greater things than they could do alone. This... is one of the more benign factions, I would imagine. The Dream is probably a test kitchen to try out plans to transcend the end of the universe, instead of just enacting the plans in the real world, regardless of the damage that might cause. These Dreamers must have been rather philosophical Axiom, by the standards of their race."

"You admire them." Shall's voice was flat.

Sebastien shrugged again. "I'd rather say... they impress me. They should impress you too. They're impressive."

"I'll start those scans, Callie." The war-drone stomped away, perhaps more noisily than necessity dictated.

"I don't think Shall likes you very much," Callie said.

"Why should he be any different than the rest of you?" He sighed. "I really can help you here, you know."

"You'd better, if you want a ride back to the *White Raven*." She went to see how Lantern and Ashok were doing.

• • •

The size of the pod meant it was easily big enough for Sebastien and Callie to both fit inside, but the curvature of the interior meant they inevitably slid together, like lovers sharing an old mattress that sagged in the middle. Callie did her best to avoid entangling with him, and he was decorous about keeping his hands to himself, but the situation was nonetheless very intimate, in a skin-crawling way.

Ashok fitted a diadem onto Callie's brow, with delicate wires running from her crown to the headset meant for Sebastien: his connection would be subsidiary to her own. They would share a sensorium, and be able to communicate, but she would be the one with agency and control over their avatar in the Dream.

"There are a lot of loose cables in here." She shoved away one dangling, wrist-thick cord that was digging into her shoulder.

"Feeding tubes and waste evacuation tubes, and a few cables for senses you don't possess," Ashok said. "We decided being able to sense radiation would just make you nervous and disoriented."

"Huh. It's fake radiation in there anyway, right?"

"Sure, but depending on the rules of the simulation, fake radiation might make your avatar throw up and lose its hair and stuff. Just like in a battle sim – you bleed, you ooze, your bones break, whatever. What happens in the Dream won't hurt your actual body, of course, though sometimes there's phantom pain from imaginary injuries, because brains are *weird*."

"The things people do for entertainment," Callie said. "Don't fry my brain, please. I'd like to survive long enough to suffer phantom radiation poisoning for years to come."

Ashok fitted Sebastien's headset. "No brains will fry. I've got enough failsafes in place here that the *worst* thing that will happen is nothing at all. You ready to go?"

Callie took a deep breath, almost said yes, then said, "Wait. How do I get out when I'm done?"

"You exit the Dream just like you exit the Hypnos – look up and to the left, and you should see a glowing door. Just nod your head toward the luminous rectangle, and poof, you're out."

"I didn't have that option when I was in the Hypnos," Sebastien said.

"Nope," Ashok said. "You didn't have any controls at all in your sensorium – therapeutic settings were enabled, on account of how you're a war criminal."

"I was an aspiring war criminal at best. I never successfully war-crimed. Unlike your dear friend Lantern, who helped murder fifty thousand people on Meditreme Station. How many people did I murder? Oh, that's right: zero people."

"And yet she's my friend and you're not," Ashok said. "Ethics sure are complicated, huh?"

Callie snorted.

"Here we go!" Ashok said. "It's *Dreaming Day*!"

CHAPTER 25

One day, when Kalea Machedo woke from her troubled life, she found herself transformed into an immense monstrosity.

Her body was *wrong* – wrong in every particular. She opened her eyes – there were four of them, taking in far more than one hundred and eighty degrees of vision – and recoiled from the wormlike roots dangling down from the filthy ceiling, brushing against her face. She swatted at the roots, and she had too many arms. The flesh on those arms felt loose but leathery, wrinkled and wattled, and her hands had far too many thumbs, and claws that sprang out and retracted as she gasped for breath. The air was hot and fetid and smelled like the bottom of a compost heap. She crouched – she had lower limbs, too, four of them, with too many knees on each one. In the course of trying to sort out the complexity of her new legs, she fell over.

She crashed into a pile of filth that squirmed away from her and fled through a ragged hole in the wall, into some outer brightness – was her bed made of vermin? Was she underground in some kind of garbage cavern? She wriggled and writhed and tried to stand, but a mind that had spent decades piloting a body with bilateral symmetry, two arms, and two legs wasn't equal to the task.

Suffering some dysmorphia, are we? Sebastien said in her mind. *It's strange, but... this body feels right to me. I never realized before that I was uncomfortable because I didn't have enough limbs. Would you like to cede control to me, just for a moment, so I can get you upright?*

That was possible, she knew – she could let him pilot the body... but then he'd have to choose to relinquish control for her to take it back. *Fuck you.*

I don't know, captain. You seem more fucked than I am. I'm just along for the ride.

Damn it. Ashok played sims all the time where he took the form of tentacled undersea monsters wrestling with sea serpents, or giant spiders competing to see who could capture and mummify the most hairy-footed humanoids in butt-silk, or literal multi-headed dragons breathing acid, lightning, fire, ice, and poison gas across rampaging undead armies. Callie, of course, never played Hypnos games like that – a gap in her experience she'd never expected to have ramifications in her actual life. But here she was.

Callie concentrated. Left front leg, left back leg, right front leg, right back leg. Upper left torso limb, lower left, upper right, lower right. There seemed to be a tail back there too. Forget that for now. She had a kind of bandolier across her chest – or thorax, or whatever – full of small glass vials, and what looked like a garden fork stuck through a loop on her "belt." She had another object strapped to her back, a long metal pole about the size and length of a broom handle, and she wrestled that off and used it to lever herself onto her myriad overcomplicated barbed feet.

Nicely done, Sebastien said, and didn't even sound ironic about it.

Callie looked at the pole in her... say hands, for convenience. Was it a tool for helping herself up from falls? No. It was a weapon. The pole had an absurdly barbed shiny black head on one end, and a hook on the other. She put it back over her shoulder and some kind of smart clamps on her thorax harness grabbed hold of the pole and held it in place, the hook and head retracting as it did. "Why do I have weapons?" she said, but the words that came out were guttural and inhuman.

Oh, my, Sebastien said. *That's an Axiom language you just spoke. There were lots of recordings on the other station, enough for me to figure out how their phonemes matched up to the written alphabet, anyway.* He sighed in her mind. *Obviously I'm glad I'm not a psychopathic megalomaniac any more, but it was nice being hyperintelligent. I've always been pretty smart, but really – I used to be a mountain, and now I am an anthill.*

My heart bleeds for you, Callie thought. *How am I speaking Axiomatic?*

There's more computing power in this station than exists in the rest of the galaxy, probably, Sebastien said. *What's a little universal translation for a system like that? We were talking in the hub, and the system might have monitored our comms before that, or even scanned the* White Raven*'s data banks. For creatures like the Axiom, such things are trivial. Look on the bright side. Now we can ask, "So where's the off switch for the gatherers?" and they'll understand us.*

"Elegant plan," she said, trying out her new voice. It

was horrible – wet and meaty and harsh. "But back to my question: why did I spawn in with weapons?"

Perhaps there are dangerous things here. Though I suspect you're the dangerous thing. Just as, once upon a time, I wouldn't leave the house without my wallet and phone and keys, what self-respecting Axiom would leave their den without a torture implement or two?

"I guess we should explore." She wondered what she looked like – some kind of immense insect? A centaur topped with a mantis body? What was her *head* like? She felt around her face with her two nearest hands and found it rough, spiny, chitinous, and horned. The mouth was a horror of mandibles and serrated edges and rows of teeth. Was this nightmare body what the Axiom looked like in their original forms? There was no reason to assume the avatar was based on anything real – it could be an imaginary form that only existed in the simulation, like Ashok's dragons and monsters from the deep.

Callie took a few tentative practice steps around the interior of the stinking cavern, getting used to her new body. She'd always been physically adroit, and soon she felt comfortable enough to crawl out of the hole. She wriggled through the gap, and emerged into a forest under a blank white sky. The trees here were large and twisted, the bark and branches black and gray, hanging with moss – except the moss looked wet, like kelp, and some of it was animate, writhing like snakes. There was no sign of habitation, of anything built at all, or of any creatures, like herself or otherwise. She turned and looked back, and confirmed she'd crawled out from a den in the roots of a tree. "Why are we here?"

Maybe this is the starting area of the Dream. Or the starting area of one realm. There's so much processing power, this could just be one planet in a vast galaxy of simulated worlds. We have no idea.

How the hell do we find the control switch then? If there was a whole imaginary galaxy of possibilities, where should she begin?

We won't find it by standing here, Sebastien said.

Callie grumbled in her monstrous voice and clumped onward, following a slope toward a ridge, where she could at least get a look at the terrain. The air was sticky and warm, but did that mean her body was just colder than the one she was used to? She smelled burning, and a distant rotting stench. A thin tendril of smoke marred the sky off to the right, so she angled that way, because she had to go somewhere.

She crested the ridge, and looked down on a battle.

There were creatures like herself down there, hundreds of them, locked in a melee with monsters of a different sort, though of roughly equal size. The enemies were more oversized millipede than centaur-scorpion, and both races were wearing armor, much of it ostentatiously spined and spiked and barbed – Callie felt suddenly terribly exposed in just her bandolier.

The creatures hacked at one another with weapons like her barbed pole, as well as oddly curved swords, and whips that crackled with electricity. The millipede-things seemed capable of spitting venom, and the centaur-scorpions whipped their barbed tails around. Callie sank low onto her segmented belly and watched, trying to make sense of what she saw. "Are those the Axiom? Is this, what, a war simulation?"

No, there are too many down there. I don't think any of them are the Axiom – I think they're all simulations.

Like the sea monsters Ashok fought, she thought.

Sebastien went on, *It could be like those games where you deploy armies, fight for resources, try to build nations. The fighters may be individually controlled, but I suspect they were just dispatched with some goal – engage the enemy, win this territory, that sort of thing.*

A centaur-scorpion pinned a millipede right behind its head with a spear, transfixing the monster to the ground. The attack seemed to paralyze the millipede, but not kill it, and the assailant drew a black crystal machete then began to methodically cut its victim apart, starting at the tail, hacking through one body segment at a time. The centaur-scorpion made a horrible high-pitched keening noise as it butchered its prey, kicking away the severed chunks in sprays of thick black blood.

Callie wanted to vomit, but this body seemed incapable of that. Instead, experimentally, she tried to laugh, quietly – and it was a softer version of the horrible noise the killer was making.

The thing down there was hacking apart a defenseless enemy, and laughing about it. *They're just simulations*, she thought. *Not players, just part of the environment, like the monsters Ashok kills in his fantasy games – he can slaughter space orcs all day, but it's not like they're real. That's just... pretend pain down there.*

Oh, no, I think they're really suffering, Sebastien said. *I'd be shocked if they weren't. Why would the Axiom bother with this otherwise? Torturing creatures that don't have interior lives – well, that sort of thing makes an emotional impact on humans. There are humans who weep when fictional characters die, because their empathy is so susceptible to manipulation. But that sort of thing doesn't work on the Axiom – they wouldn't derive any satisfaction from hurting something that only* acted *like it felt pain. If they're tormenting someone, they want that person to truly suffer. I think the Dream is so powerful that it can create simulations who possess sentience, or even consciousness, at least of a rudimentary sort – the creatures fighting down there believe themselves to be real, and can experience pain, and fear, and probably hope, since hope dashed is a very satisfying torment. Isn't that fascinating? In this place, the Axiom truly are as gods.*

Why? Callie asked. *What's the point? Are they modeling some kind of assault on a planet we don't know about? Testing out a battle plan against another civilization, in another galaxy? Or…*

Then she saw something that baffled her – a centaur-scorpion chopped down one of its own kind, to save a millipede, and then the two waded into battle again side-by-side. She'd assumed this was a battle between different species, but was there some other organizing principle at play?

Sebastien said, *It's a bit hard to follow the action, I know. Here, look up and to the right.*

Why?

Can't you just do as I… fine. Because there are controls there. Options we can toggle on and off. How do I know more about using the Hypnos interface than you do? I was born five hundred years ago!

I have better things to do than play pretend. She looked up and to the right – and a series of glyphs she couldn't read appeared, glowing in different colors. *What do those say?*

The automatic translation doesn't work in that direction,

hmm? Interesting. All right, look hard at that squiggly green one and maybe blink one of your eyes – there we go.

A visual overlay appeared on the battlefield below. That augmented reality was the first thing that had broken the illusion that this experience was entirely real. Now small dots floated over each of the creatures on the churned, smoking mud of the battlefield, living and dead, though the dead had a black circle around their dots. Roughly half the dots were red, and the other half were blue.

Sebastian started to laugh, and kept laughing.

What's so funny? What's it mean?

They're teams, Sebastien said. *Elder Trogidae thought the Axiom in the Dream were running simulations of brutalist utopias in here, or conducting experiments too dangerous or resource-intensive to attempt in the real world. But they're not. Captain, they're not in here trying to transcend heat death – or at least, that's not all they're doing. They're playing a* game, *and it should not surprise you to discover that Axiom games are violent ones.*

That is some bullshit, Callie thought. Then: *Wait, what color am I?* She craned her head back. A green dot floated above her. *Is that... am I neutral?*

The Axiom don't believe in neutral, *captain. If I had to guess, I'd say that dot means "unaffiliated," and thus, fair game for anyone to slaughter. Here, look right again. There may be a legend or some kind, or a help file.*

She did as he asked, focused on the glyph he indicated, and watched as the sky filled with fast-scrolling black letters. *Mmm, I see,* he said.

Just then, a centaur-scorpion pointed its spear in her direction, and began hustling up the hillside.

"Oh, shit." Callie looked up and to the left, and there was the door, glowing and white, a brighter rectangle against the pale sky.

You don't need to run, Sebastien said. *I was wrong about the dot. It means you're a… player, for want of a better word. Someone real. If you were a player affiliated with either faction, there would be a ring around your dot in the corresponding hue, but there's not, and that means you're a high-value target, so they'll all try to kill you. Lots of points or prestige or rep or whatever, for killing a player.*

Then I do need to run!

You can't die here, Sebastien said patiently.

I can feel pain, though! The enemy was still charging toward her, but his claws and barbed feet were having trouble getting traction on the steep, muddy slope. *Unless there's a way to turn off pain responses, like there is in the Hypnos?*

A way to turn off pain? Now that wouldn't be very Axiomatic. You have more options at your disposal than these simulated peons, though, captain – you're a better class of bug-monster. I looked at the specs, and the basic weapons you started with are vastly superior to anything the cannon fodder down there gets. Point your spear-thing at our friend.

Callie obeyed, and the barbed head and the hook sprang out. *Now what?*

There should be a button on the pole.

Her lower right hand felt an irregularity, and she pressed it.

Without fanfare – no beam of light, no booming sound, no puff of smoke – the centaur-scorpion's head exploded, and its body fell down. None of the other battling creatures noticed – one more death on this battlefield barely rated attention. Callie slunk lower and crawled down the far side of the hill, away from the battle.

She examined the spear. There was another button, near the base of the staff. *What's that one do?*

Oh, it would have exploded the head of your enemy... and all his, mmm, affinity-mates? They can form squads, and gain collective bonuses, but those advantages are counterbalanced by vulnerabilities to certain weapons. You could have wiped out a hundred of them at once, tilted the battle decisively, and made yourself an enemy and... well, another enemy, of the players controlling those armies. Obviously the Axiom in charge of the routed army would be angry at you, but I'm sure the leader of the winners would be, too, since it would appear they needed help from a mysterious benefactor, and any sign of weakness is... not a good thing in this culture. I think you've escaped notice for now, though.

Callie closed her eyes. She did not want to come to the attention of the Axiom. She just wanted to find the control room, push a button marked "deactivate swarm," and get out of this hellish place. *What do we do now?*

Get somewhere safe where we won't be bothered, and let me read these help files. There might be some kind of local intranet, too – surely there's some way of organizing these skirmishes, and leaderboards or rankings? The Axiom like to gloat – I can't imagine they devised a system of competition that doesn't have a forum for the winners to lord it over the losers.

Callie was ashamed of how happy she was to crawl back into the filthy hole under the tree. She settled down among the wriggling verminous things – something told her she could eat them, and that they'd even taste good, but she refrained – and stared at meaningless glyphs streaming by in her vision, stirring only to open a new set of files for Sebastien when he asked. *This would be faster if you let me run the body,* he said. *What do you think I'll do, run off and join the monster army?*

I'd rather not find out what you would do, thanks. Especially since he had access to information she didn't, and could keep secrets without her even knowing it. *Hurry up and read.*

It took hours – or what felt like hours. She wondered if time ran at the same rate in the Dream as it did outside. In the Hypnos time wasn't malleable that way, but the Dream was a whole other level of technology.

I'm done reading, Sebastien said eventually. *Alas, we're fucked.*

CHAPTER 26

How so? Callie asked.

I was right. The Dream is a game. There are forty-seven players. They each control an entire spacefaring civilization, and they can engage in commerce with one another, command armies, hire mercenaries, commit genocides, and build cities — all in addition to having feasts, torturing defenseless simulations, and pursuing other Axiomatic hobbies. They periodically have battle royale tournaments, where they wage all-out war on one another, and the winner of that tournament gets to be the ultimate emperor, and live in the best palace and enjoy all sorts of extra advantages and pleasures. Although even the player who finishes next-to-last in the rankings gets to live a life of unimaginable luxury and rule over an entire civilization.

What happens to the last-place finisher?

It's unclear — the notes are written as if everyone already knows the penalty for being the ultimate loser. There's reference to "suffering slime" and "the torment of millions," neither of which sounds pleasant. All I can tell for sure is that, if you lose, you stay on the bottom, without a civilization to rule, until the next tournament, and then you get equipped with some lousy basic starter resources and a little time to build them up. It must suck being the suffering slime, or else it gives you a lot of time to think and plan, because the same player rarely loses twice, though they often finish near the bottom – there are whole forums devoted to the inspired stratagems the losers came up with to make sure someone else would finish just a little bit lower. The difference between last and next-to-last is vaster than the difference between first and next-to-last, in terms of quality of simulated life, for sure.

I don't care about Axiom games. How do we turn off the stupid swarm? Was *that* in the help file?

That's what I'm trying to say. Sebastien didn't even sound exasperated, which exasperated her greatly. *The winner of the tournament is in charge of all sorts of high-level elements of the Dream – adding new civilizations, spawning star systems, populating new regions of their imaginary multiverse – they have sole dominion over adding new parts to the simulation. Which, in practical terms, means they can create new things until they run out of processing power, and then they can deploy the swarm to increase the Dream's capacity. Which the current ruler has done.*

Callie nodded, though her body did something else that involved wiggling its horrid tail instead. *Does that ruler have a name?*

Now there was a hint of exasperation. *The Axiom don't have names the way you mean. Or, it's more like they have a hundred names. They know who they are. They understand everyone else solely in relation to themselves, so their nomenclature is context-sensitive and ever-changing, and they're more like titles than names – rival, ally, contemptible servant, brood-mate, exalted murderer, and so on. The emperor is just named "the ruler," from our point of view. They have a palace in a hollowed-out planet at the center of the Dream's most populous galaxy. There's a control center in the middle of that palace that controls the gatherers, and also has the interface used to create new simulated planets, stars, people, engines of war, everything.*

So let's sneak into the palace, Callie said.

Apart from the fact that we would definitely be captured and tortured for eternity if we tried, it wouldn't help. Only the ruler can activate the controls. See? We're fucked. We can't even join the game, because the other players would start asking who we were and where we came from – showing up millennia *late to a party is bound to get us noticed. You couldn't pass for Axiom under close questioning – not even I could.*

I thought you said they didn't care about newcomers?

They care about threats! Sebastien said. *Join the game and you become a threat, at least potentially. We need to implement Plan C.*

Not yet, Callie said. *Maybe we just need a different approach to Plan B.*

Callie made a door, and opened her eyes in the pod. Ashok leaned over her. "What's wrong? Did it not work? Were the sensory inputs incomprehensible?"

Callie lifted off the diadem, then took Sebastien's arm off her hip and climbed out of the pod as he blinked and came out of the Dream. "No, it worked fine. The sensory input was *too* comprehensible, if anything."

"You were only in there for a few minutes, though," Ashok said. "You didn't happen to materialize next to a big emergency power shutoff for the swarm, I'm guessing?"

"We were in there for at least several hours," Sebastien said. "Subjectively."

"Really? I don't quite understand how that works," Ashok said. "You should've brought a neurologist. But that's... Wow. The Dream must have been running for, like, billions of years, then, in terms of subjective time. What are they *doing* in there?"

"War-gaming," Sebastien said.

Ashok's ocular lenses spun; it was the equivalent of Callie widening her eyes. "Oh yeah? Was it cool?"

"They... play games?" Lantern gazed around the room. "All this power, all this potential... and they play games?"

"Games of conquest and subjugation," Callie said. "Axiom games." She went through a series of stretches while she talked. Maybe it had only been a few minutes of real-time, but she still felt stiff and uncomfortable, like she'd slept all night in a bathtub... next to an objectionable stranger. "Sebastien pointed out they could have galaxies in there, or even whole universes, so it's entirely possible they're doing other, more nefarious shit too, and the games are just what they do to unwind or pass the time. It's awful, though, even the little bit I glimpsed – simulations who think they're real and feel pain, dying on a battlefield in a literally pointless war. It's just fought for *points*."

"But the points do buy you power in the real world." Sebastien explained the ruler's ability to control the swarm.

"So what do we do?" Ashok said.

Callie grinned. "We find the leader's pod. We stick a knife in their brain or heart or whatever vital organs the Axiom have, rip the wires out of their head, and plug me in to take their place. Then I stroll through my palace to the control center and switch off the swarm and any *other* defenses this space station has."

"I thought that might be your idea," Sebastien said. "It's not bad. Except... how do we know which pod is the leader's?"

They looked up at the galleries rising around them. "There's no way to tell from out here?"

Sebastien shook his head. "Alas, there's no game file to access here, no options I can toggle to make helpful glowing icons float over the pods and identify their inhabitants. There was nothing in the files or discussion boards inside the game that talked about the location of the pods, either. The Axiom probably haven't even *thought* about their pods for billions of years, in their time. The Dream is all that's real to them now. It has everything they need. They'd be unlikely to give away any information that could be used against them, anyway."

"There are only forty-seven choices," Callie said. "Worst case, we do trial and error. How's the threat analysis going, Shall?"

Shall's war-drone crouched on the next level of galleries, manipulators doing slow passes over one of the pods. "I've only been working on it for five minutes, Callie. There are countermeasures and anti-tampering devices of various sorts in this pod alone. Give me some time."

Ashok picked up the dangling diadem. "Do you, ah, mind if I have a go?"

Callie thought about it, then shrugged. "Don't do anything to draw the attention of the actual players in there, but sure. And try to remember, the creatures you encounter... they can experience anguish. They might even have interior lives. They think they're real, even if they're not."

"I'm not a hack-and-slash carnage player, Callie." Ashok sounded offended. "I specialize in stealthy no-kill runs." He paused. "Except in games where pacifism isn't an option. Even then, I lean toward sniping." Ashok touched one of the metal plates on the back of his head and it slid open. He pulled out a wire, blew on the connector as if it might have gotten dusty in there, and plugged it into Callie's diadem. Then he settled himself down on the floor and crossed his arms over his chest. "Hello, cruel world." His glowing ocular lenses went dark.

Callie prodded him. "He looks dead. Did I look dead?"

"This is how it looks when he sleeps," Lantern said.

"I thought he *didn't* sleep, or that he only slept one hemisphere of his brain at a time?"

Lantern fluttered her pseudopods in the affirmative. "He used to do that, but I convinced him to take some aptitude tests and demonstrated that he was less efficient and effective when he operated under those conditions than he would be if he slept completely for five hours in a row, and was fully engaged while conscious. The difference was only a few percentage points, but say what you will about Ashok – he doesn't sneer at good data."

Callie said, "You, ah, spend a lot of time around him when he's sleeping?"

"I sleep even less than he does, so, sometimes." Lantern appeared entirely oblivious to Callie's subtext, though it was hard to tell with her: Lantern had been a truth-teller, devoted to honesty, for almost her entire life, and that had required her to develop all sorts of skills of tact and diplomacy, so she could avoid lying while maybe not telling the whole entire truth. Answering exactly what was asked, and ignoring whatever might be implied, was probably a core competency for her sect.

"You two are... close, though?"

"Ashok is my closest friend among the humans," Lantern said. "We have a great deal in common, and I've spent many happy hours in his machine shop. I miss him when I am away on my station."

They were circling closer to the source of Callie's curiosity now. "There's no one else you feel that close to?"

"Elena is a good friend as well. She's very kind. She is fascinated by the Free – by the idea of sapient alien life in general – and does not hide that fact, but she also doesn't look at me like I'm a specimen for study. She treats me as a person, whole and complete in myself. When we speak, she truly pays attention."

"You're right about that," Callie said. "We're lucky to have her in our lives." She cleared her throat. "So... where do I rank?"

Lantern said, "I have not ranked all the humans of my acquaintance on a scale from closest to least close, so I can't answer that question precisely. I respect you greatly, Callie, and believe that you respect me too. Your dedication to our mission is inspiring to me, and when I find myself doubting, and wavering, or being overwhelmed by the magnitude of our task, I take comfort in your strength and determination. I don't think you would argue if I said our relationship is less warm and convivial than some others, but if we were to spend more time together, and discuss our thoughts and feelings in an unguarded moment of peace, that might change. Considering that when we met we were mortal enemies, and that you nearly killed me more than once, I would say we've come a long way. I hope to see the trend continue."

Callie nodded. "I think that's fair. I respect you, and like you, too. I've just never been great at making friends. Ashok and I still mostly bond by making fun of each other. Elena... well, that's different. When it's romantic, or love, that sort of thing. You let your guard down more. Sometimes that's good, and sometimes that's bad. So far, with Elena, it's been good."

"Love," Lantern fluttered her pseudopods thoughtfully, in slow s-waves. "Humans are interesting. My people aren't mammalian. We do not huddle together for warmth. We have no hormonal reinforcement for such behavior. Once upon a time, we reproduced sexually, though we were capable of changing our sexes as needed to create the ideal ratio of fertilizers to egg-layers, and most of us spent time as both over the course of our lives. The concept of gender, as it exists in humans, with associated behavioral or social roles, existing independently from but often strangely entwined with sexual roles... frankly, it's all baffling to us."

"It's kind of baffling for us, too. These days, most humans just accept that people can identify as whatever feels right to them, and if they want to go to graduate school or a therapist to dig deep into *why* a given gender identity or blend of them or absence of them feels right, they're welcome to do so. People who've thought about the subject mostly agree that gender roles don't have any inherent basis in biology, and that gender is a social construct... but so are borders, laws, and money, and you can get killed for transgressing any of those, too." Callie cocked her head. "But... you go by 'she.'"

"Sometimes we choose to use particular pronouns, as I have done, but only for aesthetic reasons, or because it makes dealing with humans easier."

"Why did you choose feminine pronouns?"

"I find the sound of them more pleasing than the masculine pronouns in your language."

"That... is as good a reason as any, I guess. If it's not prying... do you have children? Sorry. Not to jump right into those deeper conversations we talked about."

"I don't mind. I have not contributed my genetic material to any offspring yet. Perhaps someday. The truth-tellers tend to reproduce by mechanical means, creating clones or mingling material from two or more elders to encourage diversity. We also take in young ones who've been orphaned or otherwise lack support."

"Romance isn't such a big thing for your kind, huh?"

"Some of the Free have embraced the concept. Among the truth-tellers, it is harder. We joke that human romance requires a level of deception that we are not permitted to indulge in."

Callie snorted.

"But we do feel... affinities for others," Lantern said. Did she glance over at Ashok? It was hard to tell when you were talking to someone with seven eyes: they were always glancing everywhere. "Closeness, and warmth. An ache when they are absent. A longing. A sense of completion when they are near. That feeling is not unknown to us. Is that romance?"

"Sounds like–"

There was a crack and sizzle, and Shall's war drone fell off the gallery above and crashed to the floor.

CHAPTER 27

Callie raced over to Shall, but the drone was already levering itself upright on multi-jointed legs. "Are you all right? What happened?"

"I was trying to circumvent some of the counter-measures in that pod. I... failed to circumvent the countermeasures. I'm all right, but if I'd been made of weak human flesh, I'd be cooked right now. That was the fifth pod I examined, and all of them have different defenses, Callie."

Sebastien strolled over. "Of course. The Axiom were deeply paranoid, except 'paranoid' implies delusion, and they were right to think everyone was out to get them. Just like they were, as individuals, out to get everyone else. They wouldn't have a single set of universal security measures. They would customize each pod for their own preferences."

Callie put her hand on Shall's armored carapace. "Are we screwed? They're unopenable?"

"Oh, I could open them. I am a one-drone army, after all. The process would destroy whatever was inside, though, and the pod might try to electrocute me or blow me up in return – and doing so might summon the swarm. Just because the swarm stopped at the door doesn't mean they *can't* come in under any circumstances. They're part of the station's security system. Right now, they still think we're penitents requesting an audience, and they're leaving us alone. If we prove to be a threat, their rules of engagement might change. There's no way to know. That said… there's one pod that's a little different."

"What do you mean?"

"Come up and see?"

Callie sighed. "Fine. Don't crush me."

Shall scooped her up in his manipulator arms, and then leapt to the next gallery, then up to the third, and on to the fourth. He deposited her gently next to a closed pod – the only occupied one she could see on this level. "See?"

Callie leaned over, careful not to touch the pod, since one of them had zapped Shall so grievously. This pod was closed, like the other inhabited ones, with a sealed seam running up the middle… but unlike the others, this one wasn't sealed perfectly. There was a puckered spot where the join wasn't perfect, a hole barely big enough to stick a couple of fingers in – not that she was about to stick any part of her body in there. It was probably a flaw dating back to when the pod was first closed.

"I wouldn't try to widen that opening," Shall said. "This pod has needles hidden inside it, and the needles are all covered in toxins. If you so much as press on the outside of this pod, the spines will pop out, and this thing will become less peapod and more cactus."

"But with poisoned needles."

"I didn't say it was a huggable cactus. That's just the first line of defense, appropriate for the crime of merely touching the thing. After that, it has nastier surprises."

Callie nodded. "That opening though... it's up near the head, too."

"You're thinking a laparoscopic approach?"

"I am. Keyhole surgery."

"Ashok has laparoscopic tools in his prosthetic arm."

Callie nodded. "I remember. When we did that escort job on, what was that planet, Illapa? Taking that oligarch to the mountain he'd bought so he could die on the summit, and we had to keep him alive for the journey, and Stephen convinced Ashok to add a suite of surgical instruments to his prosthetic, just in case. It was a good thing, too."

"Stephen was remote-controlling the surgical tools, though," Shall said. "They came out of Ashok's arm, but Ashok wasn't running them."

"That's all right. I wouldn't want Ashok mucking around inside my body, but this is basically an engineering problem. He needs to reach through that hole, disconnect the necessary cables, draw them out through the hole, and plug us into this Axiom's avatar."

"We probably can't do that while the Axiom in the pod is alive, though," Shall said. "It might wake up, or have a seizure, or who knows what."

"Ashok isn't a killer," Callie said. "I don't want to ask him to do that part."

"I try to see the Axiom as more of a malignant tumor to be removed than people with rights to be respected," Shall said. "Would you like me to do the... dishonors?"

"Can you?"

"Philosophically? With some difficulty. But if killing the thing in here proves too distressing, I'll just erase the memory of the experience. That's one of the advantages of being a machine intelligence."

"How about practically?"

"Oh, I can do it. Some of the pods have life-support alarm systems that trigger countermeasures if the body inside dies – I assume solely for purposes of vengeance – but this one doesn't appear to. Even if it does... I'm tough."

"I hate to ask you to do it–"

"Then you can be glad I volunteered. Can you get down by yourself? I'll... take care of this." Shall extruded something needle-thin and flexible from the end of one of his manipulator arms.

Callie patted his armor again, then went to one of the nearby pillars. They had spiraling ramps inside, leading up and down, and she walked back to the ground floor, thinking. If they succeeded in their overall goal, and exterminated the Axiom, all of them, that would be genocide. A crime the Axiom was guilty of ten, twenty, a hundred times over, to be sure. Were all the Axiom evil, though? The data they had certainly seemed to indicate the Axiom took active joy in slaughtering those they considered inferior, which was everyone... but she couldn't be sure. What if there was a group of good Axiom, somewhere, just peacefully relaxing in deep space, meaning no one any harm?

If there were, Callie would probably never notice them, and they could keep right on slumbering. These particular Axiom were devouring spaceships and the people inside so they could create an expansion for their favorite video game. Those acts of murder weren't even necessary to further their goal – the swarm could have gotten by just fine by converting non-living matter. The Axiom had programmed the swarm to avoid attacking Axiom vessels, so they could just as easily have programmed it to avoid living things. They hadn't, because they didn't care.

She was still glad she didn't have to ask Ashok to murder anyone in their sleep, though.

Lantern showed her the button that woke Ashok up, and he groaned. "Aw, really? I just stole this sort of flying war chariot thing, and I was doing a low flyover and checking out the territory. That battle I woke up near was just a minor skirmish, groups of scouts clashing, I think. The main battle was farther out, and they had these war machines, and this sort of, I don't know how to describe it, mobile corpse desecration factory? I guess it was meant as psychological warfare, or else it was an engine actually powered by corpses, I don't really understand the mechanics–"

"Ashok," Callie said. "Focus up. We've got a pod with a crack in it, and a dead Axiom inside. Can you reach in and snake out the cables so we can take its place in the Dream, with those tools Stephen set you up with?"

Ashok got to his clanking feet. "Sure thing, cap. Dead, huh? I'm guessing not from natural causes?"

"I'll tell you exactly as much as you want to know, Ashok."

"That's OK. I'm good. Where to?"

"Go up there with Shall." Ashok and Lantern gathered their tools and set off toward the nearest spiral ramp.

Callie beckoned Sebastien, who was staring up at the ceiling thoughtfully. She didn't like it when he thought. He joined her. "Yes?"

"We've got a player we can take over."

"And a one in forty-seven chance it's the ruler. Not wonderful odds, are they?"

"They're not. Assuming we're unlucky... how long until the next tournament?"

Sebastien gave her a chilly smile. "You want to play the game."

"I want to *win* the game."

"You don't lack for self-confidence, do you?"

"The fate of Owain is at stake. What possible good would doubt do me?"

"You have a... most remarkable mind, Captain Machedo. All right. As I understand it, any player can declare the start of a tournament. Everyone tries to be in a state of constant readiness, so they can compete successfully when someone does. Sometimes there are subjective years between tournaments, with all the players attempting to become as unstoppable as possible, and no one willing to trigger the event, and sometimes a new tournament is declared mere weeks after the last one, with those players who have some advantage attempting to strike fast before the others can develop their resources and replenish their forces."

"So, what, you just say 'one, two, three, four, I declare interstellar war'?"

"The process is a bit more formalized than that, but essentially, yes."

"How long do the tournaments last?"

"Hours. Days. Months. It depends. Those who feel

they can't win will offer their services as vassals to the players they think are stronger, because if the one they support wins, they are guaranteed a better place in the rankings – well above the bottom, anyway. But of course, betrayals and attempts to wrest control of alliances are commonplace. It's not just a battle game, captain. It's diplomacy, of a peculiar Axiom sort. It's logistics, supply chains, bluffs, double-bluffs, espionage. These creatures ruled a galactic empire. Everyone who wasn't Axiom was a slave, or they were dead. You really want to go up against them in a game of empires? You are... competent, in your way, but you're a fugitive hunter, a businesswoman, a ship's captain – not a queen."

"I beat you, didn't I?" she said.

Sebastien's expression didn't change. "I was beaten. You were there. I'll concede that much. I don't want to argue. I suppose winning the game is your only hope. I *do* admire your audacity."

"Your admiration is the thing I crave most," she said sourly. "Look, we can plug Shall into the game – he can offer advice on tactics and strategy, using his big computer brain. And aren't you half-Axiom yourself, in your head? That gives us an edge, surely."

Sebastien gazed up at the distant ceiling again. "I understand how the Axiom think, to some extent. But the implants they put in my brain, the things they did to me, the augmentations... they weren't meant to make me Axiom. They were meant to make me a useful slave. They didn't make me as smart as they are – they made me as smart as their *servants* should be. I understand the Axiom the way they'd want a servant to, so I can anticipate their needs and desires. That does give me insight, absolutely. But no. I'm not half-Axiom. I wish. The Axiom are engines of greatness, directed toward terrible things. If I had their resources, I would direct those energies elsewhere."

"You're starting to sound a little galaxy-conquery again, Sebastien."

He gave a sad smile and shook his head. "No. I'm done with all that. I would make the galaxy a better place, for everyone, and not just myself. I would build a better world."

"The first step toward a better world is keeping the current world from being eaten by tiny robots. Can you help me do that?"

Sebastien nodded. "Let's play, captain. Let's play for the lives of everyone on Owain."

Callie and Sebastien had to lay on the floor this time, since the pod they were hijacking was still occupied by the dead Axiom. She'd asked Shall if the creature was definitely deceased, and he'd said, "I was thorough. I'd rather not talk about it."

They still didn't know what the alien in the pod looked like. They'd never seen an Axiom in the flesh – no living being had, apart from other Axiom. Ashok's laparoscopic tools had cameras, of course, so he could see what he was doing, but all he saw was close-up bits in passing. "Its flesh is dark green, in parts," he said. "Unless I was looking at clothing. I didn't see anything that looked like eyes or a mouth or a nose. Lots of bumps that might have been sensory organs, but alien biology is more Elena's department. I just disconnected the wires and got out of there."

Once the cables were properly arrayed, Ashok hooked the diadems up to Callie and Sebastien, then ran an ancillary cable into Shall's central processor.

"It's going to be crowded in the avatar," Sebastien said.

"You'll just have to squish over to make room." Callie closed her eyes. "Let's get in there and see if we're the king."

CHAPTER 28

Callie rolled over in a pool, and smaller creatures rushed away from her, and then fluttered around, making alarmed chirping noises. The water in the pool was black, and warm – it wasn't even water, was it? Her body was immense, tentacled, buoyant – and hungry. The twittering things were much smaller than her, a bit like dark purple seahorses with arms, each with a single, large eye above its snout.

Sebastien translated. *They say you passed out. They're asking if you're all right.*

"I'm fine." The sound that emerged from her mouth – mouths, she had many, all over her body – was a grotesque bubbling. "Just drifted off for a moment. Carry on."

Unfortunately, "carry on" apparently meant feeding her, because they reached into the water and lifted out disgusting pink slug-eel things and started throwing them into her mouths. She swallowed instinctively – the worst part was, the slimy monstrosities tasted delicious, salty and fatty and luscious, and the texture was nice too, even though the slug-eels wriggled on their way down her many gullets. She was intellectually if not physically repulsed, and shouted, "Enough! I am full! Leave me!"

The attendants all disappeared beneath the water and didn't reemerge. *Where did they go?* She probed around under the black slime with her tentacles and found openings in the wall and floor in various directions – tunnels, leading elsewhere in... wherever they were.

She hauled herself out of the pool, which was easy, because her strength was as titanic as her body, and she had so many tentacles some dragged behind her, unneeded. She left a trail of black ooze as she tentacle-walked toward a huge arched doorway. The pool room was round, with a domed ceiling, and the next room was round, too, but seemed to be a shower of some kind – as soon as she stepped in, clear fluid sprayed from nozzles all around and above, washing the slime away. The fluid wasn't water, though – it was viscous and oily. But her body responded to it well. It felt good, relaxing, and restorative, like a good rub-down with lotion.

She moved into the next room, and there were more attendants there, though these were less aquatic, and furrier. There were squishy cushions everywhere, and tanks situated on pedestals every few meters, holding the eel-slug things. Bowls of snacks? The attendants chittered at her, and she bellowed for them to leave her alone. She dropped onto a vast cushion when the room was unoccupied, arranging her tentacles as comfortably as possible beneath her.

This is so gross, she said. *Am I the ruler?* She looked up and to the right, and Sebastien told her which glyphs to access.

Alas, no, he said. *You came in twenty-third in the last*

tournament – firmly in the middle of the pack. You were a vassal to the current ruler in that bout, but you held out a while before you pledged fealty – hence the lower standing.

Crap. Well, it could be worse. At least we didn't pick the loser.

How can I review our current resources? Shall asked.

Sebastien directed her to open the proper directories so Shall could catch up. Callie was annoyed that she couldn't read anything herself. She was fine with taking expert counsel, but it would be nice if she could at least read the material herself, too.

After a long time spent looking at information she couldn't parse, she said, "Well? Any preliminary findings?"

This world is largely aquatic, Shall said. *That seems to be your... the player's specialty – resource extraction and development of alien oceans. When it comes to protecting your territory, you're in good shape. You have vast navies of bioengineered leviathans, tiny infiltrating parasites, and all sorts of things in between. You're in an excellent defensive position across the breadth of your holdings.*

Your spacefaring assets are middling, Sebastien added. *Mostly a fleet cobbled together from your various temporary allies over the millennia. You wouldn't embarrass yourself in a fight, but you wouldn't be able to beat anyone in the top ten, either.*

Looks like our host has gotten ambitious lately, though, Shall said. *We've managed to get... they're little creatures, sort of like flukes... into the bodies of some of the enemy generals and officials, and they could be triggered to make their victims sick, or even to kill them. The whole biotech thing is solid for us. We've got some bioengineered spacefaring creatures, too, that feed on radiation. They're intended as ship killers, but they're still in the R&D phase.*

"Can we win the tournament?" Callie said.

Normally, the Axiom take a long view, Sebastien said. *They're not just thinking about the next tournament, or the next ten. As long as you don't come in last, you're still the ruler of a vast civilization, and you can position yourself for greater glories in the future. Think of how the Axiom behave in reality – they're already planning for ways to survive the heat death of the universe, and that's, what, trillions of years away? They are the ultimate long-term planners. But if we* don't *think about anything beyond the immediate future…*

I see what you mean, Shall said. *If we threw every single thing we had at the fight, burned every advantage, called in every marker, used up every resource, went absolutely entirely all in, even if it would leave us utterly emptied out and vulnerable at the end… What do you think?*

It's not like I'm an expert in Axiom game theory, Sebastien said, *but… I think we'd be competitive.*

"Let's do it," Callie said. "Let's survey our resources, deploy them as strategically as possible, and then declare war." Without even thinking about it, she reached into one of the tanks, snatched out an eel-slug, and munched it down. She'd wondered why the Axiom would choose to inhabit an avatar that could get hungry, but being hungry made eating so much more *satisfying*, didn't it?

She ate another one.

Sebastien and Shall looked over her resources while she explored the rest of her palace. She was underwater, in the interior ocean of an ice planet – shades of Ganymede – and there were ample observation areas in her palace. She reclined on cool tile and watched city-sized monsters sport in the fluid beyond, which was so clear it was like seeing demon-whale hybrids fly through the air. She ended up in a room with a pool of clear fluid in the center of the floor, and an attendant asked her if she wanted to go for a swim, according to Sebastien's distracted translation.

Callie agreed, and dropped into the water (probably not really water), finding it warm and pleasant, then she dove. The seahorse attendants followed along, trailing behind her, but she ignored them as she explored the depths, the grottoes and caverns, the reefs and stone forests, the spawning laboratories for the leviathans... and the punishment pits, where attendants who'd displeased her darted beneath metal bars, dodging to escape the unfurling jaws of predatory beasts like serpentine sharks. Bits of dead creatures and clouds of whatever they had for blood floated in the water there. "Set the prisoners free," she shouted, sending up streams of bubbles. "All is forgiven today."

The attendants were hesitant, doubtless expecting some sort of trick, but they obeyed, and the freed creatures fled. The predators chased after them, and Callie reached out with her mighty tentacles and crushed them, eating half of one before she even thought about it. Her body had its own imperatives, and if she didn't exhibit conscious control, she defaulted to them.

The thought depressed her, so she returned to the palace, and sat in seclusion while Sebastien and Shall plotted.

They were there for days of subjective time. Callie swam, sometimes, and tried to do good works – setting enslaved underwater miners free, feeding the hungry in the grotto-ghetto where a race of starfish people lived – but mostly she just kept to herself in the palace, trying to ignore her titanic and endless hunger. They discussed tactics and strategy, and she demanded supplies so she could draw on the walls of her meditation chamber, marking out the positions of various forces, because it was far too much to hold in her head.

She slept, sometimes, and Sebastien did, too, but Shall was tireless. On the twentieth day, he said, "I think it's been about eight hours in real-time. I should go back and let Ashok and Lantern know we're all right, and see if you two need to wake up to eat." Their bodies were being hydrated with IV drips, but Callie had told them not to resort to feeding tubes just yet.

Once Shall disconnected, Sebastien said, *Finally, we have a private moment to talk.*

Callie groaned, a titanic and bubbling sound. "What can we possibly have to talk about that you couldn't say in front of Shall?"

I'd like to make a deal.

"Oh, would you? Do tell."

You don't like me. You don't want me on your ship. I don't feel particularly welcome as a result. There are still drones hovering around my head, even now, when I'm in here, just in case I somehow find a way to make mischief. It's… wearying. I could attempt to win your trust, but I doubt I ever will – not completely.

"You're probably right."

Then let's part ways.

"When we're done here, I'll drop you off in the system of your choice."

You needn't go to that much trouble. You can just leave me here.

"Here? On Owain?"

Here, in the Dream.

"We're going to destroy the Dream, Sebastien. We're going to blow this whole place up."

No, you aren't. The White Raven *isn't a planet-killer, and this place has more mass than a planet. You couldn't actually destroy the whole engine, any more than you could bring down a skyscraper with your fists. There's no need to destroy it, anyway, once you turn off the swarm — the engine itself is harmless. Deactivate the swarm, and murder all the Axiom in their pods — I heard Shall say he can do that much — and then simply plug me into the Dream.*

"You'd starve to death."

There are feeding tubes, and waste elimination systems. The Axiom have varying sorts of physical bodies, so the feedstock must be adaptable. I'm sure things can be configured to work for my body. Ashok would find it an interesting engineering challenge.

"Assuming it's even possible... why do you want that?"

Because in here, I could build. *I can use the tools of the great masters to create something new, just for me. Even if you're right, and I am still a raging megalomaniac who wants to conquer the world... why not leave me in here and let me conquer something imaginary?*

"I'm not leaving you at the controls of a swarm of self-replicating machines and a bunch of terror drones, Sebastien."

He made a sound of frustration. *Damn it, Callie. You can destroy the terror drones when they're disabled. The swarm might be harder to switch off permanently, but you have a wormhole generator – you could come here and check up on me every week. You could leave drones monitoring me, and if I misbehaved, they could kill my body in its pod. You could wrap my arms around a bomb when you sent me to sleep, and blow me up at the first fluctuation in the station's heat signature. I don't need the swarm if I have multiple universes' worth of territory ripe for exploration – my body isn't going to live forever, just for decades. I won't run out of space. This could work, and you know it. This is a good solution.*

"I'll admit, maybe the practical problems could be overcome. But... this world, it's a bullshit place, Sebastien. It's not real."

What's real? It's whatever your senses tell you are real. I believed the simulation you woke me up in on the ship was real at first, and the Hypnos is primitive compared to the Dream. For a long time, I wasn't sure the real world wasn't a simulation, that you weren't testing me again – I had my doubts until you plugged me in here, honestly, and even now, I'm only ninety-nine percent convinced. This... it's real enough for me. I've lost everything. Let me gain something, please.

Callie shuddered at the thought of staying inside a simulation, where nothing was real and nothing mattered, alone. "Won't you go insane with loneliness? Even you?"

The Dream can create people.

Ah. There it was. "People you can control. So you're still dreaming the dream of mind-controlling the masses?"

The Dream can create people who think they're people, who act on their own initiative, who do what they want. I could even recreate my old life on Earth, with the loved ones I miss all around me. I could recreate the Anjou, *and we could finish our mission. I could—*

"You'd recreate your goldilocks ship? You'd make... a version of *Elena*? In here?"

Don't get emotional.

"A version of Elena who thinks she's the real Elena? Who still has a crush on you, maybe even falls in love with you, since in this new reality you'd never try to murder all her friends?"

So what if I did create a version of her? It wouldn't be your Elena. It wouldn't affect you at all. Is it that important to you, to deny me happiness?

"Maybe you'd have a version of me in the Dream too. A simulation that thinks it's me, one you can maybe chain up in a basement somewhere and torture?"

I AM CURED! he shouted in her head. *I was arrogant, I could be insensitive, I could be smug. I accept all that, but I was not a sadist, or a killer, or a criminal. I wanted to make beautiful things, wonderful things, for the satisfaction of the work and the acclaim of those I admired. I am now hated, despised by the only people in the galaxy I know, looked upon with pity at best by the woman I had feelings for, adrift in time and space and my own life. I just want to retreat, Callie, to a place where I have some control. Can't you understand that?*

Callie was silent for a long moment. *Yes. I understand.* Another moment. *If we win, I'll talk to Shall and Ashok and Elena about it, and if we think it's feasible, and there's a way to do it safely... yes. You can live in the Dream.*

Thank you, he said.

Don't mention it. Callie didn't like the idea, not even a little bit – when she'd realized he wanted to simulate Elena, he was lucky he didn't have a face in here she could punch – but she needed his help, and this would certainly motivate him. It would be nice to have him off her ship, and out of her life, by whatever method.

She looked up and to the left, and the door appeared. *Let's get something to eat, and then come back in here and win this stupid game.*

When she sat up, Ashok and Lantern were playing chess on a tiny board with tiny pieces. "Did you have that chess set hidden in your prosthetic leg?" Callie said.

"It's not all mini-drones and flash-bangs in there, cap," Ashok said.

"Where's Shall?"

"He went to send an update to the ship, upload his experiences to his main mind, and all that." Ashok moved a knight. Lantern chortled. Ashok said, "Aw dang. I didn't see that."

Shall came back – fast, his legs a blur. Callie leapt to her feet, thumbing the weaponry mounted on her suit to active. "What's wrong?"

"The *White Raven*," Shall said. "It's gone."

CHAPTER 29

Stephen was in the galley with Q and Elena, all of them doing their best not to worry about what was happening inside the blank silver sphere of the station. Callie and the others had been inside for two hours. Shall had promised to update them after eight. Time was crawling.

Q was telling them about her house and gardens on Owain, and how there was only a notional difference between inside and outside – the walls and ceiling were all retractable and windowed with smart-glass, so she could close them against wind and rain and opaque them for privacy, or open everything up to the sun and breeze and flowers. A creek trickled through her house, running under a transparent floor in parts, and open and accessible in others. Stephen thought it sounded heavenly. He hadn't realized how much he missed having soil under his feet, after all these years living on artificial habitats, but once upon a time, he'd loved gardens. How much of the past decade had been him punishing himself for his failures? Isolating himself so he wouldn't feel hurt again?

"We're getting a distress signal, XO," Janice called. "Somebody's having a real bad day on the other side of that asteroid belt."

Stephen groaned. He hated being second-in-command, because when Callie took a hands-on approach, it meant he was *first* in command. But what was the alternative? Drake and Janice wouldn't take the job – neither was willing to take orders from the other, for purposes of shared-body peacekeeping, and they couldn't do it jointly, because urgent command decisions couldn't necessarily be arrived at via gradual consensus building. Ashok would be the first to admit he'd be terrible as an executive officer, and Shall said if it was up to him they'd all retire and run a coffee shop on a nice peaceful space station somewhere. Stephen was the best and only man for the job. "Details?" he said. "Did someone run afoul of the swarm?"

"Not yet, but give them time," Janice said. "It's a wide-band distress beacon from a ship called the… *Malted Milk*? That's a stupid name."

"No. Oh no." Q put her head in her hands. "'Malted Milk' is a classical blues song. That ship belongs to a musician, one of the congregants who went missing – who died, out here, on a surveying trip. His son has been talking about going out to look for him, and I told him not to, that I'd handle it, but he must not have listened."

"Is he a teenager?" Stephen said.

"Ha. No. Jabar is thirty. He knows better. The *Malted Milk* hasn't flown in years, and it barely made it to Owain from the bridge in the first place."

"Sounds right," Janice said. "Their engines died, though they made it way past the bridge, maybe halfway

to the asteroid belt. Looking at these coordinates...
they're almost certainly in the path of the swarm."

"Oh, no." Elena hugged herself. "Those poor people."

"Has anyone responded to the call?" Stephen said.

"Not really," Janice said. "Everyone is so nervous
about the disappearances that there are no ships
anywhere off the planet right now, except the one at the
bridge station, and the port authority won't leave that
unattended. The people on the ground are arguing about
who should go fetch the *Malted Milk* back, but there's
no sense of urgency – the ship has working life support,
and supplies. Everyone figures they'll get bored, but they
won't die."

"Everyone doesn't know about the swarm," Q said.
"How close is it to the disabled ship?"

"All we have are projections," Shall said. "If we believe
what Elder Trogidae said about the swarm heading to
the planet right away... we don't have long before the
gatherers reach the *Malted Milk*. Maybe as little as an
hour. No ship could make it from Owain in time to save
them, anyway."

"They'll die." Q put her head in her hands. "I know
Jabar. I know his cousins, and I bet they're with him,
too. Jabar didn't think I was doing enough to find out
what happened to his father. He thinks my loyalties were
divided – that I care more about Almajara Corp than
about the church. Than I care about *him*."

Stephen didn't like being in command, but that didn't
mean he shirked the responsibilities. "We'll go rescue
them."

Elena looked alarmed, but didn't say anything.

"How?" Q said. "We're days away."

"We have a bridge generator," Stephen said. "We can jump to a point just out of their sensor range, and pretend we happened to be in the area. We'd better get moving. Saving you was all the last-minute rescues I want to engage in."

"Really?" Q said. "You're going to help them?"

"Captain Machedo is likely to be occupied for a while anyway. Shall? Janice? Can you get us a safe distance away from the station and then open a bridge? I don't want any motes of the swarm inadvertently slipping in after us."

"Aye, aye," Janice said.

Elena cleared her throat. "Can we leave... some sort of message for Callie, so she knows where we've gone? Like a beacon? In case she comes looking for us?"

"Good idea," Stephen said.

"I'll deploy a radio beacon now," Shall said.

"Calculating coordinates," Janice said.

"Engaging engine," Drake said. The ship hummed and began to move away from the station.

"Oh, shit," Janice said. "The swarm just ate the radio beacon."

"Yes, it did," Shall said.

Stephen closed his eyes for a moment. "All right then. We'll just have to hurry back before Callie misses us."

"Do we need to strap in, or anything?" Q clutched at the arms of her chair.

"No, it's just like going through the public bridges, in most respects," Stephen said. "Except... come to the observation deck." He rose and beckoned, and Elena and Q followed after him. "We can't see anything through the cameras, but if we look through the glass when it's transparent... you'll see."

They reached the observation deck and went up to the windows just as the bridge began to open, an inky blot of spreading darkness in space, edges uncurling and reaching out to envelop them. Their ship was pulled into the dark–

And then there was light, or rather lights. Rings of glowing white, set at regular intervals in the tunnel. "It's not dark." Q pressed herself up against the glass, as if to get a closer look. "The bridges... they're always dark. What *is* this?"

"We have no idea," Elena said. "Maybe all the bridgeheads lead through tunnels like these, and the others are just... badly maintained, with lights that don't work any more."

"It does make it clear these are structures that someone made, though, doesn't it?" Stephen said.

"The Axiom?" Q said.

"Maybe." Stephen watched Q watching the lights flash past, her face alternately dark and illuminated. His lady of brightness and shadow. His vision and his guide.

Q reared back from the wall. "What was that? Did you see? It looked like a hatch, or a window, in the tunnel wall, and there was something looking at me, with one eye – a blue eye, it glowed?" She looked at them searchingly

Stephen exchanged a look with Elena, and she shrugged. "I'm sorry. I didn't see anything," Stephen said. Maybe the stress was getting to her. But... hadn't Callie mentioned something similar about her journey with Shall through one of these bridges, after they destroyed the Axiom station last year? A feeling like someone was watching her?

Q kept staring out the window. "Can we... Is there a recording we can check? That was really creepy." They emerged from the tunnel and into regular space, and Q visibly relaxed.

"The tunnel can't be recorded," Shall said. "Just like the public bridges. We don't know why. You can look at it in real-time, if you're lucky enough to have biological eyes, but nothing shows up on the cameras, and according to my sensors, there's nothing out there at all. That's fine. I don't care. I have a mind as vast as a star. I'm not jealous of your meat-body eyes, with all your jelly and humors."

Stephen looked at the stars, but he was no astronavigator. "Are we in the place we're supposed to be?"

"We are," Janice said.

Q turned and looked at Stephen. "You really did it? We're here? That worked? It's... it's all true?"

"You saw the Axiom station. You still doubted my story?"

She shook her head. "Not intellectually. But the idea that you have your own personal bridge generator... It's like, if you told me you had a magic wand, and I smiled and nodded, and maybe even believed you, because sure, why shouldn't you have a magic wand – but then you pulled out the magic wand and *did magic with it*." She leaned against the window. "It's just really hitting me, is all. We can save Jabar. He'll be OK. I mean, he'll still be an asshole, but he'll be OK."

Janice said, "Want me to tell the kids on the ship that rescue is incoming?"

"Please do." Stephen sighed. "We're going to have

to stick them in a cabin and keep them away from our viewscreens. There's not time to take them home before we go back to the Axiom station."

"Why not?" Q said. "You can travel anywhere in the galaxy in twenty seconds!"

"We can't just open another bridge," Elena said. "The bridge generator has to recharge – it takes about seven hours."

"Your magic wand has to recharge," Q said. "I guess nothing's perfect."

"If we could get to Owain in seven hours, I'd take them home, and jump back to the Axiom station from there," Stephen said. "But it's too far away, so they'll have to ride along. We'll pick up your friends, move well away from the path of the swarm, and then jump back to the Axiom station as soon as we're able."

Elena nodded. "I'll make sure the spare cabin has everything they need, and oh, Shall, we have to kill the artificial gravity, can't have them finding out about that. And we should think about dinner, too, with more mouths to feed – can you cook, Q? It's Stephen's turn, but he's going to be busy XOing..."

Stephen smiled. "Maybe you should be XO. You have the energy for it."

"Just because I'm five hundred years old doesn't mean I have seniority." Elena bustled away.

Q came and leaned up against him, and he put his arm around her. "Is that all right?"

She leaned in closer. "It's a good start," she said. "I feel like everything I knew has been... explosively decompressed. It's good to have you here. Something solid. A place where I can stand."

"You can always count on me," Stephen said, and meant it.

Stephen and Q stood by the airlock and waited for Shall to link them up with the *Malted Milk*, a banged-up transport shuttle the approximate shape of a dented tin can. Without the canoe, they couldn't ferry anyone over, so they had to use an umbilicus to do a direct ship-to-ship transfer, and it was fiddly, making everything line up right.

"What are you going to tell Jabar?" Stephen said. "About his father?"

"I don't know. I don't want to give him false hope, but I don't want to lie, either. Though... I don't know for *sure* that he's dead. It's not like the swarm leaves bodies to bury. Maybe he just got lost, or stranded, or broken down, like the *Malted Milk* did."

"It's possible," Stephen said, and she nodded sadly. They both knew possible and likely were a long distance apart.

The airlock opened, and three people floated through. "Jabar." Q went to him with arms open, and after a moment's hesitation, he embraced her, the contact making them spin a half-circle in the air. Jabar was a lean man with a shaved head, skin dark brown and gleaming, face all sharp planes and angles. The other two were younger, but looked related – the cousins, probably.

"Q! You're really out here looking for my dad?" Jabar said.

"In a fancy ship flown by specialists, sent by Almajara, no less," she said. "I *told* you. After all we've been through, bringing Owain to life, building our world, you couldn't trust me?"

He hung his head. "I'm sorry. I just... needed to do something. Waiting was killing me." He looked at Stephen, eyes hungry. "Are you the captain? Have you found anything yet? Any sign of the missing surveyors?"

"I'm the XO," Stephen said. "The captain is off in our shuttle, investigating some unusual readings on the far side of the belt, while we search around here. We haven't found anything yet – no ships, and no people, but also no wreckage."

"You're the one who's part of the church?" Jabar said.

"I am," Stephen said.

"I'm glad. You know how important this is – how important community is. How we're all part of a whole. We can go on when we lose someone, but we're *diminished*. We are better whole. Thank you, for looking. It makes me feel better, knowing there's a person of faith out here, someone who thinks of my father as a person and part of the mind of God, and not just a number on a balance sheet." Jabar moved toward Stephen and opened his arms. "Is it all right?"

Stephen drifted into the man's embrace, and his cousins came in and hugged too, and Q as well. They stood silently, and they shared fellowship, and Stephen wished desperately that he could do more to help. But even this, even sharing his warmth and his presence with these people, *his* people – even that much mattered. Giving comfort wasn't nothing. Sometimes it was the only thing.

"Come on, J," Q said, breaking the embrace. "Let's get you and your friends settled. We'll get you back home soon, but we want to finish our investigations out here first."

"Of course," he said. "Keep looking. Can I do anything? I want to help."

"We'll let you know." Stephen watched Q lead them away – Elena was setting up a room for them, and she'd soon have them basking in her warmth, too, he had no doubt.

He missed warmth. He hadn't realized how cold he'd become.

"They seem nice," Shall said.

"Don't they?" Stephen said. "Can we give their ship a little nudge, send it spinning a bit, so the swarm doesn't eat it? The poor man has lost enough."

"I'll dispatch a couple of repair drones to tow it out of the projected path," Shall said.

"Thank you, Shall. After that… get us out of the way, too, and open a bridge back to Callie as soon as you can. Do you think she'll kill me for abandoning my post? Or will she understand?"

"She'll understand," Shall said. "Which doesn't mean she won't also kill you."

CHAPTER 30

"The ship wasn't eaten," Shall said, before Callie could even suggest the horrifying possibility. "The first thing I did was scan for energy signatures, and it looks like they left under their own power, through a bridge."

"Why the hell would they do that?" Callie scowled. "They must have had a good reason. Stephen isn't the sort to go joy-riding. Maybe there was a medical emergency and they had to get back to Owain, or the terror drones woke up again, or something. We just have to trust that they'll come back as soon as they can. We don't know when they left, so go check the door every half hour, Ashok, would you?"

"It doesn't even cross your mind that they've abandoned us here to die?" Sebastien said. "That they realized this endeavor is futile, and decided to save themselves?"

Ashok actually laughed. "Sebastien. You are, just... you're the worst. Stephen wouldn't do that. Shall – the other Shall, still on the ship – wouldn't do that. Janice might think about it, but Drake wouldn't even do that much. And Elena. Come on. *Elena*?"

Sebastien nodded. "I'll grant you Elena. The others I can't speak to, but... you're right. She'd die before she abandoned someone she cared about."

"That's the only reason you're here right now," Callie said.

"Yes. Consider me reassured. It would be nice if they'd left us a message, though."

"That, I agree with," Callie sighed. "All right. The plan hasn't changed. There's just some... extra background terror now. Let's eat, and then we'll go back into the Dream, and we'll win this game."

Callie floated in a sphere of liquid at the center of her royal battle cruiser, the feeds from every likely theater of the tournament projected on screens on all sides. "Is everything in place?"

We're ready, Shall said.

"Then let's do it." Callie opened the communication channel shared by the players, and spoke ritual words that essentially meant, "I now declare the tournament open," though there were more insults, threats, and bravado to pretty it up.

There was some strategic advantage to being the one to start a tournament. You were able to move your forces into place and declare war at the precise moment of your choosing, and there was a chance to catch the other players on their back feet (or tentacles, or whatever).

Of course, there were spies everywhere, and it was hard to mobilize forces on a galactic scale without someone noticing and preparing their own contingency plans. Callie, Shall, and Sebastien had set up lots of feints and false trails, and made it look like they were going to strike hard at the ruler, when in fact they were going after the one who came in number two in the last tournament, a player who'd declared their loyalty to the ruler early on because they knew that, despite impressive ground forces, they were vulnerable to orbital attacks.

Callie launched those orbital attacks now, dropping rocks from space down gravity wells, and devastating infrastructure on key logistics and resupply worlds.

Didn't you tell Ashok not to kill a single simulated soldier on a battlefield, because you respected their consciousness and their inner lives? Sebastien said. *And now you blithely massacre billions.*

"At some point you have to choose the real over the unreal," Callie said. "These simulations live in a nightmare world of endless conflict and torment. I'll end all their suffering soon enough, when we shut down the swarm and delete the Dream."

Still, they believe themselves to be alive – as alive as you or I. It's interesting that you consider me the criminal, when I never took a single life.

"Is it interesting?" Callie said. "I'd find it even more interesting if you shut the fuck up."

Reports poured in from all over the galaxy. Her infiltrating parasitic flukes had activated seconds after she declared the tournament open, and decapitated the militaries of two-thirds of the other players. That forced many Axiom players to stop focusing on the big picture and step in to deal with tactical decisions personally, in every individual theater of war, turning their attention to tasks they'd long since delegated to simulations of great military minds.

Every planet that had significant bodies of water near populated areas had been seeded with leviathan eggs, now full-grown and activated, and amphibious kaiju were wrecking all the coastal capitals and archipelagoes and lakeside resorts and river shipping hubs.

Callie's interstellar game was good, too: she'd poured tons of resources into finishing her spacefaring monsters, and they were playing merry hell with supply lines and destroying wormhole bridges and space stations all over the sprawl of empire, devouring radiation and growing larger and more destructive with every reactor they blew up.

Ten other players reached out to her, impressed by the ferocity of her opening gambits, and offered to ally themselves with her. She accepted them all – Sebastien and Shall had accurately predicted ninety percent of the offers, so she even had plans for how they should deploy their forces, to shore up places where her own resources were thin.

After two days without rest, swimming in a tank full of stimulants, they were gaining momentum, and had added three more vassals to their team. Her people were doing coordinated attacks now, pincering in around the ruler's faction, and knocking out key strategic targets, all with losses within acceptable parameters.

"We're doing this!" she shouted, devouring a dozen eel-slugs in celebration.

Things were going so well, until they weren't.

On the third day, one of her vassals betrayed her, attacking an allied force from the rear and destroying a whole fleet. That was fine – they'd expected some disloyalty, Axiom being Axiom, and Callie blew up the traitor's lead ship as a show of her displeasure. The player wouldn't die – they couldn't – but they'd have an unpleasant time drifting in the void until they could be rescued by allies from the other team.

Callie set her contingency plan in motion... but the contingency plan failed when the planet she'd intended to take over as a beachhead for the next stage of her invasion was simply gone.

They blew it up, Shall said. *The whole planet.*

Sebastien said, *I'm scanning now, and it looks like they destroyed... all our next targets for conquest.*

Callie was stunned. "They blew up their own planets? But... there were factories, soldiers, all sorts of resources..."

But you were poised to take them, Sebastien said. *The Axiom would much rather destroy something precious to them than allow someone else to have it.*

"How did they know what we had planned?"

You had to share some information with your vassals, Sebastien said. *They probably pooled their knowledge, and then simply extrapolated your next moves. The Axiom are very good at this.*

Callie was exhausted, and more than a little demoralized. "Crap. I thought we had this. But we're playing checkers, and they're playing chess. OK. Let's implement our fallback plans–"

No, Sebastien said. *We're playing hit-ourselves-in-the-head-with-a-rock, and they're playing Go. Our fallback plans have fallen apart, too. We just lost our home base. The ruler led a full assault on our royal planet, and took over the leviathan factories… which means control of the leviathans. Air, sea, and space. It appears an agent of the ruler promised our servants freedom if they cooperated, and our servants took the deal.*

That hurt. Callie had been trying, in her way, to make life better for the people of that world, but a few days of kindness (interrupted, she had to admit, by frequently yelling at them to leave her alone) couldn't counteract millennia of oppression.

The ruler executed the servants, of course, Sebastien said. *Killed the entire species, actually. Eradicated them from the simulation. The Axiom does love genocide.*

Those poor little seahorse-things. She hoped they hadn't suffered, but she knew better than to ask. "What do we do now?" Callie said.

I'm not sure, Shall said.

I am, Sebastien said. *We lose.*

They dropped in the rankings swiftly as all their vassals abandoned them, rushing to join with the ruler's faction while she was still accepting turncoats. Callie reluctantly opened a channel to offer surrender and support to the ruler, so she wouldn't come in last – there were a handful of unaligned players who would then fall beneath her in the ranking.

But the ruler wouldn't even acknowledge the communication, and soon all the other players had pledged as vassals to the ruler, or to the ruler's closest lieutenants. The tournament was over. Callie hadn't won. She hadn't even placed. She'd come in last.

Callie lost control of her vessel. A face, of sorts, loomed up on all sides of her tank, filling the screens. It was closer to a preying mantis's head than anything else, but more geometric, and made of shiny metal – like an abstract sculpture of a mantis, made into a gleaming cyborg. Words, full of buzzing and wretched harmonics, filled the room.

She's gloating, Sebastien said. *There are insults, too, but mostly it's gloating.*

I've got a handle on the translation now, Shall said. *Let's mute them, and I'll translate in real-time.*

The buzzing stopped, replaced by Shall's voice, sometimes halting as he wrestled with a translation, his tone never matching the content of the words. "Has your pod malfunctioned?" the ruler said. "Do you have, ah, brain rot – dementia? You wasted everything on this gambit, and for what? You offended me with the transparency of your attacks. You were duped by my vassals – why would you believe their overtures and promises? We attempted to trick you, and you fell for the first layers of the stratagem, when we'd planned such complex betrayals to come later – effort wasted on the assumption that you had some deeper plan. We have never seen such a pathetic, amateurish showing. You were never an inspired player, but you were always competent. After this, no one will even accept you as a vassal. You will be the suffering slime for centuries."

"OK, I get it," Callie said. "I made a big play, and it didn't work. I lost. You won. Let's move on with our lives."

"Such impertinence." The metal face was blank. "You will learn respect, of course. How long has it been, since you were the suffering slime? Almost a hundred million years, isn't it, and then only for one cycle? You always were good at floating along in the middle, following the safe path, avoiding the depths. That's why your boldness surprised us. I confess, I thought you must have some deep strategy in mind, because your actions were so incomprehensible, and I didn't imagine you could be as stupid as you seemed to be. But turns out—"

"Yes, OK, I'm bad at the game, I get it." Callie despaired over the failure of her plan, but her pride was also banged up pretty bad. She was reckoned a solid tactician by her peers in the security services, and while she probably shouldn't feel bad about being bested by hyperintelligent alien monsters with billions of years of subjective life experience... she did.

"Do not speak to me as an equal! Show proper deference, or your torments will be greater even than those usually inflicted on the slime. You will have ample time to think about your idiocy. We have talked, the other players, and we won't declare another tournament for at least a thousand years. Enjoy your time in the muck, ah, I'm going to assume that's some kind of vile expletive."

The screens went black. "Sorry about that, Callie," Shall said. "I moderated some of the nastier language, while still trying to give you the gist."

He made her sound practically polite, Sebastien said.

So what now? Shall thought. *Some of the pods have less formidable defenses than others. Do we try to crack one open, and hook ourselves into another player's avatar? Hope we hit the leader?*

"I was thinking..." Callie began, and then stopped talking, because she left her immense tentacled body, and she was in another body, and then she couldn't talk, because she was screaming. Sebastien was screaming, too. Callie couldn't even process the source or nature of the pain: there was blood in her eyes, she had no eyes, she was on fire, she was drowning, there was acid in her guts, she was buried alive, she was being chewed up in a great mouth, her limbs were being wrenched from their sockets, she was being shocked, she was being vivisected.

She tried to make the door open, to leave the simulation, but there was no looking up and to the left – she couldn't look anywhere, because she couldn't even understand what body she was in, and with Sebastien's screaming, and her own, she couldn't concentrate.

But Shall spoke in her mind, insistently, softly: *Go to the place without pain. Focus on the place without pain. Go there. Move away from the pain.*

Agonies surrounded her, but there was a part of her… not body, because she didn't have a body, or she had too many bodies – there was a part of *her* that didn't hurt. That wasn't in anguish, at any rate, and everyday pain was relief compared to most of her existence. She tried to focus on that part, to move toward the place of lesser pain. It was difficult. It was like trying to focus intently on the thumb on your left hand, while your right hand was being pounded into mush with a hammer.

Gradually, she focused, and narrowed her attention, and moved in some way that didn't involve actual movement, and that small space without pain grew larger. She drew that absence of pain – was there any greater pleasure? – around herself like a cloak, and she huddled. Sebastien was still screaming, and she called out to him: *Here, come here*. His wails slowed, and diminished, and then he was there, with her, in her mind.

"There" was huddled by a small fire in the dark

beneath a broken bridge. A river burbled nearby, stinking
of toxins, and the air was bitingly cold. The only light
came from the fire, and the two moons in the sky, both a
long way from full. Callie looked down at her body. She
was furry, with two forelimbs, one of them wrapped in
a bloody rag where the paw was missing. She had a tail,
and a pouch like a marsupial's, and her snout was long
and pointed, and the teeth inside it hurt. The gaps where
several teeth were missing hurt, too... but that pain was
nothing, nothing at all, compared to the horrors she'd
escaped. There was a rushing noise in her ears, the call
of distant torments, still there, just... put aside. "What
the fuck was that?"

*I have more experience with distributed consciousness than
you do*, Shall said. *When they ripped you out of your avatar,
they didn't just put you into another body. They put your mind
in many bodies, all at once. Hundreds of thousands, at least.
Maybe millions.*

The suffering slime, Sebastien said. *This is what it means,
to lose in a game of utter domination and humiliation. We've
become the oppressed. We're the ones who suffer.*

Shall said, *I've scanned the skies, through all the bodies
we have that are capable of looking at the sky just now, and
we're all in the same place. I think it's the ruler's hollow palace.
That's not a sky at all – it's the interior of her world. Those
moons are her personal residences.*

"The suffering slime are... the inhabitants of the
ruler's home world?" Callie said.

It makes sense, Sebastien said. *The Axiom love domination
over others, and their personal freedom, above all else. Being
trapped inside millions of slave bodies, forced to experience
those wretched lives, made powerless and subject to the will*

of another? That's probably the greatest humiliation the Axiom can imagine. Forced to serve, and to be casually, cruelly tormented? Because the mental capabilities of the Axiom are so far beyond ours, they would likely experience that whole gamut of suffering, all at once, for the entire period of their servitude. It's only our mental limitations that allow us to focus into a single body this way. For the Axiom, doing this would be like trying to feel just one single cell inside their body, and ignore everything else.

"You're telling me our punishment for losing the game of empires is that we have to be the downtrodden proletariat?" Callie said.

Basically, Sebastien said. *We are the tired, the poor, the huddled masses, the wretched refuse of the teeming shore, the homeless, tempest-tossed—*

We're the ones who are going to win after all, is what we are, Callie said.

CHAPTER 31

They left Shall in the Dream, because if the teeming masses suddenly became uninhabited, the ruler might notice. Shall had experimented a bit, and theorized that the suffering slime – ugh, the Axiom were awful – could go about their lives independently to some extent, following rote paths, but that they lacked the independent consciousness that other simulated inhabitants of the Dream possessed. The slime could forage for food and sleep and pick through garbage and hide without direction, but unless the overriding mind made them do something else, that was *all* they'd do, endlessly looping. Shall spread out as much as he could – he could direct a hundred or so bodies at a time – and tried to allay suffering where possible, but it was hopeless. There were toothed machines hunting them down. There were torture chambers. Furnaces. Drowning tanks. Pits full of monsters. Bloodsport. Hungry predators. The ruler's world was an engine of suffering, by design.

Callie sat in the canoe, hovering just outside the sphere, and waited for the *White Raven* to arrive. Her wait wasn't that long – they must have wormholed away not long after she first entered the station, fortunately. She opened a comms channel as soon as they appeared in the distance and began to approach. "Don't forget to radio the access code," she said.

"Thanks, captain," Janice said. "What would I do without you? I brushed my teeth with an arc welder the other day. I wish you'd been there to save me from myself."

"I suppose you'd like to know where we've been," Stephen said.

"I'm a little curious. Was someone hurt?"

"Some people from Owaln went looking for the missing surveyors, and their ship broke down, right in the path of the swarm. We went to help them. We have them on board, playing in the Hypnos... and completely unaware of our current location."

Callie said, "You did the right thing, except for the part where you didn't leave me a radio beacon with a message."

"We did," Elena broke in. "The swarm ate it. It's not our fault. Also I love you."

"Must you be romantic over an open channel?" Janice said.

"How's it going in there?" Stephen said. "Any luck?"

"It's a long story," she said. "But basically, right now, I need to know: how many drugs do you have?"

Stephen and Q joined her in the canoe, and they returned to the hub. "We have ample supplies – I stocked up on Ganymede," Stephen said. "But are you sure you want to do this?"

"Shall says my idea is sound," Callie said. "What's the

worst that could happen?"

"You could spiral deep into your own psyche, and discover dark, transformative truths about yourself?" Q said.

Callie shrugged. "That sounds fine. There's nothing in me I'm scared to face."

They landed inside the hangar, and the glowing clouds lit their way again.

Q huddled close to Stephen as they walked. "This is so bizarre," she said. "This place wasn't made by humans *or* Liars. What are the Axiom like? I mean, what do they look like?"

"The ones here, on the station? No idea. They're all snugged up in life-support pods. Inside the Dream, they appear in various avatars, but... they're not pretty, as a whole." Callie would never admit it, but she did kind of miss her tentacles: that sense of titanic strength had been intoxicating.

They reached the central hub, and everyone said their hellos and shared the general opinion that Callie's plan was ridiculous, but marginally better than no plan at all.

Callie jabbed her finger at Sebastien. "I need you. You're going to get some autonomy. Don't screw me over."

Sebastien leaned close to her and whispered, "Does our arrangement stand?"

"Yes. If we win, you get your stupid playground."

"Good. I would help anyway, because I am cured, and full of altruism, but I appreciate your willingness to help me in return."

"Shut up and take your drugs."

Callie, Sebastien, and Ashok made themselves

comfortable while Q and Stephen murmured together and discussed appropriate dosages. "Have you ever done anything like this before?" Sebastien asked her.

"No. I had a little fling with stimulants and focus-enhancing drugs in my younger days, but substances with more recreational or spiritual purposes never appealed to me. My doors of perception are already plenty wide, thanks."

"How about you, Ashok?"

"I have a button I can push that gives me a burst of pure euphoria," he said. "Thanks to an electrode nestled in just the right spot, deep in my brain. I had to put a governor on it, or else I'd just press it, all day long. That's enough drugs for me."

Sebastien nodded. "I did DMT once in college, and found it... very unsettling. I avoided other psychedelics after that. I suppose a drug like that must seem barbaric to you, Stephen," he called.

"Please don't blaspheme," Stephen said. "My mother was in the church, and I was named after Saint Stephen Szára, who studied the psychotropic aspects of dimethyltryptamine. Manske and McKenna are venerated by our sect as well. But, yes, compared to the sacraments we have these days, DMT is... it's a bit like comparing the *Spirit of St Louis* to the *White Raven*. This isn't much like DMT, though." Stephen held up a small vial that contained perhaps a half ounce of bluish fluid. "It should help with your too-many-bodies problem. It's the sacrament we use in the rite of separateness-and-merging, when many branches of the church gather together for a single Festival."

Q approached Sebastien with the same sort of vial.

"Open up. We'll dose you, then plug you in. The effects come on fast."

"Let's go storm the Bastille," Sebastien said.

"I never know what the hell you time refugees are talking about," Callie said.

Callie was hit with that all-encompassing pain again, but it seemed muted and distant, somehow – like taking dissociatives for oral surgery. The pain existed, and she could see it, but it didn't matter much. A warmth spread through her body – her bodies, so many bodies – and then a tingling effervescence that made all her limbs feel buoyant, like she just might float away. She laughed, a pure drunken sound of joy, and heard that laughter emerge from ten thousand throats. She looked around, and saw other faces, of all sorts – furred, scaled, feathered, insectoid, metallic, luminous – and some of those faces were looking at *her* faces, and it was like standing between two mirrors and seeing herself reflected into infinity.

That wasn't all she felt, either. Besides the vast but finite curve of her own selves, there were other psyches in there with her. Ashok was in her head. Wonderful Ashok, sweet Ashok, the irrepressible, the exploratory, her partner in adventure. And Shall, her Shall, better than the man he was based on, who would die for her, but who would much rather live for her.

And Sebastien. She was struck by an overpowering wave of sympathy for Sebastien. He'd lost all the same things Elena had lost, but unlike Elena, he'd gotten nothing in return – certainly not love. He'd suffered at the hands of the Axiom more directly than anyone else, and he continued to suffer. Was he kind of a jerk? Yes, sure, but Callie herself could be abrasive and impatient and uncompromising. Did she deserve to be an outcast for that? Did he? Did anyone?

The Axiom did. The Axiom were the cold spot in the haunted house, the black hole at the center of the galaxy, the necrotizing spot in the healthy flesh. No. The Axiom were what demons would be if demons were real: creatures intent on torment for torment's sake. Good. Callie had been afraid the sacraments of the Church of the Ecstatic Divine would make her into a touchy-feely-love-everyone-equally idiot, but it didn't. It just made her feel connected to other people, and other living things, and if anything, it made her more angry, more boiling over with fury, at anyone who would knowingly cause others to suffer. The sacrament ramped up her empathy, it expanded her perception–

It allowed her to make ten thousand bodies turn as if they were one. Their separate pains and maladies and injuries all merged and flowed, and she let peace and warmth and belonging spring forth from the center of her, and pass into all of them. She could focus, if she had to, through one set of eyes (or other sensory organs; why was she so focused on sight, when smell and hearing and the vibrations of the air on skin were just as informative, if she paid attention?). Or she could see the vast panoply of the ruler's world through many bodies at once.

Ashok was hooting with joy, somewhere in her head. *Some of us can fly!* he cried.

Sebastien was in her head, weeping, saying, *I'm sorry, I'm sorry, I'm so sorry, I didn't know*, over and over.

Shall said, *Well, you're definitely all tripping. Do we have a plan here?*

I have ten thousand bodies, Callie thought. *How about the rest of you?*

About that, yeah, Ashok said.

Sebastien?

I... What? Callie? I didn't understand, I couldn't feel it – it's like if someone says they're freezing but you don't feel especially cold, of course you think it can't be that bad, that probably they just want attention, or else they're weak, or a whiner, or they love to complain, but really they're just so cold–

Shh, she said. *It's OK. You're warm now. Can you do this? For all the people on Owain?*

I can do this. I have... yes, thousands and thousands.

Callie smiled with ten thousand bodies, in a hundred different ways: blinkings of eyes, wagging of tails, undulations of tentacles. *And Shall can run the rest of them, jump around, put them on paths, have them do the big messy diversions, right?*

That's right, Callie, Shall said.

Then long live the revolution, Callie said.

There were millions of them. Shall sent the masses he controlled against all the ruler's enforcers, torturers, overseers, and lieutenants. His hordes tore open the jails and the pits, the arenas and factories, the oubliettes and snuff brothels, the drowning pools and experimental domes. Those newly freed ran when they could, or flew, or jumped, or limped, or were carried by their fellows. Every object that could be picked up became a weapon in the revolution... and there were surprisingly few simulated guards to stand against the uprising. The Axiom didn't believe in the power of the masses. It had taken a different kind of mind to conceive of the collective strength of the tormented and the voiceless.

Callie, Ashok, and Sebastien focused their thirty thousand on a different outcome: not general mayhem and devastation and disruption, but a targeted strike. Callie had worried that focusing while under the influence of the sacraments – the *drugs* – would be difficult, but in fact she could look at something with more depth and precision than she ever had before, perceiving more detail, and discovering overlooked nuances. If anything, she risked looking at things *too* deeply. But Shall was a murmuring voice, guiding them, reminding them, stirring them from the reverie of gazing at ten thousand paws or hands or claws and marveling at the way they moved just because you *wanted* them to – wasn't that a kind of magic?

The ruler lived in twin moons floating at the center of a hollow sphere, but there were ways to get there: teleporting booths, and trams, and huge flying transport ships, because sometimes the ruler entertained in her palace, and sometimes that entertainment required large numbers of the suffering slime to endure some hardship or humiliation. Parts of Callie's consciousness were already in the palace, acting as servants or weeping in cells, and she coordinated those to throw open the doors and turn off defenses. Many of her bodies were killed by the palace guards for their insubordination, but there were more on the way, pouring in through loading docks, crashing down through skylights, battering down doors, and every body she lost just allowed her to pick up another. There were millions of bodies. They were too many to stop.

Callie's and Ashok's hordes engaged in battles with the vastly better armed forces inside the palace, but the ruler's people couldn't stand against the onslaught of thirty thousand enraged peasants. Sebastien's horde smashed up the communications systems and seized control of the palace's defenses, cutting off contact to the outside world and destroying the few defenders who tried to rally to their leader's aid. This was the inner sanctum of the most powerful Axiom in the Dream, after all, and while the hollow moon's defenses against any outside attacks were probably undefeatable, no Axiom expected this sort of attack from the *inside*.

Callie's horde smashed down the barred and locked doors that guarded the ruler's private suites, and poured through.

Callie didn't have to jump from body to body or shift her attention around any more: she saw everything, all at once, through all her eyes. There were corpses decorating the walls here, in various stages of mutilation and decay. There were implements of death. There were holographic displays of past, grisly triumphs.

The mantis-like ruler scuttled out of a pile of twigs and dirt the size of a cottage – its bed – wielding a scepter. "So, the suffering slime rises up," it said – or so Shall translated. "A new gambit, and one I did not expect. There is no tournament now, slime. This will not help you in the game. Is it just revenge, then? I'd thought better of you. Not much better... but a bit."

"We have demands." Callie tried to speak from just one mouth, but she was too spread out now – too dissolved in the sea of bodies – and so a hundred voices shouted it.

"Do you?" The ruler lifted the scepter, a rod of greasy-looking black topped with a one-eyed skull cast in silver. "I don't have any demands. But I have a weapon that will kill all of your bodies in a single stroke... except for one. One single cell of suffering slime to contain the vastness of your mind, sibling. And, oh, the fun we'll have." The ruler swung the scepter.

CHAPTER 32

Callie said, "Are you done?" through a hundred throats.

The ruler reared back on its scuttling multitude of legs, then swung the scepter again, hard and downward, more viciously. Then it shook the scepter, like it was a flashlight with a loose connection, and swung again.

A dozen of the horde darted forward and plucked the scepter from the ruler's hand, dashing the weapon against the stone-like floor. They seized the ruler's limbs and began to drag it across the room, toward a disc in the floor that served as an elevator to the lower levels. "Impossible!" the ruler howled.

"I had bodies in the palace," Callie said. "I had bodies *in this room* – those are some of me, in pieces, pinned up on your walls! You think I couldn't creep in while you were elsewhere and break all your shit? I broke all your shit." Another ten or twelve of the horde crowded onto the silvery disc. "Take us down."

"No," the ruler said.

Callie tore off one of the ruler's legs and threw it across the room. The ruler howled. "Did that hurt?" Callie said. One of the horde, with deft fingers on four hands, brandished a set of syringes, then jabbed them into the joints between the ruler's legs. Callie ripped off another leg, and the ruler screamed until it ran out of breath, and then just gasped. "You've been injected with pain enhancers. A favorite technique among your torturers. We gave you a quadruple dose."

"This is pointless," the ruler panted. "You can't kill me. None of us can kill one another."

Callie concentrated hard and sent one body to stare into the blank metal diamond of the ruler's face. "Kill you? I am the suffering slime. I know as many torments as I have bodies, and I will visit them all on you, if you don't give in to my demands. You say I can't kill you. I know. Isn't it wonderful? No matter what I do to you... you'll never die." She reached out – this body had a stump of a paw, wrapped in filthy bandages. Was this that first body, the one she'd found refuge in right after she lost the game? That would be nice.

She caressed the ruler's metal face with the dirty bandage, leaving a smear. "You're one of the best of us. You've never finished lower than twelfth place. You've been ruler more often than anyone else. This is going to be a new experience for you. Isn't it wonderful, that after all these billions of years, you can still experience something *new*?"

Callie ripped off the ruler's mask. It wasn't just something the leader wore – it was attached, somehow, embedded, and when it came free, flesh ripped. The visage underneath was horrific, all squirming meat full of eyes and mandibles.

"Tell me what you want," the ruler said.

• • •

The control center was less grisly than the ruler's private rooms: a round, cozy space, with a console at the center, and various screens and interfaces. The leader hunched over the controls, mouthparts moving, and Shall's voice translated their words, with occasional pauses as he pondered word choice. "This is absurd. I'll accept almost anything within the context of the game, the only rule there is to win at all costs, but what you're asking... You know there's too much at stake, sibling. We need those processors for the next stage of the simulation. We have to finish testing the efficacy of the... something... tunneler. Quantum tunneler?" The leader turned their head and looked at the horde, in what Callie assumed was a baleful fashion. "Just because I'm leading the project, you want to spoil it? You're that upset at the prospect of a thousand years of torment? The Dream has made you weak. Or... were you a spy all along? Have you been waiting all this time for an opportunity to disrupt the great work? I knew you were too close with those... ah, rewinders? Those-who-go-back? Something like that. You spineless spy, you treacherous scum, etc., ah, wait, this is interesting – they're coming, aren't they? Your old friends. Coming to destroy our work before it can interfere with *their* plans."

It thinks we're working for a rival faction of the Axiom, Sebastien said. *It doesn't even occur to the ruler that we could be anything else. Certainly not some lesser species.*

I like flying, Ashok said dreamily. His horde was outside, guarding against interruptions, in theory.

"Just do as you're told," Callie demanded from a score of throats.

The leader stroked the screen. "It's done. The others

will know something's wrong, you know. The… encourager of efficacy? Efficiency expert? Something like that… will wake in the engine of the Dream and tear open your pod and kill you. You'll–"

The horde grabbed the leader and dragged it bodily into the corner while Callie took her one-handed body to look at the screen. *I don't know what I'm looking at,* she said.

She felt Sebastien's attention shift, and he was in this body with her, an intimacy that would have been repulsive not so long ago, but now felt, if not good, then at least natural. *The ruler did as it was told,* Sebastien said. *Recalled the gatherers, and told them to go inert. Stood down the terror drones and the station's other defenses too.*

That stuff about an efficiency expert? Callie said. *That sounded… ominous.*

We'd better get back to the waking world, Shall said.

Callie sobered up fast – Q gave her something that counteracted the effects of the sacrament – and found herself faintly embarrassed by the banality of her epiphanies. We are all one, everything is connected, none of us are free so long as one of us is in chains… it was the stuff of inspirational posters, but it had burst in her mind like divine revelation.

Maybe some of it was a little bit true, she conceded to herself.

"So, what do you think the odds are we make the whole station blow up?" Ashok said. "One in four? Worse?"

"The Axiom hate each other," Shall said. "I don't think they'd allow the destruction of one of their pods to trigger some self-destruct sequence that would destroy all the others. They're probably in there plotting to murder each other's real bodies all the time anyway."

"Sure," Ashok said. "But one of them could have set up a failsafe thing, you know – if I can't get mine, you won't get yours either. They could have sewn atomic bombs into their bodies. There's no telling."

"That's reassuring, Ashok, thank you," Shall said. "Just plug in the thing, please?"

Callie wobbled upright. Shall was still in the dream, keeping the ruler under control, but he was out here too, splitting his attention, directing Ashok to set the last charge.

"We have to go fast," Callie said. "Minutes in here are hours in the Dream, and the other players will start to wonder what's going on when the ruler stays incommunicado. If they realize there's a threat to the station, in the real world... I don't know what will happen."

A pod on the lowest level burst open with a shrieking tear, and a limb – an arm? a tail? – unfolded from the torn seam, joint after knobby joint, extending upward. Spines ran along the length of the arm, and at the end, a mechanical claw whirred and spun. The encourager of efficacy? Suddenly, Callie wasn't curious at *all* about what the Axiom really looked like inside those pods.

"Now!" Callie shouted, and Shall set off the charges.

They'd used directed explosives, their energies pointing inward, but even so, the flashes of light and heat that filled the space left Callie dazed and blinking even though she'd closed her eyes. When she could see again, she was impressed: there was just a black shadow of ash where the splitting pod had been, and a fragment of arm, or tail, or whatever, with a twisted metal claw at the end, smoking a few meters away. "Very efficient," Callie shouted over the ringing in her ears. "The expert would approve."

She did a quick check, to make sure all the inhabited pods were ash. The Dream engine was now populated by forty-seven dead Axiom. That was a good day's work, and, if Lantern's estimates were correct, a not inconsiderable percentage of the race's total population.

"Should I switch off the simulation, Callie?" Shall said. "I've got access to the root controls in there. I discovered a whole different set of admin privileges, related to being a project leader, instead of just winner of the game – which our overthrown ruler was, apparently. The admin panel was locked with biometrics, but fortunately, the ruler's body is still in here, so. I've already taken the liberty of turning off the… something… tunneler project. It was occupying fully seventy percent of the station's processing power. The game was just what the Axiom did to pass the time while that program was running, I think. Like a coder playing video games while they wait for their code to compile."

"Good work. As for turning off the simulation… give me a minute."

"Give you a subjective *hour*, you mean. Communicating with myself across non-matching timescales is very disorienting, Callie."

"You'll live." She walked over to Sebastien, who sat, knees drawn to his chest, hugging himself. Q and Stephen were on either side of him. "Is he OK?" she said.

"He doesn't want the counter-sacrament," Q said.

"I don't want this feeling to end." Sebastien looked up at Callie, his eyes shining with tears. "I haven't felt like this since I was a little boy, with my mother holding me and singing me to sleep. Maybe not even then. I... Everyone else always seemed so *thin*, Callie. Sometimes they were interesting, usually they were boring, but always like they were made of tissue paper and popsicle sticks."

"Ha," she said. "I always knew you were a psychopath."

He winced. "I don't know about that. Maybe just... self-centered."

"A narcissistic personality disorder was also on my list of informal diagnoses," Callie said.

Sebastien hitched out a sob. "I... I didn't know I could feel this way. Like I'm *part* of something. Like I have a purpose within a greater context. When the drugs fade, will this go away?"

"Most members of the church report positive long-term outcomes, psychologically speaking," Q said. "They self-report as being more thoughtful, more empathetic, and more aware of the impact of their actions on others, after taking these sacraments."

"The intensity fades, of course," Stephen said. "And there can be a let-down as your brain chemistry adjusts. Sometimes serious depression. But that's why we have meetings, and fellowship, and lesser sacraments, as well as the Festivals. To help us refocus and re-center. The sacraments reveal the truth, that's all: we're stronger as a community. We're better together."

Sebastien just nodded, still crying.

"I'm glad you're getting in touch with your feelings," Callie said. "Do you want to go into the simulation, or what?"

"What?" Q said.

"We made a deal," Callie explained. "If he helped, he could stay in the Dream, the only real boy in puppet-land, and enjoy exploring his God complex. Shall's in there with his finger on the 'delete' button, Sebastien. So does he switch off the universe, or leave a light burning in there for you?"

"I don't want to dwell forever among shadows," Sebastien said. "Even if the people I created in the Dream thought they were real, they'd just be aspects of myself. Reflections. Hopes. I want... to find my place in this world. Could I come to some of your meetings, Q?"

"All are welcome," Q said. "Unless they act like total assholes. Then we kick them out."

That's gonna be a high bar for Sebastien to clear, Callie thought. "Shut it down, Shall," she said.

Back on the *Raven*, they set more explosives on the terror drone asteroids, and moved a safe distance away from the station. "Let her rip," Callie said. She watched through the magnified viewscreens as torpedoes sped toward the hub. Destroying the Axiom was just step one. They needed to make sure no one else wandered by and plugged themselves into one of the other pods. It was true they couldn't annihilate the station entirely, but they could fuck up the central sphere beyond repair. Without that control center, the rings were just broken computers with all their data wiped, incompatible with all other operating systems anyway.

The sphere exploded, flinging debris out through the no-longer-spinning rings, smashing chunks of them into whirling fragments. The asteroids and terror drones were nearly vaporized, the charges Ashok and Shall had planted probably complete overkill, but they didn't want chunks of even partly intact Axiom war machinery falling into the hands of passing explorers.

There was a deactivated terror drone in the cargo hold, though, because Ashok had begged, and he'd been a good boy all year. He just wanted to take it apart and see how it worked, not conquer the universe or anything. From him, Callie believed it.

"Good enough?" Callie said.

"There's a debris field, but people will assume it's some Liar artifact if they encounter it," Shall said. "The swarm appears to be just inert matter now, and with the Dream deleted and access to the simulation cut off, there's no way to turn them back on."

Callie swiveled her chair and faced Q, who'd requested a front-row seat to the destruction. "Well, supervisor? Did we fulfill the terms of Almajara Corp's contract?"

Q nodded. "You did."

"What's your report going to say?"

"That you discovered an abandoned facility with automated defenses, presumably built by a group of unknown Liars, out near the asteroid belt, and that you destroyed it. We didn't find any of the missing surveyors or auditors, but based on their coordinates at the time of the disappearances, we're confident the abandoned facility was the problem."

"Don't be afraid to recommend us for a bonus." Callie switched to shipwide comms. "Mission accomplished, everyone. Good work. Take it easy on the ride back to Owain. We'll drop off Q and our friends from the *Malted Milk* and then, unless anyone has a better idea, the rest of us will head back home to count our money."

"About that," Stephen said on her private channel. "Could we talk in person?"

CHAPTER 33

Elena sat on her bunk – she almost never used her room, since she tended to sleep with Callie – and leaned her head against Sebastien's shoulder. "I just got you back. I just *barely* got you back."

He leaned his head against her own. He could do that, now that hummingbird-sized drones weren't buzzing around him all the time. "I know. You can visit me, though. I'd like that. But there's work for me to do on Owain. The things I joined the goldilocks mission to do – create settlements, set up infrastructure – they need that kind of work here. There's a church, too. A community. I think I need that, to keep myself from getting… lost inside my own head. Are you sure you don't want to stay? It's beautiful there, from everything Q has told me. Like a dream of what Earth could have been. A paradise."

"I've got my paradise already."

"Captain Kalea Machedo. I… don't know what you see in her, Elena."

"Pfft. Sure you do."

He chuckled. "She is formidable. I can imagine, if she was on my side, instead of against me, that would be comforting."

"She's also hot as hell. And a good person, Sebastien. She never pretended to like you, but she kept you on her ship, and gave us resources to help you, and she never complained – much – even when saving you seemed hopeless. She did all that for me, because you were important to me, and I'm important to her."

Sebastien kissed the top of her head. "Then you're lucky, and I'm glad for you. Will you visit me sometimes?"

"Of course. Owain is just a wormhole away, and it's not even going to be eaten by nanobots any more."

Callie and Stephen sat in his quarters – the second-best on the ship, after hers – and sipped glasses poured from an ancient bottle of bourbon he'd been carrying around since he left Earth. "Never had the right occasion to open this before," he said. "Cheers."

"Fuck you." She slumped, staring into her glass. She'd coveted this bottle for a decade, and now that she had a glass in her hand, she couldn't even enjoy it.

"Don't be like that. You don't have to cash me out all at once."

"Fuck you. You think this is about money?"

"Then what is it about?" he said mildly.

"It's about me and you," she said. "You were the first person I hired, XO. I was full of fire and rage, and I was going to be the best, the fastest, the most feared captain in every system I touched. Then you came along, solid as bedrock, and kept me from getting myself killed or arrested or arrested and then killed in jail."

"There were some near misses," he said. "That one time on–"

"Fuck you. Don't reminisce. You're *leaving* me."

Stephen sighed. "I'm older than you, Callie. I thought all this sort of thing... caring about someone, this way... I thought all that was behind me. Even when I met up with my congregation on Meditreme Station, even during the Festivals... I barely felt anything, to be honest. I did it because feeling something was better than nothing. A part of me always stood back, though, and watched. I observed myself having feelings, instead of just feeling them. Q... I don't know. She lights up parts of me that haven't been lit up in a long time. She wants to see where this goes. I want to go where she does. You understand."

"She can come on the boat," Callie said. "We got rid of Sebastien, so there's room. We could use, I don't know, a logistics and supply person. We need logistics and supplies."

"She has work to do on Owain." Stephen enfolded Callie's hand in his own. "Good work. They need surgeons there, too. They have entirely too many paintbrushes and not nearly enough scalpels down there. The work you're doing, against the Axiom, is crucial, and I respect the hell out of you for doing it, but... I don't want to die in space, Callie. Not when I could live, really live, on the ground. What would you do, if Elena wanted to settle down?"

Callie slumped. "I don't know. I think part of why I love her is because she *doesn't* want to."

"I wish you both all the happiness in the world," Stephen said. "Can you wish the same for me?"

"Ugh. Yes. Fine. But you're not rid of me. I'm going to visit you, old man," Callie said. "And you'd better not put me in a guest house that's shaped like a boot or some shit. You'd better find me a *house*-shaped house."

"It's been an honor serving with you, captain." He raised his glass.

"Fuck you," she said again. But she clinked her glass against his.

They had a raucous farewell dinner on the way to Owain. The crew of the *Malted Milk* regaled Stephen and Sebastien with tales of life on the planet, and everything they had to look forward to there – the projects, the plans, the parties. The crew told Q all the funniest stories they had about Stephen, which usually involved him being long-suffering and doleful in the midst of various sorts of chaos, devastation, and danger.

"This cuddlebot smuggler put a *gun* to his head," Ashok said, "and Stephen goes, so deadpan, 'Could you please point that elsewhere? I keep my brains in there, and someone in this room should retain the ability to think.'" Laughter, and drinks, and toasts all around. It was a good farewell.

Callie and Elena sat in the corner, and watched. "You're going to miss Stephen, huh?" Elena said.

"He was like... a non-shitty stepfather to me." Callie shook her head. "Anyway. It is what it is. How about you and Sebastien? He's like his old self again, huh?"

"He's arguably better than his old self," Elena said. "But I never expected him to stay after we cured him. It's hard to see quite how he would fit in on the ship."

"Ha. Yeah, that wouldn't work out. He's too much like me."

Elena turned and looked at her. "What do you mean?"

She shrugged. "Confident, sometimes to the point of arrogance. Smug. Always thinks he's right." She grinned.

"Too pretty for his own good."

"You're prettier."

"You look upon the Machedo nose through eyes of love."

"If it's attached to your face, it's the best of all possible noses." Elena sighed. "I'm going to have to study my ass off, Callie, if I'm going to be the ship's doctor. Stephen showed me a lot, and he's given me all the resources I could ask for, but I want to do this right. There are classes I can take in the Hypnos, and eventually I can try to get properly licensed. I'm going to be busy for the next couple of years."

"You're going to be even busier than you think," Callie said. "I talked to the crew earlier today. We're all agreed. You should take over as executive officer."

Elena sputtered and almost spit out a mouthful of punch. "What? That's... I just got here. I'm not qualified."

Ashok clattered over and sat down. "Did you tell her? You told her. Ha." He saluted drunkenly. "Aye, aye, XO."

"Him! It should be Ashok," she said. "He's worked with you for years, he's experienced, he knows the ship–"

"He doesn't want the job," Ashok said. "By he I mean me. Besides, I have to keep the ship running. I'm busy. Drake and Janice won't do it, and Shall's got enough to do, and he worries too much about what Callie thinks to be a good second-in-command anyway."

"Hey," Callie said warningly. "How many times did you push the joy button on your skull tonight?"

"As often as the mechanism allowed." Ashok smiled at Elena. "We like you, Doctor Oh. We trust you. You're gonna be great." He lurched off to rejoin the party.

"I don't even understand how the ship *works*," Elena

said, looking around as if dazed – seeing the ship through the eyes of incipient responsibility.

"You can learn," Callie said. "To be XO, you just have to be able to make decisions when the time comes, and you can do that. I've seen you do it."

"But how do I know it's the right decision? How do *you* do it?"

"You trust your experience, your intuition, your conscience, your moral compass, and when all else fails, you just give it your best guess."

"That's it? That's your guide to executive officering?"

Callie shrugged. "Heavy lies the head that wears the crown occasionally when the head that usually wears the crown is off the boat for some reason."

They overnighted on Owain, and kept the party going. Elena got a little drunk – people kept buying her drinks to congratulate her on her new position – and she ended up in the corner of a tavern (which looked, for some reason, like an immense terracotta chicken from the outside), sitting beside Lantern.

"Lantern!" Elena said, too loud, and then too softly: "Lantern. Tell me. Are you in love with Ashok?"

"Ah. Is that what Callie was working up to asking me before?" Lantern said. "Now I understand. No, Elena, I don't think so – not in the way you mean. We are just very good friends."

"Oh." Elena slumped. "That's too bad. Everyone should be in love with someone. It's very fun and interesting."

"I never said I wasn't in love with anyone, Elena."

"What? Who?"

Lantern's skin scintillated and shone prismatically, but just for a moment. Elena's brain was sluggish with alcohol but she remembered reading about that physiological response when she researched Liars: it was an involuntary coloration, the equivalent of a blush in humans, and could indicate embarrassment or acute self-consciousness. "I'll… see you later, Elena." Lantern scuttled away across the bar.

Elena decided she was too drunk to think about that.

Callie elbowed Ashok at the bar. "So. You. Lantern. Is that, are you, a thing?"

"Wait. What? You mean… a thing? Like a you-and-Elena thing, a Stephen-and-Q thing, kind of thing?"

She nodded. "Yes. I thought about it. I'm OK with it. It's no weirder than everything else about you."

"That is very open-minded of you, cap, but no, I'm not in love with Lantern, or doing sexy things with her. I don't even know how we'd, like… go about it. I have not looked into the subject. We're just friends."

"Lantern might be in love with *you*, though."

"Nope. Her heart – or hearts? I think she has like six of them – belongs to another."

"The shit you say? Who?"

"I'm sworn to secrecy, cap."

"Bah. Well. Too bad. I was hoping you were, you know. Having some fun. Assuming that's the kind of fun you like to have. I don't even know. It's probably sexual harassment to even ask you that."

"Could be!" he said cheerfully. "If you're asking if I'm asexual, no. I'm just super picky." He raised his glass in the direction of Sebastien, who was laughing and talking with Q and Stephen. "I am not attracted to Liars. I'm attracted to *him*, though. I would climb all over that."

Callie stared. "Sebastien? He's your type?"

"Pretty much. He was way hotter when he had a metal spider-brain implant embedded in the back of his skull, though." Ashok slapped her on the shoulder. "I gotta go empty the waste containment units, cap." He lurched off through the crowd.

Space is big, Callie thought, gazing into the depths of her drink. *There's room for all kinds of things in it.*

The remaining crew returned to the *White Raven* the next morning, popping anti-hangover pills and groaning at the bumpy ride up in the canoe.

"How's my ship?" Callie demanded, strapping into her chair in the cockpit.

"Refueled and resupplied," Drake said. "Our ammunition has been topped off, too. Courtesy of Almajara Corp. Your ex sends his thanks and regards, and says if we want another job, give him a call."

"Acknowledged."

"Is Stephen settling in OK down there?" Drake said.

"I don't know," Callie said. "He's in love. Maybe it'll wear off and he'll call us to come get him in a few months, but I doubt it."

"I'm going to miss the old man," Drake said.

"Can we have his room?" Janice said.

Callie snorted. "I'll think about it. For now, let's just get through the bridge and back home to Glauketas."

The pirate base was much as they'd left it, with Lantern's starfish-ship hovering near the *Golden Spider*. There was a message on the station system from the Jovian Imperative, acknowledging that the asteroid was now duly registered to the Machedo Corporation. "We own real estate now, everybody," she said over the PA. "Try not to wreck the place too much."

Lantern bid everyone farewell and set off for her station, to check on the younglings and make a report to the central authority of the truth-tellers, informing them that Elder Trogidae had gone mad and killed those under his care, and presumably destroyed the Axiom facility in his sector in the process. Lantern hated lying, but she'd do it, if she had a good reason.

Everyone who remained on the station retreated into their respective domains. Elena plugged herself into an immersive medical school simulation in the Hypnos, where she was planning to spend hours every day, apparently. Ashok dragged the terror drone into a disused machine shop on the far side of the asteroid, accessible from the living quarters only via a maintenance tunnel, so if the thing blew up when he took it apart, it probably wouldn't kill *everybody*, just him. Drake and Janice hooked into the Hypnos in their own quarters (where it was not, and never would be, Gravity Day), and dreamed their own private dreams. Shall reintegrated his consciousness from the ship into his consciousness on the station, and after a long moment said, "Wow. You all had a much more eventful time out there than I did in here."

Callie chatted with Shall as she checked the station's systems, making sure everything was operational, stowed, and ship-shape, and finally went to her own quarters. She'd come back from the dead, saved Owain, killed fifty space monsters, and gotten the company accounts back in the black. She'd earned a nap.

There was something on her pillow. A note. A piece of actual paper, with actual writing on it. Callie didn't touch it – just approached slowly, as if it might attack her. "Shall. Who put this note on my bed?"

"What? I... let me review the security records... Callie, I don't know. It just appeared, sometime last night. I didn't notice it before."

"Someone put it there, Shall. Someone was in my room, leaving things on my bed."

"There's nothing on the security footage, no indication that anyone boarded the station... I don't understand. My diagnostics don't indicate that anyone has tampered with my systems, either."

"Scan for wormhole radiation," Callie said. She possessed a short-range teleporter that worked much like the wormhole bridges, but with a range limited to kilometers, and with strict mass restrictions. It wasn't the only one in the universe – some of the truth-tellers had them.

"There are... traces of radiation consistent with a point-to-point short-range wormhole generator in your quarters," Shall said. "But there's still nothing on the cameras."

"Those little person-sized wormholes open and close fast," Callie said. "And there are ways to trick cameras." Her own stealth suit could do that much – the telltale subtle shimmers wouldn't even show up on the cameras.

She looked down at the note. In spidery black-ink handwriting, it read:

I've been watching your progress, checking in on you occasionally since you set out for Ganymede in that ramshackle pirate ship, and watching you closely once you reached Taliesen. Did you sense me? I thought you might have, once or twice. You're very perceptive, for a human. You did excellent work dismantling the Dream. For your next project, you might visit the Vanir system. What you find there should interest you... and certain members of your crew.

Well. It was good to know she hadn't been suffering from space madness when she glimpsed all those shimmers. It was less good to know they'd been spied on by a mysterious secret admirer.

"What does it say?" Shall asked.

"It says we should go to the forbidden system." Callie decided the note probably wouldn't hurt her, and picked it up, staring at the page.

"Who sent it?" Shall asked.

"It's signed 'the Benefactor,'" Callie said.

"Why don't I find that reassuring?"

"I don't either." Callie was even more troubled by the little drawing underneath the signature, though it was just a couple of thick strokes, in ink of bright hue: a circle, with a smaller dot inside. Stylized, but instantly recognizable.

The drawing was a single, bright blue eye.

ACKNOWLEDGMENTS

Thanks first, as always, to my wife, Heather Shaw, and our son, River, for their patience and support. They make this book-writing thing possible.

Thanks to my agent Ginger Clark for taking care of the business side of things, and to the Angry Robot team: Marc Gascoigne and Phil Jourdan and Penny Reeve and Nick Tyler and Mike Underwood. I quite literally couldn't do this without them, since they publish and edit and promote and market these books. My thanks to Paul Scott Canavan for bringing the *White Raven* to life again with his marvelous cover art. Paul Simpson once again saved me from myself with his deft copyediting. Q Fortier donated generously to the Worldbuilders fundraiser in exchange for having his name used for a character in this book, and I'm grateful for his generosity.

I went on a little book tour for previous volume *The Wrong Stars* (three cities in three months!) while I was writing this book, and want to thank Emily and Connor Lane for letting me crash at their place up in Portland, and Jenn Reese and Chris East for keeping me company there. Thanks to Greg van Eekhout for driving me around in San Diego, and to Sarah Day for keeping me company on the trip. I love booksellers, and the ones at Borderlands in San Francisco, Powell's in Portland, and Mysterious Galaxy in San Diego made me feel welcome and sold a bunch of books for me, so many thanks to them as well.

Several loved ones very tolerantly listened to me ramble on for months about Ganymede and Simon Marius and the peculiarities of various hallucinogenic drugs and twenty-first century medical procedures and whether I should murder characters or let them retire, and they offered advice, encouragement, expertise, and side-eye as needed, so thanks to Aislinn Harvey, Amanda Leinhos (I stole your *Brandenburg Concertos* joke), and Katrina Storey (Sarah and Emily, mentioned above, put up with a lot of that stuff too).

The majority of the first draft of this book was written in an unprecedentedly productive interval at the Bayou Retreat in Louisiana, and I offer my profound thanks to Melissa Marr and Kelley Armstrong for inviting me, and to all the other attendees for making me (one of the newcomers), feel welcome and supported. Thanks to my boss, Liza Groen Trombi, and my co-workers at *Locus* (especially Francesca Myman and Josh Pearce and Kirsten Gong-Wong) for making it possible for me to *go* to that retreat, even though it took place during deadline week on the hardest issue of the year; they did a bunch of my work for me while I was gone. Seventeen years in, being an editor at *Locus* is still the best day job a writer could ask for.

We'll do it all again next year for *The Forbidden Stars*…